Capital Ladies' Club

A NOVEL

To: Jeri

With Love

Gurdie

Gurdie Corell

ISBN: 1494925931
ISBN 13: 9781494925932
Library of Congress Control Number: 2015912015
CreateSpace Independent Publishing Platform
North Charleston, South Carolina
This is a work of fiction. All of the names, characters, organizations, places, events, and incidents portrayed in this novel are the products of the author's imagination or are used fictitiously. Any resemblance to actual events, locales or persons living or dead is entirely coincidental.

To my sister Gail,
because you believed in me
before I knew how to believe in myself

And to our mother Shirley Rosita,
who taught us how to be good women,
your memory lives on forever

Everybody wants to find a love,
somebody who will always care.
But we get locked up in our own worlds,
with feelings and secrets we're afraid to share...

—Bette Midler

Chapter 1

Washington, DC
September 2012

Coco Runni awoke to a chilly morning in the nation's capital, a sure sign that winter was coming and that the days ahead would soon be just as cold as her bed. She wondered who was the smartass that said Washington, DC., was full of sex and power.

Well, there were no signs of any of that coming from her Egyptian cotton sheets. Just depressing memories of what had or should have been.

She stretched her perfectly toned body, turning over for another ten minutes of shut-eye before she had to start her day. Gently running her hand over the pillow beside her, she looked around her well-appointed bedroom. She desperately longed to find someone to love and to be there for her, someone who wanted and needed to share his life with hers. She wanted a family of her own.

Her house, like her life, was a shrine to all things feminine, with soft pink silk walls and matching window treatments. The entire house was decorated to resemble the Hemingway Presidential Suite in the Gritti Palace in Venice, with Louis XVI furniture, Murano chandeliers and antiques she had purchased while on holiday in Europe. Her bedroom had exquisite foliate moldings that had been painted cream with just a hint of pink and gold-leaf accents.

The house and all of its furniture had been given to her as one of many gifts from the handsome international lawyer turned casino owner, Michael DeSalis. She still kept a silver framed picture of him on her bedside table. Coco couldn't help remembering him and their time together. He was the true love of her life and for better or worse, she still hadn't gotten over him.

Coco had the face of an angel, clear creamy complexion, high cheekbones, a button nose, pouty lips and aquamarine blue eyes. All framed with thick Swedish blonde hair that bounced when she walked. She was a dead ringer for actress Lana Turner.

Her petite frame of five feet four inches didn't allow her many jobs as a runway model, but her beauty ensured her the cover of every magazine in the seventies and early eighties. She was on a modeling assignment at Mike's casino when they met. It was the opening of the DeSalis's wedding chapel and ballroom. How ironic it all seemed now that she had met him while modeling a wedding dress. Coco had fallen head over heels in love with him, but she never got a chance to be a bride in real life.

She had enjoyed a lucrative career as a model until she met Mike. He put an end to her working immediately. No woman of his would have to work. The truth was that he needed to control everything about his women and he thought models were cheap and easy. Well, life surely made him pay for that belief. Mike died of a massive heart attack between the legs of a raven-haired model while vacationing in St. Thomas.

Every Christmas Eve, he'd made Coco a promise that the next year he would marry her and with every fiber of her being, she believed him. Holding on to that glimmering ray of hope that she was worthy of marriage and a family of her own.

The painful truth that Coco would not allow herself to believe was that Mike collected women the way he collected his prized Franck Muller watches. This time it was the beauty from the cover of Maxim magazine. With each affair, the women got younger and to Coco's heartbreak more beautiful.

As memories began to flood her mind, it all seemed like yesterday. Why do people tell you the grieving process gets easier with time? It was going on four years since Mike's death. For Coco each day brought her some painful memory of her dashed hopes and forever-lost dreams of being Mrs. Michael DeSalis.

Mike called her the morning of his trip saying, "Coco, I will be away for a few weeks, another boring business trip. Believe me I have back to back meetings. Nothing special about this one."

"Oh Mike sweetie, I will miss you. I've been looking forward to seeing you." said Coco.

Mike responded, "I will make it up to you soon."

He even suggested that they make plans to attend her favorite event, England's Royal Ascot horse race. Telling her to start looking for a fabulous outfit and a showstopper hat. She had placed a call to Britain's top millinery designer William Chamber.

The sound of Mike's voice still echoed in her head like a nightmare that she could not stop reliving. Haunting her dreams, leaving her wondering if she'd missed something in his voice. Why hadn't she known something was wrong that could've somehow foretold their future?

As usual when Coco was not permitted to travel with him, Mike would have his driver bring her a gift with a handwritten note.

> Bella Coco,
> Will see you when I return.
> Have some champagne and caviar ready for me, mia bella ragazza.
> Caio Amore,
> Mike

The gift this time was the famous red and gold box from Cartier. Inside she found two pear-shaped diamond ear studs set in platinum, each weighing in at two and a half carats.

How could she have known it would be the last time she would receive a note or a gift, or hear that sexy voice again? She had long ago stopped caring about the presents. She just wanted Mike to spend time with her, make her feel like she was the only woman in his life and that she was the person he wanted to grow old with.

There had been some bad times over the years. Mike had a bad temper for sure, he was a real hothead with a short fuse. It had taken some time, but Coco had learned how to keep the peace with him.

Mike was her obsession, and no matter how absolutely foul his behavior became, Coco tolerated his abuse and even made excuses for his outbursts. She just would not allow herself to believe that he was the worst kind of abuser.

He was taking her youth and leaving her with mental scars for her future. She reasoned that taking the bad with the good was what love was all about. Her mother had always told her that to have a great life with a successful man, sometimes you had to take some bad to live so very good.

Four days after Mike left on his business trip his attorney Jonathan Birmingham, phoned her saying, "Mike is dead."

He announced it as if he were a press agent doing damage control for some misbehaving member of the NBA, not like a trusted friend delivering the worst possible news. His call showed little to no regard for her feelings, what Mike had meant to her, or the life and the affair he was witness to. Jonathan had seen with his own eyes how much Coco loved Mike. And he knew how much pain she had endured because of her love for him.

Jonathan just gave her cold instructions of what she was to do and not do, and what would be in the morning papers. Every business reporter would surely be covering this story: The Death of a Billionaire, Michael "TV Mike" DeSalis. Mike had more business interests than Coco could ever keep up with—hotel, casinos, real estate, transportation companies the list went on and on.

Mike had been credited for the economic turnaround of Atlantic City and now everyone wanted to book their next event at DeSalis Casino, Resort and Spa. Professional boxers, headline performers everyone wanted a piece of the DeSalis magic.

He used the media like he used everyone and everything to his benefit. Not content to be one of the leading businessmen in the country, his craving was celebrity and he would do just about anything to get it. No expense was spared to ensure coverage of his business and charitable activities. He hired a top New York public relations team to make sure his picture was in some publication or newspaper daily.

Every move he made was calculated. He'd instructed his human resources staff to only hire, "Pretty people" rudely telling them, "Fat people are lazy and ugly people will keep my high rollers away."

His hand-selected charities were only the hottest cause, or as he would say, "Everyone has a need for something. Mine is to be known as the best of everything." This all made him a lightning rod for good and bad press coverage. He was completely obsessed with seeing his name in print. If the media coverage was bad, he would only ask, "Did the motherfucker spell my damn name right?"

Mike viewed life as a chess game and he was the king.

There was no doubt the story of his death would make all of the print media outlets *Baltimore Sun, Washington Post, New York Times, Wall Street Journal* and the *New York Post*'s gossip column, "Page Six"—as well as television coverage from around the world.

Jonathan also instructed Coco not to make contact with Mike's grown children until after the will had been read. No problem there. His children could not tolerate a minute in Coco's company, not without a promise from their dear Daddy for a fabulous present or tickets to a sold out show something for their trouble. To them Coco was just the whore who had broken up their parents' marriage and for that they hated her.

Coco could not understand what was happening or what Jonathan had just said to her. All she wanted to know was where Mike was and what had happened to him. Her world was coming to an end. The room started to spin and she fell to the floor, crying uncontrollably. She lay there motionless for hours.

Chapter 2

Anita de La Cruz knew something was wrong. You don't come from where she had the worst ghetto in El Salvador and not have a sixth sense for trouble.

Each morning Coco greeted Anita at the front door with a smile, welcoming her into her home and then they would go over her list of duties for the day. Anita would make Coco a cup of vanilla tea with soy milk and a drop of honey. Some days they would talk about their problems, share the joke of the day or read the latest Pickles cartoon and laugh.

Before she was Coco's full-time maid, Anita had worked for a local dry cleaner, which taught her a lot about tailoring and the care of fabrics. If Coco was going out to one of her ladies' luncheons or a fancy soirée, she would go over her outfit and have Anita press or steam something.

Some days, Anita would have to clean up after Coco and Mike had a fight. But that was less and less frequent in the last few years.

Anita made little effort to cover up the fact that she did not like Mike. She feared he would really hurt Coco one of these days. He was a real mister fancy pants, slick as grease and mean as a hot snake. Coco had told her he was away on one of his private business trips.

Anita was getting very anxious. Her stomach began doing flip-flops. She said to herself, "Something must be wrong. Why is Ms. Coco not answering the doorbell?" She took out her cell phone and tried calling, but it went immediately to voicemail. Then she remembered what Coco had told her. If ever she did not answer the door, she should use the keypad next to the garage to get into the house. Once inside she would find a spare house key hidden under the broken clay flowerpot.

With shaky hands, Anita reached into her bag to find her little coin purse, where she kept her bus fare, prayer beads and spare change. There it was the folded piece of pink paper with the garage door and the house alarm codes. She stopped to say a quick prayer. "Lord, please let my Ms. Coco be okay." When the garage door opened there was Coco's car. Anita's stomach tightened again. It was too early for Coco to have gone out for a walk. Last evening when Coco telephoned Anita saying, "Hello Anita, would you please come early tomorrow I have so much for us to do. Mike is away on a business trip but when he returns he is taking me to London. I need to pull out all of my best travel outfits and hats. I am so excited maybe I will see the Queen, see you early tomorrow morning."

Anita knew something was big time wrong. She quickly opened the door and yelled out, "Ms. Coco, I am here!" No answer. She made the sign of the cross and went up the stairs, hearing not a sound. Everything was in place, but there was no sound of life, no TV, no music and Coco was not answering her.

Climbing the stairs to the next level, again she saw nothing out of place. There were no signs of a fight or a break-in. She called out to Coco again, but again no answer. Walking down the hall, she looked in every room, bedrooms, bathrooms and closets, but there was nothing just dead silence.

As she slowly opened Coco's bedroom door, she saw her lying on the floor. Anita screamed out, "Oh Lord, Ms. Coco! Ms. Coco!" She ran to her, touching her head and checking to see if she was alive.

Finding Coco's faint pulse, she began shaking her. As Coco regained consciousness she whispered, "Mike is dead."

Anita, yelled out, "Oh sweet baby Jesus, Ms. Coco, did you kill him?" She quickly thought, "*No, no, Ms. Coco couldn't kill anybody let alone anyone as full of the devil as Mike DeSalis.*" Anita knew he was straight from the pits of hell.

Coco's pale complexion had turned ghostly white, her eyes were red and puffy and her whole face was swollen. She was lying on the floor, defenseless as a broken-winged bird. Anita had never seen her look so weak and helpless.

Anita said, "Ms. Coco, you can't stay on da floor like this." Coco was so weak that when Anita tried to move her, she could barely get her to the chaise lounge.

Immediately after Anita placed the receiver back on its base, the phone rang. Not knowing what else to do she answered it, "Runni residence."

It was Mrs. Sadie Von Kinley. Anita knew her to be one of Coco's best friends. Sadie was a bigwig in town and a board member of the Capital Ladies' Club, a very special private club that ladies from the community and wives of the diplomatic corps could only join by invitation from another bigwig.

The main goal of the club was to learn the fine art of public speaking, public image and what was expected of you in a city filled with demands. It was a kind of finishing club for grown women. But the real benefit of joining this tight-knit circle were the friendships these fancy ladies were able to build with other fancy ladies from the community. Sadie was now the new club president and that position came with many responsibilities. For the next year she would be expected to host luncheons, teas and the annual Winter Ball.

She was always calling to check up on Coco and invite her to some event. To be honest, Anita was sick to death of hearing about the grand events of these fancy people. And it was clear that Coco wanted so much to be one of them.

Sadie asked Anita if she could please speak with Coco.

Anita said, "Lady Sadie, I'm sorry but she no can come to the phone now; she in a bad way."

Sadie said, "I will be right over. Don't let anyone in the house. And darling, please don't take any more phone calls."

Within minutes, Sadie was dressed, with her makeup on and her hair in place. She jumped in her Rolls-Royce Phantom Coupé and sped down George Washington Parkway. Turning onto Route 495 and taking the River Road exit on two wheels, in record time she was at Coco's bedside.

Sadie explained to Anita that it was being reported that Mike had died of a sudden heart attack. And without thinking Anita said, "Dat's really something. I thought you had to have a heart to have an attack. That devil was born heartless."

Sadie gently placed her hand on Anita's shoulder. At that moment she knew how much this woman cared for Coco and what she must have witnessed during her years working for her. What Anita lacked in formal training and the proper use of the King's English, she made up for in complete loyalty.

Sadie asked Anita to go to the bathroom, turn on the shower, and make sure the water was lukewarm. Together they got Coco undressed and under the soft water. Coco was still in a state of stock. She just stood under the running water and begin sobbing and mumbling, "He's gone. He's dead."

Anita could not stand to see her friend and employer in such a state. So before she started crying herself, she went to the lingerie closet, pulling down the first thing she saw. The colorful silk kaftan from LaPerla. She laid it across the vanity bench.

After about ten minutes in the shower, the color slowly began to come back to Coco's face. Wrapping herself in a warm towel that Anita handed her she walked over to the vanity table and took a seat. Looking in the mirror, she could not stand the sight of herself. Cupping her face in her hands Coco began sobbing.

Sadie said, "Now, now Coco it's okay. Go ahead and cry. Sometimes our healing comes through our tears."

As Anita slipped the kaftan over Coco's head, the soft fabric fell to the floor. Sadie brushed Coco's hair, and together they walked her back to bed. Sadie asked Coco if she wanted anything to eat or drink. She just nodded her head, "No." Coco eyes were void of any real life just grave sadness.

She slipped under the covers without saying another word, laying her head on the soft silk pillow and closing her eyes. Sadie had brought along a couple of her diazepam pills and a flask of her best Russian vodka, just in case Coco needed a sedative. She thought this was one of those times in life when a pill and a shot of booze would help numb the senses. After witnessing this much pain if Coco didn't need it. Sadie thought she might need one herself.

Sadie had never seen anyone so dead and yet still alive. She was witnessing overwhelming, disastrous pain, and it was the most heartbreaking thing she had ever seen. Just as Coco's head hit the pillow, the phone rang. This time Anita let Sadie answer. It was Coco's sister, Barbara.

Sadie assured Barbara that Coco was being looked after. She also told her that Coco was asleep. Sadie knew the tension between these two sisters and didn't think this was the time for the "He's gone—now what?" conversation.

Barbara said, "Well, maybe now Coco will get over that bastard and move on with her life. She never had a true chance with him anyway. I've listened to Coco, cry too many times over him."

Barbara told Sadie, "I am sorry Sadie, but I will not be crying on this loss of life. I only have one question: what took so long?" She then told her that whatever Sadie thought was best would be just fine with her.

Sadie asked if Barbara knew anything more about Mike's death, where his body was, and whether Coco should go to meet the family and fly back with him. No one from Mike's family or his office had called to say anything more. Sadie didn't feel it would be appropriate for her to call them. She was there to comfort and take care of her friend.

Barbara said she had not heard anything, and that Sadie should not expect that they would receive any additional information from the DeSalis camp. She said, "Sadie, he didn't give a shit about Coco when he was alive. Do you really think his staff or his family will give two shits, now that he's dead?"

Sadie did not understand the coldness or the matter-of-fact tone in Barbara's voice. They were talking about her sister who was devastated and heartbroken. How could she be this cold? Sadie began feeling this call was a complete waste of time, so she quickly said her good-byes.

After she had hung up the telephone, she said, "Well, if I never speak to that cold-hearted bitch again, it will be just fine."

After pulling and straightening the covers over Coco, Sadie stepped out into the hallway to place calls to the girls, Winnie Pettridge and Nancy Hadid. She needed to bring them up to date. Winnie was in San Francisco, attending the opera's opening-night gala. Nancy was away with her family at their weekend-retreat home in Biddeford, Maine.

The four ladies Sadie, Coco, Winnie, and Nancy were closer than blood sisters. They were soul sisters. If one hurt, they all hurt. Men might come and go. But soul sisters would always be there for each other.

The city was filled with people with hidden agendas. They would do anything, including befriend you for contacts, money or position, all in the hopes of making it to what they considered Washington's inner circle. But not this group of friends. These ladies loved each other.

Tears began trickling down Sadie's face. She could not believe the weak and vulnerable state Coco was in. She thought, *"Powerless" is what's left of a woman when she has given her all to a man and been left with nothing to hold on to but the memory of love."*

Sadie thought of her life with Lonnie and how much she loved him. How grateful she was that he still loved and cherished her. He made her feel loved and protected every waking minute.

She wanted that for her friends. Every woman needs to have a love that makes her feel complete. Then the memories would leave you with the power to sail through the rest of your life and not deflate your sails.

Coco was now shipwrecked.

Chapter 3

Anita went down to the kitchen, grateful that Sadie was there to take charge of things. She pulled out Coco's favorite Herend Queen Victoria tea service, some silverware, and two linen napkins with lace trim. She went into the pantry to grab the Harrods white tea, some buttery shortbread biscuits, and the raspberry jam.

Anita suddenly had an epiphany. Coco's house was really a beautifully decorated shrine full of tears, pain and sadness, which produced a feeling of suffocating loneliness. Never a home, just a house built on the hopes of a fairytale that never came true.

Every day on Anita's ride home from work on the Metro bus, she would do what her mother had taught her. When she was worried about someone, she would send up the timbers. It meant praying to God for a person's complete happiness. She hoped that the next morning Coco would tell her that she had ended her affair with Mr. Mike. Anita thought, "If old fancy pants was finally out of the picture, Coco would be able to move on and finally find the happiness she deserved."

Anita filled a kettle with water and began preparing the breakfast tray to take upstairs to the ladies. She turned on the television, hoping to hear some breaking news anything that would take her mind off Coco's sadness.

The lead story was the death of Atlantic City businessman Michael "TV Mike" DeSalis. There he was, smiling back at her from the television screen. Anita thought there was just no escaping this devil of darkness.

They showed pictures of him with the governors of Maryland, New Jersey and Delaware, as well as several photos of him with former US Presidents and foreign Heads of State. They played video clips from his casino television commercials, he appeared all "*spit-shined and polished*," smiling from ear to ear. Like a snake charmer, he invited the humbled masses to visit his casino. He called it the ninth wonder of the world. When the casino had first opened, the commercials ran with such frequency that the media nicknamed him "TV Mike." Multiple news stations were running footage of him walking around his famous casino, introducing himself to hotel and casino guests. There was footage of him eating in the main dining room while laughing and shaking hands with people on the Atlantic City boardwalk.

In each set of photos, Anita noticed a dark-haired woman with him. She wondered who she was, maybe someone high up that worked for him? It was hard not to notice this woman, because of her exquisitely made-up face and perfectly tailored clothes. Even from the television screen, you could tell she was somebody of importance, but behind her eyes there was a steely harshness. Anita was sure the chick did most of her work on her knees. There was something in her body language that suggested she was more than just an employee to Mike.

To Anita's surprise, they only showed one picture of him with Coco and that was with a large group of people at some big party. The reporters' coverage made no mention of Coco. They just said that he was survived by his two children from a previous marriage which had ended in divorce, that his parents were the owners of Luck's the famous restaurant in Baltimore, Maryland and that he was survived by two sisters, nieces, nephews, and a host of friends. It was as if Coco wasn't even a part of his life. The reporters' coverage of Mike DeSalis was so glowing that if you didn't know him, you would have believed he was some kind of saint.

Anita did not know the Mike that the television newsman was so gallantly reporting on. The Mike DeSalis she knew was cruel, with an oversized ego and a sadistic violent temper. She believed the one she knew was very closely related to Satan, just brilliantly robed in London's finest Turnbull and Asser. Anita believed Coco had really wasted her time, youth and beauty taking heartbreak and abuse from that well-tailored demon.

Coco had worried and fussed whenever he was coming to the house. She would prepare for his visit as if he were a member of the royal family, painstakingly attending to every detail. Everything had to be perfect.

He'd convinced Coco that she could not cook. So she would have RSVP Caterer's prepare and deliver his favorite foods to the house. That way all she had to do was transfer the food to her china. Every room in the house had to have fresh flowers. She trusted Daniel Espejel of Flowers by Daniel for the perfect floral arrangements. No detail was overlooked, even down to the temperature in each room.

There had been times that after Coco had extended all of her energy, care and effort in preparing for him, he wouldn't even bother to show up. Always with an excuse that he was working late. And no matter how transparent the lie, Coco would believe him.

She would say, "Mike works so hard. I am so lucky that he loves me." When he did grace her with his presence, he would find some fault in the room, the meal or even Coco that was wrong. He was always belittling her, calling her names like "stupid ass" or "pretty dumb cunt."

Anita wondered why someone as beautiful as Coco would stay with such an evil man when she could have had any man she wanted. Why this one? What kind of hold did Mike DeSalis have over her?

Coco loved children and wanted a child so badly, but he wouldn't allow her to have his baby. Mike once told Coco, "I am afraid our child would be born as dumb and stupid as you are. Your only assets are your mouth and her perfectly round ass." It was painful to watch a woman be so demoralized.

One morning while they were having breakfast, Coco made the mistake of questioning him about something that had happened the night before.

Mike started yelling calling her a crazy, jealous, ungrateful bitch and telling her she should be happy that he still wanted to spend any time with her. He screamed, "Coco, I am around beautiful women all day, every day, they are much prettier and smarter than you. Do you think I need to come here and listen to your shit, you lazy bitch? All you want is money. You are no better than a street-walking whore! If I am fucking every showgirl at my goddamn casino, its none of your motherfucking business. Do you understand, you dumb bitch? Don't you ever question me about another woman again! Do you understand me, bitch? Do you?"

Coco cried out, "Mike, no! Please, please, don't hit me Mike! I am sorry please Mike!"

Hearing the commotion Anita left the laundry room and went into the kitchen. She walked in just as he was raising his hand to hit Coco. But in mid-air he stopped and looked right at Anita. She had her hand firmly wrapped around the handle of a marble rolling pin. They locked eyes. She didn't blink. Her stance let Mike know that she was not afraid of him he thought "she looked ready to do battle." They stared at each other with a look of pure hatred. He understood she would not stand by and let Coco be beaten or abused. He knew better than to try Anita.

Lowering his hand he bent down so he was right in Coco's face. And in a low voice he said, "I have had enough of your jealous shit. I can't stand to look at your crying face for another minute you dumb cunt. All you do is cry about something. Go wash your face! Sometimes you make me hate looking at you. This is why I don't come here more. It's because of your jealous shit! You keep this shit up, and you will never see me again. You dumb bitch!" He then picked up Coco's favorite Herend china teapot and threw it against the wall, shattering it into a million pieces.

Coco just set there, shaking and crying. When Mike belittled her this way, it took her back to being a young girl and how her father had treated her, how he would punish her and not her sister when their mother went away to take care of their grandmother. Her sister did not get late-night visits to her room from their evil father only Coco. He always told Coco she was just a "pretty nothing" girl. Not smart like her sister, just pretty and that she would only get through life because of her beautiful face. The memories of that horrible time and now Mike doing the same thing made Coco tremble. She thought, "Why did men only want to hurt me? Why couldn't someone just love me for who I am?"

Anita could stop him from physically abusing Coco in front of her, but the verbal assaults were harder to control without Coco taking a stand to protect herself. When he was finished delivering his final verbal blows, he walked out of the house, slamming the door behind himself.

Anita could not believe her eyes as Coco ran after him, crying and begging him to please come back, saying she was so sorry and that she would never ask him anything about another woman again.

Once safely in his car, Mike made a mental note to have someone on his staff call the immigration department about Anita. He thought she needed to be fired, deported, and taught a lesson about getting in other people's business. He knew that Coco would never let her go, so he would have to take care of it.

Seeing Coco being belittled and watching her begging and pleading with him for forgiveness made Anita want to quit her job. She wondered why in the world anyone would be such a fool for a man. Where was Coco's self-worth? Where was the Coco who got dressed in designer labels and threw her head up so high in the air, she could have gotten a nosebleed? Where was that Coco? Where was that Coco now, when she was being degraded down to the level of a gutter rat? Anita thought there must be something wrong with this Coco, because this Coco appeared in need of an exorcism, this Coco was surely possessed.

Anita was certain that access to unlimited spending accounts was one of the reasons Coco took his shit. Mike deposited $25,000 into her bank account every month. But no amount of money was worth being demoralized. So for the cost of Coco's monthly expenses, she would allow this man to do whatever he wanted to her, whenever he wanted to do it. The power of love and money was now the cost of Coco's self-respect.

Anita believed in love, but she understood the truth about love and money, and she knew it was plain to see and understand if you were willing to be truthful with yourself. Love, like money does not change you; it only makes you more of who you already are. If you are a fool, you will be a fool in love. If you are an abuser, you will be an abuser in love. Mike's money allowed him to be an abuser, and Coco happily played the role of his love-sick fool.

Coco spent the rest of that day in her bed. Crying like a love-sick teenager, calling his cell phone leaving messages, begging him to please talk to her. She did not hear from him for two weeks. That was his way of punishing her.

After witnessing their fights, Anita never liked to be around when he was coming over. She was very afraid of what he might do to Coco, or what Coco would do to herself. Anita didn't believe in the old saying that love is blind. She strongly believed that love wasn't blind, but it damn sure needed a seeing-eye dog, and Mike and Coco's love affair needed a crash helmet.

Now he was dead. Images of him continued to shine through the TV screen, and no matter what the news anchor said, all she could remember was how much "TV Mike" had hurt her boss. Maybe now Coco, would find some happiness.

Chapter 4

Sadie spent the entire day at Coco's bedside, quietly placing calls to her staff. She called the girls, Winnie and Nancy, to give them updates. When Coco woke up, Sadie explained her plans. She wasn't sure if Coco clearly understood her. Coco just thanked her, gave her a hug, and then went back to sleep.

By nightfall, Sadie knew Coco was still not in any shape to be alone, so she asked Anita if she would please stay with Coco through the night, and to have them both prepared to take a little trip to Florida the next morning.

To make sure Anita felt secure, Sadie assured her that the Von Kinley family would be taking care of any and all expenses for the trip, as well as her salary during this time. Sadie's staff would have their hands full with the schedule of events she already had planned. There would be no way they would be able to look after Coco, making it an absolute necessity that Anita accompany her for the trip.

The Von Kinley's held several annual gatherings during the high social season in Palm Beach. Every year during the four months that Lonnie and Sadie were in residence, they hosted a board meeting and cocktail party for the hospital, a luncheon for the local chapter of the American Cancer Society, a seated dinner for the Marvis Center, and a high tea for the Palm Beach Opera Company.

All of the scheduled events were to be held at Jewels, their palatial seaside home located on a street the locals called billionaire row. Sadie had been planning these festive soirées for months. It would be impossible for her to cancel them at the last minute, especially since Sadie was secretly hoping to be asked to serve as board chairman of the Marvis Center. The next board of trustee's election was coming up soon. She knew it would be hard for the board not to appoint her, after she and Lonnie had just presented them with a check for five million dollars.

Over the years since they'd purchased Jewels, Sadie and Lonnie had developed many wonderful friendships now the Palm Beach community was their second home. They loved every minute of their time there. The weather was always perfect for playing golf and tennis with their friends. Sadie could not imagine anything that could separate her from the wonderfulness of Palm Beach.

That's why the best course of action was to take Coco and Anita with her. She had discussed it with Lonnie, and he was not completely sold on the idea. He knew firsthand how much work Sadie put into their entertaining, and he also knew how much drama Coco always brought with her. She was not one of Lonnie's favorites. But Sadie thought Coco needed to be away from all of the memories until she was stronger, so she moved forward with her plan.

When Sadie spoke of Jewels, it was as if the house was a person or a spa with special healing powers. Sadie was generous with her invitations to special friends—just another testament to her level of graciousness. But this amount of special care spoke to how much she loved and cared for Coco, she thought of her as a younger sister.

Anita agreed to have herself and Coco packed and ready the next day. Sadie told her she would have to be getting home to have dinner with her husband. She left her private telephone number and instructions for Anita to call her anytime during the night if she needed her.

Once Sadie left, Anita telephoned her boyfriend, Hector, letting him know what she needed in terms of clean clothes. She explained to him that things were bad with Ms. Coco, and she did not know when she would be returning home. Coco needed her and right now that was all that mattered. Well, that and the fact that the Von Kinley's were paying her time and a half for being there to hold Ms. Coco's little heartbroken hand. The free trip to Florida was an additional bonus.

Anita started to think that things were really beginning to look up for her. Old fancy-pants Mike was gone and she was heading down south for a few days of fun in the sun. Hector promised to bring the items over to the house as soon as he could get them packed.

When Sadie got into her car, she placed a call to Felix, her butler and estate manager. She gave him a long list of things she needed, including arrangements for four houseguests. She informed him that two guests would be arriving with her and two more ladies would be arriving within a couple of days. All would be staying for a week.

Her instructions included which foods to have prepared, along with which flowers, chocolates, candies, and nuts should be in each guest's room. Coco loved Maryland lump crab cakes, so they would be having them for dinner on her first night. And for breakfast, she wanted the guests to have tropical fruit salad with fresh mint, individual egg and fresh herb soufflés along with freshly baked mini-croissants. This was no time to count calories. She asked him to telephone Harrods in London and have the vanilla lavender tea that Coco enjoyed shipped overnight. She was an excellent hostess, no matter how sad the houseguest.

Sadie ran her homes with the precision of a military officer. Every member of the Von Kinley's domestic staff had attended and graduated from the International Guild of Professional Butlers in the Netherlands, which specialized in the art of formal house management for career domestic specialists. She expected the best from her staff, and she rewarded them well for outstanding service and loyalty.

Just as Sadie had said, the next morning a limo was waiting outside of Coco's house. Coco and Anita walked out together, and the driver took their bags to the car. Anita secured the house. She wasn't sure what the future held for her and Coco, but she knew it had to get better than it was right in this moment. The car moved swiftly down George Washington Parkway to Reagan National Airport. They were taken to a special section of the airport for persons traveling by private planes.

Sadie greeted them on the plane. Coco didn't look much better after a long night's sleep. In a low voice, she said, "Sadie thank you for being such a good friend to me. I haven't heard anything from Mike's family or his office." Sadie was surprised to hear that Coco hadn't received any information about the funeral plans. Something seemed wrong, Sadie didn't want to upset Coco, so she said, "Coco I am sure you will hear something soon. I am truly sorry that your having to go through all of this pain. I know you really loved Mike. Nancy and Winnie will be joining us later."

After they took their seats, the hostess bought them a cup of freshly brewed coffee. Coco took one sip, laid her head back against the fine hand-crafted leather headrest, and looked out the window. Looking up as another plane ascended to the air, she said, "I wonder where those people are traveling to. If any of them are in love, did their lovers leave them? Where does your heart go, when you have no one to love anymore?"

Sadie and Anita looked at each other, and Anita said, "To Florida on a private plane."

Coco did not respond.

Anita said, "Ms. Coco, maybe while you are in the Sunshine State, you will find a really nice, good man, to treat you the way a good man treats a good woman. Now don't dat sound better?"

Coco said, "Anita, I can't think about meeting someone now. I still love Mike."

Anita looked up to heaven and said, "*Dios, por favor déme la fuerza. Esta mujer es loca como el infierno.*" ("God please give me strength, this woman is crazy as hell.")

Coco didn't speak Spanish, but Sadie was fluent in several languages. Sadie smiled at Anita and said, "Anita, why don't you have some breakfast? I need a minute to chat with Coco."

Anita was more than happy to be relieved of her babysitting duties for a couple of hours, or for however long it took them to reach Florida.

Sadie called the hostess over and asked her to please take the coffee away, and to bring them something stronger, like champagne. As soon as the hostess set the chilled flutes of Perrier Jouët in front of them, they both drank it down in seconds, finishing off half a bottle before the plane taxied down the runway. As the pilot announced their takeoff, the hostess replaced the empty glasses of Jouët with a chilled one. Coco fastened her seatbelt and closed her eyes, she wanted to remember the good times with Mike. Remember how he felt in her arms, she thought, "*Could it be possible that this is all a bad dream.*" As Coco got lost in her day dreams of a perfect life with Mike that never was. Sadie opened a binder with notes from her last board meeting. She needed to do some quick catching up, so she would be prepared for the upcoming meeting.

Anita had never been on a private plan before, she was determined to enjoy every second of this ride. She relaxed, took off her shoes, and filled a plate with fresh fruit, a large slice of the delicious spinach and crab quiche, and one of the petite cinnamon and raisin breakfast pastries that were made with the lightest, buttery dough that melted in her mouth. She washed it down with a glass of champagne and orange juice that the hostess had set down in front of her.

The Von Kinley's plane was a new Gulfstream V, everything on the plane sparkled and shined like new money. Anita felt like she was in a glamorous movie starring Lady Sadie Von Kinley and her emotional wreck of a friend, the very sad Coco Runni. Anita could not understand Coco's emotions. She understood loving a man. She had loved several, but none of her men had ever treated her the way Mike had treated Coco. Anita also understood the pain of losing someone you loved.

Which made her strongly think that Coco needed a reality check and a session with a priest. Because from what Anita could see, and what she had knowledge of, she thought Coco still had a great deal to be grateful for, starting with the fact that after taking so many beatings from Mike, she was alive. Anita knew of women that had died at the hands of their lovers, husbands, or boyfriends. Coco should be grateful that she was one of the lucky ones. She had been through hell and was alive to tell about it, and she could start her life over again.

Anita hoped that if nothing else, Coco was thankful for her wonderful, supportive friends. And for this moment in time, she was onboard a jet on her way to sunny Florida. Oh well, if Coco was not grateful, Anita would be for the both of them.

In less than three hours, their plane landed at Palm Beach International Airport. Once the plane came to a complete stop, the staff moved into place.

A limo was waiting for them at the gate. The driver greeted them and helped them into the car while their luggage was taken from the plane and placed in the trunk. Seamlessly, everything was just taken care of.

Sadie checked to see if Coco and Anita were comfortable. When she was sure everyone was okay, she motioned for the driver to take off. It was clear she was in charge and in control of her life. During the drive, Sadie placed and received a few calls. She received a call from one of her sons, and the smile that went across her face was the expression of pure mother's joy. Not only did Sadie have to plan events for the charities she supported, but she had a large family who loved to be around her, so they were calling to see what she had planned for them. Anita was so proud to see a strong, elegant woman handling her life with ease and no drama. She only hoped that Coco was taking mental notes.

Anita stared out the car window taking in every second of this experience. She enjoyed the sight of the tall palm trees, lush green landscapes, and the smell of the ocean air, most of the houses along the route were the size of small office parks.

The car heading south turned off route A1A, Ocean Drive, and then onto a private driveway that led to beautiful iron gates. When the gates opened, they unfolded to majestic gardens and a seaside palace. It was like nothing Anita had ever seen. Over the years she had overheard Coco talking about how luxuriously the Von Kinley's lived and how much she wished to have a life like Sadie's. But damn it, Coco forgot to mention that the Von Kinley's property looked like Fantasy Island. Anita was not prepared for anything this grand. It took every bit of her strength to keep her mouth from just hanging open.

Anita had never seen anything as beautiful as Jewels. The main house was over nineteen thousand square feet of elegant wonder, with eight bedrooms, ten baths, two guesthouses, and indoor and outdoor pools. There were professional tennis courts with a viewing stand, two kitchens, a full ballroom that could easily seat 150 guests for a formal dinner, with a hand-painted dance floor and huge Austrian crystal chandeliers. A movie screening room with a professional popcorn machine and candy-bar stands kept guests entertained. Off the main hallway was a gallery that proudly displayed the works of great artists like Edward Seago, Ernest Geiger, Romare Bearden, and George Loftus Noyes. In the two-story English library there were first-edition books, some signed by the authors. Another wing of the house held a beauty salon equipped with the latest of everything, a professional three-lane bowling alley, and a yoga room. In a separate detached building, there was a six-car garage, above which were beautifully appointed staff quarters. Jewel's was enough to make the sultan of Brunei proud.

They were taken to marvelously decorated guestrooms overlooking the pool and the ocean. Once there, the staff unpacked their luggage, while another group of staff members bought up trays of tea sandwiches, small pastries, and more champagne.

Anita was not sure what to do, so she gently tapped Sadie on the arm and asked, "Do you mean for me to stay here too?"

Sadie said "Yes, oh my dear if it's okay with you. I think it would be best for you to stay close to Coco for the night."

The plan had been to have Coco stay there until after Mike's funeral arrangements were completed. The girls, Winnie and Nancy, would be joining them for a couple days of rest. Then they would all be flying back to Washington, DC, aboard the Von Kinley's plane.

However, this was not to be. Two days after they arrived, Jonathan, Mike's faithful attorney, made a surprise visit, requesting a private meeting with Coco.

The Von Kinley's did not take kindly to uninvited guests. Sadie was beside herself with anger. Who did this man think he was dealing with? How dare he come to her home? And how foolish of Coco to tell him where she would be staying. This was not a good sign and Sadie knew it. She left him sitting in the vestibule for over thirty minutes, until she got Lonnie on the phone to ask if she had to let this joker see Coco.

Lonnie said, "Sweetheart you can't protect Coco from whatever this man is there to speak with her about you can only support her. I think you have to let Coco meet with him. Everything will be okay baby. We are just finishing up our golf game, I will be home soon." Sadie said, "Okay if I have to, I will let him see Coco, but Lonnie I just don't feel good about this."

Lonnie gently said, "Nothing between Coco and Mike has ever been good, and you are doing everything that a good friend can do." When they ended the call Lonnie knew for sure that the drama he thought would happen with Coco was coming to a head and Sadie was right in the middle of it. Lonnie was unhappy about this turn of events, Sadie was his queen, and she alone held his heart. He even had the slogan "a happy wife is a happy life" engraved on small silk pillows that had been placed in the grand foyers of every one of their homes. He wanted all guests who came for a visit or a stay to know the rules.

He was also keenly aware of how much these ladies meant to Sadie. And for some reason, she felt the need to take care of them. So he would make himself available for whatever she needed.

When Sadie tapped on the guest room door, she found Coco dressed and having tea with Anita on the balcony adjacent to their room. Coco was beginning to look a bit better. The Florida sun and the ocean breeze did magical things for the soul.

Sadie said, "There is someone downstairs to see you, Coco. His name is Jonathan. He said he is Mike's attorney."

Coco replied, "This must be about the final plans for Mike's funeral services. I have been waiting and hoping to hear something soon."

Anita said, "He came all the way to Florida to tell you. What? His phone not working?"

Like an actress preparing for her cameo role, Coco flew into action, moving at breakneck speed and with a renewed zest for life. She said, "How sweet of Jonathan to deliver the itinerary to me in person. Maybe I should plan to return to Washington with him. What do you think Sadie?"

Sadie said, "Coco, I don't know what to think of any of this. I do not know why this gentleman is here or why you didn't tell me to expect him. After all, that would be the only way he would have known your whereabouts. You had to have given him my address. I only know that he is an uninvited guest sitting in my library, waiting to speak with you."

Coco completely ignored Sadie's comment about the uninvited guest. She just said, "The worst is over. Mike is dead. What else could possibly happen to me?"

Sadie sometimes thought Coco's naïveté was too much to handle. She was willing to always believe the best about anything having to do with Mike and his friends who operated like a band of cutthroat pirates.

Anita gave Sadie a look of complete bewilderment. Feeling the tension in the air, she said, "Mrs. Sadie, I didn't know anything about this man coming to your house. I am sorry if it upset you." Then she went to get Coco's YSL make-up bag. She handed it to Coco.

Coco applied pink-colored lip gloss that matched her tunic and silk pants perfectly. After brushing her hair, she turned to Anita and Sadie and said, "Okay, ladies, let's go get this over with."

Sadie had a bad feeling about this meeting, but she was helpless to stop it. She led Coco downstairs to the library and then asked her if she wanted her to stay. Coco lightheartedly said, "No, I will be fine. Jonathan and I go back years. Right, Jonathan?"

Sadie studied Jonathan's face, looking for any sense of warmth or kindness toward Coco. She only saw a cold business facade. She said, "Really? Well okay, Coco. If you're sure, I will leave you to your business meeting."

As she turned on her Chanel ballerina flats, she shot Jonathan a look of complete disdain. She wanted her look to verbalized to him how much she despised him for his uninvited intrusion into her home.

Once Coco and Jonathan were alone. Coco began talking rapidly and animatedly, thanking Jonathan for coming to see her in person, telling him it would only take a couple of minutes for her to be packed and ready to leave with him. She also told him that she was traveling with her housekeeper and she hoped that would not be a problem. If it was, she could make arrangements to have Anita take a commercial flight back home.

Jonathan could hardly believe her aimless chatting. She was going on and on about Mike: how much she had loved him and how she would find a way to forgive him for being with another woman. The more she talked, the faster her chatting continued.

He had to take control of this situation. He stood up, walked over to her, placed his hands on her shoulders, and said, "Coco, please sit down. Please, Coco, you need to listen to me."

Jonathan took a deep breath and then said, "I am sorry to have to tell you this. Truly I am." He stopped knowing that what he had to say next would cut deeper than any steel knife. When he continued he said, "Coco, I am sorry... but you can't come to the funeral service. Mike didn't want you there. He left clear instructions that you were not to be allowed to take any part in his memorial. I am sorry, Coco. It was Mike's wish that the service be private, and only for his family."

His words took the air out of her lungs. Again, Coco could not believe what she was hearing. Mike had taken the time to write out plans before he died. She pushed Jonathan's hands off her, and she fell back into the soft leather of the sofa. For a minute, she could not speak. Her mind was spinning. She thought, "*There is no way I am hearing this correctly. There must be a mistake.*" When Coco finally found her voice again, she asked, "What...what did you just say? When did Mike tell you that? I don't believe you. Why are you lying to me?"

Jonathan informed her that, as Mike's lawyer and the executor of his estate, he could assure her with complete certainty that these plans had been put in place a couple of years before at the request of Michael DeSalis. He was simply there to enforce them.

As Jonathan started to repeat what he'd just said, Coco stood up and started pacing back and forth. She said, "No, no, you are lying to me! You just want to keep me from him. You always wanted me away from Mike. You never thought I was good enough for him!"

Jonathan said, "Coco, these are Mike's words, his plans, his orders—not mine, it's all here in writing, along with a copy of your trust and the deed to your house, here read it all for yourself."

Coco started yelling, "No, you can't do this to me. I will not let you take him away from me again. No, no, no! Mike is my man, and he loved me. Do you hear me, Jonathan? Mike loved me, you son of a bitch!"

Jonathan told her that, after his last heart attack, Mike had revised his will and had been meticulous about all aspects of his final services.

Coco still refused to believe what she was hearing. “What are you talking about? What heart attack?”

Jonathan said, “Coco, Mike suffered a heart attack a few years prior. He’d never told you because his children and his family did not want you at the hospital. Do you remember the time that Mike sent you away on a little nip-and-tuck vacation. You stayed at the Inn and Spa at Loretto in Santa Fe, New Mexico, you were there for two months.”

Coco said, “Do I remember are you kidding me. Yes I remember, I had to have plastic surgery to repair my nose after that motherfucker broke it and gave me a black eye. After all the shit I took from him, you are telling me that I can’t come to his damn funeral. Do you have any idea what I went through with him—what he did to me? Do you? Well, do you?”

She remembered her trip to New Mexico well. She was concerned that she hadn’t heard from Mike the entire time she was away. When she called his cell phone he didn’t answer and when she telephone his office, his secretary told her he was away on business and could not be reached by telephone.

When she finally saw him more than three months later he looked thin, tired and pale, but still so very handsome. He passed it off as stress, telling her to shut the fuck up with all the questions and not to put any more pressure on him. He didn’t need the extra stress.

After that visit, he spent less and less time with her, always telling her he was working or traveling abroad. When she asked to visit the casino, he would tell her that it was not a good time. It didn’t make sense to her, but she was always afraid of upsetting him, so she just went along with his program, constantly forgiving him because he always called her and sent her lovely gifts with handwritten notes. Now she knew that every minute with him had been a lie.

Coco asked Jonathan, “What else have I been kept in the dark about, Jonathan? What don’t I know about Mike?”

Jonathan looked at her and said, “Coco, when it mattered, you never asked questions. Now it does not matter anymore. He is dead…and there really is not much left for us to discuss.”

Coco started to cry. Could any of this possibly be true? Had Mike lived a life completely apart from her? What did all of this mean? As her mind began spinning around, she started yelling, "No, no, no! This is not true! This can't be true! Why would Mike do this to me? Why? Why? No, you are lying! I will not let you get away with this, you bastard!"

Sadie was in the dining room going over the plans for that evening's reception, when she heard Coco yell. She ran from the dining room, and Anita ran from the hall powder room. Together they pushed open the library's heavy walnut doors to find Coco in tears.

Coco turned to Sadie and yelled, "I can't go to Mike's funeral! I can't say good-bye to him. They will not let me near his body or the Church!"

Sadie wrapped Coco in her arms. She then asked Jonathan, "Is this true?"

He calmly said, "Yes. Mr. DeSalis requested that Ms. Runni not be allowed to attend his funeral services. The services are to be private, for his family only."

Jonathan then said, "I am sorry, but Ms. Runni no longer has a place in Mr. DeSalis life."

Then he turned to Coco and said, "Coco, Mike truly wanted you to move on with your own life. Your affair has been over for some time. Now it's closed for good. We all want the best for you. I am sorry, Coco. Truly, I am sorry."

Coco said, "You don't know what you're talking about, Jonathan. Mike loved me, and who are you to tell me when my affair is over? You were not the person he promised to marry, I was! So get the hell out of my face, you uptight asshole!"

Jonathan just looked at her and said, "Coco, I have always tolerated you, but now let me tell you something, you dear, foolish girl. You were never the one. You were just one of his fancy female showpieces…and you have been paid well for it."

Coco lunged at Jonathan. Sadie grabbed her to hold her back. Coco spit right in Jonathan's face, and then she said, "You are just jealous because I wouldn't let you fuck me! Now you think you are paying me back, you no-good bastard. I hate you! I always hated you."

Sadie said, "Coco, that's enough."

Jonathan took his silk pocket square and wiped his face. He then said, "You alley cat, that's why this is happening to you."

Sadie called out to Felix, asking him to have Jonathan removed at once. Felix was in charge of all things having to do with the entire estate. This meant that on occasion he was in charge of having to remove an unwanted guest.

Anita was standing next to Jonathan, holding a large vase high in the air. Ready to strike at any minute, she said, "Lady Sadie, can I hit him? Please let me bust him up."

Sadie said, "No. Please, no hitting in my house." Sadie once again asked Felix to please get Jonathan out of the house.

Felix was now standing between Coco, Sadie, and Jonathan. He gently pushed Jonathan toward the door.

Jonathan was taken aback by the protective force Coco had surrounded herself with. He'd always thought she had no one, and that was the reason she had hung on to Mike. He looked at Coco, Sadie, and the team of domestic staff standing at the library door, ready to execute him at any minute should Mrs. Von Kinley give the order for his beheading. He had expected this would not be a friendly meeting. How could it be? But he never thought for a minute it would have turned out this badly. Coco was more delusional then he had been prepared for. To Jonathan's surprise, Coco really somehow thought she'd had a future with Mike.

If any of them knew the real Mike DeSalis, they would know this was all for the best. Coco could finally move on with her life—or do whatever the hell mistresses do when they lose their sponsor. If only she knew how much he hated these meetings, and how many he'd had to make on behalf of the late Mike DeSalis estate.

Coco was not the only woman in Mike's life. She never had been. She was one of many. Jonathan still had to have two additional face-to-face meetings before the funeral services. If Coco had not been so crafty at making Mike feel guilty, as if he were responsible for taking care of her for the rest of her life, he would have ended the relationship years before. Coco was a very manipulative woman and a skillful master at being the constant victim.

The sad reality was that Coco really only knew one side of Mike. At best, he was a complicated person with many insecurities. His obsessive addiction to sex controlled him. Mike always had a variety of very young lovers which varied from young girls to beautiful women, and then the occasional beautiful young man.

Now Jonathan was left with the task of meeting with Mike's whores. There was the model who had fucked Mike into the afterlife. Mike wanted her after he watched a videotape of her taking it up the ass from his own son. And because of that, she would be receiving a hundred thousand dollars to keep her mouth shut. If she didn't—well, let's just say she would no longer be so pretty.

The last one was sure to be a challenge: the beautiful Russian brunette Natasha, who used to work in Mike's public relations office. Mike's nickname for her was "Leather and Lace", she was reportedly into all kinds of sex acts. She would be receiving the largest settlement: three million dollars. Natasha had worked closely with Mike and knew a great deal about his business dealings especially since she made the arrangements to have young girls and underage boys brought to the casino's high-roller suites.

Mike responded to strong women and Natasha was as strong as they came. She played his game better than he did. Natasha was just as tough and ruthless as Mike. She had threatened him that if he ever laid a hand on her, she would have her friends in the Russian Mafia cut off his dick and mail it to his mother. Mike believed she would keep that promise, so he made sure to take good care of her—during life, and now in death.

Natasha was a master player in the game of fucking your way to the top. Only two months after she announced that she was carrying Mike's child, she met and married a newly widowed billionaire who was old enough to be her father. Her new husband had been one of Mike's financiers for the casino. She knew Mike's Achilles heel, and she loved torturing him, telling him that her husband was richer and smarter than Mike could ever hope to be. She also informed him that her marriage did not let him off the hook financially. He would still have to send her fifty thousand dollars a month or else. She would send the baby to visit Mike's saintly mother and highly respected father, and tell them what their prized son was really all about.

She had secretly taken pictures of Mike in all kinds of sex acts. If the photos went public, Mike would have done hard time. He could not get enough sex, he had become completely addicted to it, the more perverse the better. That and his abuse of prescription drugs, which was one of the reasons for his violent mood swings.

If the public ever found out about any of this, he would have lost everything he had worked so hard to build. Knowing how much his public image and the respect of his family meant to him, he quickly made arrangements to have Natasha receive every penny she asked for monthly. Her new husband loved baby Mayi, and treated her like his own child. He never knew that Mike was the baby's father. Mike made sure he never saw the child.

As Jonathan headed to the door, he turned and said, "Coco, I am truly sorry, but this never would have ended the way you wanted it to." Then he laid a large envelope on the desk.

Jonathan wished Coco would stop crying, because her relationship with Mike had been one of Mike's many covers. Because of her beauty, he would bring her around when he needed a good, classy-looking girl on his arm. She satisfied the need some men have to do the manly thing; she was a showpiece. If Coco was honest with herself, she knew their relationship never really had a future.

Sadie said, "Please leave my house now. Please go."

Anita held up her fist. "Get out man, or you will get it, man. You hear da lady. Get out now, man. Get out!"

Felix turned to Jonathan and, in his most formal English accent, said, "Dear sir, I don't believe your services are of any more use here, so kindly follow me at once." Felix was a trained third-degree black belt and ready to protect his boss at any time, against any threat unlike this woman standing next to him with the vase in her hand. She was clearly not trained in anything but Felix admired her loyalty to her mistress.

Felix pointed to the door with his left hand, and with his right hand he removed the vase from Anita's tight grasp, gently placing it on the end table all without any sign of distress. He walked Jonathan and Anita out of the library and closed the doors behind them.

Coco handed the envelope to Sadie and asked her to please read it.

Sadie asked, "Are you sure, Coco?"

Coco said, "Please Sadie, I can't handle any more."

Sadie carefully read each line. She could not believe her eyes. This son of a bitch had thought of everything, and damn it, Coco didn't have a leg to stand on. Sadie was mad as hell. She hated it when women were treated like yesterday's garbage. The worst thing about this was that Coco had allowed this to happen, through the ultimate sin of not being in control of her own life and not demanding more for herself.

Along with the deed of trust the envelope contained a letter which was a formal document of what Coco's relationship had meant to Mike and what it had all been worth. It was a strong warning that if she made the slightest move to sue his estate, she would lose her home, forfeiting the million dollars that had been placed in a trust for her. It was a take-it, or leave-it deal, and there was nothing else on the table.

Sadie thought, "*This is why you don't date a man for a lifetime. You marry the bastard*." She believed there were many reasons for marriage, and love was only part of it. There was respect for each other, kindness to each other, the need for companionship, the building of a life together. The everyday, forever stuff, and the give and the take. Marriage meant building a team that you called a family and gaining the respect that the world grants to married couples.

Coco was no more than a mistress to Mike, and he was handling her from the grave. With one swift movement of his pen, he was finished with her. She wasn't even worth a formal good-bye. Locking her out of his funeral was the final blow. Checkmate Coco, this game was over. There was nothing and no one who could make this right.

Chapter 5

When they reached the front door, Felix turned to Jonathan and said, "I presume you remember your way out." Jewels security team had assembled at the front entrance with the guard dogs.

Anita picked up a white rock and with perfect aim hit Jonathan on his temple above his right eye, causing a small amount of blood to run down his face.

Jonathan grabbed his face. When he saw blood on his hand, he said, "I am bleeding, you bitch!" He jumped in his car and sped down the driveway.

Felix turned to Anita and asked, "Was that really necessary?"

Anita smiled and said, "You bet your tight English ass it was."

A security team member laughed. Seeing no immediate danger, Felix dismissed the security detail back to their posts. Then he asked Anita to please follow him.

Anita hesitated for a minute, and then she told him she needed to take care of Ms. Runni.

Felix assured her he had already assigned Bethany, the newest member of the Von Kinley's domestic team, to look after Ms. Runni, and that she was in very good hands. Felix could sense that Anita had some reservations about meeting with him.

He very softly said, "Miss Anita, if it's not asking too much of you, would you be so kind as to join me in my office for a little chat? My office is right off the kitchen. I would be happy to have our chef prepare you a bite of lunch."

There were several matters which concerned Felix, the first one being that she would now be staying in a lovely private room in the staff quarters, because, after all, she was staff. The Von Kinley's staff quarters were just as lovely as the rest of the house, well…minus the priceless artwork.

The other matter had to do with Ms. Runni. Felix was concerned that with her emotions going up and down so quickly, that maybe she was on some kind of medication. He needed to know how to best handle someone in her fragile mental state. He also needed to know what all the screaming and hitting of guests was about. This just didn't happen at Jewels or any of the Von Kinley estates. They took great care to carry themselves with dignity.

He had to get things back on course, and quickly, because the Von Kinley's other houseguests would be arriving soon. In a mere matter of hours, Jewels would be filled with prominent members of the Palm Beach community, celebrity guests, and board members from the Marvis Center for the Performing Arts and the Palm Beach Opera.

It was Felix's responsibility to ensure that all activities were executed without incident, or Mr. Kinley would surely discharge him of his duties. Felix prided himself on his position as head of the Von Kinley's domestic life, and he was hell-bent on living up to his reputation as the finest estate manager in the country, but to do that he needed to have all of the information possible about the people around him. Over the years he had learned that food was a wonderful truth serum. Jose, the executive chef at Jewels, was a master at preparing the very best in culinary hypnotic delights guaranteed to relax, and satisfy.

Felix was sure that after enjoying one of the chef's famous dishes, this mess of a maid would tell him everything he needed to know, including the details of why the beautiful house guest was so sad. No one that beautiful should be that emotionally distraught. Felix remembered Coco visiting the Von Kinley's a few times in the past, and while she was never the most gracious of houseguest, she was never an emotional powder keg, either.

Anita followed him into the main kitchen, which was the size of a hotel lobby. He asked her to please take a seat at the kitchen table, while he handled a small matter concerning the evening's activities.

Once she was seated, a member of the kitchen staff placed a chilled glass of strawberry lemonade in front of her. It was made from fresh strawberry puree and lemons that had been picked that morning. She instructed Anita that the beverage was unsweetened, offering her some fresh honey. Jewels had its own honeybees, and Anita learned that fresh honey, like everything else at Jewels, was just divine.

Anita watched Felix handling his team members with respect. They all seemed to like working with him. She admired Felix. He was uptight, but the guy was all about his business. This was the first time she had been in the presence of professionally trained domestic artists. She thought of them as artists because of the way they had perfected their craft, taking everyday, ordinary items and turning them into a stunning, shining art. They did it with food, flowers, and linens. They made everything look and taste marvelous. Just being around them made Anita want to be better.

She would not admit it, but she needed a minute away from Coco. All of the crying was really starting to get to Anita.

She could tell Felix wanted to know more about Coco. Given all of the drama, who wouldn't want to know more about the lady at the center of the whirlwind that had just upset their nice tranquil home.

Anita was convinced that some of Coco's crying had to do with not knowing who was going to take care of her. There was just no way anyone could be that brokenhearted over someone who regularly kicked their ass and treated them like shit.

Anita thought Coco was crying about money, not love. Coco may be able to fool these rich people, but Anita knew the real Coco, and that Coco was a very good actress and an even better liar. She had lied to herself for years, believing the dream in her head and not the truth about Mike. Coco was Mike's mistress, plain and simple.

Anita loved Coco but she knew Coco better than anyone. She thought, "*Ms. Coco's got more tricks up her sleeve than a circus clown.*" But Anita had no plans to share that bit of information with Felix or any member of this smart, well trained, domestic team. If they were as smart as Anita believed them to be, then they would be able to figure Coco out soon enough.

Anita followed Felix into his office, which was just what she expected: organized and very clean. He had charts and diagrams for every part of the house and grounds. There was a bulletin board that held bits of information and photos of every guest, including their likes and dislikes. There was something about everyone who came to Jewels. She was amazed and in awe of the level of detail that went into Felix's job.

Once she was seated, a junior chef gently placed a lovely lunch plate in front of her. It was a delicious organic free-range chicken salad sandwich, made with nonfat natural yogurt, sweet currants, and roasted pecans, all on a freshly baked croissant, and with a small fruit salad on the side. The plate was arranged so beautifully that she was not sure whether to eat it or take a picture of it.

After the first bite, Anita started talking, which was something she normally would never have done. But there was a feeling of safety and comfort about Felix; she trusted him. Anita told Felix how old fancy pants Mike DeSalis had died with another woman. She told him about Coco and Mike's fights and how badly Coco tried to cover up the truth about Mike.

With tears in her eyes, she said, "It's just wrong to treat anybody that way. And I cannot understand any woman allowing herself to be mistreated, and the physical abuse was just as bad. I just don't understand it."

She looked away so Felix could not see that she was about to cry. After she gathered herself, she said, "Ms. Runni is a nice enough lady, but she is very troubled."

When she finished telling him everything, Anita said, "Now, with old fancy pants being dead and all, I ain't sure if I will have a job for much longer. Ms. Coco, I mean Ms. Runni, don't have any other way of stocking paper, means of income, that I know of. So I don't know if she will be able to pay me. But don't worry about me. I will find a job somewhere. I have always worked hard."

They continued to chat for about half an hour. By the time Anita finished her lunch, Felix's opinion of her had changed. He suddenly felt sorry for both women. Ms. Runni clearly didn't know her own self-worth. Anita was a good woman with a big heart. She just had not been properly trained. When they were finished Felix walked Anita to her new room. The room was nicer than anything she could have imagined staff quarters to be. Suddenly, she felt fortunate to have the opportunity to get to know Felix and his team. They had all gone out of their way to make her feel at home. It occurred to Anita that she would be happy to never leave Jewels.

Chapter 6

Bethany assisted Coco back to her room. Having a good read on people, Bethany did not like Coco. She thought, "*This Ms. Runni is a drama queen.*" It was clear she was nothing like Mrs. Von Kinley. It was surprising that they were friends.

As soon as she got Coco back to her room, the tears stopped. Coco started ordering Bethany around, telling her, "Hang up my sweater. Don't you see it on the chair? It's very expensive. I know you wouldn't understand that, but pick it up now, and when you are finished, clear those dishes. I hate to see dirty dishes." She never once said *please* or *thank you.*

Bethany thought, *"Mrs. Von Kinley never spoke to anyone in the tone that this Ms. Runni was speaking to her."* Bethany complied as instructed, she just wanted to get out of Coco's presence as soon as possible. She intended to tell Felix about this lady and the poor acting job she had just witnessed.

As soon as Bethany was finished Coco dismissed her, telling her, "That will be all for now. Please leave me alone, and please tell the staff not to disturb me."

Bethany thought, "*The staff. Who in the world does this woman think she is?*" But she only said, "As you wish. Please ring should you need anything."

Coco needed to be alone. She could not believe what had just happened to her. And it had all played out in front of Sadie.

How could Mike cheat her out of a final good-bye. Moreover, how would it look to everyone who knew her. Who knew them.

Coco's mind was racing. She thought his funeral would be her last chance to be seen with him publicly. Now she had been robbed of the chance to have her picture taken and to hold court at his casket. She had been looking forward to playing the role of the grieving widow. And if not his legal widow, she was whatever you call a woman at her age who is not married to the man when he dies. There were titles, and she didn't like any of them: girlfriend, lover, mistress, friend with benefits. Whatever the title, she had again been robbed.

She said out loud, "Damn, damn, damn! Why does this shit always happen to me?" Her absence would tell everyone that she was not his fiancée, that all these years she had lied to everyone, telling them that she was going to marry Mike. Now everyone would know the truth, that Mike was never going to marry her.

Coco suddenly felt dirty. She took off her clothes and went into the shower. Under the running water, she said, "Oh my God, it's true. He was never going to marry me, never, and now the no good bastard is dead, and I can't say good bye. Oh God, what will I do now?"

With that ugly truth so plain for the world to see, Coco let go of all pretenses, and she truly cried for every promise that Mike had broken and for every pain she had felt at his hands. Coco cried until her whole body was shaking. Then she dressed, poured herself a strong drink from the small bar in the room, and lay down across the bed. She could not sleep; there was too much going on in her head. Sleep was the last thing she could think of. She just laid there, thinking about everything that had happened.

Chapter 7

Sadie needed a few minutes to herself. She was feeling overwhelmed and annoyed with Coco. She was doing everything she could think of to help her, and then Coco went and gave out Sadie's address to that joker Jonathan without even asking her if it would be okay. That was just rude, and something Sadie would never have done to Coco.

Sadie did not do well with confusion. She liked things to run according to plan. It seemed that Coco's life was filled with drama, and a great deal of it was her own doing. She could not understand Coco's thinking that this way of life was good or a desirable way to live, with no husband, no future, and no means of support.

Sadie's mother had always told her, "Women who make their living on their knees always end up broke, on their ass." Coco was living proof of that statement. But she wanted more for her friend. She just didn't know what to do to help her.

Sadie began to wonder what was keeping Nancy and Winnie. They should have arrived half an hour ago. She had no idea what was taking them so long. She needed to get an update on their arrival time, so she placed a call to their cell phones.

She was only able to get through to Winnie. As usual, Nancy was busy talking to an event planner about her next Republican fundraiser. Winnie told her their plane had just landed, and they would be heading her way soon.

When Sadie bought her up to date, all Winnie said was, "Oh holy shit." She told Sadie not to worry they would be there shortly.

After disconnecting the call, Winnie turned to Nancy and said, "You will never believe what just happened."

Nancy quickly ended her call to her event planner.

Winnie repeated what Sadie had told her. Nancy said she was not surprised, because from what she had heard, Mike and Coco's relationship was a hot mess with no future. Mike was just Coco's ATM.

Nancy had heard rumors about Mike's sexual appetite, he was rumored to make out with a snake if you held its' head still. Woman or man—he didn't care, as long as he got off.

They asked the driver to please hurry. They had all been scheduled to come down to Jewels for a little relaxation before the emotional funeral services. Now that the shit had really hit the fan. Nancy and Winnie felt bad for Coco but they were delighted, they would not be attending Mike's funeral services. They both had strong feelings about Mike and could not understand Coco's masochistic obsession with him, having heard rumors for years now that when things in his life went wrong, Mike used Coco as his punching bag. Afterward, he would buy her marvelous gifts and send her to some fabulous spa. Whenever they tried to talk to Coco about it, she would tell them she was fine, and that she and Mike were more in love than ever. Then they wouldn't see her for a few weeks. And when they did, she would always look great.

Winnie was certain that the reason Coco tolerated Mike's abuse had something to do with Coco's childhood. Someone had hurt her and left her emotionally deprived and unable to fully handle a real relationship. That was the only explanation for why Coco always followed after what she herself knew she could never possess.

Nancy and Winnie's car pulled up to the gates of Jewels in record time. Sadie greeted them at the front door with her arms outstretched, giving them big bear hugs, and then she took them upstairs to their guest rooms. The ladies had adjoining bedroom suites, both decorated in hues of icy green and peach. Their rooms were next to Coco's. The three suites shared a gorgeous balcony with stunning ocean views, adorned with classic wicker furniture, with luxurious cushions in calming shades of icy teal and cream.

The staff had already set up refreshments on the balcony for them to enjoy. As soon as Coco heard Nancy's voice, she stepped out on the balcony and walked next door to greet her friends. At the sight of Winnie and Nancy, Coco started to cry.

Sadie could not tolerate another moment of Coco's emotions. So she reminded them that she would be entertaining her board in a few hours, and she needed to leave them to get ready.

Thankful that Winnie and Nancy were there to take care of Coco, she hugged them again and made her exit. Nancy could sense that Sadie was uptight, so she told her they would stay out of sight and maybe have dinner down on the beach. Sadie was so grateful to Nancy and Winnie. They understood what life was all about, and what she had to get done. When Sadie left the room, they all went out on the balcony.

Winnie flopped down on the wicker chair and said, "Coco, girl, what is going on? Are you really not allowed to go to the damn funeral?"

Nancy said, "This is really some major drama bullshit, Coco. Are you sure you can't sue that bastard back to life?"

Coco had no answers. She knew they wanted to hear something from her, like what her next plans would be, but she had nothing to give them. She gazed out at the ocean waves. Right then, she had a sad thought that maybe her father had been right when he told her she would never amount to anything. That she was nothing, that no good man would ever want her. She hated her father for many things. One was telling her she would never amount to anything. Deep down, Coco hated herself for allowing this to happen. Coco was broken in more ways than one, and she had been for a long time.

But she truly had no idea how to correct her past or make a new life for herself. She believed they wanted to hear a grand plan, but she had nothing but tears.

Right now, sitting in front of her super-successful friends, she felt stupid and so very afraid for her future. What would she do now, without Mike to take care of her? Again the tears started to flow down her face.

Winnie took Coco's hand and said, "Don't cry anymore. We are here for you. Together we will get you through this."

That evening, while Sadie and Lonnie played host to their board members. Winnie, Nancy, and Coco had a picnic on the beach, the warm evening breeze felt great and the sound of the ocean was tranquil. The cook prepared a wonderful feast for them, with barbecued lobster tails, grilled corn on the cob, sweet and tangy coleslaw, and individual peach pies. It was marvelous, after they had eaten every morsel of food and finished off two bottles of Krug, Clos du Mesnil 1979. Nancy announced that she had booked them all on a twelve-day Mediterranean cruise, aboard the five-star Crystal Cruise Line. If everyone agreed, they would be leaving in three days.

Coco just stared at Nancy, she didn't know what to say.

Nancy said, "Coco, nothing can heal a broken heart like sunny, lazy days aboard a five-star cruise ship."

They would be meeting the ship in Barcelona, Spain, and heading to Venice, Sorrento, Rome, and finally ending the voyage in Monaco.

Nancy gave Coco a very serious look and said, "Coco, I know you are hurt, surprised, shocked and all the things one feels when something like this happens, but you have to pull your shit together and move on with your life. Yes, Mike hurt you, but it is not the first time, and we all know it. But he didn't leave you with nothing, so take lemons and make lemonade."

Coco looked at her friends. Both of them had known all along, and they never interfered in her relationship but they had always been there to help her.

Winnie said, "The best revenge is moving on and replacing him with someone who's richer and smarter. This time around, let's pick a kind man."

Nancy said, "If you are truthful, Coco, your life was not a bed of roses with Mike. Now let's go on this fabulous cruise and find you another man, or at least a marvelous lover."

Winnie laughed and said, "At this age, a lover does not sound bad. Less mess." She and Nancy burst out laughing.

Coco just smiled and asked how much all of this fun would cost. Nancy said, "It my gift to us, think of it as a birthday present."

Coco said, "Really Nancy thank you. I would be delighted to go."

Winnie said she needed to check with her producer, but she was due a vacation, and now would be a perfect time. They all agreed. Raising their champagne glasses together, they said, "Crystal Cruises, here we come."

They didn't need to worry about clothes or anything. They would take what they had already packed. If they needed something else, they would just purchase it on the ship.

Over breakfast the next morning, they told Sadie about their cruise plans. It all sounded glorious, and she would have loved to join them, but due to her overwhelming social and family commitments, she would not be able to leave right away. She said, "How about I meet you in Monaco and we can all stay at my place."

The Von Kinley's had a duplex on Princess Grace Avenue. Sadie would have Felix arrange everything. The apartment would be ready for them when they ended their days at sea.

Now that they would be leaving soon, Coco would have to make arrangements for Anita to fly back to Washington, D.C. She told her she didn't know when she would be returning home, but she needed her to check on her house every day, and to take in the mail and dust. She would let her know when she would be heading back to the States.

Anita was very sad after hearing the news that she would be leaving Jewels sooner than she had expected. She had become very fond of Felix and the rest of the staff. They were good people who had taught her a lot in the few days she was there. She told Felix that if he ever needed an extra hand, she would be more than happy to work for him. He was touched and to tell the truth, he did not want her to leave either. He had given her some small tasks to do while she was there, and she had shown an incredible pride in her work. That and her wonderful sense of humor made her fun to be around. The entire staff had become very fond of Anita.

On the day when she was due to leave, Felix gave her two envelopes. One held a check signed by Sadie for a full month's salary. The other envelope had seven hundred dollars cash and Felix's business card. He told her that if things didn't work out and she needed a job, he would help her find one. He drove her to the airport himself, helped her with her bags, and told her it was his honor to get to know her better.

Felix's words made Anita feel like a lady. Without thinking, she reached up and gave him a big hug. Felix blushed and said, "Okay, okay, enough of all of that." They smiled, and she walked into the terminal. A friendship had developed. He meant it, if she needed him he would help her. He knew that Anita was a good woman.

As she boarded the plane Anita thought, "*It's true that when you feel all is lost, sometimes you are handed a gift that will change your life.*" Coming to Jewels and meeting Felix and his team had changed Anita's life. She wanted to learn more and be more, to take pride in her profession and herself. She would stay on and see Ms. Coco through this mess with old fancy pants, but then she would start looking for a family that needed her help. Some of the Von Kinley staff had shared with her that they had full medical, dentals benefits, and they had retirement. Ms. Coco didn't offer any of that to Anita. How could she. She didn't have it for herself. Anita was working on her plan for the rest of her life.

Chapter 8

On the night before they left for their cruise, Coco could not get to sleep, so around two o'clock in the morning, she went downstairs to get some warm milk, which always relaxed her. As she wandered through the house, looking at the Von Kinley's family photos and priceless artwork, her feelings of envy and jealously were heightened. Sadie's life just seemed so damn perfect.

Coco wondered why she hadn't been the one to live in this magnificent palace and have this fabulous life. Why her friends? Why not her? What had she done wrong? She was angry with life and her choices, which had made her suffer.

Earlier that evening, Sadie and Lonnie had entertained their fashionable Palm Beach friends around the pool. Being the perfect hostess, Sadie invited them to join the party, but Coco declined, saying she was tired. The truth was that she was feeling resentful and depressed.

Watching from her window, she looked down on the festivities. She could see that no detail had been overlooked. There was even a live band, everyone was smiling and enjoying themselves. Well, everyone but Coco.

Lonnie pulled Sadie into his arms as the band played "Satin Doll," by Duke Ellington. They danced under the stars like young lovers. Sadie looked wonderful in wide-legged pants and a silk-and-cotton top from Chanel's resort collection. She wore her hair up in the back, which showed off her breathtaking diamond earrings. Everything about the evening looked perfect. Coco was happy for her friend, and saddened at the same time.

Being in this house was like walking through a fairy tale, a picture book of Sadie's perfect life. Every step she took in Sadie's domicile was pure perfection. And dammit, Coco deserved this life, not Sadie and not the rest of her friends. As she lifted a family photo up for a closer look, Felix walked up behind her and said, "Ms. Runni, is there something I can help you with?"

Coco was startled and none too happy. She scolded him, saying, "What is wrong with you, frightening me like that?"

Felix, said, "Excuse me, Ms. Runni, but when one of our houseguest is walking through the house at this hour in the morning, it is my duty to assist them. Now madam, is there anything that I can get for you?"

Coco pushed the framed photo at Felix and then said, "I just wanted some warm milk. You can bring it to my room at once." She turned and walked away, again never saying, *please* or *thank you*.

Felix could tell what was really wrong with her. He knew the look of green-eyed jealousy. His staff had already informed him of some of Coco's rude demands. So he just smiled and nodded his head, returning the photo to its correct place. He then went to the kitchen to make her a hot toddy, one of his special recipes. He poured almond milk, a double shot of thirty year old Glenfiddich private vintage whiskey, cinnamon, a drop of vanilla, and a large spoonful of honey in a saucepan. When it came to a simmer, he transferred it into a small silver coffee server and placed it on a tray with a couple of freshly baked, chocolate-chip cookies. Felix knew she had a sweet tooth and that she loved cookies. He made sure to arrange the china, linen, and a fresh flower on the tray with special care.

When he knocked on her door, she opened it, never making eye contact with him. They both knew what was really wrong with her. Coco was feeling ashamed of herself.

Felix placed the tray on the table nearest her bed. He poured the steaming liquid in a china cup. Then he turned, looked right at her, and said, "Good night, Ms. Runni. I do hope you sleep well. You want to be fresh for your flight in the morning."

Coco never looked up until she heard the door close. The tray was perfect. His special drink was the most delicious toddy she had ever tasted. Before she knew it, she'd downed the whole pot and finished off the cookies. She felted more relaxed and calm. Looking around at her lovely surroundings, she again wondered, *Why not me?* She was relieved to be departing this seaside oasis. Being on the cruise would be good for her. She needed the open seas. She felt guilty for her feelings of jealousy toward Sadie and she could tell that Felix could read her every thought.

Losing Mike, and then being a witness to Sadie's perfect life. It was just too much for her. She needed to get the hell out of there, and soon.

Chapter 9

Nancy, Winnie, and Coco left for the airport early in the morning. They flew first class to Barcelona, Spain, where they met the ship. Once aboard, they all had penthouse suites with balconies. There was nothing like an adventure aboard a Crystal cruise, where every amenity was available, and the staff was trained in the art of customer service. It was just what Coco needed. She was grateful Nancy had given her this marvelous gift.

The ladies booked spa treatments and signed up for enrichment classes. They took shore excursions and shopped in quaint stores, picking up gifts for family members and friends. Well, Nancy and Winnie bought gifts for their families. Coco spent her money on herself.

Each day they made time for some real heart-to-heart talks with Coco about her future, money, and life after Mike. Winnie could not help but feel there was something about this whole mess, that Coco was not sharing with them. Coco never talked about missing Mike. She only whined about her financial future. Winnie was starting to believe that Coco was not in love with Mike, just with Mike's money.

Over breakfast one morning, Winnie shared her thoughts with Nancy.

Nancy said, "Well, Winnie, isn't that what a mistress is supposed to do, worry about the money? If Coco really was worried about her future, she would have gotten a real job, or made that bastard marry her."

Winnie said, "Girl, I thought a mistresses job was to pull, suck, and swallow. Well, all I know is I never wanted to be one. It just never seemed like enough."

Nancy said, "Now, you know they charge extra for swallowing." They burst into laughter.

Winnie said, "Okay Nancy, really how are we going to help Coco? She just doesn't seem to get it."

Nancy, always being the one with great wit, quoted Oscar Wilde, "The truth is rarely pure and never simple." She then took another sip of her Bellini and said, "Winnie, to tell you the truth, I have no earthly idea what we can do to help Coco. She needs to find a way to help herself now that she is free."

Winnie said, "Freedom has always had a price."

Nancy looked out at the sea and then back to Winnie and said, "The sad truth is Coco has already paid a damn high price for her freedom. She is now a veteran of her own war, but she has to pull herself up. She is better off than most abused women. She has a couple of dollars in the bank, a house in her name, and her health. She can make this work, if she wants to. But she has to want it."

Every minute on the cruise was magical, and the time went by so fast. On the last night of the cruise, they had been invited to be guests at the captain's table. He was delightfully charming. His knowledge of art, world affairs, and history was enchanting. He danced with each one of them. Who would have expected a sea captain to be so light on his feet?

Nancy said, "Well, if I wasn't already married, Captain, you would be on my list. You're the real deal, my dear man."

He blushed and said, "Well, that would be the best proposal of my life. Your husband is one lucky man."

Nancy quickly answered by saying, "I tell him that all of the time."

They all laughed.

The ladies admitted to each other that they didn't want to leave the heaven they had found aboard their ship. They had all been restored and rejuvenated. These were really the best days they had spent together in some time.

They would be meeting Sadie at her place at 21 Avenue Princesse Grace, Monte Carlo, Monaco. It was a five bedroom duplex with breathtaking views of the principality and steps away from marvelous beaches filled with beautiful people, savoring the best of what life had to offer.

Sadie, Winnie, and Nancy stayed on for five days. Coco was in no rush to return home. Sadie invited her to stay as long as she needed to. And while she was there, she begged her to please find a good man. Sadie gently warned her that she could not hide out forever. She would need to get a plan for the rest of her life, and soon.

Over dinner on their last night together, after Sadie had downed two gin martini's. Sadie said, "Coco, I know you want what we have, or more to the point what I have. Well, here's some advice. You are going to have to work with a better plan than the one you are currently using."

Sadie saw the sadness in Coco's face. She didn't want to hurt her friend, but she needed Coco to wake up to the truth: that up until now, she had been lucky. As silence fell over the room, Sadie continued. "Living well is only achieved with a good plan and some good old-fashioned hard work. The older a woman gets, the less luck has to do with living well. We are all here to help you, but you have to get a plan, and fast."

Coco didn't say a word, and Sadie was hoping what she had told her was finally sinking in.

Nancy said, "Alcohol is still truth juice."

Winnie could not stand for them to be upset with each other, and she did not want anyone to get their feelings hurt, so she changed the subject.

Winnie said, "Sadie, your place is beautiful. How long have you owned it?"

Sadie said, "For close to twenty years now."

Coco finally spoke, "Ladies, I love that all of you are so successful. I am proud of you, and I promise that I will be okay. I just need a little more time."

Nancy said, "Coco, Jesus, we have always been here to help you, but Sadie is right. You have to want more for yourself, and you have to pursue your own happiness stop looking for a man to give it to you."

No one said anything else. It was late, so they wished each other good night and went to their rooms.

There is a delicate balance, of admiration, adoration, and respect that goes on in female relationships, and normally this group had the gift of perfect balance, but the green-eyed jealousy monster that Coco was feeling was starting to show. She knew that she needed to get it together, because she loved Sadie, and she treasured their friendship. She just needed life to give her a break and shine some of its wonderful blessings on her.

Sadie, Winnie, and Nancy left earlier the next morning, not bothering to wake Coco. They just left her a note that said, "We love you, but please love yourself. We will see you when you come back home."

Sadie left instructions with her staff and a neighbor who lived in the building. She and Sadie had become friends over the years. She wanted her to look out for Coco and check in on her from time to time.

Coco stayed on in Monaco, enjoying the quiet elegance of the small island town. She relaxed poolside, walked the beach every night, and made some new friends. She needed the time away to get her mind back on track. She thought of nothing but why and how her life had turned out so badly.

Sadie's apartment was fully staffed. The Von Kinley's employed a live-in husband and wife team who took care of the apartment year round. The wife, Helena, cleaned and organized and she cooked the most wonderful French dishes, while her husband, Jacques was the chauffeur and all around mister fix-it. They spoke perfect English and several other languages. They had lived in Monaco all their lives, so they could tell her everything about their beautiful homeland, and they could get her anywhere she needed to go. The Von Kinley's kept a late-model Jaguar there, so getting around town was no problem.

On Coco's second week she met a lovely American neighbor who lived in the building and spent every summer on the island. She took Coco to the opera house to see a ballet, to the Monte Carlo Casino for a night of glamour and card playing, and on Sunday they went to the Chapel of Mercy. The splendor of this historical old chapel gave Coco a sense of peace and comfort. During the rest of her stay, she visited the chapel often. It was there that she finally realized she had to move on with her life.

She wanted to believe that life and love were worth trying for again, but she just didn't know with who, so she prayed for God to give her a heart of forgiveness for everyone who had hurt her, starting with her father and then her mother. Finally, she prayed for Mike, for his evil soul and that somehow she could forgive him for everything he had done to her and to be freed of his memory.

No matter how much she prayed, she just could not get Mike off her mind. She replayed every moment with him, the highs and the lows, the fights and the making up. How he had always been so sorry afterwards, and how he had always told her that he loved her. Promising her that if she would just hold on a little while longer and be a little more understanding, things would work out.

Over the years, their relationship had turned from sweet and loving to dark and unfulfilling. The sex had started out tender and then turned into rough, unfeeling, and unsatisfying. She thought about every violent episode, how she used his bad behavior to get what she needed financially. It was her way of making him pay for hurting her. She completely hated him and loved him at the same time. Her relationship had been damaged from the start, and thanks to her father and now Mike, she felt she would always be damaged goods.

On her last morning there before she left for the airport, she went back to the Chapel of Mercy. She prayed that she would be able to leave all of her hurt on the altar. She wanted and needed to believe that when she boarded the flight home, she would be a new Coco, healed and cleansed from her past pain and hurt.

Monaco was her hiding place until she was strong enough to handle what would be waiting for her.

Chapter 10

After two months and one week, Coco returned home to face the real world. Her friends had protected her all they could and she loved them for it, but now it was time for her to move on with her life, to pick up the pieces and try to find that elusive happy ending.

Coco started with making an appointment with her Frank Templeton investment advisor. She needed to find out how much money it would take to live on for the rest of her life. She also placed a call to her tax accountant to see where she was financially in terms of her property.

After what she had recently learned about Mike's other life, she needed to be sure there were no outstanding liens or unpaid taxes on the property.

Coco was thankful she had taken Nancy's advice a few years back and opened an investment account. Nancy called it a rainy day fund. She told Coco that every woman, no matter what her marital status, should have a rainy-day fund.

Coco funded the account by using half of her monthly allowance from Mike. She never let Mike know about her investment accounts. To make sure he would never find out, she had the statements mailed to her sister Barbara's house. Barbara hated Mike, so she was more than happy to help Coco with her emergency cash account.

Coco's advisor had been helping her purchase stocks for a while now. That money, along with the million dollars in her new trust account, would give her just under two million dollars. She would still have to cut back on her spending, because now she would be responsible for paying all of her living expenses.

Since the day she'd met Mike until the day he died, he had paid for all of her expenses, everything including her newspaper subscriptions every month. Her spending habits were the only thing he never complained about. No matter how high the credit-card balance, his office would just pay it off at the end of each month. Mike never said a word to her about it.

Coco was still very disappointed in herself. She should have been more mindful of her future and not just lived for the day or, in her case, the fashion season. Why had she been so foolish to have fallen in love so hard, hoping that one day he would turn around and start to appreciate her and value how much she loved him. In a lot of ways, Coco had enjoyed being a kept woman. It was just sad that the benefits had ended so soon.

Coco's meeting with her financial advisor left her even more depressed. She learned that her estate would have to pay inheritance and capital gains taxes on the cash that Mike had left her, and on the market value of her home. When Mike died, the house was transferred from his name into her name. The taxes she would have to pay immediately added up to over 30 percent of her net worth. She knew little to nothing about taxes, only that she had to pay them. The amount her investment advisor and accountant quoted her was overwhelming. Now she would have to sell some of her stock to pay off her tax bill. The only good part of the meeting was learning that she could now get full health insurance on her own. One step forward, three steps back. It was just her life.

Coco still could not believe that Mike was dead and that he had locked her out of his life. He had promised her forever. Well, so much for that. She telephoned Nancy to tell her about her meetings. To Coco's surprise, Nancy agreed with her advisors and told her that she was lucky.

Coco said, "Lucky? Nancy, how is this lucky? Please explain that to me."

Nancy said, "Coco, you have something to start with. Build on that. You can do it; just settle down and focus."

Nancy really didn't have time to talk to Coco about this again. She had other things to do and she was getting real good and tired of giving out the same advice over and over again. So she just wished Coco well and told her she was busy and she promised to get together soon. Winnie and Sadie had been busy with major projects as well.

Coco felt like she had no one to turn to. It was clear her friends were tired of hearing about her problems, they were also busy running their lives while Coco's life was running her. When she called her sister, Barbara, all she said was to get a job and start taking care of herself.

While that was easy for everyone to say, the reality was that she was a former model who was past her prime, and she had no office skills. She could not type, and her knowledge of computers was minimal at best, she wasn't well read, she didn't have any political insights. She only knew how to look good, and shop not skills you can put on a resume.

She hated the helpless feeling that was now her constant friend. It was at times like this that she felt she really needed a man to advise her on what to do. Mike had been a brilliant businessman, and she had trusted him. What a complete fool she'd been. How could he leave her after everything they had been through together. He had left his wife and then waited to be granted the divorce, and the huge settlement, not knowing if he would have to sell his casino to satisfy his wife's demands. His divorce had been such a nasty fight, and it had all played out in the media.

Coco had given him the best years of her life, waiting, hoping, and praying that one day she would be able to wear the wedding gown she had secretly purchased and kept stored in the back of her closet. Just in case Mike said those magical words, "Coco will you marry me today?" She would be ready, and she would have the perfect dress. She'd waited so long, hoping this would be the year she would become Mrs. Michael Francisco DeSalis. When her friends asked her, "Why do you love Mike so much?" Coco couldn't explain her attachment to him, hell sometimes she didn't understand it herself.

As she started thinking about her life nothing made sense to her, from her childhood to now as an adult woman, everything had always been a mess and now she didn't know what to do next.

She only knew that after all the shit had gone down with her parents, after she confronted them about her father's sick late-night visits to her room, her mother had called her a whore and a devil. Her father grabbed a kitchen knife and started coming at her. If Barbara had not been standing between them, using her body as a shield, Coco was certain her father would have killed her.

She ran out of their house that night and never returned. Barbara took Coco to her best friend Ann. Coco lived with Ann her entire senior year of high school. The week before her graduation, her father called Ann and told her that if Coco came to the graduation, he would burn down their apartment building. To prove he meant every word, the day before the graduation ceremony, he set a stack of newspapers on fire in front of their building. Coco and Ann were frightened, they knew he meant business. Coco didn't walk across the stage. He had taken away her innocence, and the one thing she felt good about: her teachers and going to school. Now she couldn't even say good-bye to them. Barbara brought Coco her high school diploma the next week.

Ann introduced Coco to a modeling scout she was dating. He got Coco signed with a good agency the next day. Ann was kind to Coco, she had come from a troubled family herself, and she understood Coco's pain.

But Coco needed to be on her own. She wanted to get away from anything that reminded her of her past life.

She loved modeling. Every assignment was different, and she got use to the attention and people treating her like she was special. She learned that she could use her looks to get just about anything she wanted. So after a couple of good paychecks, she got her own apartment in a luxury building in the southwest section of Washington. It was near the water and close to everything. Her new independence was wonderful. She was making good money and spending every penny she made. That's the thing about trying to buy happiness; it's very expensive.

She had dinner with Barbara once a week. They never spoke of the fight or anything about their parents. She would just tell Coco that she loved her no matter what had happened. When Barbara announced that she was getting married, Coco planned a trip out of the country, so as not to make Barbara have to choose between her parents and her. When she told Barbara about her plans, they both cried. Barbara wanted Coco to be a part of this special time in her life, but she also knew how much pain it would cause everyone.

After Coco met Mike, her life changed. He purchased a condo for her in the elegant Elizabeth building in Chevy Chase. For the first time, she felt like she had something of her own. She got settled into her new life, setting up house and spending her days shopping.

One day when she was out running errands, she saw her mother leaving the Claire Dratch dress shop on Wisconsin Avenue. She wanted so badly to say hello but when her mother looked up and saw Coco, she just turned her head and walked right pass her. That was the last time Coco ever saw her. The next year, her mother passed away, and six months later, her father died in his sleep.

Coco was overwhelmed with grief and loneliness. She went to their services, but she could not bring herself to go into the church, so she sat in her car and cried. When the funeral cars were leaving the parking lot, Barbara saw Coco and gave her a small wave. She understood her pain, but she did nothing to comfort her. It was the only time that Coco felt Barbara blamed her for breaking up their family. Coco never forgot that feeling of separation. It made her parents' deaths even worse.

When all the mourners had gone, Coco walked into the church. She took one of the programs and read the obituary. It didn't mention Coco. There were no pictures of her with the family, only Barbara. It was as if Coco didn't exist. Coco sat in the church for hours, until a kind old priest came over to comfort her. It was dark outside when she finally left. When she got home, she had three calls from Barbara. Coco didn't return any of them. She needed some time apart from the painful memories.

She was afraid to tell Mike everything about her relationship with her family or what had happened with her father. Pushing her feelings for her family as far back in her mind as possible. To her, that part of her life had died with her parents. Her relationship with Barbara became strained and very uncomfortable. Making Mike happy had become her new life.

When Avenel, a planned upscale community in Potomac, Maryland, was being built, Coco asked Mike to go look at the development with her. He did one better than that, he purchased the largest end-unit townhouse for her, wanting to prove to Coco that he truly cared about her and wanted to start a life with her. He paid cash for the property and requested a ten-day escrow. Those were the good days with him. It was after she had moved into the townhouse that things started to change.

Mike started taking prescription drugs, and he began having mood swings. It was then that Coco started to see the violent side of Mike. Sometimes after she hadn't seen or heard from him for weeks. She would come home, and he would be sitting in her living room. He would have gone through her mail, her calendar, and her closets, pulling out clothes he didn't like. He would question her about where she had been and who she was with. If he didn't like the answer, he would start a fight. After the fight, he always demanded sex angry sex was his new favorite. In the morning he would leave before breakfast, and later in the day he would send her a gift. Sometimes the gifts would be an entire new wardrobe of clothes. He loved jewelry, and giving it to her made him happy. Every three years he gave her a new car, always a Jaguar. Coco had become use to the roller-coaster ride that their relationship had become.

What a lovesick fool she had been. She would make the next man pay for all the heartbreak she had suffered. In her next relationship, it would be all about her. She did not give a damn about anyone else—just herself.

She made herself a promise that the next time around, Coco Runni would win. No matter who got hurt in the process, she would win.

Life Goes On

Chapter 11

Coco thought, "*Lying here daydreaming is not getting anything done.*" She needed to get a move on. She reached for her remote control and turned on Channel 19. She always started her day by watching Winnie deliver the morning's breaking news story.

Winnie was a loyal, caring friend. She was also the only African American woman on the executive board of the Capital Ladies' Club. Not that it mattered, but it just demonstrated how old-fashioned the Capital Ladies' Club still remained. It was thanks to Nancy, Coco, and Sadie's votes well, mostly Sadie's that the board had finally approved Winnie's application for membership.

Over the years, the club had established rules on the requirements for membership. One rule was that no members of the working media would be allowed to join. It wasn't easy convincing this group of old-guarded Washingtonians that having Winnie as a member would be good for them.

Sadie had lobbied hard, and finally they reasoned that because Winnie did not represent print media, she was a highly respected TV news anchor, that accepting her membership request would be a feather in their cap.

The nominating board was very impressed with Winnie's academic accomplishments. Having graduated with honors from American University's School of Public Affairs, where she majored in communications, after graduation, she had gone on to Harvard Business School and finished first in her class. Her list of awards was beyond impressive. She was smart, rich, and having traveled the world as the wife of an industrialist, she had international contacts.

Winnie was a third-generation Washingtonian, her parents had been exceptional members of the community. Leaving her a proud heritage of the highest educational accomplishments, along with a proud history of civic leadership. Her mind was only matched by her beauty.

Winnie had a flawless complexion the color of caramel, silky chestnut-brown hair that fell to her shoulders, and large almond-shaped eyes with long, thick lashes. Her beauty was the benefit of a mixed cultural heritage. Her father was Portuguese and American Indian. Her mother was Creole, a mixture of Spanish, French, and African. All of this made for a regally beautiful woman. She took great pride in herself and her appearance. Always perfectly groomed and manicured, she carried herself with an air of elegance that came naturally.

She had married and divorced twice. The last marriage had left her with a broken heart. After her divorce was final, she returned to the Washington area, and purchased a house in the Cleveland Park section of the city. She had the house decorated by a world-renowned interior design team that was known to have worked on the homes of several former US presidents and a few Hollywood stars.

Winnie traveled among a very elite group of friends. Her picture had been published in *Town and Country*, *Vogue*, and *Vanity Fair* magazines. Her circle of celebrity friends included number one-ranked athletes, fashion designers, movie stars, and music powerhouses. But Winnie treated everyone special. It didn't matter if you were a celebrity or just an everyday person; if you were in her company, she made you feel like you were the most important person on earth. She was beautiful inside and out, and she only wanted the best of everything for her friends.

Chapter 12

Coco sat up when she heard Winnie detailing the latest fight in Congress, involving the disarmingly charming Senator Moyer, a Republican from Virginia. Moyer was a recent widower. His wife had passed away after a long battle with breast cancer. He'd been by her side every minute during her sickness. The Moyer's were a large family, with three daughters, two sons and twelve grandchildren. Moyer seemed to be a very devoted husband and father, but his time had always been divided by his work in Congress. Losing his wife had taught him the importance of family. Now he made every effort to spend more time with them.

That day, the good senator was using his powers of persuasion to lobby members of Congress and the American public on the benefits of a bill entitled 18 USC 919E, the Natural Gas Pipeline Reform Act. His powerful television presence and convincing manner would likely gain him enough votes to get his bill passed. It would be a narrow victory, but a win is a win.

Now that he was one of the most eligible bachelors in the country, and due to the fact that Coco loved a challenge. Senator Moyer had become her new obsession. He had shown some attraction to Coco but had yet to ask her out on a formal date.

She had no way of knowing that he'd already done a background check on her, and her past relationship with the casino owner was not good for the senator's pristine public image. His staff had informed him that Coco had never really done anything of substance. For a short time she'd had a promising modeling career, she had never married, had no children, and had no formal education past high school. She hadn't served on any meaningful boards or contributed to the community, other than attending flashy parties.

Their investigation did reveal that her name had been included in the divorce of Michael DeSalis. She'd been described as his mistress.

With this information the senator would be content to only flirt with Coco. He could not allow himself to get any closer than that. To him Coco had high negatives. Moyer had his eyes on the White House, and Coco was not first lady material.

He was amused by the fact that she would not take no for an answer. Her constant positioning and flirting had become very amusing to him. Like many women, Coco made herself available too soon in the game of catch the available man which rendered her uninteresting.

She made sure to be at any event that she knew he would be attending. Coco thought if he saw that she was interested in the same causes that he was supporting, it would make her look more interesting. All it was doing was making her seem needy.

Landing Moyer would be the only thing that could make up for all the loneliness she now felt, or the heartbreak Mike had left her with. Being married to a member of Congress would rocket her to the top of the social ladder.

To Coco's friends, she was just displaying more of her self-absorbed, self-destructive behavior. They had all asked her to please stop following the senator around. It was very plain to see that he was not that interested in dating anyone at the present time. For Coco that was like a red flag in front of a raging bull.

She had even volunteered to organize a fundraiser for the senator, but he turned her down, sending her a note to thank her for showing interest in his campaign. When Coco told the girls, they all weighed in with their advice for her.

Nancy said, "Money is like mother's milk to a politician. If he turned you down. Coco, he is trying to tell you nicely that he is not interested."

Winnie said, "Coco, please let this go."

Sadie said, "Darling Coco, please don't get yourself listed as a stalker. If you do, I will have to end our friendship."

Chapter 13

Winnie was reporting on local politics, and she mentioned the senator's upcoming annual barbeque. His campaign hosted the family-friendly event every year around his birthday. Coco quickly telephoned the senator's campaign office to purchase a ticket.

She would need something, elegant, chic, and classy enough to make her look like the next Mrs. Moyer. She made a mental note to call her saleslady, at Saks Jandel. Coco loved the boutique and had shopped there for years. They treated everyone the same; it didn't matter if you were the wife or the mistress. As long as your credit card was good, and you carried yourself like a lady, you were welcome in the elegant fashion haven on Wisconsin Avenue.

She left a message that she would take the lemon-yellow poplin Valentino pantsuit with matching cotton camisole. She had tried it on just a couple of days before. She also made a mental note to drop by Ann Hand's boutique. She needed a new eagle pin. Nothing said proper political elegance like something from the Hand collection.

Turning her attention back to the television, Coco was impressed with how much the camera loved Winnie. Her friend radiated grace and elegance. Winnie's look was impressive, and it was the only look that got you attention in this town.

Winnie was a good friend to have for many reasons. Coco would be seeing her in a couple of hours and would hopefully find out the latest comings and goings in the city. Coco used everything that her friends brought to the friendship table, anything to better position herself for the next opportunity.

Coco had heard rumors that a Grammy Award winning, Rhythm and Blues singer. Famous for his love songs and crazy-sexy eyes, was coming to town and staying in Winnie's guesthouse. Coco would love to be invited to one of Winnie's famous dinner parties.

Invitations to Winnie's parties were sought after. She mixed her guests with people from the worlds of fashion, sports, politics, religion, and of course she always had a Hollywood celebrity or two in attendance. Winnie's parties were not the usual Washington dog-and-pony show. They added that special magic to the evening.

Well, if it were true, Coco would have to gently invite herself, and hopefully, if Winnie was even a little grateful for her efforts, small though they might be, at getting her on the board of the club, she would invite Senator Moyer, and seat them together.

Coco made a point of making everyone around feel like she was in need of help, and that they should be the one to help her. Coco reasoned to herself that, after all, now that Mike was gone, she was without a man to take care of her. They were her friends, and they were all rich, and she was...well, prettier than they were. So they should be happy to help her find the next Mr. Right. They all had strong enough opinions about Mike being Mr. Wrong. Now was their chance to help her out. She didn't care what they thought about Senator Moyer not being that interested in her. Coco knew that given the right opportunity, she could change his mind.

Chapter 14

Kicking off her silk duvet and dangling her manicured toes over the side of the bed, Coco started thinking about her outfit for today's club meeting. Stretching again, she picked up her Natori robe, wrapping it around herself. She was proud of her body. She worked hard at making sure she didn't lose her hourglass shape. Coco believed that exercise was the true secret to a youthful life.

As she headed to the bathroom to begin her morning beauty routine, looking at herself in every mirror along the way, she was pleased with her fresh-faced glow. Her beauty routine included LaMer cleansing cream. She kept the entire LaMer collection of facial products as close as a priest keeps his Bible.

No one could tell that she'd had her nose broken a couple of times, and her jaw had been reset more than once. Her front teeth were now beautiful caps because her teeth had been broken in one of her nasty fights with Mike. Because of him she had a wonderful Beverly Hills plastic surgeon on speed dial. Her face didn't tell the trauma that she'd lived through.

She maintained a careful routine of weekly visits to Karma, Erwin Gomez's fabulous spa. It was the only appointment that she never canceled, no matter what. She loved the entire team. They were artists and worked magic on her with every visit. There she had regular facials and full-body pampering. A visit to Karma made life worth living. That, along with plenty of water, sleep, and vitamins, kept Coco's physical scars hidden. The emotional ones were a little harder to hide, and some days they were in full view for anyone who cared to get too close.

She headed to her closet, which was the entire length of the back of her house. Even with its enormous size, there still wasn't enough room for her collection of designer clothes. She only kept two seasons at a time; the rest of her clothes were sent to storage. Her evening gowns were stuffed in a walk-in closet on the third floor of the house.

She was not sure what to wear that day. She had several new outfits hanging in the closet with tags still on them.

The Capital Ladies' Club's first luncheon of the social season was a very important occasion. She knew that all the ladies would be wearing some fabulous outfit from the latest designer collections. Some members planned all year for the opening of the social season.

Her new mega-rich friend Sarah Talbot would be her guest for today's luncheon. Sarah was the third wife of an international businessman. All Coco knew of him was that he did a great deal of work in Europe and had something to do with world finance. They lived in one of the most opulent homes in Potomac, Maryland. He traveled a lot, leaving Sarah alone, so she and Coco had befriended each other.

Sarah didn't know about all of Coco and Mike's drama. Coco was very careful not to tell too much. Having Sarah around gave Coco someone to hang out with when her other girlfriends were not available. It was important to have über-rich friends in this group, and Sarah Talbot was one of the richest after Sadie Von Kinley.

For someone like Coco living on limited funds, the costs of the party invitations alone could send you to the poorhouse, not to mention the wardrobe necessary to keep your picture on the pages of *Washington Life*, *Capitol File*, and *DuJour* magazines.

Just the week before, Sarah had invited Coco to be her guest at a benefit fashion show and luncheon at Saks Fifth Avenue in Chevy Chase, Maryland, where Designer Jason Wu was making a personal appearance.

After the show, guests were encouraged to shop. Coco purchased a pretty purple dress and coat. She selected it because the color was vibrant, and the details were elegant. Coco did have an eye for great tailoring and fabrics.

She knew the Wu outfit would be a perfect choice for today's event, pulling out her new Jimmy Choo plum suede pumps and the purple ostrich Birkin bag with gold hardware. For her jewelry she chose her lovely Elizabeth Gage Tatyana necklace, made of south sea pearls, set in 18K yellow gold, with a bold antique William IV pendant, circa 1835. Just to finish off the look, she reached for one of her many Hermes scarves and a couple of the Hermes enamel bracelets.

Standing back to review her selections, she thought, *Perfection*! She would make heads turn today. No matter what Sadie or Nancy wore, she would look the best. There was no harm in some friendly competition; they had the money, the homes, and the husbands. She could have the fashion well, for as long as she could afford it anyway.

Coco's dressing room with its adjacent bath was designed to look like Mariah Carey's airy boutique-style boudoir. Marble flooring and lighted shelves added touches of glamour and drama.

Her clothes hung in brightly lit sections and were arranged from bright white to midnight-black. Her vast collection of shoes and handbags took up one third of the space. It was truly a diva's closet, and Coco had designed it to be just that.

There was a secret door in her closet that she kept locked at all times. It was there that she hid the costumes she had worn for Mike. She had a French maid, a schoolteacher, a chef, a cowgirl, and a nun's habit, along with several sex toys, movies, and books. He would make her dress up and act out his fantasy. If she didn't, he would beat her into submission. She had learned to just go along with whatever he wanted, and that was a lot because Mike had a very vivid imagination. Some of his fantasies left her with bruises. Using the scars to make him feel guilty, she would say, "Does your mother know how her little boy is acting out, you dirty little bastard. You make me sick. Now beg me for forgiveness. Do it now!" Mike would become emotional, like a little boy wanting and needing absolution. She used it for all it was worth. His mood swings were epic. He could go from a crying little boy to a raging bull with fists flying within minutes.

Coco could admit if only to herself that both she and Mike were very damaged people.

Chapter 15

Just as she finished pulling together the final touches for today's outfit, her doorbell rang. A quick glance at the wall clock let her know it was surely Anita. After their time together at Jewels, Coco was certain that Anita wanted to leave her and find another person or family to support. But Anita had stayed on, Coco could not imagine life without her trusted friend and maid.

Coco had a long to-do list for Anita today. She ran down the hall and took the elevator to the main floor. Having an elevator was the great thing about the townhouses in Avenel. It was the amenity that Coco loved the most about the property.

She opened the front door to a chilly breeze and Anita's warm smiling face. Coco thought, *"This woman is always happy; it has to be great sex or dynamite drugs."*

Anita said, "Good morning, Ms. Coco. You look beautiful today and with no makeup." It was true that Coco was one of those truly beautiful people. As soon as Anita stepped inside, Coco went over the day's to-do list.

Anita looked over the list and then said, "Okay." She asked Coco if she wanted anything for breakfast.

Coco said, "Yes, can you bring up a small breakfast today. A boiled egg and a slice of wheat toast, along with my normal cup of tea."

Coco had to get back to getting ready for today's event. Just as she finished with Anita, her telephone rang. All of a sudden, her house sounded like Grand Central Station. Looking at the caller ID, she saw it was Sadie calling.

Usually she was happy to hear from Sadie, but today she just didn't have much time, so she would have to make it a short conversation.

Sadie was calling to remind Coco that she needed her at the club early to greet the ambassador of France. Thanks to Sadie's international flair and long-standing position on the social register. She was able to secure prominent speakers like his excellency to deliver the keynote address for today's luncheon.

Of course, Coco would be on time, as she believed the ambassador to be single. She loved to flirt with handsome men. She never really knew which luncheon or dinner would be the one where she'd meet her next lover or sponsor. And the way things stood now, anyone would be better than the ghost of Mike.

As soon as she hung up the phone from speaking with Sadie, the phone rang again. This time it was the director of development for the Symphony. She was a polite young woman. She was calling to see when Coco had time to meet with her to discuss the Women's Committee's upcoming fundraiser.

Sadie and Nancy had both served as president of the Symphony's Women's Committee. Because they were friends, people just automatically thought that Coco was charitable or had an interest in serving on a board. If only they knew that she was very close to needing a fundraiser for herself.

Coco quickly got off the phone, explaining that right then was not the best time for a chat. She would check her schedule and call back when she had a moment to chat about the upcoming season.

Not one to let an opportunity go by without a little self-promoting, Coco informed the young woman that she was having lunch with the ambassador of France that afternoon. Failing to mention that he was speaking to the entire club and not just her. It was just like Coco to use any opportunity to sound more important than she really was.

After Coco ended the call, she yelled down to Anita, asking her to please answer the phone on the first ring and to tell callers that she was not available. Anita said, "*Deje que esa mierda ir al correo de voz. Estoy ocupado, maldita sea*!" (Let that shit go to voice mail. I'm busy, dammit!)

Coco turned on some music, hoping to clear her head. It was getting late, and she was not ready for her day. Running her bath water, she added a generous amount of Laura Mercier fresh fig honey bath cream to the warm water. She needed to think of a way to encourage her moneybags friend Sarah Talbot, to purchase a table for the symphony and, of course invite Coco to be her guest.

She would work on that today at the luncheon. It helped Coco's budget that the club kept their luncheon prices under one hundred dollars per person. She always used that as her giveback. It was not of equal value to a fifteen hundred dollar gala dinner ticket. But a girl has to use what she has at the time.

What Coco did not have was an endless checkbook or a large home to entertain in like all of her friends. She was becoming more and more resentful of their blessings and her misfortune. Sometimes life was just not fair. Why hadn't she made a fortune in the stock market or married a great guy who would take care of her forever?

While the soft sounds of Celine Dion's, "Taking Chances" played in the background. Coco slipped into the warm water and started to recount her list of tasks and all she needed to get done today.

Again, she thought if only Mike had left her more money, or if she had been able to file a suit against his estate for a share of the casino, things would be so different for her. She had often wondered whether their relationship would have ended differently if she had been able to keep the baby.

When she told Mike she was pregnant. He started a huge fight, yelling at her that she was just trying to trap him. He called her a gold digger and a whore. She'd never seen anyone look more like a devil than Mike on that evening. He started in on her slamming her head against the wall and then throwing her on the floor. She'd fallen down the stairs trying to get away from him. He ran after her. In his rage, he punched and kicked her in the stomach. When he finished beating her, he went to the bathroom to wash her blood off his hands. Then he yelled at her, "No babies, bitch! Do you understand me? No fucking babies!" He walked out, leaving her lying at the foot of the stairs.

Anita found her several hours later and took her to the hospital. Coco suffered a miscarriage. Her dreams of becoming a mother ended that day. The next day she flew to Beverly Hills, California, to see her cosmetic dentist and plastic surgeon. She needed a "freshen up." She didn't speak with Mike for two months after that. When she did, he said he was sorry for what he called his blowup, and then he blamed her for their relationship troubles.

When she returned home Mike sent her a Boucheron gold-enamel-turquoise and diamond necklace in the shape of a serpent, with a note that read:

> Ciao, mia bellissima Coco,
> Love can be deadly. Try not to get bitten.
> Mike

They never spoke of that incident again, Coco never wore the necklace.

Chapter 16

Sadie O'Hara had it all, brains, beauty, and sweet Southern charm, with perfect porcelain skin, thick red hair that hung to her shoulders, large green eyes, and full lips. Her long slender body, tiny waist, full bosom, and shapely legs that went on for days.

The O'Hara's were an immigrant family. Their ancestors had come to this country from Kildare, Ireland. Having been mostly mill workers, they traveled to America with only the shirts on their backs, in hopes of a better life. They worked hard, went to church every Sunday, lived within their small means, and respected their neighbors. Sadie loved them but she wanted more for her life than what her loving parents could provide.

People had always told her she was pretty, so she joined one beauty pageant after the other, winning each time. She used her prize money to take piano and dance lessons. She also took classes in manners and grooming. She learned how to walk, talk, and carry herself as if she belonged. Her mother told her that if she was willing to work hard, and if she looked the part, doors would open, and for Sadie they did.

She had everything she needed to succeed in life, holding tight to the core values that her family had taught her, treat people the way you want to be treated, watch your manners, and always send a thank-you note.

You couldn't help but fall in love with her, and that is just what Lonnie had done the moment she walked on stage for the Miss Tennessee beauty pageant. Lonnie had been asked to serve as a judge. Something his father would have been presiding over, but this year the senior Von Kinley was away on business, so Lonnie stepped in to help.

After the swimsuit, evening gown, and talent portions of the competition were completed, it was time for the all-important question from the judges, and as luck would have it Lonnie's question was presented to Sadie.

As with everything in life, Sadie was prepared and ready. She looked right into Judge Von Kinley's eyes and answered the question with grace and the elegance of a woman far older than her years.

Judge Von Kinley asked Sadie, "What do you think a woman's life goals should be?"

Sadie responded, "First and foremost to be a good wife and mother, and then to help her community, because charity begins at home and spreads abroad."

Dang, dang, dang! Lonnie was seeing stars and hearing bells. He had been hit by Cupid's thunderbolt.

Sadie won the pageant.

After the crowning, Lonnie walked backstage to meet Sadie. She was surrounded by well-wishers and some of her pageant friends. As Lonnie approached the happy group, they all seemed to move along, leaving Sadie and Lonnie alone. She greeted him with her sweetest Southern voice, saying, "Good evening, Mr. Von Kinley. Did you enjoy the pageant? I am most grateful for your support, and I promise to represent this fine state with pride and dignity."

Lonnie was speechless. He just stood there staring at her. After what seemed like hours, he managed to say, "Will you have dinner with me tonight?"

Sadie was startled but never without a backup plan. She said, "Not tonight, but how about lunch tomorrow?"

Before he could answer her, Sadie's parents, Arthur and Sallie O'Hara, came over to congratulate their daughter and introduce themselves to the Von Kinley gentleman.

Lonnie immediately knew that he needed to make this moment count. He said that he would be honored to take the O'Hara family out to lunch the next day. That was, if they could make time in their schedules. Arthur O'Hara instinctively knew that this was not just a gathering to celebrate Sadie's becoming Miss Tennessee. He could tell by the way the young Von Kinley was looking at his daughter that he had other plans. Men just know that about other men. Mr. O'Hara also noticed that Sadie had not taken her eyes off the young man.

Lonnie asked Mr. O'Hara if he knew where the Von Kinley estate was, and if they could arrange to meet him there for a celebratory luncheon the next day. Everyone in Tennessee knew of the Von Kinley estate. But the O'Hara's had never been asked to visit before. The O'Hara and Von Kinley families did not drink from the same watering holes. They were separated by several million dollars and a few thousand acres, to say the least.

Sadie had entered the competition to fund her college education, because her family did not have the money to send her to the school of her choice. Nor did they have the wardrobe to dine at the Von Kinley's estate. Through Sadie, the family was introduced to another world, and things were beginning to move fast.

Sadie's father was a proud man. Normally, he would have turned down this kind invitation. But he didn't want to be the reason Sadie did not get ahead in life, so with much reservation, he accepted the invitation on behalf of himself and Mrs. O'Hara. There was no need to bring along Sadie's nine siblings.

Sadie was beside herself with joy. She couldn't wait to get home to tell all her brothers and sisters about the handsome, regal, and charming Von Kinley. By Sadie's calculations, if she did everything her mother had taught her, she was sure she would be married by this time the next year.

The pageant director walked over to shake hands and announced that he needed Sadie to take pictures. As they excused themselves, he told them Sadie would be very busy for the rest of the evening.

Lonnie spoke up and said, "She needs to be free for lunch tomorrow as she will be dining with my family."

The pageant director already had a list of events that Sadie needed to attend, but knowing how much the Von Kinley family supported the pageant, the director could not say a word except, "Yes, Mr. Von Kinley, she will be there."

By the time lunch was over, Lonnie was completely in love with Sadie and the O'Hara family. He couldn't wait until after Sadie's one-year pageant term was over to ask for her hand in marriage. The months went by fast. Sadie was busier than a one-armed paper hanger, and she loved every minute of it. She was also falling deeply in love with Lonnie. They talked daily about what they wanted out of life, what they needed in a mate, how many children they wanted, and where they would live.

Lonnie had a promising career in the air force, and Sadie wanted to be an officer's wife. She gave up all thoughts of college and a career in television broadcasting to be Mrs. Lionel Von Kinley, until death did them part. They married at the First Baptist Church in front of five hundred of the most prominent families in the south.

To ensure control over the guest list, the Von Kinley's insisted on paying for all the wedding expenses. Mr. O'Hara had a real problem with this. He never wanted it said that his family could not afford to marry off this eldest daughter. But the truth was that he could never afford the kind of over-the-top extravaganza that Mrs. Von Kinley wanted.

She had watched President Nixon's daughter get married at the White House, and she was now determined to recreate the elegance of that day. It was to be a White House wedding, southern style, and the reception would be under a beautiful tent at the Von Kinley estate.

She had their back yard and the tent decorated to look just like the White House rose garden. The wedding made all of the social columns, which greatly pleased the senior Mrs. Von Kinley.

Sadie was just perfect for Lonnie, and theirs was a deep and passionate love affair. You could feel their love whenever you were around them; it was like electricity in the air. Sadie wanted to be the perfect wife, she learned how to prepare all of Lonnie's favorite meals. She was determine to make her new husband proud of her domestic talents.

Lonnie was focused on pleasing Sadie in every way possible he wanted to be the best husband, son-in-law and brother-in-law, so he learned the names and the likes and dislikes of all of Sadie's family members. As a wedding gift, the Von Kinley's give Sadie and Lonnie a check for one hundred thousand dollars, and hired them a maid.

Lonnie took Sadie on a month-long honeymoon to Half Moon Bay, Jamaica. Wanting to start their family right away they were delighted to learn that Sadie was pregnant when they returned home. Sadie gave Lonnie three healthy sons each born within two years of the other.

As Lonnie's military career began taking shape, he was decorated with one promotion after another. They traveled the world and moved twenty-three times, finally settling in McLean, Virginia, where Lonnie reported to the Pentagon every day. They had both enjoyed the life of a military officer, but it was hardest on their boys, who had to consistently make new friends.

But it taught them a great deal about the world. They carried themselves with worldly knowledge, and with respect for different cultures and people. Sadie had become very popular among the military wives, and she was a favorite bridge-club member. No matter how busy she was with outside activities, she always made her family her number-one focus. She was at every school event the kids had, and she also made time for Lonnie's needs, never letting anything or anyone come before her family, home, and marriage.

It had been a wonderful life, but after serving twenty-five years, Lonnie retired from active duty.

His father was deeply disappointed when Lonnie did not want to return back to Tennessee and take over the family tobacco business. Lonnie assured his parents that his brother Eugene was doing a great job. He had worked hard and deserved the right to be the new CEO of VK Tobacco and Feed. Relieved of the pressures from his family, Lonnie followed his own dream and founded LVK, a defense contracting company specializing in the design and development of radio systems in all defense aircraft.

Within a couple of years, the company had grown into one of the most successful defense-contracting companies in the nation. It's growth and profitability had gained the attention of wealth followers after the glowing coverage in *Forbes*, *Time*, and *Life* magazines.

Sadie started volunteering with local charities in the metropolitan area. Over the years they had come up the social ranks to become an A-list couple in Washington, D.C. The Von Kinley's chaired all the good events: the Meridian Ball, Lombardi Gala, National Symphony Ball, Washington Ballet Gala, and the Kennedy Center Spring Gala. Sadie was passionate about her work with Art and Preservation of Embassies an organization through the State Department that supports American Embassies around the world. Together Lonnie and Sadie had served on several boards and had donated millions of dollars in support of universities, hospitals, and museums within the metropolitan area.

Chapter 17

Nancy Hadid was a petite blonde with fine, delicate features and a fiery personality. She was also a loyal friend who always went out of the way to protect the people she cared about. Sadie had chosen Nancy to be vice president of the Capital Ladies' Club. Sadie's reasons were simple, for one thing she could trust Nancy, and the other was because Nancy had one of the most beautiful houses on "S" Street near embassy row. And Nancy prided herself with knowing everything about everyone in town. It was well known that Nancy Hadid was a big gossip. She was also best friends with the former President's sister and had been invited to a number of White House State Dinners and the Presidential Retreat Camp David on several occasions.

Nancy loved hosting lavish fundraisers in her home to support her favorite political candidate in the Republican Party, or anything having to do with the Restoration of Blair House the President's official guest house. She had also been very successful at raising millions of dollars for any charity or cause she supported. Having been married several times, which had left her very comfortable. Her current husband was Dr. Salim Hadid, one of the nation's leading urologists, a medical research specialist, and the chief designer of the three-piece penile implant device that had sold in the millions in the US market alone.

She liked to say, "For years that Cinderella bullshit really messed up my head, but I finally found and kissed the right frog."

The fantasy may have messed up her head, but it had done marvelous things for her financial future. Nancy was worth millions in her own right. She established the Nancy Madison Trust. Putting the trust in her maiden name allowed her the appearance of coming from wealth, which could not have been farther from the truth. Nancy had graduated as valedictorian from her small-town high school and had been offered full scholarships from several colleges and universities. Her parents wanted her to accept the scholarship to Vanderbilt University, but that was too close to home for Nancy.

So she happily accepted a full scholarship to Stanford University in beautiful sunny California. She had her bags packed when she and the family came home after her graduation ceremony. Her mother and sisters could not stop crying. Nancy told them she would always have a place for them, but she needed to see God's beautiful world and she couldn't do that from the only home her father could provide: a run-down, rusty mobile home in the trailer park named Buttercup. It was one of Memphis's finest trailer parks, but Nancy made herself a promise that she would never set foot in one of them again. It was a promise she planned on keeping.

She loved the west coast and was determined to make it work for her, she worked part-time at a local diner and took a full load of school courses. In her senior year, she fell in love with a handsome young man whose family was one of the major donors to the school. He would turn out to be her first husband, that marriage ended in a quick divorce. But that didn't stop Nancy she was determined to have everything that she'd missed as a child. Nancy worked her plan, and she married up and up, until she met and fell in love with Salim. Now she never wanted to marry again, Salim was the one.

Nancy was not only good at picking husbands, but she was also excellent at reading Wall Street and could trade stocks as well as any day trader. She used her Wall Street money to fund what she called NRM (Nancy's Rainy Money). The NRM had grown so large that she was now using the money to donate to local charities that supported women and children.

Nancy loved to make people laugh, and she had a story for every occasion. She never seemed to have a bad day, unless you messed with her beloved Salim or their daughter, Paulina. The Hadid family hosted a Memphis-style barbecue each year at the end of the social season. It was a major hit. The entertainment included an Elvis impersonator who performed with a full band called themselves the Memphis Enforcers. Nancy kept the menu simple: Southern-style barbecue with all the trimmings, all served picnic style. The fun never stopped until the last guest left around midnight. Everyone looked forward to being invited to the Hadid's home the first weekend in June.

Sadie placed a call to Nancy to discuss their upcoming Capital Ladies' Club board meeting. Keeping the membership of this ladies' club happy was very important to Sadie. The club members would be voting on two very sensitive bylaw amendments, and Sadie wanted to know if Nancy had heard of any infighting. Nancy said all was clear. She had not heard of any complaints or knew of any brewing upsets. Nancy was very confident that everything was fine.

The French ambassador was a great choice, and the ladies were all very excited to spend an afternoon hearing about the latest happenings between the U.S. and the French government.

What Nancy didn't have the heart to tell Sadie was that everyone in town was whispering about how much Sadie was drinking. Nancy had received a number of calls concerning Sadie's frequent inebriation. It was no longer their inner-circle secret. She would have to keep an eye on Sadie at the luncheon today. She could not handle the thought of something happening to her dear friend.

With all her details covered, Sadie began to get dressed. She would be in her trademark Dior couture suit, a black-and-white windowpane-checked dress with a three-quarter-sleeve jacket and a large black-leather belt. Her jewelry would be simple, the Van Cleef and Arpel's retro gold-and-diamond necklace designed with two large eighteen-karat yellow-gold omega bands and brilliant-cut diamonds set to form a triangle shape at its center. During the day she only wore her seven-karat eternity band, and her diamond-bezel Cartier tank watch.

Sadie employed a full-time social secretary named Emmie. She and Sadie worked well together. Emmie had worked for the State Department and the German embassy and was well versed in protocol and the requirements of social entertaining.

She called into Sadie's dressing room to ask if there were any changes to today's seating arrangements. She was preparing the place cards for Sadie's two tables. Sadie quickly went over the list of names, and thankfully, there were no changes. She asked Emmie to tell the driver she would be driving herself today, so she needed her car brought around. She also instructed her to prepare thank-you cards to guests who had attended the luncheon honoring Sadie for becoming president of the Capital Ladies' Club.

Sadie also needed letters sent to her generous friends who had responded to her fundraising letter in support of the upcoming Princess Grace Foundation Gala Awards Dinner taking place in New York. Sadie had supported the lovely event for several years now. She respected the mission of the foundation and the amount of support it gave to the arts community. She told Emmie that all correspondence needed to go out in today's mail. She would review them when she came downstairs to her office.

Sadie carefully went over her speaking points, along with everything having to do with the day's meeting and luncheon. She was a real stickler for all details being carefully checked. She required that every "*I*", be dotted and every "*T*", be crossed. No detail would be left unattended to; that was just the way things had to be in Sadie's world. She put an enormous amount of pressure on herself, always needing perfection.

Her last instruction was the most important one. She asked Emmie to please have a Bloody Mary sent up to her room. Sadie never started her day without what she called a mild one. After a late night of socializing, a Bloody Mary with just one dash of hot sauce over crushed ice. Her breakfast tray consisted of a boiled egg, a slice of whole-wheat toast, a cup of coffee, and a mild one.

In the last couple of months, the tray was returning to the kitchen with everything untouched, but the glass containing the mild one would be empty. Sadie was taking in less than a thousand calories a day. She was down to less than one hundred twenty pounds, and she was beginning to look too thin.

Chapter 18

Winnie had been up since three o'clock in the morning, covering the local news. All she really wanted to do was go to the Four Seasons Spa for a quick workout, something she did every day after she wished her viewers a great day and signed off the air. She would then check with her producers for any breaking news stories. If all signals were a go, she would head directly to the spa.

Unfortunately, there was no chance of that today, because the rest of her morning and her afternoon would be taken up with the Capital Ladies' Club's first meeting of the season. It was a very important meeting, and her attendance was required. She knew it because throughout the morning, she had received calls from Coco, Nancy, and Sadie. Her cell phone was full of messages from them.

Capital Ladies' Club had a long-standing history of supporting young women in their hopes of a career in public policy or in the field of communication, with scholarship money to complete their educational requirements. This was one of the reasons Winnie had agreed to join the club. Winnie was hoping to use her new board position to increase the amount of scholarships given out annually to deserving young women who were majoring in the field of communication.

Time was moving fast. It was already ten o'clock. Now she would not have time to run home and change into another outfit. She had prepared for such a problem when she packed her large Chanel tote bag this morning. She would just change her jewelry, adding the Seaman Schepps multicolored Rio necklace, made her plain red vintage Chanel dress pop. She also changed her shoes to match her Chanel handbag. Now, with her outfit complete, she was ready for the Capital Ladies' Club.

Just as she was taking a final look in the greenroom mirror, her cell phone rang. It was Phillip Lay inviting her to join him and his wife for an early dinner that night at their lovely home, Riverview, a historical home in McLean, Virginia. Winnie kindly thanked him and Donna for thinking of her, and then she told him she was very sorry, but tonight she was not available.

As she hung up the phone, she wondered what Phillip Lay wanted with her. Why this sudden interest? She had received a number of invitations from the Lays recently. She knew no one in this town spent that much energy on social invites if they didn't want something. Whatever Phillip wanted, one thing was for sure; he was very married, and Winnie did not have affairs with married men. She believed that it was a well-documented fact that men got caught because they didn't know how to handle love affairs.

Over the years she had seen the Lays at social events but had never really been introduced to them until a couple of years ago, when she saw them at the International Red Cross Ball in Palm Beach, Florida. Since then, they seemed to run into each other at every social event. That same year they had both attended the San Francisco Opera's Major Donors Weekend.

Phillip was married to a petite blonde named Donna, with razor-sharp features and a personality to match. She seemed unable to relax, smile, or just be in the moment. Clearly she needed a better plastic surgeon and a personality transplant. Her permanent look of complete disinterest made you wonder what had happened to her to make her so unhappy, and what was behind that sadness.

As one of Washington's power couples, the Lay's had chaired several charitable events, mostly having to do with cancer research. Phillip had lost his brother to cancer and was now fighting to find a cure. They built a wing on the local children's hospital, dedicated to kids and their families suffering with cancer. Phillip was a member of the famous Lay jewelry family. But he had made his own fortune in real estate development, having built most of Chevy Chase, Maryland. He was Cary Grant handsome, tall, with a beautiful smile and playful eyes that longed to find some fun again and someone to play with.

When you saw the Lay's together you wondered what had happened to them. They always looked so sad, lonely, and bored with each other. Seeing them together made you wonder if some heartbreaking truth left them unable to find joy in each other's company. Winnie thought, "*Oh well, it's not my problem, and I am not available to be Phillip Lay's confidante.*"

Winnie sat down at her computer to catch up on e-mails before she left the station. As she was clearing off her desk, she noticed a thick envelope from the National Gallery of Art. Her assistant had left it on her desk. Inside was a lovely engraved invitation, inviting her to the opening-night exhibit of the French impressionists, followed by a donors' dinner. The event was taking place in a couple of days. This was a major invitation and a big surprise. Invitations from the National Gallery of Art were as covert as invitations to the White House. She immediately called the gallery's Circle office and responded that she would be honored to attend. Winnie loved the arts.

She stuffed the gallery invitation into her bag and headed for the elevator. When the doors opened, she ran into her station manager, who greeted her with his normal dry expression.

He said, "I attended a reception at the British embassy last night. I ran into your friend Sadie Von Kinley. She was feeling no pain and had to leave the party early."

Winnie nodded her head and said, "Really? Well, I hope that didn't stop you from having a wonderful time." She stepped into the elevator and prayed the doors would close quickly to end their conversation.

Station managers always carried an air of superiority about themselves and loved any reason to put down on-air personalities. They wanted you to be loved by the community, and at the same time, they hated you for being popular. It was a fist-in-glove kind of relationship, and the best way to handle it was to keep your distance.

This was the second time someone had told her that Sadie was drunk in public. Winnie wondered what the hell was going on with her friend. She would have to call Nancy and Coco when she got in the car. Together they had to find a way to help Sadie.

Winnie slipped behind the wheel of her new champagne-colored Maserati Quattroporte GTS. As she headed down Connecticut Avenue toward the country club, she could not think of anything but Sadie. She placed a call to Nancy's cell phone, and as usual Nancy did not answer. The call went to voice mail. She then called Coco, who, after the word "*hello*", started talking about herself and what a mess everything in her life was. Winnie thought, "*Damn, this girl is completely self-absorbed.*"

As soon as Coco stopped to take a breath of air, Winnie jumped in. She asked Coco if she had attended the reception last night at the British embassy. Coco said, "Yes."

Before Coco could start with what she had worn or who was there, Winnie said, "Coco, please tell me if Sadie was drunk."

Coco said, "Well, yes, very much so. Lonnie had to get her out of the embassy fast before the ambassador noticed. You know, it's because Sadie never eats anything. She downed two extra-dry gin martinis without any food in her stomach. How did you find out about it?"

Winnie said, "It doesn't matter. The fact that I've heard means people are talking about our friend, Coco."

Coco said, "Yeah, right. Well, okay." Coco then went back to talking about herself. She started in on her inquiry about what was going on in town and if Winnie was having any special dinners with a very hot recording artist.

Winnie thought, "*How in the world had Coco found out?*" And then she remembered that the town gossip queen, Nancy Hadid, was at it again. Nancy had seen Winnie with Morris Gray, the latest hot R&B recording star, when they had dinner at Café Milano's in Georgetown. Milano's was Washington's hottest restaurant.

Winnie loved Nancy, but damn, the woman could not keep her mouth shut, unless it was about her personal business then Nancy's lips were sealed. Winnie knew that Nancy and Salim were having major problems in their marriage but Nancy was not forthcoming with what was the root cause of the problem. She had kept that secret well hidden.

Winnie told Coco that Gray had left Washington for meetings in New York. However, she would let her know if he would be coming back to town. And if she hosted a dinner party, Coco would be invited, and yes, she would extend an invitation to Senator Moyer.

Winnie then said, "Coco, when are you going to give up on that man?"

Coco said, "As soon as I find another single member of Congress who's still interested and able to have a good time."

With that, Winnie said, "I will see you shortly." Disconnecting the call, she marveled at just how much social climbing Coco was able to do within a couple of minutes. If she'd only spent that much time focusing on finding a job or a new man who was available and interested in her, maybe she would get over the memories of that damn Mike DeSalis.

Some time back, Winnie had suggested that maybe Coco could get a job in Moyer's office. She thought Coco was going to faint at the mere thought of having to go to work every day. Winnie could not understand what was happening to Coco. Since Mike's death she had become such an unrepentant user, always with a story of something that had happened to her, or how someone had wronged her. She wanted and needed constant attention and sympathy. Coco's new thing was telling people about her health concerns. If you told her you had a cold, she would top you by saying she had just gotten over the flu. If you had a pain, hers would be worse.

But she would and could recover within a mere fraction of a second if you invited her to a party. Coco's never-ending complaints and concerns about her finances would come to a quick stop if you told her it was a black-tie affair. Then she would make her way to Saks Jandel's for a new outfit. Coco's actions had become very transparent, even to the people who loved her the most.

When Winnie spoke with Sadie and Nancy about Coco, they all shared the same stories. Sadie was complaining about how she was feeling used by Coco, and she'd stopped inviting her to most of the Von Kinley parties, saying, "Now don't get me wrong. I love Coco more than anyone, but sometimes the aftermath of a broken love affair can hurt the bystanders, so if you don't mind I will put some distance between me and what is going on with our friend. I am here if she really needs me, but this everyday complaining and not doing anything to make it better…well, I am out of ideas."

Nancy just said, "God love Coco. She can't get out of her own way to find real happiness, so she is content to ride on our coattails."

Chapter 19

Winnie and Coco arrived at the country club at the same time. Only to find the ambassador of France standing in the vestibule chatting with members of the Club. Coco had let Sadie down by not arriving early as promised.

The minute Coco spotted the ambassador, she turned on the charm, and like magic he was under her spell. Coco took him by the arm, moving the other ladies to the side, she quickly apologized, and explained that the staff at the Club did not tell her of his arrival.

Coco sweetly said, "Please come with me, Mr. Ambassador. Oh, how I love your suit. My, my, do you look handsome! You know, I have always thought the French are just more fashionable than us poor old Americans."

Winnie could only laugh to herself about Coco, the girl had a gift. Winnie walked into the ballroom to find Nancy and Sadie busy checking out their table location and going over last-minute details. Winnie needed a minute with Nancy, but this was not the time.

Nancy waved and motioned for Winnie to come over. She had seated her and Coco next to the head table. Sadie was complaining about the club being embarrassed by Coco's arriving so late. And now the hostess committee wanted to take pictures with the ambassador before the luncheon got started and no one could find him or Coco.

Winnie assured Sadie that there was no need to worry. All was well, Coco was on her job, and the ambassador was being well taken care of.

Sadie smiled and said, "Well Winnie, if you say not to worry, then I will not worry anymore."

Winnie could smell alcohol on Sadie's breath. She asked Sadie, "How was the reception last evening at the British embassy?"

Sadie responded, "It was lovely. We all missed you." Then she quickly changed the subject, asking Winnie about the table centerpieces and if she liked them.

Winnie thought, "*Table centerpieces? Really, Sadie? Table centerpieces?*" But she said they were very tasteful and perfect for the event. The centerpieces were made up of large American beauty red roses. In the center of the flowers there was a small American and a French flag.

As more club members started arriving and Sadie went into club president mode. She was so gracious to everyone, remembering details about their families' illnesses, marriages and deaths. Winnie wondered how Sadie did it.

Nancy stood beside Winnie and they were both looking at Sadie and thinking the same thing. Nancy said, "We have to watch out for our club members. They could get drunk just by inhaling Sadie's breath. Lordy, lordy, can that woman drink!"

Winnie said, "Nancy, don't make fun. We need to sit her down and talk to her."

Nancy turned and looked Winnie right in the eye. "You and what army, my dear friend? Sadie has been drinking since she was young. If we even began to bring up the subject with her, she would never speak to us again."

Just then several members walked over and started talking to Winnie about the stories she had covered on the news that morning. They all wanted to take pictures with her and Nancy. The subject of Sadie's drinking was closed for now. But Winnie knew that their friendship was based on truth and trust; they had always been honest with each other. They could not let this get any more out of hand. Still Nancy was right. They had to handle it with care.

Winnie walked into the reception area to get a glass of water and ran right into Donna Lay, Phillip's wife. As usual she did not look happy, just perfectly groomed and dressed to impress.

Donna said, "Good morning, Winnie. I was hoping to run into you today."

Winnie asked, "Why?"

Donna had a quick response, "Phillip would like you to join us this evening for dinner. It will be at our house—just a small group of friends."

Winnie didn't know she was a friend of the Lay family. She thanked Donna for the kind invitation but said that she would have to decline as she needed to be in bed early that night. "Remember, I have to be up early to go to work," Winnie explained.

Donna did something that Winnie had never seen her do she smiled. Although it was a stiff, freakish smile, it was a smile nonetheless. And then she did something that Winnie was completely unprepared for. She said, "Oh yes, work. I sometimes forget about you girls who have to punch a clock. Oh well, I will tell Phillip you can't make it. After all, it was his idea to invite you. You know, I am always telling people that you are so much thinner in person than you look on TV. It does add those extra pounds. Oh well, have a good day, dear Winnie." With the precision of a trained mercenary, Donna had hit her target.

Winnie just stood there, thinking, "*What in the world, is wrong with this little anorexic bitch? She is just evil. That's why she only smiles when she is ready to attack someone."*

Donna walked away with the confidence of a prizefighter who had just won a championship match. Winnie didn't understand why that was necessary when she had never done anything to Donna Lay. She barely knew the mousy devil, much less wanted or needed to spend any time in her presence. She made a mental note to herself that the next time Phillip called her, she would be much obliged to tell him what a bitch his wife was—and never to invite her to their damn house again.

That was the alluring and dangerously deceptive secret of some Washington women. They may look pretty, soft, and perfectly groomed, but underneath their tailored couture suits were hearts as cold and hard as glacial ice.

The luncheon bell chimes rang, and the receiving line began. It was time for the first luncheon of the Capital Ladies' Club's season to begin. As expected, the ambassador gave a delightful speech, followed by questions and answers from the ladies. He surprised them all by giving them each a gift of a full travel-size bottle of Jean Patou's Joy perfume, along with a coffee-table book of the famous House of Patou. It was a well-known fact that everyone in Washington loved a good favor bag.

Winnie had been up for so long that she was starting to feel dizzy.

Sadie walked over to her and asked if she would like to join her for a glass of champagne to celebrate a great season opener.

Winnie thought, "*Are you kidding me?*" Winnie was still upset from her exchange with Donna Lay. She said "Sadie, I am sorry but I will have to take a rain check. I am really tired. Let's talk tomorrow morning great event." She kissed Sadie on the cheek, said good-bye to Nancy and Coco, and headed for the door.

Before she could make it out of the ballroom, Coco put in another reminder bid for an invite, should Winnie be hosting something.

Winnie thought, "*God love her. Coco never stops. It's amazing the heights and depths a social climber will go to be in the know.*" Coco didn't even know Morris's name or his list of musical hits, but she knew she wanted to be at "the something," as she called it.

Winnie just smiled and made a hasty exit, almost running to her car. She had to get out of this beautiful clubhouse.

Driving down Connecticut Avenue, she was thankful the country club was not far from her house. It was a large house for a single person, but Winnie had fallen in love with the Tudor-style layout. The house was built in the 1930s. It was grand, with nine bedrooms and ten bathrooms, a large backyard with an in-ground pool, a pool house, and a two-bedroom guesthouse. And as an extra bonus, the entire estate was gated.

Winnie was passionate about her home and loving interior design, she'd hired the very best design team in the country, the fabulously talented William R. Eubanks of Palm Beach, Florida. They had completely gutted the property and remodeled it. The new layout was much lighter. The rooms opened to sunny, bright interiors, using colors in the hues of white, cream, and a hint of green, with colorful fabrics and art. Each room was large and welcoming. The enlarged master suite included his-and-hers baths, separate dressing rooms, steam showers, a closet that was the size of a mini boutique, and a massage room. On the main level, the embassy-sized living and dining areas were perfect for entertaining. One of Winnie's favorite rooms in the house was her large library and her office. The house also had a chef's kitchen and wine cellar. She'd lost three bedrooms in the redesign, but she didn't mind. It was all worth it.

Since her divorce, Winnie had dated some of the most eligible men in the country. But she just didn't want to get married again, so for now, she was satisfied with the single life. When a man started talking about marriage, she would break off the relationship and move on to another equally handsome, well educated, and accomplished gentleman. She was just not ready to marry again.

When she walked into the house, her housekeeper, Maria, told her she had received some beautiful flowers. They were in the living room. She was surprised to hear flowers had been sent to her, but right now she was too tired to really care. It would have to wait until later. Winnie said, "Thank you Maria, I am really exhausted I am going right to bed."

Maria answered, "Ms. Winnie you have been up for a long time, I made your favorite spinach salad. If you're not hungry I will place it in the refrigerator for later. Will you be needing anything else this evening?"

Winnie said, "No, just a hot shower and to go to bed. Thank you Maria for everything."

Maria and her husband Vince were live-ins, and they took care of everything. They both felt so blessed to have found someone as kind and generous as Winnie to work for. She was very fair, and she paid them top dollar. She even paid for their vacations twice a year. They had full health and dental insurance, along with an IRA.

Winnie believed in the old saying, "If you stay ready, you never have to get ready" , she required that her house be run on schedule, with everything in its correct space, and that the house be kept in "turn-key condition", at all times.

Winnie took the back stairs up to her room. She never saw the flowers.

Walking into her dressing room, she kicked off her shoes, removed her necklace and earrings, replaced them in their pretty boxes, and then closed and locked the safe. She still could not understand why Donna Lay had been so unnecessarily catty to her. She undressed, laying her dress and undergarments on the silk stool. She would hang them up later. Turning on the water and watching it pour out of the golden Sherle Wagner showerheads, she stood right under the warm water, wishing it could wash away the heaviness of the day. Closing her eyes, she finally felt relief coming to her. Water was Winnie's magic potion and showers were her escape. After thirty minutes of wet heaven, she stepped out of the shower, wrapped herself in a thick robe and slippers. And headed to her large California king-size bed. Thank goodness the house was completely silent. She could get some much-needed rest. She pulled back the covers and slipped into bed. Pushing the remote-controlled window shades that blackened out her room and then closing her eyes, she could still hear Donna Lay's voice in her head. She needed to forget about Donna, and that's what she did as she fell peacefully to sleep.

Chapter 20

Nancy, Coco, and Sadie were the last to leave the country club. They always stayed back to chat about the event and catch up on all of the latest gossip. Sadie and Nancy had received lots of praise from several long-standing, hard-to-please, true pain-in-the ass members for securing the ambassador. Sadie invited "the girls," as she liked to call them. To join her for a celebratory drink.

Following her lead they walked from the ballroom across to the private dining room. It was closed until dinner, but Sadie was sure no one would mind. They only needed a quiet table and a cold cocktail. She headed for the table nearest the window, which gave them a perfect view of the golf course. The rolling greens and tree-lined fairways looked more majestic than ever. Every detail of the clubhouse was filled with Old World charm. It gave a feeling of a bygone area.

There was simply no mistaking the distinct difference between real wealth and being rich. Wealth afforded you this kind of luxurious atmosphere, posh surroundings, and the refinement of everyone speaking softly and answering you with polite kindness.

Coco was always taken by the sheer splendor and understated elegance of the club and the golf course. She quickly scanned to see if there were any new faces. With any luck, she might meet a new single member. She sometimes thought it wasn't fair that Nancy and Sadie enjoyed the privileges of membership to this perfectly landscaped wonderland, while she was only allowed entry when the Capital Ladies' Club had their six annual meetings.

It was times like this that made her mad at every man who had been in her life, starting with her father. If only she had ended her affair with Mike years ago and married any one of the many men who had shown her some interest, then maybe she would be a member too.

How many *maybes* would life require Coco to accept? It was always *maybe* for her—maybe this or maybe that. Would she ever really know what it felt like to have a loving, devoted husband? Had her father's prediction for her life been true?

Coco would kill to be a part of the country-club lifestyle, but you needed big money and an even bigger name to gain membership. Coco didn't have any of that right now. For now she would just have to be content with being a well-dressed freeloader.

After they were comfortably seated. Coco said, "Let's make it a small drink, since we had wine with lunch. I would hate for us to overdo it."

Sadie said, "Well, that's nonsense. We have a lot to catch up on."

The headwaiter Eric Lance knew these ladies well and they always took very good care of him and his team especially Mrs. Von Kinley. She took the time to get to know the staff and always sent them holiday cards and presents. She even knew their birthdays and she seemed genuinely concerned about everyone. Mrs. Von Kinley and Mrs. Hadid were two very special ladies and Eric was pleased to serve them.

Sadie made eye contact with Eric and with the slightest nod of her head, he came over to their table. She was happy to see him and greeted him with a warm smile, quickly asking how his day was going and if his family was doing well.

After dispensing with the pleasantries she said, "Eric my dear man, would you be so kind as to bring us three chilled flutes and a bottle of Veuve Clicquot, please? Thank you so much."

Eric said it would be his honor, and he quickly left the table. He instructed his teammates to take extra care of these ladies.

Sadie asked Nancy about her weekend. The Hadid's had a beautiful lake house in Maine. It had taken Nancy over three years of hard work and a small fortune to bring the once deserted spiritual retreat back to life. The restoration resulted in a showpiece of rustic elegance that had been featured in *Architectural Digest* magazine.

Nancy looked away from her friends to gather the strength to keep herself together. She still could not believe how badly their weekend had turned out. She and Salim had spent the entire weekend trying to make some sense out of their daughter's recent rebellious behavior. The guilt and pain were tearing them apart.

The Hadid's world came crumbling down around their shoulders after Paulina had gone through Salim's wall safe and found her adoption papers. Things had not been the same since that day. Nancy had not only withheld the truth from Paulina, she had never told anyone that they had used a surrogate.

Nancy had to have a hysterectomy when she was only twenty-three years old, due to a medical condition called menometrorrhagia and uterine fibroids. The surgery not only left her unable to become a mother. It ended her first marriage.

Salim was Paulina's natural father, but a kind woman named Paula Madden was Paulina's natural mother. Paula had given Salim and Nancy the most miraculous gift, and becoming parents had changed their lives. It was an indescribable scene of joy, wonder and explosive love that nothing else on earth could give a person. Paulina was the center of their world and the most important person in their lives.

Nancy had always wanted to tell Paulina, but it never seemed like the right time. Deep down inside she knew that she and Salim were playing a very dangerous game of, "hide the truth." Every time she told herself this was the time to have the discussion. Nancy decided there was another reason to wait. Their final decision not to tell her had broken their family into pieces, and now Nancy was not sure if they would ever be right again. Paulina was suffering the most, she no longer knew who she was or what in her life was true. She was acting out in every way she could to hurt them.

Nancy had walked in on Paulina giving their tennis instructor a blow job, and as if that were not enough to send any mother over the edge, Paulina did not seem the least bit ashamed of her behavior. It was as if she were trying to get caught.

She just looked up and said, "Damn. Do you mind? Please knock before you enter a room. We were not finished. He hasn't come yet."

Nancy belted out a loud "Get the hell out of my house, you're fired!" The poor boy ran for his life. Paulina stormed out of the room, crying that she did not have any privacy.

Nancy ran after her yelling, "If you want privacy, grow up, finish college, get a job, get your own damn house, and you can blow the entire Wimbledon tennis team, just not under my roof!"

Paulina stopped, turned and looked Nancy right in the eye and said, "You mean my father's house, don't you? Remember, you are not my real mother, and adoption papers do not give you the right to tell me what the fuck to do. So please go plan another one of your luncheons, you fat bitch."

Nancy was so shocked she just stood there with her mouth hanging open. What had happened to their sweet little girl? Then she thought, "*Am I fat? Why did she call me fat?*"

Paulina ran to her room, slamming the door so hard the entire household staff came running to see what was happening. Nancy dropped her head, walked right to the bar in the library and poured herself a strong drink. She picked up the phone to call Salim, who as usual was in surgery.

Being married to a world-renowned medical doctor was great for your lifestyle. But it was hell when family problems came up. It meant you were a single parent for all emergencies not having to do with immediate medical care.

After the waiter set down their glasses and uncorked the champagne, Nancy looked around to see if there were any other members or staff in earshot. When she knew the coast was clear, she slowly began telling Sadie and Coco about her troubles with Paulina and their recent blowups. The latest was that Paulina had moved out of their house and was now living with one of her friends.

Sadie reached over, took Nancy's hand and said, "I am so sorry you had to lose a good tennis instructor over this and your game was just getting good."

Nancy could not believe her ears. Clearly Sadie was too drunk to think straight. Nancy really needed some good advice right now. Sadie knew Paulina better than any of Nancy's friends. They had always seemed to have a good relationship. And Sadie was the first person she had called after Paulina had found the papers.

Coco asked if it would be okay if she reached out to Paulina. Coco said, "Nancy, I have never understood why you didn't just tell Paulina when she was much younger that you were not her natural mother. Then you would have already gone through this. Well, if it would be okay with you and Salim, I would like to invite Paulina to join me for the Lady Gaga concert coming up at the Verizon Center."

Coco had been given the tickets and did not have anyone to go with, so this would work out for her as well. Nancy was touched by Coco's offer to help, and she immediately said, "Yes." Anything that helped her child would be much appreciated.

Sadie said, "I don't understand how taking Paulina to a concert is going to help her understand or come to terms with the fact that the people she loved most in the world have lied to her, but oh well, let me know how that all works out."

Coco said, "I want her to know she has a friend in me."

Sadie said, "Coco, you are making this about you, and it needs to be about Paulina."

Coco said, "Sadie, I am not making this about me. It's just that spending time with someone like me could be good for Paulina."

Sadie turned to Nancy and said, "You need to get her to see a family counselor, not a singer who wraps herself in raw meat. Don't get me wrong. I love Gaga and think she has the best voice out there today, but Paulina needs the help of a trained professional."

Sadie asked if Salim knew about the tennis guy. Nancy said, "Yes, we talked it all out over the weekend while we were at the lake house."

Nancy said, "Salim is very hurt. He broke down crying. But he wants to blame me for everything. He said it's my fault that Paulina has gotten hurt. It's my fault for withholding the truth about her birth mother. Suddenly everything that is wrong with our family is my fault. All he has to say is I have given her everything, including love and lots of time and attention."

Sadie said, "Oh my word."

Nancy said, "That is when all hell broke loose. It really pissed me off when Salim used the, "I or we" card when trouble comes up in our marriage or family."

Nancy thought, *"I hell!"*

Salim had made little to no time for Paulina in the last couple of years. He worked constantly, traveling around the world, giving speeches on the advancements of male infertility treatments and the benefits and risks of the penile implants.

Nancy told the ladies that she did not hold back on him. That it was the first time in their marriage that she had really let Salim have it. Her mouth was a weapon of mass destruction and he was her target. She had enough of being the nice, quiet wife and letting him get off with the "I am the big doctor. I am too busy for these problems at home." Nancy had reached her limit with both Salim and Paulina.

By the time they packed the car to return to Washington. Salim was silent, and the distance between them was much greater. Not only was Paulina missing him, but she was as well. They hadn't had sex in months and although he was a man who specialized in the advancement of the penile implant, she was not getting any of his these days.

Sadie scolded Nancy. "You cannot let that happen. No matter what, you must fuck your husband twice a week. It's necessary for a good marriage. Really! And I mean twice a week, Nancy. Twice a week. Do you hear me?"

Nancy and Coco were completely shocked to hear Sadie use the F-word.

Sadie realized what she had said immediately and apologized, saying, "Sorry, but there really wasn't any other word to express it better."

Nancy had always been curious about Sadie and Lonnie's sex life. They were the older couple in the group and they always seemed so in love and into each other. So now was just as good a time as any to ask.

Nancy cleared her throat and leaned in closer to the ladies, quietly asking, "So Sadie, how often do you and Lonnie well, you know?"

Without a moments delay, Sadie proudly announced that she and Lonnie had a healthy sex life. He still brought her to mind-blowing orgasms. She credited it to the fact that she had taken the forbidden mask off sex. Her mother had given her a copy of Xaviera Hollander's book, *The Happy Hooker*, as a wedding present. She had read it cover to cover about five times. She'd learned what really makes a man happy. Hollander was a former call girl and madam. Sadie's mother thought she would be able to tell Sadie things that she herself didn't know. Sadie smiled and said, "I have become very good at it." She and Lonnie enjoyed every minute of their married life together. She then told them that most marriages ended over two things, money or sex and both were necessary for a person to have a good, balanced life. She said, "I love and need both. That's what it takes to keep me happy."

Sadie also understood marital problems and how hard it was to keep everything running smoothly at home. She wanted Nancy and Coco to understand that it was hard work. No one has it easy, and no one in this life gets away without paying a price for whatever they have. She and Lonnie worked at their marriage every day. She was grateful to the love gods that Lonnie still loved her so much and that he still did it for her. Even after over thirty years of marriage, to her he was still the most handsome and loving man in the world.

Two hours flew by like seconds. Sadie looked at her watch and said, "Oh no, I must be getting home. Traffic will be horrible. Lonnie is home tonight, we're having Chinese takeout, watching a movie and going to bed early." And with a Cheshire cat smile, she leaned in and said, "It will be a good time for all."

They all laughed out loud like schoolgirls sharing a secret.

Nancy said that Salim was home tonight as well, so maybe they could talk about Paulina's problems.

Sadie responded, "Have you heard anything that I have said? Make tonight about you and Salim. Order his favorite meal, put on something sexy, and fuck him like you are trying to kill him. Tomorrow you can talk about Paulina. Right now you need to rekindle your love affair with your husband." Then she added, "Always save yourself first. Only after that can you save someone else."

Coco again asked, "Nancy, why didn't you just tell her about using a surrogate, and why did you keep the secret from us?"

Sadie said, "That answer will take us all night. The question is not how they got into this mess. It's how will they get out of it." Sadie had been very upset with Nancy when she first learned of the adoption papers. She could not understand anyone doing that to their family. And she secretly agreed with Salim and Paulina that Nancy had placed far too much attention on activities outside of her home, and she needed to fix what was wrong inside of it.

Nancy quickly signed the check, and the ladies thanked the staff and made their way to the valet. Their cars had been driven to the front entrance, and the attendants were waiting for them. The ladies hugged and wished each other a good night.

Chapter 21

As soon as Coco got into her car, she called Nancy, explaining that she was worried about Sadie driving home. Nancy asked her what she was doing the next Wednesday evening. Coco did not understand the question. She was telling her that their friend was too drunk to be driving herself home. And Nancy was asking her about next week.

She said, "I don't have any plans, what's going on."

Nancy said, "Well, I would like to invite you to be my guest for the Snowflake Ball."

The ball supported research for children's cancer, and it was the opening of the social season in Washington. It welcomed the new and returning members of the diplomatic corps to the nation's capital. Coco loved the event and said she would be delighted to attend.

Then Nancy asked her what she would be wearing and mentioned that maybe she should go to Tyson's Corner that evening and look for something. Coco then understood what Nancy was doing. Coco would follow Sadie home, and when she made the turn on Crest Lane, Coco would continue on Chain Bridge to Tyson's Galleria, taking care of both things at once.

They chatted for a little while longer, now that they both felt better about Sadie. Coco said she would call her if anything went wrong and thanked her again for the invitation to the ball. Nancy asked if she thought Winnie was okay. She left the luncheon before their normal catch-up chat session. Coco said she didn't know; maybe she was just tired.

Nancy said, "Okay, enjoy your shopping. And by the way, I am wearing white to the ball—just so you know."

They both promised to check on Winnie in the morning and again wished each other a good night.

Coco followed Sadie and was surprised that she only hit gravel once. She made it home without any problems. She knew that they would have to speak with Lonnie soon about Sadie's drinking. It was really getting out of control.

Coco parked and walked into Neiman Marcus. She loved the store. Many of the sales staff recognized her and came over to say hello. If they only knew that she really could no longer afford to shop as she had in years past, they would not be so friendly to her. It was a sad truth that in this town, you needed money to be popular. "Money talks and bullshit walks," is what Winnie had always said about the city, and it was really true.

Right now, Coco's bank account balance was problematic. Since Mike's death, she was down to less than half a million dollars in cash and only three hundred thousand in stocks. Which was not enough money to live on for the rest of her life.

As she walked through the store, she cautiously selected a fun pair of fluorescent-pink leather pants with floral cut-outs up the side of the legs and a matching off-the-shoulder silk-and-cotton top for the Lady Gaga concert.

She also found a soft pink gown that would be perfect for the ball. It fit her like a glove. She wouldn't need any alterations. She had only been in the store for thirty minutes and she had spent over four thousand dollars. Coco could not help herself. Shopping was just in her blood. Being a Neiman Marcus circle's club member, she earned points for her purchases. She had received a five-hundred-dollar gift card from previous purchases, which she now would use to purchase a thank-you gift for Nancy and Salim, since they were her free meal ticket to the ball.

As the saleslady carefully packed up her items, Coco dropped several names of events that she would be attending in the coming months. She needed to let this woman know that she was someone special. Coco was the worst name-dropper in town. She didn't get it that most people hated it. Name-dropping was a sure sign that the person did not have any real power. Powerful people never had to drop names.

On the ride home, Coco's reality set in. How was she going to pay for the items she'd just purchased? If only she had a rich husband like Nancy and Sadie, or a big job like Winnie's, she would be able to take care of these matters for herself. But she didn't.

Chapter 22

Winnie did not wake up until around 8:00 p.m. She went to the bathroom and then downstairs to get some water. Maria had left some telephone messages and the mail on the desk in the kitchen. Winnie gathered it all and walked toward the front hall of the house. When she looked in the living room, she noticed the large floral arrangement. Who in the world had sent her this massive gift—and all of her favorite flowers?

She sat down and read the card. It was from Phillip Lay, asking her to be his guest at an upcoming event in support of the Washington National Opera. Winnie thought, *"What in the world do the Lays want from me?"*

She crumbled the card in her hand and walked back upstairs to her bedroom. She would have her secretary send him a note in the morning declining the invitation.

She remembered the National Gallery of Art dinner was in a couple of days. Walking back into her dressing room, she went to the evening-gown section, and pulled out the new Valentino, a green long-sleeve, V-neck gown she had purchased in New York during fashion week. It was perfect: slick and elegant. She would wear the Martin Katz large emerald-and-diamond earrings with the matching ring and no necklace, and she'd carry the crystal Tembo elephant minaudière clutch by Judith Leiber. For shoes, she pulled out the Manolo Blahnik gold-and-pearl mules. She needed to instruct her secretary to hire a car and driver for the evening. No time like the present. Winnie sent a text and an e-mail to her secretary, letting her know what she needed taken care of for the Gallery dinner and to send a response to Phillip Lay immediately declining his invitation.

Winnie looked at her telephone messages, and saw that there was one from her sister, Tina. She would have to call her back in the morning. They were planning a family trip to the Greenbrier Resort for Thanksgiving.

Tina was such a lovely friend and sister and they had a great time together. Like Winnie, Tina was well educated having focus on her career she had worked hard and made a small fortune in real estate, and was now happily married to her third husband, a very nice and quiet man who just loved Tina to pieces. They lived in a lovely home on Fox Meadow Lane, in Potomac, Maryland.

Chapter 23

Coco knew she only had two choices: she could pull more money out of her principal investments, which had already taken a big hit, or she could call up her friend-with-benefits, Saul Baumann. Saul was the founding chairman of a private equity firm. He had amassed a fortune of over eight hundred million dollars.

They met one year after Mike had passed away, when Coco ran her shiny baby blue Jaguar into the back of his brand-new Porsche Panamera Turbo at the corner of Wisconsin and Massachusetts Avenue. Completely beside herself, Coco didn't have any idea what to do next. She just couldn't deal with any more problems, so at the moment she just sat in her car and cried. Saul wasn't hurt, but he was pissed off. He had just left the dealership with his new toy. After checking the damage, he saw that it was mostly to Coco's car. The Porsche had taken the crash well.

When he walked over to Coco, he couldn't believe just how beautiful she was. To him she seemed like the most beautiful, helpless creature he had ever seen. She was clearly in over her head at that moment. Afraid she may have gotten hurt, he asked her if she needed to go to the hospital.

She said, "No. Oh please, I am sorry. Are you hurt? Please don't tell me that I hurt you and you're going to sue me. Really? Are you going to sue me? Oh Jesus, I don't have enough for a lawsuit. I will be homeless, right on the street…homeless…did you say that you were hurt?"

Saul said, "It's okay, now first, what is your name?"

"I am Coco Runni. And you?", said Coco.

Saul felt sorry for her he said, "I am Saul Baumann, and I am not hurt, and I am not going to sue you. It looks like your car got most of the damage."

Coco sadly said, "That's just like my life right now."

"Oh my, I am really sorry to hear that", said Saul.

Before Saul could say or do another thing, Coco started to cry again. He knew that these tears were about something other than their fender bender, he needed to get to the airport. But he couldn't leave her. She was just too pretty and too helpless.

When the police arrived, Coco and Saul exchanged insurance information, and Coco's car was taken away by a tow truck. Saul's car only had a small amount of damage to the rear bumper. He asked her if she needed a ride home or if he should call someone, like maybe a husband or boyfriend. That's when she really broke down crying.

She said, "No, I have no one to call. No one will care what happens to me...no one."

He said that he would be happy to drive her, but he needed to catch his flight, so he hailed her a cab. Something about her had touched his heart. He wanted to take care of this lost, crying soul who just happened to be the most beautiful woman he had ever seen.

That evening, Saul called Coco to see if she was okay and again asked her if she needed anything. He told her he was very worried about her, and if she needed anything to please call him, day or night. He also told her that he was taking care of her car, and there was no need to report it to her insurance company.

The next day, his office sent her a large flower arrangement with his business card enclosed and a note that said, "You're not alone. Someone does care."

He made arrangements to have her car repaired, detailed and the floor mats replaced. It looked and smelled like a new car. After a week had passed, Saul called her to ask if she was interested in meeting him for a drink. Coco's problem with Saul was that he was not her normal super handsome guy. His face reminded her of a tuna fish, and she only liked to be seen in the company of movie star handsome men. But she didn't have anyone else asking her out right now. She turned him down three times. But he continued to ask her out, so on his last call she agreed to have dinner with him. Saul made arrangements for them to go to his favorite spot, The Palm, on Nineteenth Street, in the heart of the city. It was a well-known establishment frequented by real power brokers who demand the best in food and wine.

He was excited about getting to know more about Coco—who and what she was all about. He wanted to pick her up at her home or send a driver for her, but Coco refused him every time, so they agreed that she would meet him at his penthouse at the Foxhall condos.

Saul carefully planned out a lovely evening for them, and he drove them to the restaurant in his Rolls-Royce Wraith. During the drive over, he kept the conversation light. She seemed interested in what he did for a living, so with gentle care he explained the Baumann Group.

When he asked her about what she did for a living, she said, "Well, I used to be a model. Now I am…well, looking for something that interests me. I love fashion and travel."

When she finished explaining her likes, a very sad and gloomy expression came over her lovely face. Saul immediately changed the subject to something light.

"Well, I should have known you loved fashion," said Saul. "You are the most beautiful lady in this restaurant this evening."

"Oh, thank you. How very kind of you to say that," Coco said.

Saul said, "Coco, I only say what I feel, and I tell the truth. You are beautiful."

His kind words made her relax a little.

Saul leaned in and asked, "Are you hungry?"

Coco gave him a big smile and said, "Yes, I am, how about you do the ordering for us today?"

Saul smiled and said, "Okay, but I will be happy to have you order. I have eaten everything on this menu, and I can tell you it's all wonderful."

Coco laughed and said, "I trust you…so have at it."

Saul ordered Coco the nine-ounce filet mignon, and for himself the prime New York strip with brandy peppercorn sauce. They shared an order of half and half, half cottage fries and half fried onions, and an order of creamed spinach. It was a heart attack on a plate, but they didn't care. Finishing the delicious meal off with a bottle of Two Angels Petite Sirah, a good red wine from California. Saul didn't like to rush a good meal, so he ordered them a glass of port from the Fonseca Bin 27 Reserve.

During the evening, Saul's eyes never left Coco. He seemed to be happy just to be in her presence. Several times during the evening, he told her she was beautiful and that he was proud to be with her. When she mispronounced something or said something silly, he never once made her feel bad about herself. Mike would have taken off her head or told her to shut the hell up.

During their meal, she lightly said something about being mistreated and misunderstood. Saul noticed that she apologized a lot for everything. During dessert, she dropped her fork.

Coco said, "Oh my God, I am so sorry! Really, I am sorry. I don't think anyone saw me do that. I am so stupid…sorry!"

Saul quickly said, "Hey, sweetheart, it's okay! Really, no big deal. It's just a fork—they have more. We are okay."

He knew then that she had been physically abused, and she was afraid of everything. When the waiter brought a new fork to the table, Saul noticed that Coco's hand was trembling.

"See, everything is good," he said. He changed the subject and asked her about the first lady's fashions. The rest of the dinner went fine and on the ride back to Saul's place they listened to quiet jazz in the car.

He asked her up for a nightcap and was surprised when she said, "Yes."

Saul was so easy to be with, Coco didn't want the evening to end, she was truly enjoying herself something she hadn't done in some time.

Saul apartment was expansive and elegantly decorated. He had purchased three units and turned them into one large penthouse home with great views of the city. He said, "Coco please make yourself comfortable."

"From these pictures it seems you go to the White House a lot, I can't tell if you're a Republican or Democratic. You have pictures with everyone.", said Coco.

Saul asked her, "Does it really matter? Well, I vote for the best person for the country. Now what would you like to drink."

Coco said, "Some pink champagne if you have any."

Saul smiled saying, "Not a problem how about a glass of Pol Roger, Rose 1985, it was a good year for the wine."

"If you say so, I don't know much about vintages of wine. I just know what I like. Saul, I am not very smart about those types of things", said Coco.

Saul said, "Your smart enough to know what it is that you like, that's half the battle in life."

As he placed the chilled flute in front of her, she looked at the pink bubbles rising to the top of the glass and then she took another look at Saul. Taking a sip of the champagne, it was perfect and just what she needed to finish off a lovely evening.

She said, "No one is this nice for nothing. You don't know me. What do you want from me?"

He told her that she was right; he didn't know her, but he would like to have the honor of getting to know more about her. He said, "Coco, what I know is that someone you loved a great deal has really hurt you, and you're having a rough time dealing with what is left of your broken heart. And for that I am so sorry. I know how you feel." They talked for another couple of hours.

Coco finished her champagne, while Saul enjoyed a glass of fifty-year-old port. When she asked him if he would kindly pour her a glass of what he was drinking. He said, "Coco are you sure? I don't want you to be sick."

Saul hated to see a woman drunk. He said, "It's really late. How about I call a cab to take you home. I can have your car bought to you in the morning."

As he was getting ready to stand up to call down to the concierge for a cab, Coco reached over and grabbed Saul's leg. She angrily asked him if he wanted to have sex with her and if that was all men ever thought about, she said, "Saul is that the reason you are being so damn nice to me?"

He took her hand and pushed it away from him. He told her that maybe she had better be getting home now. When he opened the door, Coco stumbled out and fell face down in the hallway. She was out cold. He couldn't let her just lie on the floor, so he picked her up and took her to his guest bedroom, where she slept off her drunkenness. Throughout the night he checked on her. When he looked down on her, he saw an incredible beauty who had somehow lost her way. There was something about her that made him want to protect and take care of her. But he did not want any drama in his life, and in his experience women like Coco always came with drama.

Coco awoke to the sound of someone talking. She didn't recognize her surroundings. She only knew that she was still drunk and feeling very lonely and embarrassed. She walked down the hall toward the sounds of the television. When she reached his bedroom, she realized that Saul was watching the movie *Bad Boys II*, starring Will Smith and Martin Lawrence. When he noticed her standing in the doorway, he silenced the movie.

There was a moment of uncomfortable silence. Then they both started to speak at the same time.

Coco said, "You know that is Will Smith and Martin Lawrence best movie. Well, that's what I think, anyway."

"He was excellent as Ali, and I think he should have won an Oscar," said Saul.

"Yeah, you're right. Okay, it's his second best," Coco said.

Saul could tell that she was feeling bad, so he put on his robe and walked over to her, saying, "Hey, how are you feeling?"

"Saul, I am sorry. I didn't mean to drink so much. I feel like a fool", said Coco.

Saul said, "You never have to feel like a fool around me, Coco."

Just then, Coco started feeling all of the liquor and rich food and covered her mouth. Saul helped her to the bathroom, where she threw up. He got her a bath towel and the guest terry robe. He thought she might need to get out of her soiled clothes. He then went to the kitchen to put on a pot of coffee.

Thirty minutes later, a very sick Coco emerged, looking a little green but much better than before.

"Okay, now how do you feel?" asked Saul.

Coco said, "Like something the garbage man left on your front doorstep. Thanks for the robe, and towels, toothbrush and everything. Saul I am sorry to have our evening end like this."

Saul said, "Coco, I just want you to feel better. Believe me you have nothing to be sorry about. I don't judge my friends."

Even now as Saul looked across his kitchen at Coco standing there sick, she was the most beautiful woman he had ever seen. As he studied her, she seemed more fragile and afraid than ever. He had to find out what was at the root of this pain. He wanted to make her feel better.

As he poured her a cup of coffee and placed it on the counter, he asked, "Do you like cream and sugar? Well, I noticed you didn't touch your coffee at the restaurant, would you prefer tea, I can make you a cup."

Coco said, "Oh, it's fine. I will take it plain. If that will be okay. Saul, please tell me why are you being so nice to me."

Coco looked at him again closely he had a great body, large kind eyes, but his face, he was just not good looking.

"Can't a guy just be nice?" he asked.

She took a sip of the coffee. Placing the cup back down on the delicate saucer, she asked him, "Are you married? This is not the kind of china a bachelor would normally have."

Saul laughed and then looked at her and then said, "Are you crazy, Coco? I have told you that I am not married. If I were you my dear lovely lady, would not be here. One thing I am is faithful. But I will thank my decorator the next time I see her."

"Now Coco, it's the early hours of the morning. Please tell me what you would like to do now. I can drive you home, because I am not letting you drive yourself, or you can go back to sleep in my guest bedroom. And let me warn you, the same decorator is responsible for the linens. Not a wife, my decorator so you tell me what would you like to do now."

Coco smiled and said, "Watch Will Smith and Martin Lawrence."

"Okay, I will carry your coffee, or would you like something else to drink? If not, follow me", said Saul.

Coco put up her hands and said, "No, please nothing else to drink...I may never drink again."

He stopped and turned to her, "Do you mind watching it in my bedroom?"

Coco said, "No, I am standing here in your robe. I think we are beyond formal pretenses."

As they took a seat on the settee in the sitting room area, he started the movie from the beginning.

Coco felt safe and comfortable with Saul. He was such an Old World gentleman. Halfway through the movie, he reached out and took her hand. She felt something powerful in his touch.

He said, “My darling, how are you feeling?”

Coco reached over, took his face in her hands and gently kissed his full lips. At first he let her guide the kiss, but within minutes he was in complete control.

They made mad passionate love like she had never experienced. Saul was an excellent lover. He was powerful and gentle, commanding and giving. Her body exploded at his touch. She had never experienced this feeling of sexual fulfillment. After their lovemaking, they showered together.

As she was getting dressed in the bathroom, Saul went to his wall safe and took out five thousand dollars in cash. He slipped the money in her handbag. Saul knew that Coco was feeling the pressure of not having someone to take care of her, and he also knew she loved to shop. He hoped the gift would make her happy, but he would not talk about it with her.

When she came out of the bathroom, she was dressed and was looking much better.

Coco said, “I think I am better now. I can drive myself home.”

Saul said, “Okay. You look lovely.” Before she could say another word, Saul took her into his strong arms and held her tight. Softly, he whispered, “You will be okay, Coco and someone does care about you, me.”

As tears welled up in her eyes she said, “You are an amazing man, Saul Baumann.”

Saul said, “You have no idea Coco. Let me know when you want to really find out.”

He walked over to the phone on the desk and called for the doorman to bring her car around front.

He walked her to the door, and they kissed good night.

She could tell that Saul really liked her and Coco liked him too. She thought if only he didn't look like a big-eyed tuna fish, maybe she could think about spending some real time with him.

It was on her drive home that she found the money in her handbag. At first she was mad as hell, and then she thought about it. She needed the money, and she loved the sex. It was the best sex of her life. She wondered how he knew that she was broke? Did she say something to let him know?

That was the beginning of their relationship or affair, or whatever you call what they were to each other.

In a day or so, he would send her two dozen long-stemmed yellow roses with a thank-you note. If he got lonely, he would have his secretary telephone Coco and invite her to the next local team's home game. They would sit in the VIP seats and Saul would take special care to treat her like a lady. Coco always enjoyed every minute of it. This is how their relationship had been now as she pushed the buttons on her cell phone she smiled to herself that she was looking forward to an evening with Saul.

In her sexy voice she said, "Hello Saul it's Coco."

"Hey Baby, I was just thinking about you. How about joining me for dinner tonight?" Saul happily said. And so the Saul and Coco dance would begin again.

The next morning she would make the deposit into her checking account and pay her Neiman Marcus credit card bill and some other smaller bills, all courtesy of Saul. The man had the face of a fish, but the manhood of a mule, and oh boy, did he know how to use it.

Saul had become Coco's dirty little secret.

Chapter 24

Nancy knew that Sadie would never tell her anything that would hurt her. She only wanted the best for them. So she took her wise counsel to heart and with rapid speed started drafting the "Get my husband back in love with me" marriage restoration plan. Sadie's matrimonial success was partially due to her having always made it clear to everyone that nothing came before her husband and her family.

Nancy felt the same way. Although, if she were completely honest with herself, she would have to admit that over the last couple of years she had spent a great deal of time promoting her candidate of choice for the Republican Party, major historical restoration projects, as well as the ballet, the opera, the Capital Ladies' Club, and the Women's Committee of the Mission Army—and very little time at home.

Her excuse was that Salim was busy traveling, but there had been many evenings when she was away from home on board retreats and campaign fundraisers, leaving him in an empty house and eating dinner alone or dining at the country club. When Salim begged her to join him on extended trips away, she always refused because of some prior commitment that she felt she had to attend. It took two to make a marriage work, and they were both failing.

Sadie's dire words kept ringing in Nancy's head: *If you don't make him happy, some tight-ass young thing will be more than happy to make him her husband...make him her husband...make him her husband.*

Nancy knew Salim would be home tonight, so she quickly telephoned his favorite restaurant, the Lebanese Tavern on Connecticut Avenue, she ordered all of his favorites, and had them delivered to the house.

With the menu taken care of, she now needed to set the mood, so she called her gardener, José, and told him to go to Johnson's Florist and buy as many fresh flowers as he could carry, and to have the maid help him place the flowers in all of the rooms they would be using that evening. Setting the mood required a little aromatherapy, and nothing delivered that better than Agraria spicy bitter orange scent. She placed candles and petite crystal bottles of its essence throughout each room.

Once everything was in place, she gave the staff the night off. Paulina had moved out of their home only a few weeks prior. Their little family was going through so much right now, and everyone's feelings were raw. Tonight had to be about finding their way back to each other. After that they would find a way to get Paulina to understand that they never meant to hurt her—they loved her too much for that.

Tonight Nancy needed to keep her mind on Salim. If her plan to restore their marriage worked out, and she prayed that it would, together they would get Paulina back on track.

The house looked perfect, like something out of a romantic movie. He would be arriving home within the hour, so there was no time to waste. Now she needed to take a shower and select the perfect outfit. She ran up the stairs to their vast bedroom suite, took a quick shower and walked into her Poliform-designed dressing room and closet. She pulled out a soft blue cashmere top and matching pants she had recently purchased at Neiman Marcus. The pillow-soft material glided over her curves and clung in all the right places. The top had a deep V neckline with a bow that tilted on one side and rested on her hip. Everything about the outfit said, "Please hug me and hold me tight." If ever she needed to be in Salim's arms, it was now. Keeping her look soft, she brushed her shiny hair back into a short, loose ponytail. She applied very little make-up—just a light smear of Dior Addict lip glow.

Tonight she would keep her jewelry simple, wearing the sapphire-and-pearl pendant that Salim's mother had given to her at their wedding. The sapphire was suspended on an eighteen-karat gold chain necklace, spaced with six pearls, each measuring five millimeters. Nancy didn't wear it much because it was so delicate she was afraid of something happening to it. The pendant fell to her cleavage like a baby resting in its mother's arms, giving her the look of both a maternal goddess and a seductive mistress—something she was sure Salim's mother had never thought of when she'd given her the necklace. After fastening it, she slipped on the eternity band to her wedding ring set. It was a true sparkler. The large diamonds were cut in rectangular shapes, and set in platinum. She thought back to their wedding day and how much they had been in love. They had promised each other forever, and that's what she still wanted—forever with her beloved Salim. She applied a couple drops of Bond 9 perfume, *The Scent of Peace*. Its floral and citrus scent was Salim's favorite. Giving herself a last glance in the mirror, she wondered how she could have let things get this out of hand and allowed her marriage to be in such a frightening place.

Washington was not the city to be unmarried in. Single women were treated like enemies. Forget Iran, Russia, or even North Korea; it was the single life that Nancy needed immediate protection from.

Slipping her perfectly pedicured toes into Vera Wang mules, she walked down the back staircase that led to the kitchen. She was pleased with everything. It was like it had been when they were first married.

As her anticipation built for Salim's arrival she couldn't believe it, but she had butterflies in her stomach. Salim loved having dinner in the family room off the kitchen in front of the TV, while watching the news. So tonight that's just where they would be eating.

The room was large, with eighteen-foot ceilings, a fireplace, and parquet floors that were covered with plush custom rugs. The furniture was overstuffed leather in a rich rum-raisin color. There were cashmere throws on the backs of the sofas to wrap themselves while watching movies on cold nights. The walls were covered with art they had collected in their travels around the world. The coffee tables were stacked high with books from their many author friends. One wall was dedicated to an eighty-inch television with all of the latest in electronics delights. It was Salim's man cave. When they first moved into the house they had enjoyed many fun evenings in this room. That was until their worlds became too full of stuff to find each other. Now she would have to do some major purging.

Just then she heard the sound of his car tires and the garage door opening. Her butterflies were in full effect now. What if he didn't respond? What if he asked her for a divorce? She steadied herself, walked back into the kitchen, and greeted her husband with a smile.

"Welcome home, my love", she said. While giving him a hug and a kiss.

Salim looked surprised. Nancy was never there to welcome him home anymore. He wondered if something bad had happened, or if she was getting ready to ask him something. He could only bring himself to respond with a dry "Hi."

She held on tight. She needed to feel him, to hold him. When she let him go, he walked past her and placed his briefcase in one of the breakfast room chairs, looking at the chafing dish on the counter.

He asked, "What's all this?" She could see his whole body tighten up. His entire body language changed, and he looked upset. He said, "Please don't tell me we have houseguests."

Nancy quickly answered, "No sweetie, it's just you and me tonight."

He said, "This is a lot of food for just us. Nancy, really I am not in the mood for company tonight. It's been a really rough day." His emotions were still raw, and the feeling of being on guard even in his own home was unsettling. He didn't want to spend the evening with anyone. He just wanted and needed a place where he could clear his head.

She was doing everything in her power to keep her voice soft, alluring, and calm. Nancy thought, *"Has it been so long that he has forgotten about the intimate evenings we used to share? Why did he seem so shocked that we would be having dinner alone?"*

There are moments in life when reality gives you a good swift kick in the ass, and this was one of those moments, live and in living color.

For years their relationship had a synchronicity to it. To them it was what being a couple was all about. Salim had loved being married, and so had Nancy. They both needed a partner to make it through life, and in each other they believed they'd found that person. Nancy and Salim enjoyed the fact that they instinctively knew what the other wanted or needed. They could finish each other's sentences, their bodies moved in tune, and they shared each other's thoughts and feelings. That is, until it all went wrong until their lie had broken the chain that held them together and made them one. Now they were shattered pieces that needed the fine hand of love to bring them back together. There was much work to be done in their marriage, but she needed him to relax and want it as much as she did.

As if he could read her every thought, he opened each chafing dish. Smiling, he turned to face her, saying, "Really, just the two of us?" He asked her if she had spoken with Paulina today. Tonight was not the night to fight over Paulina. So she just said they had texted each other. She didn't say any more about it, and neither did he.

Salim walked back over to her, gave her a kiss, and said, "Thank you. All my favorites."

It was the first sign that maybe this evening would work out. Nancy thought, "*The way to a man's heart is still through his stomach*." She hadn't seen him smile since before their big fight during their family vacation in Maine.

Nancy said, "Darling, how about we eat in the family room tonight?" She knew how much he loved it. He quickly agreed and asked her if he could just run and change his clothes. He would be back in a minute. Faster than the speed of sound, Salim had taken off his Canali suit, washed his face and hands, put on his favorite pair of old jeans and a T-shirt, with no shoes, just a pair of sweat socks, and soon he was in the family room watching CNN.

He called out to her asking, "What would you like to drink?"

She answered, "Whatever you are having will be fine with me."

He said he would be having a double scotch on the rocks. She answered, "Then make mine a glass of red wine, please."

Salim walked down to the wine cellar and selected a bottle of 2007 Concha y Toro Carmín de Peumo Carmenere, a superior wine from the cabernet family. Its rich velvety notes of currants, butter, and green olives were a perfect balance to Nancy's dinner selections. After letting the wine breathe for a few minutes, he took one of the tulip-shaped stemless crystal glasses from behind the bar and poured her a glass. He was touched by Nancy's efforts to make this a nice, quiet evening at home, and he wanted her to know that he appreciated it.

Maybe they could get over the hurt, pain, disappointment, and damage they had done to each other. No matter how he tried, he could not forget the hateful words she had said to him. Fighting with Nancy was like going ten rounds with Sugar Ray Leonard. When it was over you needed rest and a doctor. For sure, you would never be the same.

They had so many problems. He hadn't been able to forgive her for not telling Paulina about using a surrogate. He'd wanted to tell Paulina the truth as soon as she was old enough to understand it. Keeping it a secret had been Nancy's idea. She had tried to hide the truth because she felt guilty about not being able to give him a child. It was convenient for Nancy not to deal with the truth, but she hadn't taken Paulina's feeling into account. To deal with her guilty conscience she became an overachieving volunteer and charity superwoman, giving to every cause you could think of. He had also come full circle on her constant need to be at the latest and greatest event. And then she complained that he was not interested in sex anymore. Well news flash parading your husband around like a Westminster show puppy did absolutely nothing to get him aroused.

Salim didn't care about social standing or any Washington position. In the last couple of years, Nancy seemed all-consumed with acquiring public attention for her charitable efforts. She packed their schedules with so many events, they were out at a black-tie affair every night he was home.

The worst offense was that she used their vacation homes for charitable events, even after he had asked her not to. He hated the idea of some stranger sleeping in his bed. The house in Maine was his retreat, and she had turned it into a charitable auction item. Salim thought, *"Who does that kind of shit to their husband? After all, it was his money that paid for the mortgage every month."*

He had been blessed to be born into a wealthy family, but he'd worked hard all his life, and his success was of his own making. He never took a penny from his family. He wanted to enjoy the fruits of his labor and didn't want to always be "on" or smiling at people he didn't give a damn about. Salim could give a flying fuck about who was in or out in this town. He just wanted a woman who wanted to be his wife and not some goddamn socialite. He wanted a mother for his daughter, and Nancy was not there for Paulina or him. But she availed herself for anybody and everybody who had a social cause.

At first he'd made excuses for her, that this was all because Nancy had grown up so poor. But Salim was Nancy's third husband. She had married and dated several men of means, prior to their marriage so that excuse no longer worked.

The truth was that she had become very affected by the worst possible disease, one he had no powerful prescription for. It was known as "Potomac fever," and if she did not find a cure soon, he was afraid their marriage would surely come to an end. He could no longer handle the pressure or the loneliness of being married to a Washington socialite. He just needed a Washington wife. He still loved Nancy deeply, and he wanted their marriage to work, but she needed to do a great deal to ensure their future. Tonight they would both try.

Nancy used the large Herend dinner plates and piled them high with falafel, chickpea fritters, shrimp arak, gulf shrimp sautéed in onions, lemon-cilantro-arak sauce, pearl couscous, lamb kabobs with spice, Lebanese rice, and for dessert, they would have the toasted-sesame crème brûlée. She headed into the family room. Placing their dinner plates on teak wood TV trays, she sat back and curled up in an oversized leather chair.

With the pride of a sommelier presenting his prize-winning selection, Salim presented Nancy with a glass of wine. Bending down, he gently gave her a kiss on the forehead. They enjoyed a quiet meal, watched all of the news show's, and as an added treat, they watched *Wheel of Fortune*.

Nancy had forgotten how sweet and perfectly boring these nights at home could be. Around ten o'clock, Salim finished off his second cocktail, and Nancy had finished half a bottle of wine. He asked her if she needed help with dishes. Before she could answer, he picked up the plates and took them into the kitchen. Nancy followed with the glasses and linens.

As the last glass was placed in the sink, Salim's telephone vibrated. He had a text message. He told her it would be a minute; he had a very sick patient and needed to speak with the physician covering for him.

The truth was that it was the divorce attorney he had met with the day after they got back from Maine. Salim took the call in his study. After listening to everything his lawyer had to say, Salim told him that he wanted to hold off for now. He wanted to try again to repair his marriage. The lawyer advised him that over the years Nancy had amassed quite a large number of investments, and that she was now a extremely wealthy woman in her own right, it seems that Nancy and her sister had been transferring all of their investment profits into Nancy's foundation. Salim was not at all surprised to hear that. He had known that Nancy had a true natural gift with money. But it would have been nice to have her tell him about the financial position of her foundation, rather than to hear it from a divorce attorney. As the attorney continued to speak about what divorce would mean to them and the cost of dividing assets. Salim thought, *"Was this really the sum of my marriage? Why do I have to find out things from a divorce attorney that my wife should have told me. Why does Nancy like to keep secrets from the people she says she loves? First Paulina now me, I wonder if there is something else that I don't know about the woman I am married too. Better yet, why do I still love her?"* He told the attorney he would get back to him, but right now he wanted to try again.

He also had a text from his new secretary a pretty blonde, fresh out of college who was very eager to help Salim out in any way she could. She had wanted to go over his calendar for the next day. Salim had to admit he was enjoying the attention. He knew this was a dangerous game to play, but Nancy was leaving him no choice but to find attention outside of their home.

Nancy finished cleaning up the kitchen. Salim was still on his call when she made her way upstairs to their bedroom. After about an hour of waiting for him, she went to her desk in her dressing room to go over her schedule for the next day. She had no real plans. There was a reception at the Italian embassy in the evening. Maybe she would meet Salim for lunch. They hadn't done that in years. She clicked on his schedule to see if he would be in town.

To her disappointment, the schedule showed that he would be leaving on a late flight to Denver for a medical conference, where he was the keynote speaker. She wondered why he hadn't said anything about it over dinner.

Nancy heard him turn on the shower. She thought, "*Great timing*." She took off her clothes and joined him under the warm water. Normally, this was when he would get a giant hard-on, and they would make love all night. But tonight he was not interested. He suddenly seemed stressed. She wondered what kind of telephone call he had just received.

She said, "My, that's a quick shower. Is there something wrong, darling?"

He said, "I am not feeling that dirty tonight…how about you?" He handed her the soap and walked out of the shower. Wrapping a thick towel around his waist, he walked into his dressing room and closed the door.

Nancy finished showering alone, feeling a sudden chill. Something had happened on that call he'd taken. She needed him to get back on the same page with her. She thought it must be the pressures of being a surgeon. Maybe she could get him to relax under the covers. Sex had always worked with Salim; in the past they had a wonderful sex life.

She dried off, slipped on a tiny silk nightgown, propped herself up with the large Euro shams, and waited for him to join her. When he came in the bedroom, she unwrapped herself like a present. Salim just pushed back the duvet, got into bed, and turned off his light. She reached down, gently taking him in her hand, and ever so softly but firmly started to massage his wonderful member.

He said, "Not tonight, Nancy. I am tired."

She responded by softly kissing his ears and face, all while continuing to massage him. After a couple of minutes he began responding. There is not a man born who can ignore attention to that part of his body, so when he was good and hard, Nancy climbed on top, mounting him with the precision of an expert equestrian, slowly lowering her silky wetness down over his throbbing, hard rod. Once she was completely filled with his love, she began riding him as if he were a Kentucky Derby winner going for a triple crown. Daily kegel exercises helped keep her vagina very tight. Tonight she used every muscle in her body to tighten her wet walls around him, applying pressure on the down stroke and loosening it on the upstroke, never completely losing her hold on him until she felt him begin to quiver and shake. Like any good jockey she was determined to bring her mighty stallion to victory. So she squeezed down even harder until he yelled out, "Oh damn, baby! I am coming!" and then he erupted in a powerful climax.

After that he said, "Thank you, babe. I really need to get some rest now."

She thought, "*That's it? Now you are going to sleep?*"

She said, "Oh, okay." Feeling completely deflated, she dismounted and went to the bathroom to clean up. Sitting on her Sherle Wagner marble-and-gold bidet, she thought, "*This is some real bullshit. I fucked him good, and he just goes to sleep. What about me?*" Spreading her legs to position the warm water to reach her love-filled tunnel she let the warm water cleanse her, and using the controls she brought herself to a lonely but satisfying orgasm. As she went back to bed, she fought the urge to smother him to death. Instead, she spent the night crying silently into her pillow.

Chapter 25

It was three o'clock in the morning. Before Winnie knew it, the alarm was sounding off, and she was up and heading to the bathroom. Maria had already seen to it that Winnie's chic ensemble was in perfect condition, making sure there were no missing buttons and that the cashmere pants had soft creases in them. No detail was ever overlooked.

All Winnie had to do was shower, do her hair and make-up, and then she'd be ready to go. The weather was cool outside, so Winnie dressed in a Max Mara tan cashmere suit and a silk blouse, with her curb-link Verdura gold-link necklace and matching bracelet watch very simple but elegant. She slipped on her tan-and-black Chanel low-heel pumps and went down stairs. She could smell breakfast was ready: Irish steel-cut oatmeal with fresh berries, and chai tea was served in her breakfast room. As she ate she gave the morning newspaper a quick once-over. She finished her breakfast thanked Maria, wished her a good day, and was off to the station.

She intended to head to the gym for a quick workout right after she signed off today, then to George's Salon for a manicure-pedicure, and today she would have her hair blown out.

She would speak with her producer today about having someone from the National Gallery of Art on the show to talk about the upcoming exhibit. That was her way of thanking them for inviting her to their black-tie event. Winnie herself had collected several nice art pieces. She loved watercolors and the work French impressionist.

Winnie was excited about the upcoming dinner, and she wondered if she would see the ambassador at the National Gallery of Art. Had Coco invited herself to that event? She laughed to herself. Coco was a real trip.

When she arrived at the station, the newsroom was buzzing. Congress was back in session, so there was a lot of news to cover, and her producer was ready to go. They quickly went over the breaking stories: a shooting in Temple Hills, a robbery in the southeast, and a possible political shit-storm involving a pay-to-play scheme with a senior congressman from Chicago.

Reading the details of the case building against the Chicago congressman, Winnie wondered when politicians would learn you can't play both sides and not get burned. The first lady was hosting a luncheon for the founders and board members of the charity Knock Out Abuse Against Women, a local charity that annually raised millions of dollars in support of women and children affected by domestic violence, they held a huge event every November that Winnie had attended many times. The president was campaigning for a new energy bill in California and would be attending a star-studded dinner that evening at the home of a billion-dollar movie powerhouse, the founder and chairman of Gatie Entertainment.

Winnie read over her script, greeted her co-anchor, and checked her makeup. She was ready. She walked behind the anchor's desk, took her seat, put her microphone on and on *three, two, one*, she smiled and said, "Good morning, Washington. This is Winnie Pettridge with breaking news from Temple Hills, Maryland, where three teens are suspected of a drive-by shooting..."

Chapter 26

When Nancy woke up the next morning, she was in bed alone. She got up and walked into the bathroom and no Salim. He always gave her a kiss on the forehead before he left for the day. Not sure what to think, she reached for the phone. Calling down to the kitchen, she asked the housekeeper if Dr. Hadid was having breakfast. She was told that he had left early without any breakfast.

Nancy said okay and that she would be heading to the gym and would not be requiring anything this morning. She knew he didn't want to face her, just as she was sure their marriage was heading in a dangerous direction. Her past failed marriages had taught her that much. Just the sheer thought of Salim not being in love with her was too overwhelming to think about. Her knees started to shake, and she felt sick to her stomach. She had to fix this and now.

Maybe in the heat of their argument, she had said too much. She was hurt too. Her feelings of abandonment in their marriage and being left alone were not easy things for her to handle. But more than anything, she wanted him to understand that he was needed and wanted. His family needed him just as much as his patients did. Nancy understood that she had to shoulder half the blame for what was happening, but not all of it.

He had to know that she still loved him. She called his cell phone, and to her surprise, he answered. She told him that she loved him more than anything.

He said he loved her too, but he needed some time to get over the things she had said to him. She asked him, "What do you mean, you need time? What are you saying?"

He said he couldn't talk anymore, and he had to go. Before she could say good-bye, he ended the call.

As she put the telephone down, her entire body felt a chill. She would have to work on a better plan, and immediately, to fix her marriage. She said to herself, "I will be damned if I let Paulina or anyone come between me and Salim."

She needed a good workout. That always cleared her head. She quickly washed up, slipped into her workout gear, and left for the Four Seasons Spa. She could work out, get a massage, and work on her "love and marriage repair plan."

As she made the ten-minute drive to the spa, she thought of everything that had happened in the past couple of months between Paulina, Salim, and herself, rethinking every minute and wondering what she could have done differently. How had she failed them so badly, and dear God how could she fix it? Over and over again she heard Sadie's words in her head: *If you don't do something soon, someone else will make him her husband...make him her husband... make him her husband...MAKE HIM HER HUSBAND.*

Pulling into the valet station, she put on her best smile. As she stepped out of the car, the valet attendant greeted her warmly, and then quickly his look changed to concern.

He said, "Good morning, Mrs. Hadid. Oh, is there something wrong? You are crying."

Nancy hadn't felt the tears rolling down her cheeks. She quickly wiped them away and answered, "No, no, I just have a cold."

She reached into her pocket, taking out some crumpled money. She stuffed a fifty-dollar bill in his hand, as if money would be the ultimate memory eraser.

He said, "No, this is not necessary, Mrs. Hadid."

She looked him in the eye and said, "I am fine. You are always so kind to me. Now please take it. I am going to the spa for a workout."

Walking as quickly as her toned legs could carry her, she made a mad dash through the opulent hotel lobby and headed to the oasis of the spa. Greeting the front desk staff, she asked if it would be possible to get her favorite Cherry Blossom Champagne treatment after her workout.

Today her workout would consist of thirty minutes on the treadmill, followed by laps in the sea-salt pool. Nancy had a lean, athletic body. She wore a perfect size six dress, but to stay that way required daily workouts. Nancy loved food, and eating gloriously delicious meals with her family and friends was one of her favorite things.

She plugged in her headset and turned on John Legend's "Green Light," featuring André 3000. She loved the song. Its quick beats allowed her to get into a fast run, and within minutes she felt lost in the music. After forty minutes on the treadmill, she changed into her swimwear and made her way to the pool. Working out completely relaxed her. She swam for over two hours until the technician came to get her for her massage. Then she wrapped herself in a thick towel and headed to the showers, and within minutes she was on the massage table.

The Cherry Blossom treatment awakened Nancy's spirit as it relaxed her muscles.

The technician told her there was an opening for a facial if she was interested. She agreed and spent about an hour in the relaxation lounge. While the tranquility of the spa helped renew her senses, she still had not come up with any additional ideas on how to get her family back on track. She went to the changing area and dressed slowly.

While she was preparing to leave, she ran into Dede Snowden, a prominent member of the community, who had recently founded a charity for missing children. Dede asked her if she could count on support from the Hadid family for the upcoming event.

Nancy said, "Which one? You have an event every month. It's getting hard to know which one to support but yes, please send me something." She said she would check their calendar, and even if they could not attend the event she would still send in a donation.

Dede never liked being called on her constant fundraising, so she said, "Oh, by the way I ran into your friend Sadie the other evening, and she was two sheets to the wind. She can really kick it back! Oh…I am sorry. What I meant to say was she was really enjoying herself. Well have a great day Nancy, and I will have my secretary send you something right away. See you soon."

Nancy said, "Thanks, Dede." Then she thought, "*Damn, what is happening to Sadie?*" She wondered where Lonnie was when all this was happening, and who these friends were who were letting her get drunk in public and not protecting her.

As she reached the door, she ran into Winnie. Winnie greeted her with that award-winning smile saying, "Hey girl, I am just arriving...but it looks like you need a friendly lunch. Do you have time?" Winnie always knew when something was wrong with Nancy.

They walked through the courtyard into the Bourbon Steak restaurant and ordered the chopped shrimp and crab salad. After the waiter left their table, the two friends began sharing their problems.

Nancy led in, saying, "By the way, Dede Snowden said she saw Sadie the other night, and she's telling everyone that she was drunk."

Winnie said that her station manager had seen Sadie somewhere, and he had the same report.

Winnie quickly turned the subject away from Sadie and back to them. She could tell that something was troubling her friend and she could see Nancy had been crying. Winnie reached over the table and took Nancy's hand saying, "What's wrong? Talk to me please."

Nancy started telling Winnie everything, even about their bedroom problems.

Winnie listened intently to every word and when Nancy was finished, Winnie called the waiter over ordered two cosmopolitans, very cold with a drunken cherry.

When the drinks were placed on the table and the waiter had disappeared, Winnie raised her glass and said, "Here's to getting real. Nancy, sometimes the only way to assess the collateral damage of breathing rarefied air is by counting the love ones you have suffocated during your climb to the top. Now I only have one question for you. Was it all worth it?"

Nancy could not believe what Winnie had just said to her. Had she made a mistake in sharing with her?

Winnie had seen the warning signs that Salim had been giving Nancy for some time now. She just could not understand why Nancy missed them, so she talked straight to her.

Winnie said, "Nancy, for the last few years you have been so busy chairing every event in this town, you have missed the most important principal of life: charity begins at home and spreads abroad."

She continued, saying, "No one keeps the kind of schedule you do and has a healthy marriage. I can't go out every night and I am single! Not and keep my home in order, not even with good help. You, my dear friend are out at every soirée, and now you're wondering what has happened. You had better clear your schedule and save your marriage and family and do it now."

Nancy said, "I tried last night."

Winnie quickly answered, "It's going to take more than one night to fix it."

Nancy tearfully asked what she should do next. Winnie knew the pain Nancy was feeling. She had been there. The difference was that Nancy and Salim had a marriage that was worth saving. Hers had not been such a union.

Winnie picked up her iPhone, telephoned her assistant at the station, and asked for the contact information of the marriage therapist that had recently appeared on the show. She wrote down the information and handed it to Nancy, telling her to call for an appointment ASAP.

Winnie was sure Salim still loved Nancy, and she hoped they could repair the damage they had done. They just needed to get back on track. Nancy suddenly felt there was some hope and she would recover from this, stronger and more in love than before.

Winnie said, "Okay, now that we have solved your problem, what can you tell me about Phillip Lay and the Lay family that I don't already know? I need the back story.

Nancy thought she knew everything about everybody in town, so she was only too happy to spill the beans. She told Winnie that Donna Lay was a member of the Capital Ladies' Club and she regularly hosted the holiday ball invitation-addressing luncheon at her magnificent home. She was known for being a good hostess but not a great hostess. It was rumored that Phillip had an affair with the wife of some ambassador, and when Donna found out she had a major fit and Phillip had to do some serious jewelry buying to get back in the house. However, their marriage was never the same.

Nancy got very sad again, and Winnie said, "Pull it together. That's their marriage, not yours. You will be okay, Nancy. Just make Salim and Paulina first again."

As they finished their salads Nancy finally asked why Winnie had wanted to know about the Lay's and whether she would be doing a feature on them for her TV station. Winnie knew better than to tell Nancy about the recent calls from Phillip Lay and the attention he had shown her, so she said yes, she was considering them for a special report on Washington's top givers. Satisfied with that answer Nancy began asking questions about who else Winnie was considering.

The waiter asked them if they wanted dessert, and they both said no. As he placed the check on the table, Nancy quickly took it, saying this one was on her. Winnie grabbed the little black folder and said no, she had asked Nancy to lunch, and she quickly took out her black American Express card to pay the bill. They both laughed because they fought over the bill every time they went to lunch. It was a standing thing with them. They were always trying to treat each other.

Heading out of the restaurant, they ran into Phillip Lay. His face lit up when he saw Winnie. He was only mildly interested in exchanging pleasantries with Nancy. She greeted him and his guest. Phillip introduced the handsome man with him. The gentleman was a well known architect and had just finished the design of the new Biltmore Hotel in Las Vegas. During the short conversation, Phillip never took his eyes off Winnie. Both ladies smiled and wished them a good day.

As Nancy and Winnie made it to the lobby, Nancy said, "That was something! You had just mentioned Phillip. He looked very pleased to see you."

Winnie brushed if off, saying, "Oh, it's just the TV thing. Everyone feels like they know you when you are in their bedrooms at five o'clock every morning."

They walked to the hotel lobby, Winnie had an appointment at George's and Nancy had to get back home. Winnie hugged Nancy and whispered in her ear, "Everything will work out. Just call the counselor. I am praying for you and your family."

Nancy said, "Thank you, Winnie. You're the best."

Winnie said, "Let me know if there is anything else I can do."

Nancy said, "Just keep praying."

As they went about their daily routine, Nancy found strength in knowing that Winnie would always be there for her.

Chapter 27

Coco placed a call to Paulina, inviting her to the upcoming Lady Gaga concert at Verizon Center. She explained how she had been invited as a VIP guest, and how many people she could have asked, but that she'd thought only of Paulina.

Paulina loved Lady Gaga and would have gone to the concert if Coco hadn't started the conversation with such bullshit. She thought, "*This is not a lady that I want to be indebted to for anything.*"

Paulina said, "Oh, Ms. Coco, you are too kind to invite me, but I have so much homework, I just can't take the time right now. But thank you."

"Paulina, I am so disappointed you can't make it. As I said, I only thought of you when I received the tickets, and you know, I'm aware of what you are going through right now. How is everyone handling it? How are you handling it? Well, I am here if you need someone to talk to. I am very busy, but I will make the time for you. I understand how parents can be." Coco wanted Paulina to know what she was missing by not hanging out with her. She wanted Paulina to feel a little regretful.

Paulina hated nosy busybodies. She thanked Coco again and quickly got off the phone. To her Coco seemed nice on the outside, but there was something about her that she couldn't put her finger on. She only knew she wanted to stay away from whatever that something was.

It hadn't always been that way, but after Mike's death, Coco had changed. She now was jealous and small minded and always seemed to want to one-up another woman. Paulina had overheard Nancy talking about some of the catty things that Coco had done to her.

Back when things were okay with the Hadid family and they were still having big holiday parties, Paulina had witnessed Coco openly flirting with

Salim during her family's annual Memorial Day cookout. She thought, "*With friends like Coco, you really don't need enemies.*"

When all of the guests, left Paulina told Nancy what she had seen. After that Coco was never invited to any more private family affairs. Nancy may have done some crazy things, but she was still a woman. And Paulina didn't like a man-stealer, and that's what she thought Coco was.

When Coco got off the phone with Paulina, she said, "Damn, now who do I have to go with me?"

She called Sarah, who just happened to be free that night. Sarah said, "Oh, thank you, Coco. What are the seat numbers?"

Coco, not knowing any better proudly read off the numbers. "Section 121, Row D."

Sarah said, "Coco, those are nice seats, but they are not VIP...I will go with you, but only after I call my husband's office and see if we can get an upgrade. You know you really should not tell people that you have VIP seats if you don't. We will have a sore neck from those seats, but we will go and have a good time. Let me call you back."

In an hour Sarah called back with four tickets for floor seats in Section 2, Row B, along with backstage passes. She had invited two other mutual friends from their "ladies who lunch" group.

Sarah said, "Coco, why don't you give your tickets to someone else and come with me as my guest?"

Coco was trumped again, and the concert had been her idea. She thought these rich bitches move fast. Now Sarah would be seen as the important lady and not Coco. Sarah had taken over her idea and had the money to show off in style.

Sarah assured her they would have a great time. She would have her driver take them down to the center. They would be Gaga-monsters for the evening.

Sarah was younger, richer than Coco, and now was outshining her yet again. It seemed like Coco was unable to get around always feeling like a red-headed stepchild. She knew what she needed: some good old-fashioned down-and-out-poor friends. Then she could be the star.

Coco looked up to the ceiling and said, "For the love of baby Jesus...how could this have happened to me again?"

Chapter 28

The Von Kinley's had been major supporters of the Snowflake Ball since they arrived in town. Sadie was now serving as immediate past ball chair, taking her role very seriously and supporting the ball by opening her home for invitation-addressing luncheons, committee teas, and special donor receptions. She loved attending the dinner and looked forward to it all summer long. To ensure the evening was not a total social affair, she carefully planned who would be given the honor of being invited to join her and Lonnie at their table. Social rating was given for having the right table guests, so she guarded her table assignment and guests selection with as much care and purpose as a congressional appointment.

Lonnie and Sadie would be playing host to an interesting group this evening: the returning ambassador of Mexico and his very young wife, a striking beauty rumored to be the former mistress to the president of Spain. Also at their table were Republican Senator Tommy Bantor of Florida, and his wife Polly. The senator was a senior member of the Senate and chairman of the Committee on Foreign Relations. Sadie played bridge with Polly, and the two families enjoyed a very close relationship.

Also joining them would be the newly appointed senior vice president of a large petroleum company and his partner, a nationally known interior designer, who had just won the contract to redecorate Blair House, the official guesthouse of the president of the United States. Balancing out their table was Avis Paulson, the new president of the Washington Opera, a middle-aged woman from Dallas, Texas where she had reportedly raised a ton of money for the arts. She would be attending with her husband, a lobbyist for a major energy company.

As Sadie was getting dressed for the evening, she received a telephone call from Avis, explaining that her husband would be unable to attend. He'd come down with some kind of stomach bug. Sadie always gracious said she completely understood and not to worry these things happen, and she and Lonnie looked forward to seeing her in a few hours.

As soon as Sadie hung up the telephone she yelled out, "Goddamn it my table now has an empty seat!"

She quickly got on the phone and called every single person she knew, but it was far too late, and no one was available. She would just have to wait until she got to the hotel and have a waiter remove a seat from the table.

She also made a mental note to never invite Avis to her table again. Sadie didn't care if she raised a zillion dollars, you don't call someone hours before a major black-tie event and cancel. You give your husband some medicine, tell him to stick a cork up his ass, get dressed and start the car.

Looking into the mirror, she quickly felt terribly bad for thinking such a thing. Who was she kidding? If Lonnie had so much as a bad cough, she would gladly stay home and take care of her man. How dare she be upset with Avis? She was at least making the effort to attend the ball.

Sadie remembered what it felt like to be needed. She would give anything to feel needed by someone again. These days the only people who seemed to need her were her charities.

Reaching for her favorite liquid boost of confidence a very dry martini she noticed her glass was empty. She hadn't remembered drinking the first one. Looking at the empty glass, she thought, "*It's okay. I am just busy, that's all. No problem here I am okay.*" She needed another martini very cold, with two large olives. For as long as she could remember, martini's had been her companion when she was getting dressed. It was part of her routine, which started with a long bath. She soaked in warm water until her stylist arrived at the house for hair and makeup. After they finished, she would enjoy a small cocktail and then slip into her gown. She'd been doing this routine for so many years.

She felt a sense of duty now. It was no longer simply about the glamour, joy, and excitement of these evenings. Sadie understood full well that the charity needed her support. It was part of the social pressure of being blessed with such a good life. People expected so much of rich people that sometimes it felt like a brick hanging around her neck. On the brighter side of it, she would be seeing some old friends who had been away for the entire summer.

Looking into the mirror, she noticed fine lines forming around her eyes and mouth. She needed to place a call to Chesapeake Plastic Surgery soon.

She was startled when the intercom buzzed.

It was Lonnie. He said, "Baby, how are you coming along? Please remember, we don't want to be late."

Sadie smiled to herself and softly assured him by saying, "My darling, I will be down in a few minutes. Can you make me a very dry one, please, sweetie?"

Lonnie said "Yes". He never said no to anything she asked of him.

She hung up the telephone. Sitting at her mirrored vanity table, she glanced at the crystal framed pictures, which reminded her of the wonderful life she had been blessed to live. She ran her finger over one of the pictures with Lonnie, Benny, Timothy, and Larry smiling back up at her. The photo had been taken several years ago, during a family vacation in St. Barts. She remembered that day as if it were yesterday, and she laughed out loud to herself at how much fun they'd had. She worked hard to make sure they enjoyed family vacations.

She missed her sons, now that they were all grown up and had lives of their own. They called often, but it would never be the same as when they all lived under the same roof. No mother could be more proud of her children than Sadie was. The Von Kinley boys had grown up to be outstanding men. They had never given Lonnie or Sadie a moment's worth of trouble. That was another reason she made daily Mass at her church: to thank God for his many blessings to her and her family.

She walked over to her dress, a strapless Oscar de la Renta ball gown, with a full skirt in red silk, from Mr. de la Renta's latest collection. The gown was very simple, well as simple as a six-thousand dollar couture gown can be. Every inch of it was unmistakably Oscar's, with clean lines and the very best silk fabric. It was hanging on a walnut hanger like a soldier's uniform, ready for a night of social battle. She gently slipped it off the hanger and stepped into it.

Tonight she wanted her accessories to speak. Lonnie, a lover of big jewels and an avid collector, had given her a new suite of masterful gems that he'd purchased at Christie's Auction House.

The lot was entitled "Magnificent Jewels." It included a Bulgari designed ruby and diamond necklace, with matching bracelet and earrings, and a large ruby and diamond ring that had been the property of a San Francisco tobacco heiress.

Lonnie said the suite was coming from one tobacco farmer and going to another. He had given it to her for their thirty-fifth wedding anniversary. Each piece was a true work of art. The stones were cut in pear, oval, and rectangular shapes and mounted in platinum, creating a look of sparkling white diamond flowers with ruby centers. To add a little fun to her outfit, she pulled her whimsical Judith Leiber Humpty Dumpty crystal minaudière handbag. Carrying a Judith Leiber was like carrying a piece of art. It made her smile every time she looked down at it. Sadie was one of the largest collectors of Judith Leiber handbags in the United States, and she displayed them in glass-enclosed cases that lined the walls of her seventeen hundred square foot dressing room.

Sadie's lady's maid, Hattie was very special to the family. She was a woman of refined elegance with lots of southern charm. She had been with the family since the Von Kinley's got married and had helped Sadie raise the boys. At one time Sadie and Hattie were both pregnant. During that time they took care of each other.

When Hattie knocked on the door, she was carrying a small tray with Sadie's cocktail. She wanted to help her finish dressing and also remind her that Mr. Von Kinley was waiting in the library.

Like Sadie, Hattie was an empty nester. Her son a fine young man had finished college, gone on to medical school and was now a doctor specializing in lung cancer at the Mayo Clinic.

He'd gotten married last year. Hattie invited the Von Kinley's to the wedding. It was a small lovely affair. Hattie had placed the Von Kinley's with the groom's family, and that had touched Sadie's heart so much that she cried through the entire wedding service.

Lonnie had taught Hattie how to invest in stocks years ago, and she and her husband had done their financial homework. She was now a very comfortable woman. Hattie's husband, Samuel, had passed away several years before. Although Hattie was alone now and no longer having to work for financial gain; she worked to keep herself busy.

As Hattie zipped up Sadie's gown and helped her secure the closure of the necklace, they talked about the family's upcoming event. Hattie smiled at Sadie and asked, "How will you manage tonight?"

Sadie responded, "What do you mean?"

Hattie said, "Well, when everybody sees this necklace, there will not be any air left in the ballroom after all of the gasping is finished!"

They both laughed.

Sadie said, "It is really a fabulous piece. Lonnie out did himself."

Then Hattie reminded Sadie to call her brother, Sam, in the morning. He wanted to talk about plans for the families to get together for the holidays. Hattie wished Mrs. Von Kinley a good evening.

Hattie left her to go to Sadie's bathroom and begin straightening up. She returned everything to its rightful place.

Just as Sadie was about to walk out of the dressing room, her private line rang. She said, "Who could this be?"

Hattie asked, "Do you want me to answer it?"

Sadie said, "No, I will get it." Sadie answered the phone. It was this year's ball chair. She was calling to tell Sadie she wanted to have a picture taken of the two of them, before the festivities get started. She also wanted to thank Sadie and Lonnie for supporting the event. Sadie told her they would be leaving the house soon, and she would look for her the minute they arrived.

Just as Lonnie was fixing himself a tight scotch on the rocks, the doorbell rang. He thought, "*Who in the world would be ringing the doorbell, and why hadn't the security gate announced a visitor?*"

Felix was on it, but before he could do anything, the door opened. It was Benny, their eldest son making a surprise visit. He was traveling back to New York and had a break in his schedule, so he thought he would drop by home and check up on his parents. His brothers had been worried about their mom. It seemed that every time they spoke to her, she had been drinking.

When Benny walked through the door, he smiled at Felix and made a motion for him to be quiet. He wanted to surprise his father. Felix pointed to the library and whispered that he was waiting for Mrs. Von Kinley to come down.

Benny walked in, and Lonnie almost fainted. The two men hugged. There was no relationship closer than theirs. They were father and son, and now that the boys were all grown up, they were also best friends. They held each other for a long moment.

Lonnie said, "Son, what are you doing here? Is everything all right?"

Benny told him about the business meeting, which had concluded faster than planned leaving him a free twenty-four hours to spend with his dear parents.

Benny said, "You know I will use any excuse to spend time with you."

Lonnie could not be prouder of his sons. They were everything he had wished and prayed for. Lonnie said, "We have a party to go to tonight. Let me speak with your mother and see if we would be missed if we stayed home with you."

Just as Lonnie was about to pick up the intercom and dial into Sadie's dressing room, she walked into the library. With the same reaction that his father had just shown, Sadie was overjoyed to see her son. But she was worried that something was wrong. Benny assured her that everything was fine, that he was free for the next twenty-four hours, and he wanted to spend that time at home with them. He could smell alcohol on Sadie, and that concerned him.

Benny looked at his handsome parents and said, "Well, looks like you two are heading out for the evening, so I will raid the refrigerator and see what delicious leftovers the chef has in the kitchen."

Sadie asked him if he would like to join them. As luck would have it, they did have an extra seat at their table. She said, "Please Benny, save us from a boring evening."

Benny was okay with it, but he did not have a tux with him. Lonnie called to Felix and asked him if the midnight-blue Ralph Lauren tux was ready.

Felix said, "I just picked it up this afternoon. It's hanging in your dressing room, sir."

Lonnie looked at Benny, "Well Son, I do believe we are now the same size, so please follow me and we will have you dressed in no time."

Benny said, "No, you stay here with Mother. Felix, please bring the tux to my old room. I will be dressed and back down here in less than twenty minutes."

Benny was ready in no time, and he looked like a Ralph Lauren model. Sadie was so proud of him and his brothers, and seeing him only made her realize just how much she truly missed the days when they had all needed her.

During the ride to the hotel, Benny got his brothers on the telephone putting the call on speaker so Sadie and Lonnie could join in the conversation. They laughed, and they all told Sadie what they wanted to eat during the holidays. For the first time, the ride to the hotel just didn't seem long enough. When they pulled into valet parking, they ended the call. Sadie thanked Benny for getting everyone on the call. She loved them all so much.

Chapter 29

Nancy was completely overwhelmed with social responsibilities and had no interest in attending tonight's ball. She hoped Salim would show up. They were still having trouble communicating, and the stress of it was beginning to show on her face. It would be hard to keep smiling when everything in her life was not so wonderful. If Salim was a no-show, it would be a sign that they were heading for separate lives. She placed a call to his cell phone. It went directly to voice mail. She simply reminded him about tonight's event and that she loved him.

As she hung up the phone, she thought, *"How many nights they had looked forward to being together at these kinds of events. They would always be the first couple on the dance floor. She could still feel his arms around her, gliding her across the floor. How had things changed so much, so quickly?"* When they had the blowup in Maine, he told her that he hated these kinds of evenings. He only did it because he was trying to make her happy. She called him a two-faced liar and told him that he didn't have to do it anymore.

She heard her cell phone ring. It was Paulina, telling her that she was going with some friends to Aspen for a weekend of skiing and she needed to use her father's credit card.

Nancy told her no, she needed to speak with her father when he came home. Paulina told her she was going, and that was that. She would find the money to pay for it. Nancy tried to reason with her to calm down, saying she was sure it would be okay, but that Paulina had to at least speak with her dad.

Paulina hung up the phone before Nancy could finish her sentence. Nancy thought, "*This little bitch has really gotten out of control.*" Her behavior was so erratic that it just didn't make any sense. Nancy wondered if Paulina had started using drugs. She understood that Paulina was hurt, but no piece of paper could change the fact that she had always been loved.

Just as Nancy was heading upstairs to take her shower and change into her gown, Salim came through the door. She was so happy to see him. He looked tired and somehow older than he had before. Their eyes met and she said, "Hello. I am glad you're home."

He said, "Why? Are you really worried you may not have a dance partner? I am here so that you don't have to worry about that tonight."

Nancy was hurt. She said, "It's not about a dance partner; it's about my life partner, the man that I love, my husband. Yes, I am glad you're home, and I want you to come home to me every night."

Nancy felt like an enemy in the line of fire, between Salim and Paulina she never knew which one would shoot her first. So she just marched up the stairs and went to her bathroom. She needed to take a hot shower to relieve some of the tension she was feeling. Her family's drama was taking it's toll on her, but she was not sure how to make it better. She understood some of Paulina's problems, but rebelling like this was not making anything better. She so much wanted to just sit her down and talk things through. But Paulina would not have any of that. She just wanted to punish them.

Salim just stood there. He had not been ready for what she had said. She did still love him, but she had killed something inside of him and he needed time to heal. He walked into his study, sat down at his desk and looked out the window. His emotions were taking him on a roller coaster ride. As he pondered his thoughts, he felt like shit. He didn't want to hurt Nancy, he loved her. Why had he said that to her? Why couldn't he let go of the anger and the hurt and begin finding his way back to her? Why did he need to punish her for what she had said in Maine?

He looked at their wedding photo on his desk. She was still his beautiful bride, still the little spitfire he'd married, still the lover he wanted to spend the rest of his life with. So much had come between them. They were facing a mountain of tension and disappointments and enough pressure to knock them down.

The question he had to answer was: Did he have the strength to knock the mountain down? And what would he find on the other side?

Just as he was about to get up to go upstairs, his cell phone rang. It was Paulina. She wanted to use his American Express card to pay for a trip to Aspen. She said she had already gotten the okay from Nancy. She needed him to give American Express the okay for her purchases. He told her no, she could not go to Aspen. She told him she was of legal age, and she could do what she wanted to do, and that he was the worst father known to humankind. And then she hung up the phone.

Salim thought, "*Dammit, why had Nancy told her yes?*" He was pissed off. He went upstairs to find Nancy in the shower, he opened the shower door. Salim started in saying, "Why in the world would you tell Paulina she could go to Aspen to ski for the weekend?"

Nancy was shocked. She said, "Hold on a minute. Paulina had just called me, and I told her no, she could *not* go until I spoke to you about it! Nancy stepped out of the shower naked, with wet soap bubbles dripping from her body. She marched over to the phone, called Paulina, put the call on speakerphone, and repeated her conversation with her saying, "Paulina, I never told you that you could go to Aspen. How dare you lie about that to your father? You my dear cannot go to Aspen, and Paulina, I am getting pretty sick and tired of these little games you are playing. You do not have the right to play your father against me or me against him."

Paulina disconnected the call. Nancy stood there, beautifully naked and looking at Salim with fire blazing out of her eyes. "How dare you think that I would ever approve of her going off like that? She is twenty years old she does not need our permission but she needs our money, and she is acting like a five-year-old!"

Paulina was at that difficult age. She was becoming an adult but still acting like a child. She still needed their guidance. Salim felt bad for being so quick to judge Nancy. He picked up a towel went over to her, and wrapped it around her.

Nancy said, "Salim, we need to sit down with Paulina and try again to make her see our side. I never meant to hurt you or her, I have always thought of her as my child."

Salim said, "Nancy, how would you feel if you just found out that your parents had kept a secret from you about who your mother was?"

Nancy said, "Remember my parents lived in a trailer park and we barely had enough to live on. So excuse me if I had the life that Paulina has enjoyed, I might be celebrating our buying the whole fucking town a drink—not going to Aspen to party on my parents' money."

Paulina was doing anything she could to hurt them. The crowd of kids she was hanging around were major risk takers. They experiment with drugs, wild sex anything to take them to the next level of numbness.

Nancy begged him, "Please work with me, and not against me. I feel like you and Paulina want to punish me and I can't handle it. Believe it when I say that you carry my heart with you. I love you and Paulina you are my world, please forgive me and let's make this work."

Salim took Nancy into his arms. She asked him directly, "Do you still love me Salim?" He whispered in her ear, "Yes Nancy, I do still love you."

Salim asked Nancy what time they were expected at the dinner, and she said seven thirty. His look told her that it was the last place he wanted to be, and she agreed, but obligation won. As they began dressing for dinner, they were both filled with an unsettling feeling of failure. They dressed in silence, and as usual, it didn't take Salim long. He waited for Nancy in the library.

When Nancy came downstairs, she was wearing a white-and-gold Donna Karan gown, accessorized with an Alveare gold-and-diamond suite by Bulgari, including the Parentesi wristwatch. She carried a small blue satin Lady Dior evening bag. Salim could not help it; she looked wonderful, and she still turned him on. They rode to the hotel in silence. They were both thinking about Paulina.

Nancy placed another call to Paulina's cell phone, which went to voice-mail, so she left a message. "Paulina baby, we love you. Let's sit down and talk about everything you are feeling. If you want to find your birth mother, I will help you, your father and I both love you. Please don't shut us out like this."

When she ended the call, Salim reached over and took her hand. They didn't need words. They each knew what the other was feeling.

Chapter 30

The air was crisp and cold, and the sky was lit up with brilliant twinkling stars. It was a perfect winter evening.

As guests arrived to the Four Seasons Hotel, they were greeted by magnificent floral displays in the shape of snowflakes hanging from the top of the valet cover.

The hotel had been transformed into a magical winter wonderland. Large flowers that looked like white doves with branches of red berries hanging from their beaks greeted the guests. No one in this universe could display flowers with such whimsical elegance and drama as the event planner to the stars, Preston Bailey. He had been contracted to transform this winter oasis at the request of this year's chairwoman.

Sadie knew just how absolutely fabulous he was to work with, and over the years they had become great friends.

Guests were taking their time as they made their way to the registration tables. Members of the Junior League, dressed in long midnight-blue gowns with large white roses pinned on their left shoulders, were serving as this year's welcome committee, directing guests to the lower level as the musical group called the Floating Violins played softly in the background.

Sadie, Lonnie, and Benny were all smiling as they emerged from their limo. As they greeted new and old friends all chatting about how wonderful the hotel looked. Lonnie noticed several of the young ladies eyeing Benny and making a beeline toward him. He always handled the attention with grace. Sadie jokingly said, "Ladies, I am so sorry, but he is all mine this evening. I am one lucky mother." Everyone laughed, and Benny planted a kiss on Sadie's cheek.

Taking the stairs down to the grand ballroom level, they mingled among the lovely items on display, Sadie and Lonnie signed up for several interesting packages. Benny was getting into the auction as well. He saw a couple of restaurant offerings that looked great and thought if he was lucky and won them, they would be great when he brought his girl down to visit his parents.

Sadie noticed Nancy and Salim arriving. They both looked immaculately turned out, despite the stress that she knew them to be under right then, since Sadie and Nancy chatted every morning. Sadie wanted to keep Nancy encouraged that things would get better.

After Salim checked them in, he made his way to the bar. Nancy walked into the auction area. She saw Sadie and gladly made her way over to say hello. Not even Nancy's flawless make-up could cover the sadness in her eyes.

Sadie said, "Nancy, my darling, please smile. You don't want people to notice the sadness on your face."

Nancy said, "Sometimes I don't have the energy to act like everything is okay when it isn't. Sadie, we had a fight before we left the house this evening. I guess I am just not a good actress."

Sadie reminded her that Washington, D.C., was built on the backs of the world's greatest actors, politicians, and community do-gooders. All giving their level best performance every time they walked out their doors. "You can do this Nancy, you have to." Sadie said.

Sadie knew that Nancy needed some words of encouragement, so she told her that things would get better. But they both had to work on it and to pray every day for grace to get through the tough times. She reminded Nancy that the tough time wouldn't last forever.

Nancy said, "I am willing to try, but Salim needs to meet me halfway."

Sadie said, "My darling, he's here. That is meeting you halfway. Do you think any husband in this wonderfully decorated hotel wants to be here?"

Salim was not in the mood to make the expected cocktail small talk, so he spent his time placing bids on items that he didn't want or need. But he was thankful that it kept him busy during the chatty cocktail hour.

Several times he noticed Nancy looking sad and lonely. He went over and stood beside her, and she seemed to brighten a little. He took her hand and led her to the auction items he was interested in, wanting to know if she liked them as well.

Just the touch of his hand was everything to her. She asked him to please never let her go. As he looked into her eyes the realness of that statement hit him. Again he saw her genuine fear of losing him. He wished that he could give her the assurance that they would make it through this, but he himself didn't know.

As Nancy had requested, he didn't let go of her hand until they were headed to their table.

Lonnie and Benny were perfect hosts, making time to speak to everyone. Some people had seen the *New York Times* story on Benny being among the new young financial geniuses. Everyone was impressed with his advancement in the financial world and even asked his advice on some global matters. Lonnie and Sadie were both so proud of their son.

As the ballroom doors opened, music filled the room as guests moved to their tables. The room was beautifully decorated. Dinner tables were covered in dark-blue silk cloths. Tall centerpieces of flowers, all shaped in large balls, were suspended on crystal vases. There were larger white flower-balls hanging from the ceiling, with crystal drops that looked like stars.

Coco arrived late and missed most of the cocktail hour. She walked into the ballroom looking like a princess in a pink Monique Lhuillier strapless petal-skirt ball gown. Her hair was piled high on top of her head, which showed off her large, oval cabochon opal and diamond earrings that fell to her shoulders. Mike had given them to her after one of their fights, when he had hit her so hard he had broken one of her ribs.

Coco spotted Senator Moyer and made a beeline over to see him. She kissed him on the lips and gave him a big full-body hug. He asked her where she was seated, and to his surprise they were at the same table. Coco was elated. She took his hand and began leading him to their table. The good senator was stopped by several important guests who needed a minute of his time, so he quickly dropped Coco's hand and turned to speak to the guests.

His aid walked over to tell Coco that the senator would be at the table soon, and it would be best for her to wait there for him. There was nothing else for Coco to do but make her way to the Hadid table alone. When she saw Salim and Nancy, she thanked them and asked if she could please be seated next to the senator.

Nancy told her that she had already taken care of that. Coco gave her a big hug. Salim greeted Coco. He thought that out of all of Nancy's friends, Coco seemed like she would do it with anyone with a net worth of over one million dollars. He really did not like Coco, and he wondered why Nancy was friends with her.

Coco noticed how sad Nancy looked, but she never asked about Paulina or if something was wrong. She just wanted to know where she and Senator Moyer were seated. Coco was single-minded. If it wasn't about her, she really didn't give a damn about you.

Winnie was the event's mistress of ceremonies and was making her way to the podium to welcome guests to the seventy-fifth annual Snowflake Ball.

Coco asked Nancy if that was a Chanel gown Winnie was wearing. She said, "Oh, I think she has worn that before."

Nancy said, "So? It's still lovely."

Coco said, "Oh yes, it is but she needs to be careful about wearing a dress more than one time when you are being photographed. Well, don't you think so? Coming from a fashion background and all, I pay attention to what people wear. I never wear a gown more than once."

Nancy thought Coco's conversation had reached an all-time low so she quickly said, "Coco, you don't marry the same man more than once, but it's okay to wear a dress more than once."

Coco just smiled and turned her attention back to the senator.

The evening proceeded as expected, with a few heartfelt speeches, announcements . Closing of the silent auction, and then the presentation of the award for outstanding work in the aid of millions of children suffering with cancer.

The conversation at the Von Kinley table was spirited and fun. Sadie was enjoying every minute of it and downing one drink after the next. She had not touched her dinner. Lonnie asked her to dance, and when she got up, he noticed how drunk she was. After about three dances, they made their way back to the table.

Over at the Hadid's table, conversation was not as spirited, but it moved along nicely. Coco danced with the senator and pressed herself as close to him as possible. After two slow dances, Senator Moyer told Coco he had to leave. It was a workday for him tomorrow.

Coco asked, "Would you like me to join you?"

The senator was surprised by her boldness. He politely declined by telling her not tonight but maybe soon. With that he gave her a good-night kiss on her cheek, and his aide led him away. Coco had been dismissed on two fronts by the good senator, and she was left standing alone on the dance floor. Coco returned to the table with little interest in anything having to do with the charity.

Nancy not knowing what had just happened smiled and said, "Well, Coco what was that all about?"

Coco, not wanting them to know that she had been turned down, turned the attention to Sadie, saying, "Look, Benny and Lonnie are helping Sadie. Do you think she is drunk again?"

Nancy turned to Coco and said, "Really Coco. No I am sure she's just tired."

Winnie had just walked over to join them when they all saw the three Von Kinley's walking out of the ballroom. The men were assisting Sadie.

Winnie said she had to leave and wished them a good night. Nancy and Salim danced one last time before leaving.

Coco made a quick exit after spotting the doctor that she had been secretly having an affair with. He was dancing with his wife. Their eyes met, and he nodded his head. Coco knew what that meant, and she made a beeline for the door. By the time the valet had brought her car up, her cell phone started buzzing. It was the doctor, who left a message that he would be over in the morning to see her. He had seen her dancing with the senator, and he wanted to speak with her about it.

He was good for ten thousand dollars, so she could not tell him no. She texted back, "Okay." She then called Anita and told her that she would not need her the next morning.

After they got home, Benny and Lonnie had a conversation about Sadie's drinking. Benny was very concerned. Lonnie said he was more concerned about her not eating. Lonnie said they would be leaving in a couple of days to enjoy the holidays in Jackson Hole and they would discuss it then. If they thought she needed treatment, they would handle it as a private family matter.

Benny was not happy with the conversation, but he knew he could not put pressure on his father. As they finished their conversation, Lonnie told him how grateful he was that Benny was there with him. He knew that since he and his brothers had moved away, Sadie had become somewhat depressed. They talked for another hour, and then they went to bed.

Benny telephoned his brothers, telling them what was happening with their mother.

Chapter 31

Senator Moyer always felt good about evenings where people were gathered in the name of a good cause. In his soul he believed in the fight for what was good and right. He loved the American spirit of providing support to anyone in need. It was his life's goal.

A hometown boy who had grown up in Virginia, he went to public schools, attended college on a scholarship, and then married the richest, sweetest girl in town. They had accepted each other and become best friends. He was the handsome showman, and she was the dutiful wife who enjoyed being behind the scenes.

She had supported him in every campaign and believed in his vision for a better tomorrow. When she was diagnosed with stage four cancer, he dropped everything and stayed by her side until she succumbed to the deadly disease. Moyer was never the same after her death. She had kept all of his secrets and was the only person he completely trusted, and now she was gone.

He was basically an honest man. He would not take a kickback or do business with anyone if he didn't think they had good intentions. He didn't need their money. But he loved the power of the political game.

Moyer's days were filled with congressional work. At night, when not out at a charitable event, he was at home in the privacy of his Virginia estate. He thought of himself as a good old Southern boy with simple needs. He completely believed that through his congressional election, he was living his life's purpose and making this country a better place for people everywhere.

The only drawback was meeting women like Coco Runni. She made such a fool of herself every time she saw him. Last night was no different. She had pressed her body so close to him he could feel her nipples.

He had no idea what it would take to get her to stop coming on to him. She just kept coming no matter how many times he let her know that nothing, absolutely nothing, would ever happen between the two of them.

Chapter 32

It was late when Nancy and Salim returned home. They were both tired and weary. They showered and went to bed. Nancy reached over to Salim to kiss him good-night, hoping that maybe he would be in the mood for some good-night sex, but that was the last thing on his mind. He gave her a peck on the cheek, turned over, and went to sleep. He wouldn't even hold her.

Looking up at the darkened ceiling, thinking about everything that had happened between them. Their fights, the trouble with Paulina, the adoption, she knew their troubles were deeper than her lie. And she was deathly afraid of facing it. Her lie, their lie, was only the lighter fluid. Their problems had been building up to this four-alarm fire for some time now.

In the still silence of the night, she asked herself again why she hadn't told Paulina. She had always wanted to, but she never thought the time was right. Why hadn't she agreed to travel with him when he'd asked her? And why had she allowed so much time to go by before she addressed their problems?

It was always something, their schedules, the feeling of being abandoned in their marriage, and Salim's loss of interest in their sex life. She worried that he might be having an affair.

She wondered if Salim would agree to a marriage-counseling session and what would happen if he did go with her. Would his version of their truth hurt too much to hear?

He rose early the next morning and left the house without even saying a word to her. Nancy knew the time had come for professional marriage advice. She dressed and went down to her office. After thirty minutes of debating in her head all of the pros and cons of opening herself to the rawness of a counseling session, she picked up the telephone, and willed herself to press the buttons. She started shaking. She could not do it, she just could not tell anyone the ugly truth that her marriage was not perfect. That she could be facing another failed marriage and that it might kill her. That not having Salim's love was worse than death.

The phone rang. It startled her. She was in no mood for idle chatting today, so she let her housekeeper answer. The intercom buzzed. It was Salim on the line, and he was in a mood. He started in on her, yelling that Paulina had taken off to Aspen, and wanting to know if she had any idea where their daughter was staying and with whom. She could not take any more of this. She could no longer be the dumping station for his frustration with their life.

She reminded him of their last conversation with Paulina the night before and then informed him that she had no idea where Paulina was staying.

Salim yelled, "Do you know anything about our family, or do we have to be a fucking charity before you notice us, Nancy? I am really coming to the end of my rope with this marriage. Can you please make time to be my wife, and Paulina's mother? Can you Nancy? Well, can you?"

He had said it, the end of his rope. As she heard the words her heart lost a beat. She could not find the breath to answer him.

He said, "Are you there? Did you hear me?"

She said, "Yes, I heard you, Salim...I am hurting too." She waited for him to say something else but he just hung up on her. When she heard the dial tone, she replaced the telephone receiver. Her legs went weak, she started sweating, and the room suddenly felt too small. She sat down on the yellow leather chair behind her desk. Her mind was racing. He had said it: he was coming to the end of his rope with their marriage. There it was, plain as day...the words she never wanted to hear, dangling in the air like a spider web.

As tears ran down her face, she picked up the telephone and placed the call to the office of Dr. Grace Redman, the marriage counselor that Winnie had recommended.

The receptionist answered, saying, "Dr. Redman's office. How can I help you?"

Nancy opened her mouth but nothing came out. She quickly hung up the telephone. She was feeling warm and claustrophobic. She needed air and something cold to drink.

Nancy steadied herself and walked out to the garden. She needed a minute to find her center and regain her calm. She was only outside for ten minutes when her gardener walked up to her and asked if she had gone over his list of recommendations for this year's holiday decorations. With Thanksgiving being just around the corner, he wanted to get everything up soon. She told him no, but she would get right on it.

Nancy walked back into the house. She asked her housekeeper to please bring a cup of chamomile tea to her office.

Once back at her desk, she picked up the phone again. This time, with calm hands, she dialed the number to Dr. Redman's office. The receptionist answered, "Dr. Redman's office. How can I help you?"

Nancy spoke in a whispered tone, saying, "I have been…oh, well…I need to be, oh…oh…I was referred by a friend, and well…I want…I really need a meeting with the doctor." Nancy had never sounded so shaky or uncertain in her life.

The receptionist asked her how soon. Nancy thought about her call from Salim and said, "As soon as possible. Please."

After the receptionist looked over Dr. Redman's calendar, she told Nancy that the doctor would be leaving for the holiday soon and would not be able to see her until the first week of December. Nancy had no choice but to accept the next appointment date. The receptionist instructed her to go online and print out the new patient forms, and bring them with her when she came for her appointment, along with her insurance information. Nancy said she would, and then she thanked her and hung up.

Now the real work had begun. She now had to get Salim to agree to go with her. She clicked on their calendars and noticed that Salim was in town that entire week and most of December. Maybe she could make this work after all. She picked up her cell phone and sent a text to Paulina, asking her to please call home.

Suddenly Nancy felt like she was moving in the right direction for her family and her life. She knew that she didn't have one without the other.

Nancy picked up the list of holiday decorations that her gardener had prepared and went over his suggestions. She noticed that he wanted to add a few additional white lights here and there. The overall results would make the house one of the most beautiful on their block. She agreed with his suggestions and dialed him on the intercom. She told him to move ahead with the holiday decorations, and she thanked him for everything he did for her family.

She needed to make plans for the holidays. This year would be difficult, so she had to add some fun to it. She thought back to the last vacation they had taken when they'd all had a great time. She remembered their time in Hawaii, thinking that maybe this year they could have Christmas on the island of Maui. In Hawaii, they would not have to act or pretend to be perfect. They could just relax and take in the sun and the ocean.

She telephoned Paulina again, and again the call went to voice mail. She wondered where she was staying and when she would be returning to the city. A mother never stops worrying about her child, no matter what is going on in her world.

Chapter 33

Coco's telephone rang at seven thirty in the morning. It was her doctor friend, calling to say he was on his way. When he arrived, she poured him a cup of coffee, and he asked her questions about how friendly she had seemed the night before with the senator. Her dancing so close with the senator had made him very jealous.

He said, "So that's what you like, Coco? You like members of Congress, do you?" She told him that had nothing to do with it. She and the senator were just friends. She needed to get him off the subject of Senator Moyer. To distract him, Coco removed her robe to show her nurse's uniform. She went over to him and took his balls in her hand. She squeezed hard on his very small member. To her surprise he quickly became erect. He moaned and started pulling her hair. He was ready for their game of "doctor and nurse."

He said, "I am ready to teach you what happens to nasty nurses, Coco."

Coco knew all too well that the only thing he had the skills to teach her was how to count to ten thousand dollars.

She sweetly said, "Okay, Doctor, show me."

He followed her downstairs to the guest bedroom that she had prepared for her new friends with benefits. She had the room decorated with blackout drapes and plenty of sex toys.

As soon as she closed the windows, he went into action. He was a real freak and loved to feel in control of sex. The poor guy had a couple of problems in the sex department. First off, he was just no good at it. His other problem was that he just didn't have the right size of equipment to satisfy a woman. Coco was amazed at just how small the doctor's manhood was. Though he was over six feet tall, and wore a size thirteen shoe, his scrotum was the size of two small, hairy, lychee fruits, and his penis was the size of a gherkin pickle and that was when it was at its happiest and ready for action.

Sometimes when he visited her, she felt like she was taking part in some bizarre science experiment. Watch the giant size man with the teeny-weeny manly stuff. She did however always find herself somewhat intrigued as to how he could receive any satisfaction with parts that small, but he seemed to respond like a normal man with the universal, "I am coming! Oh, oh, damn, I am coming!"

She was thankful for that announcement. It was the only way she knew when to make her proper response, "Oh yes, you dirty doctor. Fill me up!"

He always liked to tie her up, and then starting with her breasts, he would pretend to give her an exam saying, "Let me have a look at these perky breasts." Then he would take them one at a time into his hungry mouth, biting down until she begged him to stop.

It only took about thirty minutes until he was finished, after which he cleaned up and thanked her for a wonderful morning visit. He got dressed and met her back in the kitchen, where he placed an envelope with ten thousand dollars cash on her counter.

Before he left, he did something that he'd never done before. He showed her just how much he did not like her with the senator. When she walked him to the door, he turned grabbed her by the neck. Pushed her against the wall, looked into her eyes and said, "If you want to keep getting that little envelope, I had better never catch you acting like a whore in public again. Do you understand me?"

She could barely breathe. She nodded her head, and then he released his hold on her. She didn't say a word. He kissed her and said good-bye, adding that he would call her in a couple of weeks.

Coco could not make out what was going on with him. How could he be jealous when he was married? She needed the money, so she would have to get something on him to keep him in-line.

She cleaned up, dressed and went to the bank. Depositing four thousand dollars in her checking account and two thousand in her money market account. The rest she would use to pay this month's bills.

Her arrangement with Saul and the freaky doctor kept her comfortable, but she knew it could not last forever. She needed a husband and fast. Coco thought of Saul which was happening more frequently these days. Out of everyone she had known, Saul was the best lover she had ever had. Their bodies just fit perfectly. The problem with Saul...well, for one he did really look like a tuna fish, and he never wanted to spend time with her unless it was with sex.

With the holidays coming up, Saul would do his normal, send her a lovely gift, and after he spent the long weekend with his family in New York. He would call her, and they would get together and enjoy an evening of great conversation, delicious food and the world's best sex. Saul never tried to hurt her and make her feel bad. There was something about him that was gentle even when he was being bad.

Nancy called Coco to ask her if she had time to meet up for a quick lunch at LaFerme on Brookville Road. They served a great country paté with walnut bread.

Coco could hear how sad Nancy sounded, she said, "Yes, of course." Coco rushed home changed her cloths and head back out to meet her friend.

Chapter 34

Paulina arrived in Aspen, Colorado, with her friend, party girl Tiffany Barnhill. Tiffany was the daughter of the latest hot Internet company founder. When their IPO went public, within hours their net worth was in the billions.

Tiffany was the only person Paulina had confided in about being adopted and all of her family's problems. They had been sharing an apartment at 2801 New Mexico Avenue. It was a two-bedroom duplex apartment that Tiffany's father rented out. The lease had become available, so they moved in.

When Paulina moved out Salim met with Tiffany's father, had a written agreement drawn up, in case things didn't work out. Which Salim was almost sure they wouldn't. These kinds of arrangements usually didn't last long. He also agreed to pay for half of all the monthly expenses to have Paulina stay with Tiffany. He didn't like Paulina being on her own but it was close to her school and to their house on "S" Street. What Salim didn't know was that Tiffany was a real party girl, with an increasing coke habit.

When Paulina wasn't studying or joining Tiffany on the party circuit, her thoughts were consumed with wanting to know more about Paula Madden and where she was now. Salim's first wife's name was Candy. She had been an OB-GYN and had been killed on Route 270 as she was going to Shady Grove Hospital to deliver a baby. Candy was speeding and talking on her cell phone when an eighteen-wheeler stopped short, and her car went under the truck, decapitating her. Salim was completely devastated. Candy and Salim's union never had a chance to produce children. She died too soon.

Salim married Nancy two years later. The adoption papers were signed by Nancy six months after Paulina was born.

For Paulina, the discovery had rocked her world and left her unable to trust or believe anything that Salim or Nancy had to say. She now had no idea who she really was. She felt betrayed by everyone. She somehow was most disappointed in Nancy because of her constant stand on family values. You would think that letting your adopted daughter know who her real mother was would be a major family value. Or better yet, how about telling your daughter, "Oh, by the way I am not your birth mother?" She could not understand why it was so hard to be honest with someone you said you loved. Now she didn't believe they had ever truly loved her. She didn't feel like she belonged to anyone, and nowhere felt like home anymore.

When she confronted Salim and Nancy, they did major backpedaling. Nancy said, "I always wanted to tell you, and I made a promise that one day when you were old enough to understand, I would sit you down with your father and explain everything. You have always been my daughter."

That was such bullshit. Paulina had just walked out of the house. Since that night, she had not found a way to have a calm conversation with either of them. She was just so angry with them. Nancy kept begging her to come with them to see a therapist. Really, why did she need to go to see a therapist? She was not the one who had lied. She didn't need therapy—they did!

Everything seemed foreign to her now. She wanted to find her real mother. She needed to know something about her. Did she have morning sickness when she was carrying her? Did Paulina have her eyes? She needed to know everything. Paulina had an exotic beauty, with olive skin, large dark eyes, long thick hair, and a wide mouth with full lips. She looked very much like her father. Now she had to know what her real mother looked like. These constant questions just kept going around and around in her head.

The only person she had to talk to was Tiffany. She listened to Paulina and seemed to understand her heartbreak. Growing up without brothers or sisters had always been lonely for Paulina. She'd met Tiffany her senior year of high school, and they had become close friends almost like sisters.

Tiffany was also exposing Paulina to a wild life filled with parties, booze, drugs, and guys. The constant partying seemed to block out her pain. If she was high or drunk, she couldn't feel the loss of her family. Tiffany seemed to have an unlimited allowance, so she was taking care of the expenses for this trip. American Express had called Salim, and he had told them not to approve the purchase for her round trip airline ticket.

They would be staying at Tiffany's family's mountain lodge at the Ritz Carlton Highlands. The condo slept eight. Tiffany had invited about twelve girls to stay with her, so the accommodations would be tight. The lodge was located near town, giving them great access to the bars. Tiffany had invitations to every party that weekend. She would be showing Paulina the ropes, as she had become her official party ambassador.

Tiffany believed in free love and everything that brought to the table, or the bed or really anyplace. Sometimes Paulina thought it was too much. But she needed Tiffany now and didn't want to offend her, so she went along with it.

Paulina was truly excited about the trip to Aspen. She loved to ski and had been doing so since she was a very young child. Salim had brought her there every winter, and they would stay for two weeks, skiing every day from early morning until the mountain closed.

She missed her family. When things were good, they had always enjoyed fabulous vacations. Nancy made sure of it. She wondered if she could ever learn to trust them again. Maybe Salim was not her father. How could he go along with the lie for so long?

Admittedly, she had been taken care of all of her life. It was time for her to grow up and learn how to be less dependent on Nancy and Salim.

Every day was proving to be an adventure some good and some bad. She was learning about the world and people, and some things she didn't want to learn. Out of all of this there was one sure thing. If she ever had a child, she would never give it away or keep the truth about its father from her baby.

They arrived at the beautiful lodge. It was large elegant and equipped with every amenity, fully staffed, and the lodge provided a heated outdoor pool. Paulina loved the floor-to-ceiling windows that gave wonderful views of the snowy mountains. Just steps away from the lodge there was a private lift to take skiers to the top of the mountain. Paulina couldn't wait to get in her ski clothes and head out.

Tiffany assigned everyone to their rooms. Paulina and Tiffany would share the master bedroom and would not be sharing with anyone else. As soon as they were unpacked, they changed into their skiing outfits. Tiffany had Chanel skis and a black-and-white Chanel ski suit. Paulina was happy using the skis that she had been given by Salim a couple of years ago.

Being in the cold, windy air was like a mind cleanser for Paulina. She hadn't realized just how much she'd missed it, until she was in the lift chair heading to the top of the mountain. Coming down a hill at top speed was a rush that both her spirit and her mind needed. They skied for a couple of hours, and then they went back to the lodge for a quick swim. After that they showered and changed for a night of partying.

Tiffany scored invitations for everyone to a party at Casa Tua Aspen, a great Italian restaurant. They would be attending the birthday celebration of one of Tiffany's childhood friends Brad Hillson. A handsome young man who was famous because his family was the first to invent the motel. Today it's believed that nearly every American has stayed in one of the Hillson Motel's at one time in their lives. Like most families, the Hillson's had their problems. The difference was that they were willing to share their dysfunction on television once a week. Brad was starring in the family's reality show.

The paparazzi were waiting outside of the restaurant ten deep, in hopes of a glimpse of Brad or any member of his famous family.

Inside the restaurant, they were taken to a private room where a buffet and three bars were set up. No one was eating, but everyone had a drink in their hand. Brad gave Tiffany a big kiss and hug, pressing his full body against her. When they finally let go, she introduced Paulina as her best friend. Brad said, "Any friend of Tiff's is a friend of mine."

Everyone in the room appeared to know Tiffany, and the attention seemed to bring out the wild party girl in her. Paulina had an idea she wouldn't be seeing Tiffany a lot on this trip. It was only a couple of minutes before Paulina had gotten the attention of a ski instructor, Darien. He promised her private lessons if she danced with him. Tiffany had left her side to go with Brad.

When the DJ put on "Empire State of Mind," by Jay-Z and Alicia Keys, the ski instructor asked her to dance. Paulina was delighted. She loved dancing, and this song was one of her favorites. The vibe in the room was electric. The party had come alive. The room was filled with young, sexy people, all dressed in the latest fashions and ready to party the night away.

The DJ mixed the music perfectly. Paulina danced to Bruno Mars, Justin Timberlake, and Rihanna. They danced for about an hour, before they both needed something to drink and headed for the bar.

Paulina ordered a lemon drop martini, and Darien went for vodka on the rocks. They sipped their drinks and looked out at the crowded dance floor. The music was so loud that Paulina could not hear what Darien was saying to her, so she pointed to her drink and he nodded in agreement. She wasn't sure if he was still thirsty or if the drink was not mixed properly, but he left Paulina and went back to the bar.

Paulina looked around for Tiffany. She saw her on the dance floor with Brad. They waved to her. The ski instructor moved on to another girl, and Paulina was pulled onto the dance floor by a young man named Scott. He was Brad's brother. He was a great dancer but very touchy-feely, and she had no plans to sleep with anyone on this trip. After they danced to Pitbull's song "Time Of My Life", featuring Ne-Yo. Scott took her hand and led her to the bar for something to drink. He told her the bartender had made a special drink in honor of Brad, and he wanted her to try it. He said it was light and she would not get drunk. So she tried it. Scott was right; it didn't make her drunk. She got so wasted that she could barely feel her feet. As the liquid cruised through her bloodstream, her head started spinning. Scott was only too available to assist her. She told him she needed to use the ladies' room. She saw some of the girls that were staying at the lodge. She told them what happened and asked them to get her out of there.

Kimberly agreed, and as they made it through the crowd and back through the main restaurant, Paulina steadied herself while leaning on Kimberly. Once outside, they tried to catch a cab. Paulina's legs felt weak, and she fell to the ground just as a tall, handsome man was coming out of the restaurant.

He helped her up and said, "That must be some party. Do you think you need some medical attention?"

Kimberly said, "No, we just need help getting a cab back to the lodge."

The gentleman said, "It may be a long wait. There are not many cab's in sight at this hour." He offered to have his driver take them home.

Kimberly looked around again for any sight of a cab. When she saw nothing, she said yes. She reasoned that since it was two of them, he would not try anything. Plus he didn't look like a rapist. He did, however, look like a prince in his blue cashmere sport coat and matching overcoat. His demeanor gave off a calm reserve that matched his movements. Kimberly knew class, and this man was covered in it, head to toe.

His car and driver pulled up fast, and he took over getting Paulina in. Once he'd settled her in the back seat, he noticed how beautiful the sick young lady was. She was rail-thin with dark features. He studied this exotic beauty. She was well-groomed and beautiful enough to be a fashion model. Her large, almond-shaped eyes were very sad, and she seemed to be afraid of something.

Her friend, on the other hand, was a confident redhead with piercing eyes that appeared ready to protect and defend at any minute.

Kimberly very suspiciously asked, "Do you live around here?"

He smiled and answered, "Not all of the time. Do you? That is, live around here?"

Kimberly liked everything about his cool demeanor. He even smelled good—rich and manly. She noticed that his eyes never left Paulina.

He asked Kimberly again, "Are you sure we don't need to take your friend to the hospital? It wouldn't be any trouble."

Kimberly looked at Paulina, who had her head against the back seat. She wasn't sure, but she said, "No, I think we will be okay. But thank you anyway."

Within minutes they were at the Ritz Carlton lodge. As soon as Paulina got out of the car, she started vomiting, and just inches from the handsome gentleman's custom-made Gucci loafers.

He jumped out of the way and said, "Thank goodness for fast reflexes."

Kimberly apologized for Paulina, saying "Oh, I am so sorry...she must've eaten something that didn't settle with her stomach."

He looked very worried and again asked, "Are you sure she doesn't need to go to the urgent care center? I am willing to take her there. Really, I think she needs to be seen by a doctor."

Kimberly told him that Paulina would be fine. She just needed to get her upstairs to their room.

The doorman helped Paulina the rest of the way. Kimberly noticed that the doorman seemed to know this mystery gentleman. Kimberly almost wished she had more time she would have been able to ask more questions. She definitely wanted to know more about him.

He asked the doorman to please make sure they made it upstairs to their room. Then told him he was not sure, but Paulina may be in need of some medical attention. After they were through the door, Kimberly turned to get another look at him, but he had gotten back into his car and was driving away. Kimberly was sad she hadn't even gotten his name to say thank you.

As his car drove away, he thought about just how crazy his evening had turned out. He had represented his client in the completion of a successful business deal, and his girlfriend of three years had broken up with him on the evening he was going to propose to her. Maybe love was just not in the cards for him.

And now he had helped two damsels in distress get home safely. There was something about the sick one that made him want to know more about her. Maybe it was the Boy Scout in him, or maybe it was just the way his father had raised him and his brothers. He didn't want to see a female in need and not help her. On his way out the next morning, he would check on the sick young lady.

He would be leaving in a couple of days. He had a few more meetings to attend before his departure. Now his prized Aspen would be the place where he'd gotten dumped, and helped a beautiful sick young lady.

Chapter 35

Back in their suite, Kimberly helped Paulina into a cold shower. Their kitchen was stocked with stuff for sandwiches, lots of fruit, cheeses, and freshly baked cookies. Paulina was so grateful to Kimberly for helping her. She apologized for taking her away from the party. Kimberly said it was okay. Her health was more important.

Paulina could still feel the effects of the sudden illness, and after her shower, all she could manage was a cold ginger ale before falling into a deep sleep.

The next morning, she did not remember a thing that had happened. Tiffany walked in the apartment around eight o'clock in the morning, looking like hell. She went right to their room and crawled into bed. It was three o'clock in the afternoon before she woke up.

After some lunch Tiffany was looking better. She got dressed and was ready to go again. She said she'd had a great time and was sorry Paulina had to leave early. Kimberly filled her in on what had happened to Paulina. But Tiffany seemed disinterested in the details. She just said, "Oh well, she is fine now."

Kimberly said, "Well, now, on that note, I guess I will head out to the gym for a quick workout." There were times when Kimberly thought that Tiffany treated all of them like disposable friends. If they didn't fit into Tiffany's plans, she didn't want to be bothered with them. One thing was clear: Tiffany's family's newfound wealth was not bringing out the best in Tiffany, and Kimberly was becoming afraid for her and Paulina.

Paulina was taken aback when Tiffany never asked her how she was feeling. She just took it all in stride. Paulina told her she thought Scott had put something in her drink.

Tiffany said, "Scott is Brad's baby brother. He would never do anything like that. I think you must have eaten something that did not agree with your stomach." It was clear that Tiffany didn't want to hear any more about it, so the subject was closed.

As Kimberly was heading back up to the apartment after her workout, the concierge gave her a note. The stationery had the initials TVK on it. There was no telephone number or e-mail address. The note read:

> Dear Barnhill guests,
> I hope you are feeling better today. Please be careful
> and enjoy the rest of your stay.
> TVK

Kimberly asked the concierge who the gentleman was. He said he was not at liberty to say, but he could tell her that he was an important young man from a very prominent family. They owned the largest home on Red Mountain, the estate was located on Hunter's Creek.

The girls dressed and went back to the slopes. Paulina was very quiet. She skied alone, only joining them for a late-afternoon snack. Tiffany asked her what was wrong, and Paulina said, "Nothing. She just had a lot on her mind."

Darien, the ski instructor, said hello and asked her if she wanted a quick lesson. She didn't but she would have done anything to get away from Tiffany at that moment. They had a few more days together. She hoped it would get better, but right now she felt somewhat discarded by her friend. She had not come to Aspen to get date-raped, and that's what was on Scott's mind and she knew it. She just wanted to have fun, ski, and take in these marvelous, breathtaking mountain views.

Tiffany was really into Brad, and they were making out every second they were together. Tiffany told the girls not to expect her back at the lodge. She was spending the rest of the day at Brad's place. She jokingly told the girl's she would be giving him the rest of his birthday gift today and laughed.

Paulina, Kimberly, and the rest of the girls told her to be safe. Then they left to take in the slopes. That night they all went out to another party. And Paulina made a mental note to only drink water.

Paulina met another guy who said he worked on Capitol Hill for a newly elected congressman from Colorado. He invited her to join him at a small fundraiser the next night hosted by the congressman's re-election team at a restaurant called Steakhouse No. 316, which was rumored to be one of the best restaurants in all of Aspen. Paulina agreed to attend if Kimberly and the other girls could come with her.

They met Congressman Alfred Flank and a host of his supporters. He looked too young to be a member of Congress. Two things were for sure, he knew how to work a room and his supporters had a great deal of confidence in his ability to represent them in Washington. He was introduced by Governor Tackett, who said that the congressman was engaged to marry his eldest daughter Belinda.

Kimberly asked Paulina, "What do you think about the congressman? He looks young. Where is that cute guy that invited us here? Do you like him?"

Paulina looked around and then said, "Oh there he is over there standing next to the stage. He is okay, but I am not looking for a relationship right now."

Kimberly agreed, "Me too. Just want to have some fun. What do you think about the Governor's daughter? She has not smiled during the congressman's entire speech."

Paulina knew how much Kimberly took in all of the details of events like this and she was a whiz at reading people. So Paulina gave the congressman and the Tackett family another quick look. Kimberly was right Belinda Tackett only smiled when her father spoke, and there was a strange vibe between her and the congressman. Paulina thought, "Oh well its none of my business, good luck to them."

Kimberly said she had overheard some people talking about the Flank/ Tackett upcoming marriage and rumor had it the union was all about money and power. When all of the speech's ended Kimberly turned to Paulina and said, "Hey you want something else from the buffet, there are some pulled pork sandwiches that are really good."

Paulina smiled and said, "Pulled pork here we come." The girls laughed and headed over to the buffet table.

While the congressman was mingling and thanking his supporters, he noticed Paulina and Kimberly.

Congressman Flank appeared to take an immediate interest in Paulina, wanting to know everything about her.

"Good evening, I am Congressman Alfred Flank and you are?"

Paulina cleared her throat and said, "I am Paulina Hadid and this is Kimberly Moore, we are visiting and received an invitation to attend your party. I am sorry but we don't live in your beautiful state."

Congressman Flank smiled and said, "It's Colorado's lost. Thank you for joining us tonight." Belinda walked up behind him and told him that they needed him to take pictures. He said, "Yes dear." And he quickly followed her to where he was needed. Congressman Flank continued to mingle with his supporters, however he never allowed his gaze to stray far from Paulina. His attention was making Paulina feel out of place.

After a few minutes she remembered that she and Kimberly had made plans to meet Tiffany at another party, so she found her host. Thanked him for a wonderful evening and told him they had been invited to another event. Keeping the conversation short, she simply said her apologizes and headed to the door.

Paulina and Kimberly hailed a cab and headed over to join Tiffany at the Caribou Club on East Hopkins Avenue. The party was being sponsored by a local glossy magazine that celebrated the art of living well. Each month it featured a celebrity who owned a home in this winter wonderland. The club was decorated in blue, white, and gray, with lots of little lights. It looked like a scene out of *Doctor Zhivago*. The club was filled with important local's and major celebrities who were winter birds too Aspen. Everyone was enjoying the people-watching.

Kimberly ran up to Paulina and said, "Hey, that's the guy who gave us the ride home. Look, over there, standing by Kate Hudson." Paulina did not remember anything about the evening so she looked in the direction that Kimberly was pointing. She saw a handsome, well dressed young man speaking with media powerhouse Jason Binn.

Kimberly said, "Let's go over and say thank you." But before they could make it through the crowd he was heading out the door.

Paulina said, "Sorry, Kimberly, you lost your chance."

Kimberly said, "Damn, he is gorgeous. Brad Pitt meets Prince William kind of gorgeous. You really need to meet this guy."

Paulina smiled and said, "No, *you* really need to meet him. I am good for right now."

The DJ was mixing the music just right. The party was turning out to be the best, and the girls were having a great time.

They went to the bar, got themselves a drink, and looked around for Tiffany who was with another guy. They asked her about Brad, and she said he left something about his sister's husband getting arrested on Hollywood Boulevard and it being on *E! News*. His mother thought it was best for him and Scott to come home to show family support.

Tiffany, never one to let any grass grow under her feet, just moved on to another guy. They had a fun evening with great food and drinks.

Later that night, Tiffany confided in Paulina that Brad was using coke, and it made him a little too violent for her. She was happy he had left. She really liked Brad and wanted him to get himself together. After another day on the slopes and more parties, it was time to return home.

On their last day, Tiffany arranged spa treatments for all of the girls followed by a special lunch prepared by the Ritz Carlton chef. They all thanked Tiffany for a wonderful day and a great winter vacation.

Paulina was not happy to be returning home. Next week was Thanksgiving and the start of the holiday season. She had nowhere during the holiday's to go but back to Salim and Nancy. Tiffany had not invited her to spend time with her family. They would be heading back to Aspen.

Paulina had no idea what Nancy had planned for the holiday's. She just knew she wanted no part of it. She listened to her voice mail messages. She had several from both Salim and Nancy. She wanted to call them back, that was the worst part because she loved them both so much.

Chapter 36

This year with no holiday plans, Coco was thinking of where she might go. It all seemed very depressing with no family of her own and only her friends families to share the holidays with. The last couple of years, Winnie had hosted and paid for Coco to be her guest at the Greenbrier resort in White Sulphur Springs, West Virginia. But Winnie had not extended an invitation to her this year.

She loved going to the Greenbrier with Winnie and her family, but Coco could not afford the expense on her own this year. Well, she could afford it, but she felt like Winnie could better afford it. Coco couldn't bring herself to just come out and ask Winnie to foot the bill, although she had suggested it several times, each time Winnie had changed the subject. Her friend Sarah Talbott had announced that her entire family would be spending the holiday at their new vacation home in St. Barts, and she would not be returning to Maryland until after the New Year. Sarah's husband had surprised her with the house as an anniversary gift. Sarah didn't invite Coco to join her family, either.

Sadie had not invited Coco to the Von Kinley compound in Jackson Hole or their home in Aspen in a couple of years. Nancy said her family was heading to Hawaii. Coco thought, "*This is crazy. I have all of these friends with lovely homes, and no one is inviting me to join them.*" So she would have to join her sister Barbara and her family, something she was not looking forward to. She liked her sister, but damn talk about uptight, proper acting show off's. Well maybe she would just stay home and enjoy her own company.

Saul's office called to invite Coco to join him at a basketball game. She had accepted the invitation and was looking forward to a night out watching the home team. During the game Coco would gently mention that she had no plans for the upcoming holiday and see if Saul would take the hint.

During halftime Coco ran into Salim and being her flirty self, she paid him way too much attention. Saul noticed the exchange while he was getting them something to eat, and he didn't like it one bit. Coco asked Salim about Paulina and told him to give her love to Nancy. Salim was a little chilly to Coco; it was clear that he didn't like her much. Everyone could see it but Coco.

When Saul walked over to the two of them, Salim seemed very friendly to Saul. Salim said, "Well I need to get back to my seat, you two enjoy the rest of the game." When he walked away Saul gave Coco a hard stare.

Coco said, "How do you know Salim Hadid."

Saul responded, "My dear how do you know him."

"I am friends with his wife we are in the same club, and we just had lunch together the other day. He didn't seem friendly to me tonight, I wonder what is the problem with him, do you think he knows we are together", said Coco.

Saul said, "What ...what did you just say?"

Saul, took a good hard look at Coco and for first time since they had met and started their relationship, Saul was ready to send Coco home and never see her again. He could not believe what she had just said. Saul looked Coco in the eyes and said, "So tell me Coco do you expect all men to be overly friendly to you? Is that the game you play?"

Saul didn't like Coco's attention to Salim. Coco was not ready for what Saul asked her next. He said, "Coco, are you attracted to Salim, do you want him?"

Coco did not say another word the rest of the game. When they got into his car, Saul said, "Coco, there are some real truths you must learn. When you are with a man, he needs to be the most important man in the room for you, not some other man."

Coco said, "Well, man I am with for the record. I have never fucked Salim! And right now I don't know if I will ever fuck *you* again. But hear this, I have had enough complicated relationships, and I am not looking for another one."

Saul knew he had hit a nerve. He thought that Coco needed to grow up, sometimes she acted too childish.

Sitting there beside him, Coco was thinking of something that she could do to make Saul pay for being rude to her. She would start with silence, and then his real punishment would come. When he wanted her to come up to his apartment she simply said, "No." So much for her plan to get Saul to invite her for the holidays, she didn't want to be in the same car with him much less spend Thanksgiving with him.

Coco said a quick "Good night Saul. I hope you enjoy the holiday's."

Saul knew he had hurt her feelings but she had also hurt his and he needed some space away from Coco.

Saul was busy the next few days, he had lots of things to do before he left town to be with his family over the holiday weekend. But he was thinking of Coco constantly he telephoned her several times, but she would not return any of his calls.

Coco was very lonely and she thought about Saul and what he had said to her. She thought, "Well so much for a happy holidays, and ho, ho, ho, to me."

Chapter 37

Winnie was finalizing her plans for the upcoming holiday season when she received a call from Sadie. "Hello, my friend. What are you doing?"

Winnie smiled and said, "I am elbow deep in holiday plans. How about you?"

Sadie laughed and said, "I have been at it all day. Every hour another family member is inviting themselves to Jackson Hole. There will not be a square inch of the place that doesn't have a Von Kinley or O'Hara sleeping in it."

Winnie said, "Sounds like heaven to me."

Sadie looked over her plans and said, "It is, Winnie. You know, I just love it."

They talked for about an hour, going over everything that was happening in their lives. Sadie asked Winnie if she was hosting Coco again this year. When Winnie said, "No, not this year." Sadie felt sorry for Coco but quickly responded, "I would love to invite her to Jackson Hole, but as I said, there is no room at the Von Kinley Inn." Just then Sadie's intercom buzzed. Her florist was waiting for her in the library. She needed to go over plans for their annual holiday open house and how she wanted the house and lawn decorated this year.

Sadie said, "Oh Winnie, I am so sorry. My holiday elves have arrived, let's talk again soon."

Winnie laughed and said, "Well, Mother Claus, don't keep the elves waiting."

They both laughed out loud and promised to meet for lunch after the holiday's.

Taking another look at her family guests list, Sadie was thankful their Jackson Hole house, had ten bedrooms, eleven bathrooms, and two large, two-bedroom guesthouses on the property.

They would be celebrating Sadie's brother's birthday and Lonnie's sister and brother-in-law's wedding anniversary during the holiday vacation. Sadie's niece announced that she was pregnant, so they would be celebrating that too. The truth was they would celebrate anything as long as they were all together. Every minute was filled with games and something fun to do and the highlight was the family talent show.

Sadie didn't drink as much when she was around family. She especially delighted in having her sons home. It was wonderful to have them near even if it was for just a couple of weeks.

Nancy, Salim, and Paulina confirmed their plans for Hawaii. They would be staying in a large timeshare at the Ritz Carlton Kapalua. To take the pressure off Nancy suggested to Paulina to bring along a friend. The idea made Paulina relax, she invited Kimberly to join them. Kimberly was very respectful, and could get along with anyone, having her there seemed to ease some of the tension. They all tried to just relax and enjoy themselves.

Nancy and Salim made love twice during the vacation. It was loving and sweet.

Chapter 38

Three months later, Sadie invited Coco, Nancy, and Winnie to join her and a few friends for an afternoon tea, to meet with a representative of the Wounded Military Spouses association. The charity had asked the Von Kinley's to support them with a small fundraiser. Sadie was using this opportunity as the first committee meeting.

Winnie declined, work commitments had her too busy at the moment. She was well versed at what these teas were all about, so she sent Sadie a check with a note that said she was honored to support the cause.

What Winnie could not support was two or three hours out of her day, sitting around and planning yet another event. She loved the girls, but she needed more in her life. These were the moments when Winnie was thankful to have a full-time job.

Sadie hosted the meeting in her sunroom, which overlooked the formal English-style garden, with perfectly landscaped lush green border boxwoods, a parterre, topiaries in whimsical shapes of teddy bears and elephants, and direct views of the Potomac River. The embassy-sized dining room was set with her best collection of finely crafted Buccellati silver and her most delicate Royal Copenhagen Flora Danica china. Her flower selections and the linens were all beautifully displayed.

Her chef had prepared a delicious assortment of finger sandwiches watercress, cucumber, curried chicken salad, and Virginia honey-baked ham with freshly baked cheddar cheese biscuits, and open-faced smoked salmon topped with caviar, delicate scones with Devonshire cream, yummy chocolate dipped strawberries, and petit fours decorated with the charity's initials in royal icing on top. This was a formal high tea, so Sadie had enlisted the help of a proper tea pourer to assist the ladies.

Sadie's flawless execution of this special gathering had Coco simmering with green-eyed jealousy. But what was sending her over the edge was how pretty Sadie looked and how gracious and gentle she was. It was impossible for Coco to understand how anyone could have such a calm, tranquil presence. Sadie was beautiful, inside and outside. She had a kind word for every guest who entered, and with her southern charm she made everyone feel at home. She had a way of making everyone feel like they were her best friend.

Coco could not stand the fact that Sadie lived so grandly, while she had to make her living on her back, her side, and sometimes standing on her head. Coco loved and hated Sadie, at the same time. She was grateful that Sadie had looked out for her after Mike's death. However, since that time she had done nothing to help Coco find a husband. Sadie and Lonnie had lots of contacts and knew several recently divorced or widowed men, but they never tried to help her.

To be fair, they had set her up on a blind date one time with one of Lonnie's golf buddies from Palm Beach, named Homer, but the date went nowhere. She had asked the guy a couple of questions about his houses, his job, his investments, and his retirement plan, and by the end of the date, he told her he didn't think it would work out between them. He reported back to Lonnie that he thought Coco was a gold digger.

Sadie seemed only too happy to deliver that bit of news back to the girls. She had called Coco early the next morning, saying, "Coco, what did you do to Homer? He told Lonnie you are a gold digger. Coco, how could you act like that in front of our friend? Lonnie is very disappointed in you—and so am I."

Coco tried to defend herself, but Sadie had already made up her mind, and from that day on, Sadie never again tried to fix her up. Coco again thought how unfair her circumstances were. She was prettier than all of these women, and everybody knew it. Why didn't she have the husband and the majestic home where she could host an over-the-top tea party?

Sadie had assembled the most sought-after members of Washington's philanthropic community. The ladies were all fashionably dressed and proudly wore their symbols of capitalism like badges of honor.

Except for Sadie, Coco had nothing in common with these ladies, and they let her know it. She wondered why Sadie had even invited her to this meeting. Did she want her to feel bad about herself? She had to know that Coco was not in a position to make large donations right now. And like a fool, Coco had accepted the invitation. She was regretting every second of that decision now.

For Coco, the sheer splendor of this glorious afternoon was all too much for her. She felt like Sadie was just showing off her wealth. Turning suddenly Coco let one of Sadie's precious teacups slip out of her hand, watching as the fifteen-hundred-dollar cup and saucer hit the marble floor and shattered into a million pieces. The room filled with chatty ladies fell silent. Everyone was looking directly at Coco and wondering what in the world had made her do such a thing.

One of the ladies, the wife of a four-star general, said, "Oh my word, is she sick?" And another lady, the wife of the founder and chairman of a large department store chain, said, "Sick is not good enough when you drop a piece of Flora Danica. I don't want her coming to my meetings."

Knowing that all eyes were now glued on her, Coco put on her most sincere acting job, saying how very sorry she was and that she would replace the cup and saucer right away.

Sadie was very calm on the outside, but inside she was wondering what in the world was wrong with Coco. She'd only invited her in hopes that Coco would find a new friend to latch onto, and maybe someone would have a single male friend to introduce Coco to. Sadie thought, *"Now this bitch is destroying priceless china."*

Sadie was not going to let this act of foolishness get more attention than it needed to. She said, "Coco, are you okay? Please be careful. No need to worry about replacing it. I just want to make sure you're okay." Sadie's staff quickly cleaned up the spill.

As the afternoon progressed, Coco started interjecting ideas about this or that trying to take over and upstage Sadie. Nancy could see that this was not going well. She didn't understand what Coco was trying to prove. Nancy was certain of one thing, this would not turn out well. Coco was making a complete fool of herself.

The final decision was about where the event would be held. It would have to be either West End Bistro or Cafe Milano's. Both locations were perfect for a wine dinner, but in the end they selected the West End Bistro. It would be a small, intimate affair with special pairings throughout the meal. They discussed the event's décor, and it was decided that the restaurant's current dining furniture would be taken out and replaced with rented tables and chairs, allowing the right number of guests at each table. Sadie wanted everyone attending to feel special.

It was decided that the dinner would take place in the middle of May, which was very short notice, and everyone agreed to work overtime to get everything taken care of and get the invitations out. Subcommittees were formed, and everyone was in agreement. Then Coco said the event should take place sooner.

One of ladies looked at her and said, "Coco, right? That is your name Coco? Well, if you had seen the social calendar, you would know that every week is already filled."

Nancy sat there, just looking at Coco and wondering, "*What in hell's name is this all about?*" She could hear the ladies whispering about Coco, and it was not good. Nancy didn't understand how Coco thought asking all of these crazy questions was going to make her look good. If Coco thought she could show up Sadie Von Kinley with this plan, news flash—it was not working. Nancy had seen Coco do some crazy things, but this was by far the craziest Nancy had seen.

When Sadie stood up and cleared her throat, Nancy knew what was coming next. She was powerless to help Coco, so she just dropped her head. Suddenly Nancy remembered the rap lyrics to one of Paulina's favorite groups, the Tag Team: "Whoomp! There it is." She thought, "Whoomp! Here it comes."

Sadie very calmly turned to Coco and said, "Well, Ms. Runni, you have been the star of today's meeting with all of your helpful suggestions. I am so glad you found the time in your schedule to join us, but suggestions are only as good as their outcome, so can we put you down on our list of event sponsors, seeing as you are so passionate about our cause?"

Coco's narcissism had taken control of her. She did not even see Sadie's move coming. Suddenly, center stage did not feel so good. She gave Sadie a hard stare and then said, "Well, I will let you know."

Again, every eye in the room was on Coco, and it was the wrong time to pull back. One of the ladies whispered, "I thought as much."

Sadie was letting everyone know that Coco was full of hot air and completely out of her league. Now Coco would have to make a donation. Nancy could feel the tension between them, and she couldn't wait for this meeting to come to an end.

Sadie invited everyone to stay and have more tea. Nancy was through with this afternoon she' d had enough. She gave Sadie a check for five thousand dollars, thanked her for the invitation, and then said her good-byes. She was one of the first guests to leave.

Coco followed her out the door. When they were outside and out of hearing range, Nancy asked, "Coco, so what were you doing in there?"

Coco said, "Well, I just wanted to give them some ideas. Now Sadie has put a price on my head."

Nancy said, "Really, Coco? Really? Get over yourself. You put that price on your *own* head when you kept opening your mouth. Coco, you were very rude to Sadie, and she has been nothing but good to you. Messing with Sadie Von Kinley is social suicide, and you just drew blood. Be careful, Coco, now all the ladies in that room are talking about you—and not in a good way."

When the valet brought Nancy's car around, she turned, gave Coco an air kiss, and thanked and tipped the valet driver. Then she pulled off, leaving Coco standing there alone.

Coco's car was brought next. She didn't tip or thank the valet attendant; she just rudely pulled off, almost running over the poor man's foot. On the ride home, she got a call from Saul. He wanted to see her that evening. She said yes, and he told her to be at his house no later than seven o'clock.

Chapter 39

Nancy didn't have the energy to deal with Sadie and Coco. When it came to her girlfriends she liked to keep things simple, and this mess was anything but simple. Coco was being a real bitch to Sadie, and it was wrong.

But today was not the day for Nancy to get involved. She had to keep her mind on getting to her counseling session. She'd worked hard and finally Salim had agreed to attend today's session, and they were addressing their issues. She now had a better perspective as to why people resisted coming to counseling. It was one thing to know your life was a mess, but to have it aired before a complete stranger was just gut-wrenching.

For today's session, Paulina would also be joining them, and Nancy was hopeful that everything would work out. After Christmas break she had gotten Paulina to sit down with her, and they had a talk about the adoption and why they'd used a surrogate. She told Paulina how much she'd wanted a child, and she gave Paulina the diary she had written in every day during those times. She asked Paulina to read it. Maybe then Paulina would come to understand Nancy's feelings, and how desperately Paulina was wanted. Nancy even told Paulina that she had hired a private detective to help locate her natural mother.

For Nancy it was all about making Paulina happy. Even if that meant they never talked again. As long as Paulina was happy, safe, and loved, then Nancy would learn to live without her.

There was still so much pain and hurt but Nancy was grateful the conversation had begun.

Winnie had asked Coco a number of times to only call her at the television station if there was an emergency. But Coco frequently disregarded her request and would call anyway.

Today Winnie was in the middle of research on an upcoming story. She thought it was rude of Coco to call her about something they could discuss later, away from her office.

As soon as Winnie said hello, Coco started in, telling her about the meeting at Sadie's and how she had only tried to be helpful. She didn't know why Sadie had asked her for a donation in front of everyone.

Winnie knew Sadie would never do that to anyone, so she just listened to Coco for a minute or two, and then she told her she needed to go back to work. Winnie was trying to be a good, patient friend, but the truth was that for some time she had been growing weary of Coco's games and social climbing.

Winnie said, "Coco, I am in the middle of something right now. Let's talk later, okay?"

Coco said, "Well, this is very important. I have been humiliated. This is serious! Winnie, what should I do?"

Winnie was getting tired of this call in a strong voice she said, "Coco, don't you have more to do with your time than go to those teas and meetings? You know what they are all about. They want donations for the community. I just sent a check with a note and called it a day."

Coco couldn't stand it when Winnie made everything sound so simple. She took a deep breath and said, "Yes, I have other things to do, but I wanted to support Sadie, so I went. Now look what happened! I was just trying to be a good friend."

Winnie said, "Sadie would never do anything to humiliate you or anyone else. Just calm down. But really Coco, I have to get back to work. Let's talk later."

With that Winnie ended the call. Now Coco was pissed off with both Winnie and Sadie. They just didn't seem to understand her anymore.

Winnie just could not understand Coco or what she was doing with her life, spending her days with "ladies who lunch" and her evenings with who knows who. Winnie had seen Coco out with Saul Baumann. Saul was a confirmed bachelor and was rumored to only keep the company of high-priced call girls. While he was not an attractive man, there were many positive things about him. For starters, he was well educated, was a old school gentleman, very wealthy, well traveled, and part of a very established New York family.

After Winnie saw Coco out with Saul, she'd asked around about him and found out that he'd really gotten hurt in his divorce. The rumor mill had it that one day when Saul came home, his wife had told him she wanted a divorce because he was the most boring man she had ever known. He later found out she had fallen in love with some young guy, and she was stealing money from Saul to pay for her lover's drug habit. Winnie's source also told her that Saul had promised to never fall in love or marry again.

She worried that if Coco was keeping time with Saul, it only meant one thing. Winnie thought, *"When would Coco learn to stop paying for her life with her body? There would come a time, very soon, when it would not be enough. But Coco was doing nothing to prepare for that day."* Well, nothing that Winnie, Sadie, or Nancy could see anyway.

Chapter 40

When the last guest left, Sadie went immediately to the library, locked the door, and poured herself a gin and tonic over crushed ice. She needed to be alone with her thoughts, and she needed something to calm her nerves.

Wrapping her long, thin fingers around the heavy crystal glass, she downed the first drink and quickly followed it with another. Finally, she could feel the warm, relaxing liquid cruising through her bloodstream, its calming powers quickly cascading through her body, giving her a feeling of sedation. The liquid anesthetic helped her steady herself.

She was wounded by Coco's behavior. It was pure jealousy, plain and simple. But that knowledge didn't take away the painful feeling of being hurt by a friend. Sadie could not understand what she had done to make Coco behave so poorly.

After the meeting, several guests asked Sadie about Coco, and why Sadie had invited her. So not only was she personally insulted by Coco's actions, she was now being placed in a position to defend Coco at the same time.

Right then, Sadie felt that Coco was no more than a guttersnipe, and she had always treated her like a true friend. She'd supported Coco, only wanting the best for her. She had even paid some of her bills, and this was the thanks Coco was showing her after all Sadie and Lonnie had done. Just as she was about to place a call to Nancy to discuss Coco's outrageous behavior, her telephone rang. It was Larry. At twenty-five years of age, he was still her baby boy.

"Hello, my darling boy! What's going on," Sadie asked, trying to keep her voice even. She didn't want to sound like she had been drinking; she desperately didn't want anyone to know.

Larry could tell right away, but he didn't want to say anything that might hurt her feelings, so he just said, "Hi Mom. How was your day?" He felt so stupid for saying that. He knew how her day was. It was only five o'clock, and his mother was two to three drinks into a bender. And he was helpless to stop her, so he just tried to focus on the positive.

Sadie quickly changed the subject. She didn't want to remember how her day had gone. And she for sure was not going to tell her family what a fool she had been to think Coco was her friend.

Larry was calling to check up on her and to tell her how excited he, Benny, and Tim were about the upcoming trip to the fishing lodge in Manitoba, Canada. He said, "I even like the name of the lodge, the Silver Bowl. You know what else I like Mother? Going to Wimbledon with you. How about we plan to go together this year? An afternoon, center court, with Federer, Williams, and your favorite son." He didn't want his mother to feel left out of all the fun with his brothers, and he knew she loved tennis.

Sadie smiled and said, "That will be wonderful. I will make plans for the entire family to come along."

When they started comparing schedules, they discovered that their all-boys trip would be the same weekend as the wine dinner for the military spouses. They hadn't been fishing in such a long time. This would be a great outing for them.

Sadie said, "Oh sweetie, it will all work out. Your father will be home soon, and you know he will handle it."

Larry said, "We don't want to do anything to take away from your event, Mother. If you need us to, we can reschedule."

Sadie's protective side came out. "I don't want you worrying about this. Trust me, it will all work out. You guys look forward to fishing with your dad. It makes him so happy, and I love it. Maybe one day I will come along."

Larry started laughing, "Mother, you fishing? Now that will be the day! Well okay Mom, I have to run now. Please take care. I love you." Larry knew for sure his mother would fix it; she always did. If only he could fix what was wrong with her.

Sadie was suddenly very sad. She said, "I love you too." She wanted to tell him how much she missed him, but she didn't want to put that pressure on him. As she hung up the phone, she started to feel like she was failing her family. Why had she agreed to chair the dinner? But it was too late for her to back out without the Von Kinley's looking bad.

She didn't want her boys worrying about anything. Lonnie would handle it; he always did. To her, Lonnie could do anything and everything.

Sadie walked over to the bar. She stopped for a moment, looking at the beautiful crystal decanters. She knew, she needed to just walk away. But as the sunlight reflected off the glistening crystal, it was like prisms carrying flashbacks through her mind of everything that had happened. She was trying to find the willpower she needed to put the glass down and walk away. As demons in her brain took over, she became powerless and helpless, standing there frozen and afraid to take another step.

She quickly thought of Lonnie, her sons, the pressure she felt, the disappointment, the loneliness. And then pictures of Coco flashed in front of her. She remembered how many friends she had lost to jealousy. If they knew how hard she had to work to keep her life looking so fabulous, they wouldn't be envious, they would be tired, as tired as she was at that moment. The pressure and the secrets were too much for her.

There were things that only she and Lonnie knew about, things that she had never shared with anyone and never would. That's the problem with secrets. They kill you from the inside out. With shaky hands she poured herself another gin and tonic. This time it was mostly gin.

As she took a sip, she said, "Problems, problems, my life is filled with problems. God help me, I am not strong enough to handle all of this on my own."

Emmie buzzed Sadie on the intercom. She needed Sadie to go over some details for a couple of upcoming events that the Von Kinley's would be hosting, sign some checks, and approve a list of presents that Sadie was sending out to family members for upcoming birthdays.

Sadie answered very pleasantly, saying, "Hello, Emmie. I will be right over. I was just finishing up on a call from my son Larry."

She needed to try sounding and walking straight, and after three strong cocktails, that was not an easy task, but it was one she had become used to.

After meeting with Emmie, Sadie made her way upstairs to her dressing room. She needed to freshen up before Lonnie got home. She didn't want him to know she'd been drinking. He never understood the pressure she was under, and she was certain he never would. After she showered, changed her clothes, and applied fresh make-up, she went down to the kitchen.

Thanking her staff for the wonderful job they had done for the tea party, she smiled and said, "It was just perfect. It's because of you that this house runs so well. I am grateful for all you do for us."

As she handed Felix a stack of envelopes one for each staff member, inside was a nice bonus check. She wanted them to know how much she appreciated everything that they did in managing her home. Felix could tell that she had been drinking again. He was worried about her; the drinking was really getting out of hand. Several times lately when the Mr. Von Kinley was away on travel, Felix and Hattie had to carry Sadie to her room.

After going over a few details with Felix, Sadie checked on dinner. She was looking forward to a quiet evening at home. She told Felix that after dinner was prepared, he could take the rest of the night off.

She wanted it to be just her, Lonnie, and her bottle of gin. It was the only threesome she enjoyed.

Chapter 41

Lonnie had been in meetings all day. He was looking forward to relaxing for the rest of the evening. On the drive home, he stopped off at a local flower shop. He wanted to pick up a small bouquet to take home. It was something he did often when he was in town. He knew Sadie would love it.

He also knew that no matter how long he'd been married, to keep their love strong, a man needed to let his wife know that he still loved, appreciated, and desired her. It always surprised him how much the small things made Sadie happy. A simple note or a spray of flowers made her as happy as a twenty carat diamond ring.

When Lonnie walked into the flower shop, the ladies behind the counter stopped and stared. Lonnie was still dashingly handsome, standing over six feet tall, with bright eyes and a friendly smile, a commanding voice, and gentle manners. Even at his current age of sixty, women still took notice.

Lonnie said, "Good evening, ladies. Would you be so kind as to help me with a small bouquet of flowers?"

The shopkeeper quickly answered and said, "Yes, Sir. What would you like?"

Lonnie knew what flowers Sadie liked and was grateful the shop had them in stock, so he quickly pointed out her favorites and then asked to have them wrapped with a pretty bow. When they were finished, the bouquet looked great. The shopkeeper at the desk said, "Well, somebody is pretty lucky to have you bringing these flowers."

Lonnie smiled and said, "No, I am the lucky one." He pulled out two one-hundred-dollar bills and told them to keep the change. He turned and headed out the door thinking of his beloved Sadie.

When Lonnie got home, he could tell that something was wrong, and he could smell the faint scent of liquor on Sadie's breath. He didn't like it when she had been drinking during the day. He presented her with the bouquet, and gave her a big hug.

Sadie said, "Oh Lonnie, thank you so much. They are beautiful, and all my favorites."

"You're welcome, my love. Is everything okay ?" He knew what she would say. She always wanted to hide her stress from him. Sadie was not the best actress. When he pushed her for details it always made her withdraw from him, he didn't want that tonight.

Sadie said, "Oh yes. Why do you ask, sweetie?"

She didn't want to tell him about what had happened with Coco. She was determined not to let Coco into her evening after she had tried to destroy her afternoon.

So she told him about the conflict with the boys' fishing trip and her military spouse's dinner. Lonnie told her he would have the boys meet him at the lodge. He would leave first thing in the morning the next day and be there before Saturday afternoon.

Lonnie, "Let's see if we can get them on the phone now."

Sadie, "That would be great. Do you think we can find all three of them?"

Lonnie smiled and said, "Let's give it a try."

They walked into the sitting room off their master bedroom, and Sadie took a seat in the silk-covered tub chair, while Lonnie placed the conference call. And as he promised, he got all three of their sons on the phone. He told them of his plan to fly out early Saturday morning and be there no later than noon. Sadie's dinner was on Friday evening, so all would be well. They continued to make jokes about the biggest catch and then wished each other a great night.

Lonnie walked over to Sadie, wrapping his arms around her. He said, "Okay, now that that's taken care of, what are we having for dinner? I am starving."

Sadie smiled and said, "All of your favorites." She loved being in his arms. She felt safe, wanted, and needed there.

Lonnie whispered in her ear, "I am holding my favorite, but what are we eating for dinner?"

They both started to laugh as they walked downstairs into the small dining room off the kitchen area. It was where they had enjoyed so many family dinners together.

They talked nonstop about family and local events, never seeming to run out of things to say to each other. The conversation was free flowing and safe they never discussed what mattered the most to them as a couple, no words felt right so they continued to ignore the obvious.

As Felix prepared to bring in their dinner, he looked at the bottle of Château Lafite-Rothschild 1983. It was Mr. Von Kinley's favorite. But Felix didn't know if it was proper for him to serve it this evening when,

Mrs. Von Kinley had already had a few drinks. Then he quickly remembered his position. It wasn't his job to live their lives for them; it was only his job to make sure they enjoyed every minute of living.

Lonnie loved meatloaf with mashed potatoes, green peas, and a glass of red wine. He said, "Rothschild and meatloaf, it's my favorite meal."

Sadie had given their chef, Lonnie's mother's recipe for meatloaf. It was perfect, and it brought back fond memories.

Sadie said, "Thank you, Felix. Now I want you and the staff to have the rest of the evening off. We will be just fine. Thank you for everything."

Lonnie polished off his first plate and went into the kitchen to serve himself seconds. Sadie enjoyed her entire dinner and even ate a slice of cornbread with butter and honey, sweet southern-style cornbread was a must-have at the Von Kinley's table.

For dessert, they both enjoyed a large slice of Hattie's famous dark-and-white-chocolate mousse layer cake with Bing cherry sauce.

Lonnie couldn't have been happier, until Sadie asked him to pour her a glass of wine. If he said no they would have a fight; if he said yes he was adding to her problem. In the end, he did what he had done so many times before: he poured her a glass of wine.

Chapter 42

Saul and Coco had dinner at Marcel's, a fine French restaurant near Georgetown. Saul enjoyed a superiorly prepared meal with great wine. After dinner they headed to the Kennedy Center, tonight was the opening performance of *West Side Story*.

When they arrived, several members of the show's production team were waiting for them. The group only wanted to speak with Saul, but he would not allow them to be rude to Coco. He said, "Excuse me, please allow me to introduce this beautiful lady with me, this is Ms. Coco Runni, she is very special to me, so do introduce yourselves."

They quickly made their introductions and then walked Saul and Coco to their box seats. Saul always made every effort to make Coco feel special when they were together Throughout the evening, he complimented her on how beautiful she looked and how sweet she smelled, and he told her he was honored to be her date. She was always touched by how attentive, gentle, and gallant he was with her. She felt relaxed, proud, and protected when they were together.

Saul held Coco's hand the entire evening. During the intermission, they went to the Circle's Lounge where they were greeted by the lovely Jovita, a tall elegant woman that took special care of the Center's major donors. Jovita greeted Saul warmly saying, "Well good evening Mr. Baumann, how are you, thank you for all you do for the Center, and who is the lovely lady with you tonight."

Saul smiled and said, "This special lady is Coco Runni. Coco, this is Jovita, she is the best reason to come into the lounge." They all laughed and wished each other a good evening. Saul had arranged to have a glass of Coco's favorite champagne waiting for her. Several patrons came over to speak with Saul. Again he introduced Coco as his lady. It was only when they were leaving that Coco understood why so many people were thanking Saul. He had underwritten the entire production. He'd also donated two million dollars to the Center. Coco felt stupid for not making the connection earlier.

On the ride home Saul asked, "Coco, did you enjoy the performance? I never asked you if you liked *West Side Story*."

Coco said, "Saul, this has been a perfect evening."

Saul proudly said, "Well, thank you, my love. I thought that I had taken you to enough sports events for a while."

He pulled Coco closer. He loved to feel the warmth of her body and smell her sweet powdery fragrance of Acqua di Parma. Coco gently laid her head on his shoulder and closed her eyes for the quick drive.

Saul said, "Coco, something is troubling you. I can feel when you are not yourself. Tell me what's wrong."

Coco said, "Oh, it's nothing really. I just had a fight with my friend Sadie."

Saul quickly asked, "You mean Sadie Von Kinley? She is such a kind, gentle woman. What in the world could you two fight about?" Saul gently turned Coco's face so he could look into her eyes, and then he said, "I am all ears. Tell me what happened. What's on your mind?"

Coco told Saul about the event and what had happened at the tea, as well as how she felt Sadie had made her feel bad about not having everything that she had, and especially for not having the money to make donations. Saul knew that there was more to the story than Coco felt ready to tell him.

Saul had seen this emotion in Coco before. It made him want to protect her and to make some of her problems go away. But having three sisters of his own, he was aware of how delicate the female balance could be.

Saul listened and then said, "This sounds bad. What would it take to make it better?"

Coco said, "Yes, Saul it was. I was treated very poorly."

Saul said, "The most important thing to remember is that you and Sadie have been friends for a long time, and good friends are hard to come by."

Coco and Saul were silent the rest of the way to his place.

When they arrived at his apartment, he went to his desk, wrote out a check for five thousand-dollars, and asked her to please make a donation to the charity. Coco was thankful. It meant a great deal to her that he wanted to help her.

Coco said, "Thank you, but I didn't tell you this for you to give me a donation."

Saul thoughtfully said, "My darling, I never want you to be unhappy, and it's for a great cause. I am here to support you, no matter what."

Coco was touched no one had ever said that to her. They made very passionate love until the early hours of the morning. Saul still sent Coco home with his normal gift. She needed the money, but she was growing increasingly dismayed at accepting his cash gifts. She really enjoyed going out with him and she no longer wanted him to think of her as just a paid companion. But the subject of money and his little gifts had never been discussed, she didn't know how to start the conversation.

One thing was certain, her relationship with Saul was now the only thing that kept her mind off her problems with Sadie. Coco was feeling bad and plenty guilty for hurting her friend.

Coco remembered something that her mother once said, "When you set out to hurt someone make sure you don't get hurt yourself." Right now Coco was feeling the hurt and pain of her actions and it was not a good feeling.

Chapter 43

Morning came too soon for Sadie. She was suffering from a nasty hangover and only able to speak softly to tell Lonnie that she would not be joining him for breakfast.

Lonnie was very disappointed. He said, "Another bad morning darling? You are going to have to go easy on the sauce. Rest well. I will tell Hattie to bring you a tray."

Sadie didn't need a lecture this morning. She needed a good cup of coffee and some quiet. She raised her hand to blow him a kiss and then covered her head with the silk duvet. He was right. This was her third bad hangover this month. She never meant to drink too much, but it just happened. When she opened her eyes, the room started spinning, and she had to run to make it to the bathroom in time. She was sick as a dog.

Lonnie quickly made his way down to their state-of-the-art home gym, where he worked out every morning for one hour with his personal trainer.

After his workout, normally he and Sadie would have breakfast together, but like so many mornings lately, Lonnie was alone.

Felix brought him the phone. It was Benny. He wanted to know if it would be okay if he brought someone special home with him over the Memorial Day weekend. Lonnie told him it would be fine, but he needed to prep Sadie. He told him that she would not be ready for an engagement surprise, if that was what was going to happen. Benny said he didn't know, but that the guest was very special to him. And he was sure his mother would fall in love with her just as he had.

Lonnie said, "Well, my son, you are all grown up, so now is a good time to start the next phase of your life. I think we have a lot to talk about on our upcoming fishing trip."

They both laughed and said, "Yes," and that they were both looking forward to it.

Benny asked, "Dad, how is Mom doing?"

Lonnie answered quickly, "She is fine, Son. Your mother is just fine." Benny knew that she was not doing fine and that his father didn't want to speak about it. It bothered Benny so much when his dad shut him down when he tried to talk about Sadie's drinking problem.

Lonnie changed the subject saying, "Just so you boys know, your old dad is clearing off a space in the study for my huge catch. I will be catching the biggest fish."

Benny laughed and said, "Yeah Dad, dream on. That will be all me."

Lonnie and Benny had to get back to their busy schedules, but it had been a great early-morning call.

Hattie brought Sadie a tray of black coffee, dry toast, and a chilled flute filled with a Cristal and orange juice. Sadie didn't move until Hattie left the room. She was always humiliated when she had a hangover, and she didn't like to be around anyone. As soon as she was sure Hattie was gone. She got up, went to the tray, and drank the coffee. Then she called Emmie and told her she was not feeling well and that she could have the day off. She called Hattie, thanked her for the tray, and told her that she would not be needing anything else for the day.

Sadie didn't leave her room until later in the afternoon.

Chapter 44

Winnie was working on a follow-up story about the latest scandal in Washington, D.C., involving homeowners losing their property due to unpaid property taxes. After the last real estate boom raised property tax assessments which put many homeowners in a position of losing their homes because they were unable to pay the skyrocketing property taxes. Many residents had been in their homes for over twenty years. Now their tax bills had risen so high that homeowners were left owing amounts ranging from a couple of hundred dollars up to tens of thousands.

One elderly couple she featured in her report had lived in their home for over forty years. The wife was sickly and on disability, and the husband was a cab driver. They had very limited income and had used up all of their savings for the wife's medical bills.

As Winnie told their story and those of other homeowners all facing possible loss, her heart went out to them. Through the power of journalism Winnie gave a voice to the voiceless, her story touched many viewer's hearts. The switchboard was filled with calls from viewers wanting to know how they could help the couple.

Winnie had been affected by the circumstances of the homeowners since she began investigating this story. And the couple had touched Winnie's heart so much that she secretly paid off their delinquent tax bill, allowing them to keep their home.

After she wrapped the show, Winnie went to her office, returned calls, and reviewed some research notes for her next story. Which involved the need for additional shelters for woman and children who were victims of domestic violence.

She checked with her producer one last time before she left the station. Then she headed to Cafe Milano's. She was meeting the winner of the auction for lunch with her at a recent charity event.

When she arrived she found the lucky donor to be none other than Phillip Lay. She was disappointed but also curious she could not understand what Mr. Lay wanted with her. She hid her disappointment with a warm smile, determined not to let this meal take too much time. After she was greeted by the charming and very handsome staff at Milano's, she made herself comfortable at the table.

Winnie smiled that award-winning grin and then said, "Hello Phillip. Wow, you are the donor. Well, I don't know what to say. Thank you, I guess."

Phillip said, "Well, let me help you. It's true that I will do anything to have a few minutes of your time."

Winnie said, "Well, I hope you are not disappointed." As she looked around the dining room, she noticed seated at each table was either an ambassador or a head of industry, which was the normal Cafe Milano crowd. Winnie said, "Phillip, I'm sure you know many more interesting people, so I can't image why you would want to spend lunch with me. I only report the news these powerful people seated in this room make the news."

The waiter approached their table offering them a delicious glass of Nuschese Pinot Grigio from the southern region of Italy, he knew it was one of Winnie's favorite wines. After they placed their order, Phillip responded, he said that he had seen her coverage on the overtaxed citizens and was grateful that she had delivered the story with such compassion. He wanted to do something to help the special couple.

Winnie told him she was pleased that the story had touched so many people, and several companies had stepped in to donate home repairs or drop off groceries as a result of the coverage. Everyday citizens were expressing their concern with all kinds of acts of kindness. They discussed the volatile character of the real estate market.

Phillip said, "Winnie, I am concerned about the couple's long-term housing problems."

She told him that the couple's taxes had been taken care of. She didn't tell him she was the fairy godmother paying their tax bill.

He was grateful that a kindhearted person had taken care of this calendar year's property taxes. He then looked deep into Winnie's eye and said, "How very kind and generous of this anonymous person."

His eyes were piercing her heart. There was something very special about being in Phillip Lay's presence.

He then asked her, "How will they be able to pay their taxes next year and stay in their home?"

Winnie had thought about that herself, but was at a loss as to what to do. She quietly looked away from Phillip as she thought about the question and the lovely old couple.

Phillip sensed her tension and he didn't want her to feel bad, so he told her he had instructed his attorney to set up an escrow account in which he'd already deposited enough money to pay the taxes on the property every year for the next twenty years, or until the homeowners passed away.

Winnie was so taken aback by what Phillip had just told her that she didn't know what to say, so she just said, "Thank you, but why would you do such a thing? Why have you gotten that involved?"

His answer was as simple as the problem itself. Phillip looked at Winnie and said, "Because I can, and because it's the right thing to do."

There was a moment of silence at the table. Then Phillip said, "Winnie, they will never know that I am the donor. I want nothing from them. I have more money than I can spend in several life times, and I want nothing in return."

She sat there thinking that maybe she had misread Phillip's intentions. Maybe he only wanted to help, she was not sure. She only knew he had done a great thing for people he had never met. Whatever he was after, she gave him credit for using his vast assets to help someone else.

What she had misread was just how delightfully funny and quick-witted Phillip was. She hadn't laughed so much in years. All of her tension and prejudice of him were slipping away.

He seemed like an extremely elegant man with a big heart. He'd come from a wealthy family, but had made his own money and had experienced some of the same things she had. As their conversation continued, it became clear that the similarities that Phillip and Winnie shared were greater than their differences.

They were both true Washingtonians. Both loved the home teams. They knew all the stats about the players and the owners. They knew who had the best chili dog in town, Ben's Chili Bowl on U Street. They both loved the arts, especially the opera and the ballet. They both loved to entertain and to garden. They were both collectors of Impressionist paintings.

Phillip said, "Winnie, every time I look at Monet's *Woman with a Parasol*, it feels familiar to me, like something I witnessed in another life."

Winnie completely understood that powerful connection to art. She shared with him her love for Alfred Sisley's *La Seine au Point du Jour* and Degas's paintings of dancers.

She said, "Art fuels our souls. I have loved it all my life and have been lucky enough to own a few pieces."

He smiled and said, "Forgive me for what I am about to say, but Winnie, no art in your home could possibly be more beautiful than its owner."

Winnie smiled. "Oh, Phillip you are charming."

As they discovered more about one another, Phillip was surprised to learn that Winnie loved nothing better than spending her Sunday's in her small greenhouse. She absolutely treasured her time gardening and had a deep love of horticulture.

She said, "There are always fresh flowers in my house. I have been very successful with orchid plants. It's all a matter of the soil and the light."

He took her hand and playfully examined her nails.

With a mock scowl, he said, "You wear gloves…these are not the hands of a true gardener."

She returned the favor and said, "Well, that fresh manicure does not suggest that you have been pulling weeds, dear sir."

They both laughed out loud.

She thanked him again for the lovely arrangement he had sent to her home with an invitation to join him and Donna for dinner. Despite her first reservations and against her best efforts, Winnie thoroughly enjoyed their lunch. After three hours of eating, drinking and laughing, their lunch came to an end.

Phillip thanked her for giving him the time and opportunity to help out someone he may never know. He then thanked the staff and left a very large tip for the waiters.

When they walked out of the restaurant, his car and driver were waiting. Phillip told her how much he had enjoyed getting to know her, and he wished her a great evening. Within seconds he was gone.

Winnie walked across the street to the parking lot, retrieved her car, and headed home. On her drive she thought about their lunch conversation. She laughed to herself thinking, "*What a delightful man.*"

Chapter 45

Paulina was not looking forward to today's counseling session. She'd been thinking about nothing else all day. She wondered if this therapy session would reveal something that she hadn't heard. She had already heard how sorry they were for lying, over and over again.

As far as Paulina was concerned, there was nothing that could be said to remove the hurt and pain of their lie. Because of their lie she had the constant feeling of not belonging to anyone, not knowing if the woman walking down the street in front of her, or the woman at the cafe, or at Starbucks was her real mother. Did her mother still live in Washington, or had she moved? Was she married? Was she happy? Did Paulina have sisters and brothers that she knew nothing about? She hoped that the therapy sessions would bring answers for all of her questions, insecurities, and her confusion about who she was.

Nancy had tried to explain, and Paulina understood her problems with conceiving a child. But how could she possibly try to rationalize not telling her that they had used a surrogate and that she was not her natural mother?

Paulina pulled up in front of the medical office building in the Spring Valley section of town, off Massachusetts Avenue. She had spent the night before partying with Tiffany. There were dark circles under her eyes. She had a headache and was terribly hungry. She parked and was heading toward the building's entrance when Nancy pulled up. Nancy yelled out the car window for Paulina to please wait, she wanted them to walk in together. Nancy parked her car and almost ran to Paulina, giving her a hug and thanking her for coming.

It was hard for Paulina to make small talk with Nancy after everything that had gone down. Although part of her mind was telling her to forgive and move on. After all, this was still the woman who had taken care of her all her life.

Deep down, Paulina knew that Nancy had been good to her. Nancy was the only mother she knew. Paulina was crazy about Salim. He was a great father. Although he was gone a lot, he always made an effort to attend some of her school programs.

Nancy never missed one play, tennis match, or any of her school concerts. Paulina had played the horn and was terrible at it. But Nancy never seemed to mind. She would just sit there and listen for hours. She had always been there to help her with homework. Why had they lied and hurt her like this? Paulina felt tears running down her face. She turned her head so Nancy could not see her wipe them away.

After they checked in, Salim came through the door. He smiled when he saw Paulina, and this time she could not hold back her emotions. Without a second thought, she jumped up and ran into his arms.

Just then the doctor walked into the waiting room and asked them to please follow her. Salim and Paulina went in first, followed by a tearful Nancy.

The doctor asked Paulina why she was crying. What was making her so sad? Paulina said she wanted a family who loved her and didn't lie to her. She missed being close to Nancy and her father, but she could no longer trust them.

Paulina turned to Nancy and said, "Tell me why didn't you love me enough to trust that if you had told me, I would still love you? Why did you hurt me like this?" Then Paulina started screaming, "Where is my real mother? Do you know? I don't believe you when you say you don't know. I can never trust you again."

Hearing Paulina say those words made Nancy break down in tears.

Salim found it painful to see the women he loved in such emotional turmoil. He thought, *"Maybe these sessions were not the best thing for them."*

The doctor asked Paulina, "If you could find your natural mother, would you forgive Nancy and Salim?"

Paulina just looked at the kind doctor and asked, "Would you?"

The doctor said, "Paulina, this has to be about your feelings. No one here can tell you how to feel. We can only help you work through those feelings in the hope that you can find peace." Then the doctor asked Paulina how she felt about Salim. He was her natural father. Why couldn't you begin there and try to find her way back to loving Nancy? She wanted Paulina to address her pain but appreciate Nancy and Salim for everything they had done to raise her. Nancy said, "I could not have loved you more if I had given birth to you."

Paulina turned to the doctor and said, "I don't like it when Nancy leaves us to go off raising money for her precious causes." Paulina knew that Nancy hated it, when she called her Nancy and not mother, so Paulina made a point to say it several times during their session.

The doctor asked Paulina to look at Nancy and tell her how she was feeling at that very moment.

Paulina turned to Nancy, and when their eyes met, she dropped her head, stood up, and said, "I can't do this anymore. It hurts too much."

Paulina ran out of the doctor's office, taking the stairs down to the lobby.

Salim ran after her. He met her at the car and begged her not to drive when she was this upset, and to please come home with them. "Maybe we can talk without the doctor there. Paulina you must listen to me and hear me, no matter what some doctor has to say or what your friends say, I am your Father, I have always been your Father and I will always be your Father. Every family has problem, and that includes ours. In life we all make mistakes, and we all will need forgiveness at one time or the other. We never meant to hurt you please believe me," he said.

Paulina reached out to hug him and with her head on his shoulder she softly said, "I just couldn't. Please understand I need more time to make some sense out of this."

Salim begged her to please be careful, and she promised him she would.

Paulina drove to Burger King on Connecticut Avenue. It was the only fast food restaurant close by with a drive-up window. While waiting in line, she telephoned Tiffany.

Paulina said, "Hey Tiff, do you want something to eat? I'm at BK's, in line now."

Tiffany sounded rushed. In her high-pitched voice, she chirped out, "Oh Pauly, get me whatever you're having. See you when you get home." She then ended the call.

Paulina thought, "Tiff is so flighty."

Tiffany always said yes to food, but she never finished a meal. She said she was on the French woman's diet: two bites and you're finished. To Paulina it seemed Tiffany just liked the idea of food. She didn't want to really eat it, just to have it in front of her.

When Paulina got to the condo, Tiffany was saying good-bye to some guy. His pants were unzipped, and Tiffany's hair was a mess. Paulina knew what she had been doing all afternoon. Tiffany never seemed to get enough sex. Paulina had to admit she had done her own fair share of the "bump and grind," but never every day with a different guy. Paulina had begun to have doubts about whether Tiffany was the right roommate for her.

Tiffany flopped down on the couch and told her the guy had the biggest manhood she'd ever seen. It curved to the left. She said, "I don't think I'll be seeing him anymore. But on the positive side, I got my protein quota for the day."

Paulina didn't want to let Tiffany see just how disgusted she was with her. The details of Tiffany's afternoon were making Paulina sick to her stomach. She asked who the guy was, and Tiffany told her he was an international student in his junior year at George Washington University. According to Tiffany, he was from well respected South Africa family that owned a diamond mine. She had met him while they were in Aspen, and they'd hooked up today over coffee…and one thing led to another.

Tiffany said, "Enough about him. How are you feeling? How was your session with your parents?"

Before Paulina could say a word Tiffany said, "Pauly girl, do you know your father calls almost every day to check up on you, and your mother does as well…oh I mean Nancy. Well, she does the same."

Paulina said, "Yeah, I know, but why did they?"

Tiffany cut her off in midsentence, saying "Pauly, I think they really love you, girl. My parents never call me. It's as if I am not their child. I would be happy to have your parents any day of the week over mine. I know they hurt you, but you really need to stop holding a grudge against them, it's time to think about forgiving them. They are really good people. They send over food almost every day. Your dad is very protective of you. My dad doesn't even remember my birthday! And even your parents' *friends* check up on you. The other day we received a box of homemade butterscotch-pecan cookies from the pretty news lady on the television, Ms. Winnie. I think that is her name."

Tiffany looked very sad for a minute. She really did wish that she had half the love and support that Paulina had. She pushed away the heavy feelings and went back to being a party girl. She jumped up, grabbed the Burger King bag, and ran into the kitchen. She said she was going to warm the food. Paulina knew better. She would smell it and throw it away.

She came back with a large brownie. Paulina asked her where she had gotten the brownie, and Tiffany said, "Your mother sent them over early this morning. They are the best."

Paulina went into the kitchen. On the counter was a large tin box. When she opened it, she saw her favorite chocolate fudge brownies, some with nuts and some with caramel. Paulina had loved these brownies all her life, and she remembered making them with Nancy. She wanted so badly to be in the kitchen with Nancy making them again. Paulina and Nancy loved to bake. They would bake for any reason, at any hour of the day or night.

They would bake pies, cookies, brownies, and cakes when they knew someone was sick or had lost a loved one.

She smiled when she thought about them in the kitchen baking holiday cookies. They had cookie cutters for every possible occasion and a shortbread cookie recipe that was loaded with butter. No matter how bad you felt, when you bit into one of these cookies, you would feel better.

Over the years Paulina had learned to love those minutes in the kitchen with Nancy. It was there that they'd had their deepest conversations about life and people, and even about boys and sex. That is why she could not understand Nancy not telling her about the adoption. They talked about everything.

Why couldn't they have talked about what was the most important? Paulina slowly replaced the lid over the brownies. She missed her family so badly. And she really missed Nancy.

About an hour later, Tiffany came into her room and said, "We need to party. It will help you let go of your heartache, if just for tonight."

She told Paulina, "It will all work out. I promise you. Now come with me, and let's have some fun."

Paulina said, "Tiff, I really can't afford to go out every night, I have a shitload of homework to do."

Tiffany said, "You know what your problem is? You are too damn serious about everything. You need to let go and enjoy life."

They hadn't gotten home until three in the morning the night before. Paulina could just barely keep her eyes open in class. She was beginning to worry that she would not be able to keep up. Paulina was determined not to let her relationship with Tiffany derail her plans of becoming a lawyer. She wanted to fight for children like herself. She felt like family law was her purpose in life.

Tiffany's cell phone started tweeting, and she happily answered. It was her contact for tonight's party. Tiffany's cell phone was a modern day party line. If there was a party within the city limits, Tiffany was invited. She told the person on the other end that she would be there, and that her friend Paulina would be joining her.

Paulina again started to protest that she had too much homework, and she really was tired and needed her rest. But before long Tiffany had convinced her to come along. Paulina was disappointed in herself. She really didn't want to go to another party.

Tiffany went to shower and dress for tonight's round of fun. They would be meeting a group of friends in Georgetown, and who knows where after that. Tiffany put on a one-shouldered tulle Versace dress. The dress was formfitting, and sheer from the thigh down to the knee. She paired it with five inch platform Versace shoes. Tiffany's hair had a ton of extensions, and she let it fall loose and flowing. She finished her look with long lashes and heavy makeup.

Paulina could not understand why Tiffany seemed to go out of her way to look cheap. Paulina pulled on a pair of clingy Gucci pants, a Dolce and Gabbana top that Nancy had given her as a gift, and a pair of Christian Louboutin Follies spike heels. Then she looked in the mirror and wondered who this person was staring back at her. She could not believe how her life had changed. She started thinking that maybe she should finish college out of state; maybe she needed some distance from Salim and Nancy. And this constant party thing with Tiffany was getting old. It had been fun for a while, but now she just wanted someplace quiet to think.

As they walked through the lobby, the front-desk clerk gave them a questioning look and the doorman murmured, "Little ladies, please be careful."

Paulina thought, "*It's official. We look like hookers*." Tiffany was so proud of herself. Paulina could only hope that no one took their picture and sent it to Joan Rivers fashion police. She could hear Joan now, "Streetwalkers or Socialites—who can guess?" It was amazing how much money their outfits had cost and yet the end result looked so cheap. Paulina just wanted to run away and hide.

They took a cab to the K Street lounge, where they met up with some friends. Tiffany greeted everyone with air kisses. The talented bartender was mixing up a new drink called Millionaire's Punch. It was made with finely distilled Kentucky bourbon, Grand Marnier, grenadine, and egg whites.

Tiffany and Paulina were both handed drinks, but after Paulina's surprise drink in Aspen, she was now very cautious. She held the drink until she was sure no one was looking. Then she went to the bar and ordered a mixed drink of cranberry, and orange juice, with a slash of ginger ale. She told the bartender to put a cherry in the glass. That way everyone would think she was drinking a cocktail.

After about an hour at the lounge, they all headed to another party. This one was at a beautiful house on "Q" Street. Tiffany was with another guy, one she had met previously at a horse event in Middleburg, Virginia. It seemed that his parents were the owners of this lovely historic mansion.

The party atmosphere was more intimate than Paulina had expected, with well-dressed young people in every room. As Paulina wandered from one room to the other, looking for anyone who was interested in talking to her, she found a huge spread from Chipotle Mexican Grill in the kitchen. She made herself a plate and then stood alone, listening to music from Katy Perry's song "E.T.," featuring Kanye West. Everybody was coupled off but Paulina, she was feeling like a third wheel. When she finally saw Tiffany again, she told her she was not feeling well, and if Tiff was cool, she would take a cab back to the apartment.

Tiffany waved Paulina off, saying she was more than cool with the new plans. Tiffany turned her back to Paulina and headed out to the garden with her new guy. Paulina had reached her limit with Tiffany and this party. She put her plate in the kitchen sink and walked out of the house. Walking over to Wisconsin Avenue and hailed a cab and went back to the apartment.

Paulina was more than just a little pissed off at Tiffany, she was determined to have a talk with her in the morning. Right now all she wanted was a shower, and a good night's sleep.

She was awakened around three o'clock in the morning by Tiffany screaming. Paulina ran out of her room and found two of the guys from the party in the living room clearly with plans to rape Tiffany. When Paulina turned on the lights, the guys were shocked that someone else was in the apartment. Tiffany said, "Help me please! These crazy motherfuckers have to get out of here."

One of the guys said, "Oh great, it's two of you bitches, more fun for us."

Paulina said, "Not in your dreams." She could see that Tiffany was high on something, so she knew that she would have to fight this one on her own.

Picking up a vase, she threw it at the guys. It startled them, but that would not be enough to get them out of there. She saw a golf club in the corner, grabbed it, and started swinging, making contact with one guy on the shoulder while the other one ran out the front door. Both guys were down the hall in seconds. Paulina closed and locked the apartment door and turned on the alarm.

Tiffany fell to the floor. Her Versace outfit was torn, and her face was red. Paulina dropped the golf club and went over to her. She was very concerned about the drugs that Tiffany had clearly taken. She wanted to make sure her friend didn't need medical help.

Paulina was afraid for them both, and she was mad as hell at Tiffany, saying, "This shit has to stop, Tiff! Those bastards could have done anything to us! I can't take this." She continued, "If this doesn't stop. I am out of here. Tiff, and I mean it!"

Tiffany was in no condition to have this conversation.

Paulina said, "Tiff, what have you taken?"

Tiffany, in her slurred speech, said, "Pauly girl, those guys are crazy... crazy! I just took a pill to give me some energy. Nothing bad, just one pill, but it was super strong."

Paulina could not believe Tiffany. She said, "Tiff, tell me, how you are feeling? Do you need to go to the hospital? Maybe you should get your stomach pumped."

Tiffany quickly said, "No...I will be fine I have taken this before, but I think I may have taken two pills tonight, I am not sure...Those guys just know how good I am in bed and they wanted to take a quick spin...but no, no, no, not tonight."

Paulina stood up. Looking down at Tiff, she was furious with her and sad for her at the same time. Tiffany was worth so much more than this, but she didn't know it. Tiffany and Paulina were broken, and neither one of them knew how to fix the other.

Chapter 46

The next morning, Tiffany was still asleep when Paulina went off to class. She was thankful that she didn't have to run into Tiffany this early in the morning. She wasn't prepared to talk with her just yet.

When her classes were finished Paulina was still not ready to return to the apartment so it seemed like the perfect time to go shopping. After shopping for a couple of hours, she went to Toka Spa on Prospect Street, for a manicure and pedicure.

With all of her shopping and beauty treatments finished, she realized that she was famished so she headed downstairs to Cafe Milano, where she ordered two pizzas, a LaScala and a Babila, and two orders of the Insalatina—butter lettuce with candied walnuts.

While waiting at the bar, she noticed the owner he walked with a commanding sense of power. In true Italian style, he was impeccably dressed and groomed.

She observed how diners were watching him. He stopped by several tables to chat and then quickly moved on to the next. There was a table reserved in the corner of the room, and she noticed that a waiter was standing near it, when the musical genius Stevie Wonder walked in. He and the owner exchanged warm greetings before Stevie sat down. The two men seemed like old friends.

Paulina was staring so hard that the owner turned and looked directly at her. He gave her a smile and nodded his head. His eyes were kind and gentle. She had never met him before but had seen several news articles about him, his celebrity friends, and the charities he supported. He was a true power player.

When the handsome waiter bought her order, she paid, thanked him, and headed home. Paulina made a mental note to visit Cafe Milano's more often. Good things were not just on the plates.

Tiffany was still in bed when Paulina returned home. When she came out of her room, Paulina noticed that she was alone, which she thought was progress.

Tiffany said she was sorry for what had happened the night before. She didn't want Paulina to move out. They shared the delicious Milano pizzas, and for the first time, Tiffany really ate. They talked like young college girls do.

Tiffany said, "No more parties for a couple of weeks."

They laughed, and Paulina went to her room to catch up on homework.

Chapter 47

After his daily workout, which included jogging through Central Park, Benny headed back to his apartment. His exercise routine was a must. It helped him relieve the mental pressures of his demanding career advising world leaders on their countries financial future. He was now a leading expert on international monetary matters, and he loved every minute of it.

Benny had graduated with honors from Princeton University, where he'd majored in global finance. After graduating he went on to Harvard University. There he earned a double master's in international monetary disciplines. All of the major private-equity firms had heavily recruited him. After much consideration and long talks with his father, Benny accepted the lucrative offer made by JP Morgan and Chase.

Life in Manhattan was exciting. He purchased a co-op at 150 Central Park South. Wanting and needing to be his own man he never accepted any help from his parents. Which made them even more proud of him.

His job required a great deal of travel, so he was seeing the world again, not as a kid with his parents but now as a grown-up, discovering the wonders of the world. And it was a delight to his soul.

Everything was going as he had planned, except he had not found the right girl. He'd dated several charming young ladies, but none of them presented the right balance of beauty, brains, and the gift of a generous heart.

Benny had never viewed himself as handsome. He just thought he looked like most guys. He was six feet three inches tall, lean, and he had his mother's smokey eyes and his father's thick hair. It wasn't until women stared at him that he thought about his looks. Usually he thought there might be something on his face, not that he looked handsome. He believed there was just so much more to life than vanity.

While standing in line at Starbucks for his daily caffeine fix, he met a lovely young woman. She was trying to balance her cell phone and three cups of iced coffee, when she turned around and spilled every ounce down the front of Benny. His suit was fresh from the dry cleaner, and he was rushing to a meeting. She burst into tears and then laugher. As she started to help him wipe the icy brew from his pants, her bracelet got stuck in his zipper. They both started to laugh, and that's when Benny noticed how breathtakingly beautiful she was. She had an all-American beauty, with silky blonde hair, large blue eyes, and a smile that could light up a room.

She continued to apologize, and then asked him if he could just get her bracelet free from his pants zipper without getting them both arrested. She laughed and said, "I am sure there must be some kind of New York ordinance against public groping."

Benny started laughing and said, "This could only happened to someone while getting coffee in New York." With a little tug, he loosened her bracelet, when she looked up at him, something happened. It was like the sky parted. He could not take his eyes off her, and he was sure he wasn't breathing on his own anymore. She was the most beautiful woman he had ever seen.

She said, " Really I am very sorry. Oh by the way my name is Amy, if you give me your contact information I promise to have your suit cleaned."

Benny said, "That will not be necessary, but tell me does this happen to you often, because I have never had anything like this happen to me before and I pray never again."

Amy looked at him covered from his waist to his feet in coffee and said, "No, I must say this has never happen to me before."

With that they again burst into laughter. He knew he should've been upset with her, but he just couldn't be she was too cute, and she clearly had a sense of humor.

He reached into his jacket pocket and pulled out a business card, never taking his eyes off her.

The manager of the coffeehouse had seen what happened. She was a regular, he knew her standing order and the fashion house she represented, he gave her a quick replacement. She grabbed her new order, took one last look at Benny on her way to the door, and ran out of the store.

Benny just stood there covered in coffee, watching her walk out of his life. The store manager asked him, "What would you like to order?"

Benny laughed and said, "How about a forty-two long?" The manager gave him a perfect cup of fresh hot brewed strong and black just the way he liked it. Benny paid for his drink and walked out of the store and into his waiting car.

His driver asked him, "Man, what happened to you."

Benny responded, "Don't even ask. You wouldn't believe it if I told you. We need to move fast or I am going to be late."

His driver asked, "Back to your place and fast."

Benny simply nodded his head.

He had a conference call in fifteen minutes and a plane to catch in a couple of hours. Luckily, the coffee shop was only a couple of blocks away from his place. So he could run home make a quick change take his call, and go directly to the airport.

He thought about Amy during his entire flight. He laughed to himself. She was a beautiful, messy whirlwind. She had his information, but he had forgotten to get hers. It had all happened so fast. He resigned himself to the knowledge that he might never see her again. So he put all of his concentration on his upcoming presentation to the financial leaders of Greece. They were facing a catastrophic, financially disastrous future if they didn't act soon to stabilize their market.

When his plane landed, he was taken immediately to his hotel. After a good night's sleep, he was fresh and ready. All of his meetings went as planned. He delivered the strategy for success, along with some cold, hard facts. It would now be up to Greece's financial leaders to make the necessary changes to ensure their beautiful country's future.

After five days of meetings, Benny was back on a plane heading home. He was looking forward to meeting his brothers, Tim and Larry, for a weekend on the town. He talked to them every day. Their bond was stronger than just being brothers; they were best friends.

Benny had told them all about the coffee shop girl. They found the entire story hilarious. Tim shared his somewhat broken heart news about Cami, his now-former girlfriend, who broke up with him over drinks while he was in Aspen, and how that same evening he had given two young ladies a ride home. One was so sick she threw up, and the other one was eyeballing him so hard he thought she was either going to kiss or attack him. But the sick one had an exotic beauty that he could not forget. Tim guessed her nationality might be Arabic or Greek. He was not sure.

He only knew that he would never forget her sad eyes. Larry was dating a bartender and model who was working at the W Hotel. Tim jokingly asked him, "Who dates a bartender?" Once again they all laughed. They couldn't wait to see each other. It was going to be great, the Von Kinley men's weekend on the town.

When Benny got home, there was a large gift-wrapped box waiting for him at the front desk of his building. It wasn't his birthday, so he wondered who would be sending him a gift wrapped box.

He opened the card and read:

> Sorry about the coffee spill,
> I hope this makes it up for the trouble…
> Amy

She had enclosed her business card. He thanked the front-desk staff and went up to his apartment. He unwrapped the box. Inside was a dark-blue suit with gray pinstripes and a cotton dress shirt with his initials engraved on the left cuff. And it was a forty-two long, the perfect size. He could not believe she had done something so nice. But how did she have his suit size and his home address? Then he listened to his voicemails. It seems she'd had the suit delivered to his office, and his secretary had it sent to his home.

He called Amy and asked her if she was interested in having a cup of coffee with him. She laughed and said, "Do you really want to try coffee with me again?" He said, "Yes, but this time he wanted to do the pouring."

They met for dinner instead, and before the main course they were both falling in love. They had seen each other every day since that first date.

Chapter 48

While the counseling sessions continued to be grueling for them. Nancy decided it was time to look for Paulina's mother so she contacted the offices of Skip Turner, one of the nation's top private investigators. If anyone could find Paulina's birth mother, Skip was the man for the job.

A retired thirty-year veteran of the Metropolitan Police Department, he'd been the star investigator of the homicide division, having a reputation for finding anything or anyone that didn't want to be found. His successful discovery of critical data in several high-profile murder cases had made him a legend.

Nancy arranged to have Paulina meet her at the Turner Recovery office located at 1225 Connecticut Avenue, in the heart of downtown DC.

His office was understated. The suite consisted of three rooms with very little to no décor, the reception area had a massive fish tank filled with deadly jellyfish. Skip's office was decorated with a cherry wood pedestal desk, a couple of leather chairs, law books, and a wall of televisions, all displaying different news shows. There were no paintings on the walls, there was nothing which told you anything about the room's occupants. Next to his office was his junior investigator's office, which was even less impressive than Skip's.

Clearly these men had one-track minds. It was all about the business of investigations, no thrills and no frills. The only thing that was surprising was how handsome Skip was. His skin was a beautiful almond brown, his gray eyes were steely and framed with long lashes, and his teeth were super white and perfectly straight. He stood six feet tall, and very well built. He looked more like a Hollywood actor than an investigator.

Looks aside, his mannerism was that of a true hard-ass, he was very direct, get to the point, cut-the-shit, I've seen it all type of man. When he spoke it was clear he'd spent most of his life dealing with hardened criminals.

Nancy had filled him in on all of the details of Paulina's mother and why they'd had to use a surrogate. As she spoke Skip's eyes never left her; he took in every word she said, as if her story mesmerized him. His intense manner concerned her and she was unsure how Paulina would react to him.

Their family counselor had warned her that the outcome may not be as she had hoped. And Paulina should not attach a fantasy to what and who her natural mother could or should be. She needed to keep an open mind and to be prepared that her mother may not want to be found, or she may not welcome Paulina's desire for a reunion.

Paulina was excited and frightened at the same time. Not knowing had taken such a toll on her self-esteem. Her life was like a puzzle with missing pieces. She could not move forward without finding the piece that she hoped would make her whole again.

Skip announced that he had already started on the case, since Nancy had sent him a sizable retainer and the last information she had on Paulina's birth mother. Skip reported that Paulina's mother was very much alive and living well. Her name was Paula Madden Shorthouse-Crumb. She was currently living in Palm Desert, California, with her husband whom she had married twenty years ago. They were members of the Monterey Country Club and lived a quiet, respectful life.

After she gave birth to Paulina, Paula had left the Washington area. She got a job as a secretary for a top-rated golf resort, and while working there, she met and married the very rich Donald Crumb. They had two children from their union, and Crumb had three kids from a previous marriage. Skip was sure that Paula's husband had no idea about Paulina and may not welcome the discovery.

He asked Paulina some very direct questions, and with his intimidating stare, he weighed her answers. He said, "Little lady, what are you going to do if Mrs. Crumb does not want to see you? What happens if she tells you to get the hell out of her life?" Paulina looked at Nancy, searching for answers to his questions. Nancy said, "My darling, this is what you wanted, and you have a right to get answers to these questions, but sometimes the answer is not what we are hoping for. Are you ready for this?"

Skip told her that once she opened this door, it would forever be open, and both of their lives would be changed. There was just no guarantee of the outcome. He had seen so many cases that turned out badly. People got hurt, and their lives were never the same. Paulina told him to please move forward; she wanted to see pictures. She just had to know everything about this woman who had given her life.

Skip said, "Okay, but remember you asked for it. It looks to me like you already have a mother who loves you. But I will take you to your birth mother. Just give me a couple of weeks to set everything up."

Paulina and Nancy left Skip's office without saying a word. They were both afraid of what may happen next.

Once in the elevator, Paulina asked Nancy if her father knew what she had done. Nancy told her yes, she would never keep another secret from anyone she loved again. She reached out and touched Paulina's hand. To her surprise Paulina didn't pull away. She took Nancy's hand and held on tightly.

When they got to the garage, Nancy asked her if she would like to go get a bite to eat.

Paulina's reply surprised Nancy, she said what she wanted was one of Nancy's big turkey club sandwiches prepared the way she used to fix them. Nancy smiled and said, "You bet I will. Just meet me at home."

Paulina got into her car, which had been a gift from Salim for her graduation from high school. It was a Mercedes-Benz C250 Sport. He had promised it to her if she made all A's her senior year. That was four years ago, and it seemed like yesterday. She would be entering law school in the fall.

She remembered when she and Nancy had studied together doing extra-credit projects to ensure she was in the top percentage of her class. Paulina recalled how happy they had all been. How much she still loved them both. She thought about how nothing could replace family. No one would ever mean as much to her, or hurt her as deeply as her family.

Her cell phone rang. It was Tiffany. She wanted to know about her meeting with the PI.

Tiffany said, "Pauly, your life is becoming so James Bond, with private investigators and secret meetings."

Paulina said, "It all feels like hell, Tiff. I want my other life back, before all of this shit happened."

Tiffany said, "Well, it's not your old life that I am calling about. It's your new life with me. Can you come with me to a party tonight?"

Paulina said, "Hey, I thought you were laying off the parties for a little longer."

Tiffany said, "Any longer and I will start to dry up!"

Paulina told her she would sit this one out. She had some family stuff to do that evening. Tiffany asked her to thank her mother for the wonderful supersized peanut-butter cookies she sent to the apartment that morning.

Paulina said, "What cookies?"

Tiffany said, "They arrived after you left for class, I have already eaten two. They are huge and buttery, and they have sugar sprinkled around the edges yummy! Pauly, your family is so sweet. I hope you can someday forgive them…because they really do love you."

Paulina told her to please be safe and not to bring anyone home with her.

Nancy raced home. She was delighted that Paulina wanted to come back to their home and spend some time with her.

She telephoned the cook, asking him if there was any sliced turkey in the refrigerator. If not, would he please check the freezer? He told her they had everything for the club sandwich, and he would whip up a batch of Miss Paulina's favorite double-chocolate brownies with the caramel centers. Nancy told him that would be wonderful. She thought it was too bad that tonight Salim was traveling. It would have made his day to see Paulina sitting at the kitchen table like old times.

Nancy didn't take the time to change her clothes. She just pushed up her sleeves, washed her hands and went to work. Whipping up a juicy, delicious, double decker club sandwich.

When Paulina arrived, the staff and Nancy were all so happy, they hugged her. Nancy put the plate in front of Paulina. It was a perfect club sandwiches, with potato chips, and a pickle on the side. She had never seen a club sandwich so tall. It was too big for Paulina to put in her mouth. She had to cut it and eat it in parts, even then she could only finish half. She saved room for one brownie.

Paulina asked Nancy a lot of questions about what she knew of her birth mother. What was she like during the pregnancy? She asked how much money, if any, they had paid her, and if Nancy thought she did it just for the money. She couldn't understand how any woman could carry a child for nine months and then walk away.

Nancy told her everything. She did not hold back on any details. As hard as it had been for her to keep the truth from Paulina. She now felt a sense of freedom to hold nothing back. She asked Paulina to please stop thinking of it in such harsh terms. Paula had done a beautiful thing for her and Salim. She had given them the most beautiful baby. Just then a sad look came over Paulina's face, and she became very quiet.

Nancy changed the subject, asking her about her new living arrangement and how she liked Tiffany. Paulina said it was fine. It was taking some getting used to, but overall she liked it. Paulina looked around the house and then suddenly and very abruptly said she had to leave. She had homework to do and she had to go.

Nancy said, "Please wait, wait a minute. Let me pack you the rest of your sandwich and the brownies for you." She walked her to the door. She knew better than to ask her to stay. They both knew that would not be happening until she had made her peace with them.

Paulina thanked her for the dinner, and then she turned and began to say something, but she stopped short.

Nancy asked her what she wanted to say.

Paulina said, "It's nothing—or maybe another time. I have a lot of homework, and I need to get to the apartment." Paulina quickly got into her car and drove away.

Nancy stood there watching her car drive down "S" Street and wondered where she was really going. What place made her feel safe now? Was there any place where her daughter could find her happiness again?

She went back into the house and called Salim. She told him everything, and he said he was praying for them, because he knew that only God could bring them back together. It was now their constant prayer. He feared they could not withstand much more hurt and pain.

Nancy went upstairs and called her sister, Lynn. She needed someone to talk to, someone who loved her and would let her cry until she felt better.

Chapter 49

Coco received a call from Saul, he informed her that his sister, Beatrice, had passed away of a massive heart attack during the night, and he needed support to make it through the services. Coco told him she would be honored to travel with him. She felt touched that he'd thought of her, and that he wanted her with him during such a difficult time. After all, their relationship was more of an after-dark kind of thing. They hadn't seen much of each other in daylight hours.

Beatrice lived on the Upper East Side of Manhattan, which was also Saul's adopted hometown. The Baumann family originated from Berlin, where they had been successful wool merchants and bankers until the war. Fearing for their lives, they moved to France and then to the safety of the United States. Saul shared very little about his upbringing or his family. Just that they had come to this country with nothing, and had worked hard for everything they had.

The sadness in his voice gave away his pain. He told her she would need clothes for a couple of days. He wanted her to look demure and elegant, not showy. He asked her to bring along only her best dresses. Perhaps one pant-suit, he preferred Coco in dresses because he liked to admire her shapely legs.

Saul told her his driver would be at her house at five o'clock that evening, and they would be leaving from Dulles Airport. He also told her that if she was a minute late, he would leave and she would never hear from him again. Coco understood how much this meant to Saul.

As soon as he ended their call, Coco went into action. She wanted to be prepared for anything that might come up. So she selected her most lady-like suits and dresses and paired them with all of the necessary accessories.

She didn't want to disappoint Saul. She packed herself, using her new Louis Vuitton Pegase luggage in Indian rose. She had just purchased the pieces of luggage as a birthday gift to herself. Never did she think her first use would be attending such a sad occasion. By the time she finished packing, she had filled three cases and her toiletry case.

Luckily for her, she had spent the entire day before with Erwin Gomez at the Karma Salon and Spa, so her nails, hair, and face were in perfect condition for up-close inspection by Saul's family. She was sure Saul's ex-wife and his two children would be attending, so she would really be on display.

Coco called Anita to tell her she would be out of town for a couple of days and not to worry about the house. She would call her when she returned. Coco was sad to hear that Saul had lost his sister. She had noticed pictures of his family all around his condo.

The Baumann family seemed like a large, happy family and from the looks of the pictures she had seen, they enjoyed a lot of celebrations together.

Coco was glad to be getting away for a few days, since she had not heard a word from Sadie since the tea at her house. For that matter she hadn't heard much from Nancy or Winnie, either. She had seen a picture of Winnie at some fancy party at Mar-a-Lago in Palm Beach, Florida.

She used to talk to Winnie almost every day, but after that damn tea, she hadn't heard a word from her.

Chapter 50

Coco sat at her makeup table feeling empty and alone. She needed her friends; they were her family. Now because of her childish jealousy and spitefulness, she had cut herself out of their inner-circle.

Coco's clothes and jewelry masked the fact that she was constantly in self-protective mode. No one understood that she was in fear of running out of money and not being able to take care of herself. It seemed that, all of her life, she had to fight just to make it from one day to the next.

She felt bad that sometimes she leaned on her friends too much, but she never meant any harm. What a complete fool she had been to let her feelings take over her common sense. She could only hope that Sadie would forgive her someday. For now she would be with Saul and maybe she could be the kind of friend to him that she should have been to all of her friends.

Saul's car was outside her house at exactly five o'clock that evening. She had her bags ready and at the door when the driver came to retrieve them. She slipped into the back seat next to Saul. He looked so sad, Coco understood his feelings and wanted to make it better for him. It broke her heart to see him in this much pain.

Saul said, "Hello, Coco. Thank you for coming with me."

Coco just smiled, and leaned into him planting butterfly kisses, as she gently placed her cheek to his and whispered in his ear. "Oh darling, I am so sorry for your loss." Even in his grief, the sheer touch of Coco made Saul's heart skip a beat. Her shiny hair smelled of honey and jasmine, and her skin was soft and silky. Every inch of Coco was blissfully smooth like melted butter. As her cheek touched his face, she awakened every fiber of his being.

He removed one shoulder of her Chanel wrap, looking her over. She was wearing an understated but ultra feminine dark-blue suit. The skirt had a flouncy thin-lace hem and the jacket had the double CC gold buttons and the same thin lace around the collar and cuffs. All of her accessories were Chanel. With a slight nod of his head, he approved of her look. As Saul told the driver they were ready to go, Coco gently took his hand in hers and didn't let go.

Saul traveled by Net Jets, a private-plane charter service. When they arrived at the airport, they were taken immediately to the plane. Once they were onboard, the pilot and team greeted Saul and extended their condolences. Saul introduced Coco, and then they were escorted to their seats. Saul ordered drinks, and told the staff he wanted privacy for the remainder of the trip. He told Coco they would be in New York soon. When the plane began taxiing down the runway, Saul took off his jacket and removed his tie.

He asked Coco to go to the bathroom to freshen up. She told him she had just taken a shower, and then she understood what was about to happen. She actually thought he would have been too grief stricken to get it up, but she assumed Saul needed some sympathy loving for the ride.

Coco did as she was told. She went to the restroom, and before she could close the door Saul was beside her. Coco's hunger for Saul was just as strong as his for her. Like two animals in heat, they went at each other. The lovely marble bathroom was not large enough for the two lovers. Saul quickly took Coco to the bedroom in the rear of the plane. Pushing her down on the bed, he covered her small frame with his muscular body.

His hunger for her never seemed to be satisfied. He needed to taste her, to feel her, to be inside of her. As the plane was reaching full altitude, Coco was reaching a powerful climax. Their lovemaking made them both erupt in a forceful orgasm. Sex relaxed him, it provided the physical release he needed to de-stress. He was gentle and sweet as Coco held him in her arms for the rest of the flight. When the flight attendant announced they were approaching New York, they freshened up and changed clothes.

Saul had made reservations at the Carlyle Hotel. They would be staying in the Central Park Tower Suite, and enjoying breathtaking views of Central Park and the Manhattan skyline.

Coco felt tentative, she needed to find her groove. Her relationship with Saul had really never required her to play the role of girlfriend, because the relationship had hinged on sex. Coco had no complaints. Saul was a magnificent lover. He knew her body, and oh how he pleased her, but the sexual heat didn't transcend into a committed relationship.

But now, this role made Coco uneasy because she was unsure about playing the girlfriend. For reasons she did not yet understand Coco wanted to be in this role more than anything she had wanted in her life.

When they walked into the suite, it was filled with fruit baskets, flowers and notes of condolence. Coco thought, "Everyone seems to know and respect Saul and his family."

Once they were unpacked, Saul ordered a couple of appetizers for Coco to nibble on. He had to leave immediately for a family meeting.

Coco didn't feel good about Saul going alone. She told him she was there for him, and if he needed her to accompany him, she would anytime, anywhere. Saul smiled and told her he would be back in a couple of hours and to try and stay awake. He then kissed her. This kiss was not his normal rush. It was smooth, warm, and very sexy. She walked him to the door.

When the food arrived, it was all things that he knew Coco liked. Foie gras terrine with endive slaw and roasted freshwater prawns in buttery lemon oil. Coco was touched. She thought, "*Here Saul is in pain, and he was thoughtful enough to order my favorites.*" Every bite was heavenly. The Carlyle was known for outstanding service, elegant appointments and exquisite food and Coco thought they were living up to their reputation.

After enjoying her meal Coco took a bubble bath, slipped into a long silk nightgown, and waited for Saul to return. She made a couple of calls and flipped through the local papers looking for news about Saul's sister.

Saul had been gone for about four hours, when he returned Coco could tell he had been crying. She thought, "*He looked more heartbroken than before.*"

Coco greeted him with a big hug. She was not prepared for what happened next. Saul dissolved into tears, right there in her arms. He was such a proud, strong man. She had never seen him like this, and it brought out a different Coco. She was loving and nurturing, which was just what he needed. Coco helped him to the couch, took off his jacket, and loosened his tie. She poured him a glass of cognac from the crystal decanter on the server. After a couple of sips, he spoke quietly and asked her to forgive him for breaking down. He said, "I never thought Beatrice would leave us. She was everything to me. When we lost our parents, Beatrice became our big sister, mother, friend, and the leader of our family. We all looked up to her, and now she is gone. I will never get over this loss."

He put his drink down and dropped his head in his hands.

Coco said, "Oh baby, I understand. Believe me I do. Would you please tell me more about her? She sounds like a wonderful woman."

Saul said, "Maybe later. Coco, I will never get over this loss, never."

There was nothing left to do but just to hold him as close as possible.

He thanked her and told her to go to bed, saying that he needed to be alone with his thoughts.

He told her there would be a private service in the morning and a public memorial service the following day. He stood up and held out his hand for Coco to follow him. He had reserved a two-bedroom suite. Coco was staying in the adjoining bedroom. He kissed her and told her, "Please be ready at eight. You will be meeting my family in the morning, I want you to get some rest now." Then he kissed her on the cheek, thanked her for the drink, and told her she smelled lovely.

Coco felt torn, part of her wanted to share his bed, and part of her was afraid of her deepening feelings for Saul. Coco went to her room, but she could not sleep. She knew that Saul was hurting and she just wanted to be near him. She could hear him pacing the floor in his room. She didn't want to crowd him, but she also didn't want him to be alone.

She was uncertain whether to play it safe and do just what he asked or go and comfort him which is what she so badly wanted to do.

Around three o'clock in the morning, Saul slipped into Coco's bed. He gently wrapped his arms around her, waking her up.

She asked him if he was okay.

He said, "Yes, I just needed to smell you again." He asked her what fragrance she was wearing. Before she could answer, he said, "Is it Nina Ricci, L'air du Temps?"

She said, "Yes."

He said, "It makes a woman smell like an angel. I would like you to wear it all of the time, Coco, please."

The room was softly lit by the moon's glow. She turned to face him. Taking his face in her hands, she said, "If it pleases you, I will wear whatever you like, baby." She had never called him *baby* before and meant it until that moment. She kissed him softly on the forehead, nose, and lips—again and again.

He told her, "I need you, Coco. I really need you."

Coco was not accustomed to hearing those words. No one had ever told her she was needed. It opened something deep within her, a feeling she had never felt.

She simply told him," I am here, baby...I am all in for you my love."

Saul pulled her closer to him, wrapping her in his arms. He didn't want sex. He needed intimacy, which was something their relationship had really never experienced. Saul had shied away from his feelings for Coco because he knew how deeply he cared for her, but he never wanted her to know. Coco lay in his arms, ready to give him whatever he needed. They drifted off to sleep and when the wake-up call came at six o'clock, they were still in each other's arms.

Saul kissed her on the forehead and said, "Good morning." It was the first time he had ever said that to her.

She returned the kiss and buried her head in his hairy chest. Saul's body was warm it was hard to imagine that he was in his early sixties. He had the body of a Greek god.

He loosened his arm and pushed back the covers. Getting out of bed, he turned and said, "I think I will go for a quick workout." He asked her what she'd like for breakfast.

She told him just tea and a slice of whole-wheat toast. Picking up the telephone, he placed the order. Then he reminded her what time to be ready for the day's activities. After she assured him she would be ready and on time, Saul went to his room.

Coco was surprised at how disappointed she felt that Saul didn't require some good old-fashioned morning sex. She got up and headed to the shower. Once the water was warm enough, she slipped out of her silk nightgown and into the soft water.

She didn't notice that Saul was watching her from just outside the bedroom door. He smiled to himself at just how lovely she was; normally he would've joined her in the shower, but not today.

There was a knock on the door. Room service entered with his fresh hot coffee, hot water for Coco's morning tea, and freshly squeezed orange juice. Saul kindly thanked and tipped the young man, and then walked over to the table to pour a cup of coffee.

He stood looking out the window admiring the life force that was New York City, and his mind went back to his journey to this promised land. He remembered his papa and mother telling him to be a good boy, and to listen and obey Beatrice. They promised they would see them again very soon, but right now, he and his brother and sisters needed to go ahead of them. His mother had taken all of her jewelry and sewn it into the linings of her children's clothing. She told them not to tell anyone, and that if they needed anything, Beatrice could sell the pieces to take care of them.

He could still hear the sounds of people just like himself pushing forward. He could still hear the chatter of adults telling their children to be quiet. He could smell the sweat and fear of people in the small detention room at Ellis Island, and he remembered holding Beatrice's hand so tightly. She had brought them to safety, and now he was preparing to lay her to rest. Nothing would ever be the same again. He would have to learn how to live without her, his big sister and his best friend.

Saul didn't hear Coco come into the room. She said, "Darling, I thought you were going to the gym to work out."

He said, "I thought so too, but right now I don't know how to feel or what to do?"

Coco walked over to him. Gently wrapping her arms around him, she said, "Maybe you shouldn't do anything at this moment."

They took a seat on the sofa and talked. Coco listened as Saul told her about his first days in New York, the old apartment that they had lived in, their fear of not having any parents to watch over them, and how strong Beatrice had been. She had been and still was everything to him.

After a couple of hours, the telephone rang. It was the front desk, calling to say their car had arrived. They went to get dressed. Coco knew that today would be very difficult for Saul.

She heard his deep voice crack when he called out to her that it was time to leave. To his surprise, Coco was dressed and ready to go. She walked over to him and gave him a hug. She then replaced his pocket square with one she had purchased for him.

While Saul had been at his family meeting, Coco had telephoned the Hermès Madison store. She purchased a black silk twill jacquard pocket square and the Gatsby handkerchief. After she explained the urgency of her purchase, the store had a courier service deliver the items to her room.

Saul was taken aback. Coco had never given him a material gift, she was all the gift that he ever needed.

He asked, "What's this?"

She said, "Something to keep me as close to your heart as possible. That way, when your heart starts breaking, it will remind you that I am here to help you heal."

Saul's eyes welled over. He could not speak; he just nodded his head. He kissed Coco on the cheek, and they walked out of their suite together.

They headed to the private service, after which there would be a luncheon for the family. He had to will all of his strength to get through the day and the rest of his life—without Beatrice. Her children had arrived, along with several members of his family. They all had special memories of their time with Beatrice.

As Saul looked over at Coco, he felt comfort in knowing that no matter what happened, from this moment in time he and Coco were a team.

Coco felt it too. It was a new feeling to her but something she loved. She slipped her hand in his. Without saying another word, she was letting him know that he was not alone.

They held hands the entire ride to Beatrice's large townhouse on Park Avenue. Everyone had arrived and was waiting for Saul, all of his siblings and their family members, nieces, nephews, and Beatrice beautiful grandchildren. When all of the family was together, the Baumann group was a large family.

Saul introduced Coco to every member of his family. When they asked her questions, Saul answered them. He was being protective of her—something no one had ever done. When he spoke, she looked at him lovingly and held onto his every word. It was not an act. Coco loved Saul's deep voice. He was smart and strong. He knew something about everything. He never made her feel stupid for not knowing as much as he did. He never raised his voice in anger; he spoke to her with loving care. Every moment they were together, in one way or the other, Coco felt protected, and now she was feeling love, real love, not just her and Saul but the love of a family, watching Saul's family and witnessing how much they loved each other made Coco want the love of a family for herself.

Once the Rabbi finished the prayer, they all headed to Frank E. Campbell's for the private service. After that they would be returning to Beatrice's house.

There was a large buffet of elegantly displayed kosher food on display in the dining room. Coco was not a big eater, but she knew she had to eat something so as not to offend anyone. So she gently tapped Saul on the thigh asking him, "Darling, are you hungry? Let me get you something to eat. You haven't eaten all day."

Saul said, "Yes, love. Just a little something would be nice."

Coco quickly prepared a plate and brought it to him. She opened the large linen napkin and placed it on his lap, then handed him the plate. She then took a glass of tea from the waiter's tray and placed it in front of him. It had been years since a woman had served Saul at least one who was not working in one of the many restaurants where he often dined.

Coco was playing the loving girlfriend, which comforted Saul greatly. When she asked to use the ladies' room, his sister offered to show her where it was. Saul knew what this was all about, Saul sister would question Coco on the way to the rest room, he could see that they were very interested in knowing who Coco was. Saul trusted Coco to handle the situation. After all of the meetings and arrangements were taken care of, they left the family at the townhouse and went back to the hotel.

Saul and Coco bid good evening to the Baumann clan.

On the ride back to the hotel, Saul thanked Coco for everything. She said Beatrice sounded like a wonderful lady. She had accomplished so much in her lifetime; it was amazing. She only wished she would have had the opportunity to meet her.

Coco and Saul returned to their suite and had dinner in bed while watching the news. They talked about their families, how they had grown up and their dreams for their lives. Coco made jokes and Saul laughed. The intensity of their relationship had Coco feeling safe for the first time in her life. She had never known this feeling of needing to be with anyone so much, for no other reason than loving to be in his company there was a purity to it that was so new to Coco.

Saul was going through such a hard time and she was giving him the kind of comfort he needed. That night she slept in his bed, they made beautiful love, and he spooned her as they fell into a deep sleep.

Chapter 51

The next morning they dressed and left for the service. Saul was understandably pensive and quiet. Temple Emanu-El was filled with celebrities, business leaders, and show-business people. Beatrice had been a costume designer for the theater and movies and she had been married to the owner of a textile mill. Together they built a life that was admired by many.

The service, like everything in Beatrice's life, was elegant. Her children spoke of what a good mother and friend she had been. An Oscar- and Tony-award-winning actress told of how Beatrice had helped her during a rough time in her life. She said, "Sometimes in life, the real stars are not on the screen or the stage. They are the people that make you shine, and my friend Beatrice made everyone shine." The last person to speak was Saul. His words brought tears to everyone's eyes, including Coco's.

As she sat there absorbing every minute of this amazing memorial service. She thought about the Baumann family, how they had already given her more than her natural family and much more than Mike DeSalis, and they didn't even know it.

Coco was impressed with Saul's family, but not because of their successes. It was the way they shared their lives with each other. His nieces and nephews looked up to him and showed him love and affection. They told her stories about how Uncle Saul never forgot a birthday, graduation, or anniversary. Saul remembered everything having to do with his family.

Saul had a daughter Giselle and a son Matthew, both very attractive, gentle mannered, well educated both were lawyers and they were both married. Saul proudly introduced them to Coco. They were kind, but not interested in having any meaningful conversation given the circumstance of the day. And Coco understood how they were feeling.

After the services were over everyone returned to Beatrice's house, to receive mourners and friends. Saul wanted a few minutes alone with his children. He asked them to join him on the terrace. They talked for a few minutes about the loss of Auntie Beatrice and what that would mean to the family. Saul wanted to give them time to express what was going on in their hearts and minds.

When they were finished talking about Beatrice. They asked him about Coco. He told them that she was very special to him, and he wanted them to get to know her.

Matthew said, "Dad, is this serious?"

Giselle responded quickly, "I hope so Daddy, I hate seeing you alone all of the time."

Saul was touched that his kids wanted him to be happy. Until that moment he hadn't thought about them having any desire concerning his life outside of him being their dad. He didn't answer them right away, he looked through the french door's, Coco was seated near his youngest sister and they were chatting she seemed comfortable, right at home with all of his family members.

He then looked at his grown children and said, "Yes, this could be very serious but this is not the time to talk about such things. Today is about Beatrice."

When Saul was finished talking to them, they all went back inside and Saul went immediately over to Coco, she took his hand. Giselle said, "Coco, it's a true pleasure to meet you and I hope we see more of you."

Coco was touched she looked into Saul's eyes and said, "I hope so too. Your father is a very special man."

Giselle and Matthew said, "Yes, he is very special."

Saul kids, along with all of their cousins, had made plans to have a cousins-only evening together, so they said their good-byes to their respective parents and made their exits. You could easily see how close they were. No matter what, they loved each other like best friends who just happened to be family.

Watching Saul's family made Coco again feel like she had missed out on so much, not having come from a loving, close-knit group like the Baumann's. She wanted to take it all in, so she just sat back and enjoyed watching, listening, and wishing she could have been born into a group of loving relatives such as this one.

After the required parts of the service, and greeting all of Beatrice's large community of friends. Saul and Coco returned to the hotel. Saul wanted to take Coco out to a really nice restaurant. But when he asked her what she felt like for dinner, she told him that if he didn't mind she just wanted to stay in their lovely suite and have dinner in bed again.

Saul was so grateful. He was feeling somewhat overwhelmed and very tired.

He ran them a hot bath, put on a CD by Ronald Isley and Burt Bacharach, it was all ballads. They relaxed in the warm water together.

Coco had never in her life taken a bath with anyone. It was the sexiest evening she had ever had. The large window over the bathtub allowed them to enjoy a perfect view of the city's skyline. New York was a beautiful place, and Coco was falling in love with everything about it. As they sipped champagne and listened to the lyrics to "Anyone Who Had a Heart."

> Anyone who ever loved could look at me
> And know that I love you
> Anyone who ever dreamed could look at me
> And know I dream of you
> Knowing I love you so

As the beautiful words and soft music filled the air, Saul and Coco didn't need words to express their desire for one another or the comfort they gave each other.

Later that night they made love and fell asleep in each other's arms. Saul woke up several times during the night. When he moved, Coco woke up too. Gently she comforted him, holding him tightly until they went back to sleep.

For the rest of the week, the Baumann family observed a period of mourning. Every day, Beatrice's house was open to receive mourners and friends. The family members wore black ribbons on their left lapels. On the last day of shiva, Saul sent Coco shopping and told her to be back at the hotel by dinner.

After Saul left to join his family, Coco received a call on her cell phone from one of Saul's nieces asking for a minute of her time. His niece wanted to let Coco know that her Uncle Saul was very important to her and that he had never bought anyone around the family before since his divorce.

She said, "Coco, please don't hurt my uncle. He is very special to all of us."

Coco said, "I understand. He is very special to me, too. I would never do anything to hurt Saul. He means the world to me."

The two women chatted for about an hour. They agreed that taking care of Saul's heart was their goal. Coco invited his niece to visit her whenever she was in Washington, D.C. They agreed to stay in touch and wished each other well.

When he finished with his family meetings, Saul said his good-byes to the family without Coco. He wanted to hear what they thought of her and to his surprise, everyone had liked her and respected that she clearly cared deeply for him. His siblings were very protective of each other and he was shocked when they gave her their stamp of approval.

On his ride back to the hotel, he asked the driver to take him by his old apartment. He wanted to see the old neighborhood. When they arrived, he got out of the car and walked around for a couple of minutes. He could still hear Beatrice calling him to come inside, that he needed to study, and get cleaned up for dinner. It all felt like yesterday. The years had passed by so quickly. He was now left with his treasured memories.

When he got back into the car, he telephoned his favorite store, telling them he needed a quick gift and that he would be sending the driver in to pick it up. Saul purchased Coco a lovely bracelet and watch.

Unbeknownst to Saul, Coco had purchased a lovely Jay Strongwater jeweled picture frame at Scully and Scully on Park Avenue. She had gotten a picture of Beatrice from his niece. And now she was having it framed and wrapped.

When he returned to the hotel, Coco was not there to his surprise. He was fearful that something could have happened to her. He immediately called her cell phone. When she answered, he was relieved. She was heading back to the hotel. He told her to please be safe. She smiled and said she would.

Having someone look for her, out of nothing but pure protection, was such a good feeling. Their relationship had changed, and now the rules would have to be reset. Coco didn't want to go back to their old relationship.

They were scheduled to leave in the morning, so tonight was their last night together and Coco was already beginning to miss this time with him. They had a lovely dinner in the hotel's restaurant and afterwards they retired to their suite. Saul and Coco talked endlessly about his family. Coco couldn't get enough of hearing about Saul and Beatrice, and the conversation gave him a great deal of comfort.

That night they didn't make love. They just held each other and talked until they fell asleep.

Chapter 52

Early the next morning, they packed and headed to the airport. When they were seated and comfortable onboard, Coco presented Saul with the gift in remembrance of Beatrice.

Saul said, "Coco, my dear what is this."

Coco looked at him with love and appreciation for all that he had allowed her to share this past week. She said, "Something small in honor of Beatrice." Saul was truly touched, he thanked her with a kiss.

Coco had shown more compassion for him in the past week than he thought possible. She had been everything he had hoped for and so much more. His feelings for her had grown so much during their time together he was afraid of how he would feel when they returned back to their separate lives. He was certain that what he felt for Coco was far more than the sexual pull that she had over him. Saul knew he was completely and totally in love with Coco.

As they neared the end of the flight Saul stared out the window, his thoughts replaying this past week. Coco was by his side as much as he would allow displaying compassion, tenderness and love not only to him but to every member of his family. Somehow she had become more to him than just her combination of beauty and sex appeal, she had invaded his very soul.

Once they landed and were in the car, Coco immediately sensed a change in Saul's disposition. He barely said anything to her on the ride to her house. She didn't want to believe that he was turning into the old Saul so she assumed he was thinking about business.

When they arrived, she said, "You have never been inside my house. Would you like to come in for a drink?"

He thanked her and said "No, but I would like a rain check." Turning to look deep into Coco's eyes he asked her, "Who purchased this house for you, Coco?"

She wanted to be truthful with Saul, but she sensed that Saul was starting a fight. He wanted out. She had served his needs and now she was back to being his play toy. Coco fought back tears. She could not believe, after everything they had shared in New York, that this was happening. As her voice started to break, she said, "It was a gift from Mike DeSalis, the man I was going to marry."

Saul looked at the house for a few minutes and when he turned to look at Coco, he was noticeably annoyed. He asked, "Why didn't you marry him?"

Coco said, "It just didn't work."

Saul answered quickly, "There must be more to that story."

Coco said, "Saul, honey, what's wrong? Have I done something to upset you?"

Saul smartly said, "Coco, when you live in a man's house, you will always be that man's woman. You know that, don't you?" Saul had turned steely cold.

Coco searched his face, hoping to find the answer to the change in his mood. But there was nothing there, just disappointment and pain.

As he handed her a wrapped package. He said, "Open it when you get in…your gifted house."

Coco said, "What is this for?"

Saul very sharply said, "It's a thank-you gift, for everything you did in New York, my dear girl."

Coco was offended. She handed the package back to him and said she didn't need a gift. She wanted to be with him to comfort him.

Saul said, "I am giving it to you because you didn't ask for anything from me, and you got me through a rough time. Please take it, Coco. Please."

He saw the hurt in her eyes, he hadn't meant to hurt her, but knowing she was living in another man's house was just too much for him. Suddenly the normally calm and collected Saul was allowing his emotions and feelings of jealousy to take over his common sense. Saul knew he was being irrational Mike was dead. But Saul wanted all of Coco, not just part of her and that could never happen with her living in Mike's house.

Coco opened the lovely wrapped box. It was a gold-and-diamond watch and matching bracelet designed by David Yurman. Suddenly she had a flashback to Mike and his gifts. She told Saul to please take it back. She then quickly got out of the car and went into her house. She didn't understand why Saul would do that to her.

As his car pulled off, Saul didn't understand why he had behaved so poorly. Or why she had rejected his gift. Had he done something wrong by giving her the present? He knew she loved jewelry and he had seen her admiring the set in a magazine. Coco had always been pleased when he'd given her gifts. What in the hell had happened?

He asked the driver to please turn the car around and go back to Coco's house. He got out of the car and walked up to her door, but he could not knock. He turned around and got back into the car and went home. He could not bring himself to walk inside the house that another man had purchased for the woman he loved. He knew he'd gone too far, but he could not stop himself.

Coco was looking out the window when his car drove back to her house. She saw him walk up to the front door and then turn and walk away. She knew she would never see him again. She just could not understand what she always did wrong with men. Why did they treat her this way? What was wrong with her, that no one could ever love her? Watching him leave hurt her deeply.

Against her own will, she had fallen in love with him. Now the old feelings of vulnerability were coming back to her. She had felt them so many times before with Mike. Foolishly she had allowed herself to relax with Saul, hoping that she would be safe with him, and now he was about to pull the rug right from under her feet. This time the feeling had only lasted for seven days.

She listened to her voice mail. There were several left by members of her club, all about mindless things having to do with the Capital Ladies' Club's upcoming events. Coco was not interested in any of it.

She couldn't believe what had just happened with Saul. What was going on with all of his questions about how she came to own this house? Where did he think she lived—the Salvation Army?

There were several calls from her tiny, teeny, weeny, miniature manhood doctor friend. She called him back and told him to drop dead and never call her again. Coco was finished with all of them, and that included Saul. She went upstairs to change her clothes and unpack. She called Nancy to check on her, but after dialing the number she was happy to get her voicemail. She was really in no mood to hear anyone's drama. She hung up, without leaving a message.

She thought, "*This is the perfect time for a quick getaway.*" She needed a couple of days away to clear her head and sort out her feelings. When she looked at the calendar, the wine dinner was coming up. She really had no interest in the social season right now, but she was afraid of receiving more of Sadie's wrath if she didn't attend. Coco was feeling really guilty for the way she had treated her friend, and worse for the way Saul had treated her.

The matter could no longer be ignored. She needed to apologize. There was no time better than the present moment, so she placed a call to Sadie's private line.

Chapter 53

Sadie was spending time keeping herself busy with her family and trying not to think about her friends. One of her nieces was getting married and she'd been asked to host a large bridal shower for over one hundred people. She was honored to do it, and she made sure it would be everything her niece could have dreamt of. But even with everything she had going on Sadie was still bothered about Coco. Sadie smugly thought Coco was the one without the family and she had been blessed to have everything well almost everything. Sadie took a minute to review all of the details of the upcoming family gathering. As soon she sat down at her desk, her private line rang. The caller ID showed "Coco Runni."

Sadie had received Coco's wine dinner donation, along with a replacement cup and saucer sent to her from the prestigious boutique on Park Avenue, Scully and Scully and a large arrangement of spring tulips with a note that said, "I am sorry for everything. Love, Coco."

Sadie answered on the third ring. After the pleasant greetings, Coco jumped in saying, "Sadie, can you ever forgive me? I don't know what got into me…I am truly sorry and I hope you can find it in your heart to forgive me."

Sadie was in shock. Coco calling to say she was sorry. Now this was a first. She was not prepared to let Coco off that easy. So she said, "Coco, to tell you the truth, I am very hurt and disappointed in you, but now is not the time. We need to get the wine dinner finished and then you and I can have a meeting—just the two of us." Sadie told her she had received her donation and thanked her for the replacement cup and saucer.

Coco had sent the check and flowers, but she hadn't sent the cup and saucer. She didn't want to rock the boat, so she just went along with the conversation. She wondered who in the world had sent the Royal Copenhagen Flora Danica.

Sadie was very hurt by several things that Coco had done to her, and to get the relationship back on track, they needed to have a sit-down meeting. But not now. Sadie didn't have the time.

Coco knew then that she had gone over the line, and Sadie may not be so forgiving. They ended the call but all was not forgiven.

Coco needed a glass of wine and something to eat. All of the drama with Saul had caused her to work up an appetite. She called Cheesecake Factory, ordered herself a large Chinese chicken salad to go, drove to White Flint Mall, picked up her dinner and then went back home to eat alone.

As Coco roamed around her empty house she realized she missed Saul and sadly nothing felt the same without him.

In the span of seven days, her life had changed, and it all had to do with Saul Baumann. She looked over at the picture of Mike that had been at her bedside for such a long time. Coco didn't want to look at him another minute. She took the picture and threw it in the locked closet where the rest of his things were. Mike's memory had remained for too long. In that moment she decided she would trash everything that reminded her of him. By the time she was finished she felt exhausted and completely alone.

She wanted to call Saul, but she couldn't.

Saul arrived home to hundreds of e-mails and voicemails. He was not interested in any of them. All he could think about was Coco. Damn, he had really played that wrong! What in the hell was he thinking? He had treated her like a whore, and she had treated him like a king. Saul could not understand why he let his feelings of jealousy overrule his common sense. He only knew that the thought of Coco sleeping in another man's house, and sliding into another man's bed unnerved him.

Saul changed his clothes and went to his desk. There he found the receipt from Scully and Scully for the china cup and saucer he had sent to Sadie Von

Kinley under Coco's name. He wanted to protect Coco from all hurt and pain, and now he had done that very thing to her. If only she knew how much he loved her.

He couldn't handle this right now, so he returned to his computer and tried to respond to the most urgent e-mails. Then he went to the gym for a quick workout. It always relaxed him and then back home and to bed.

Saul awoke around midnight, with only his thoughts and memories for company so he decided now was a good time to read the letter from Beatrice. She had left a letter for each one of her siblings. Saul had waited to read it until he got home. He'd hoped to have Coco there for support, but he had truly messed that up.

So he poured himself a strong scotch, sat down and opened the letter, and began reading:

> To my baby brother Saul,
> If you are reading this letter, I am in heaven with Mother, Father and my Arthur. You must know that I always loved you as my baby, my brother, and my friend. You were so young when our parents were killed. I often worried that you wouldn't remember them.
>
> If you did, you would treasure the love that they shared for one another. And you would know that you need that in your life. I know you were hurt in the divorce, but please, I beg of you, don't let that stop you from giving your heart to someone else. Loving someone and being loved in return, each and every day, will allow you to enjoy the wonderful success you have worked so hard to build.
>
> Saul, I love you more than anything or anyone. Please open your heart and let someone love you back. Please don't live the rest of your life as a single man.
>
> Now, one more favor, please watch out for the rest of the family.
>
> Until I see you in heaven, I love you always,
> Bea

There were tears running down his face, and he had never felt so alone and heartbroken. Saul sat at his desk for hours rereading the letter. Finally he placed it back in its envelope and put it away in his safe. That night all he could think about was Beatrice and Coco. He slept on the couch. His bed didn't feel right anymore. He wanted Coco beside him. He missed the smell of her, the feel of her, and the sound of her voice. He didn't get a moment of rest the entire night.

The next morning he tried to get the strength to call Coco. But he just couldn't do it. He was afraid she would reject him, and right now his heart could not take it. So he went to the gym and worked out for hours, until his body was sore, and he could no longer feel the pain in his heart.

When his workout was finished he went back to his office and did some research on several companies he believed to be in position for a merger. He went over several new product patents that would become IPO's in the very near future. With any luck, Saul would be positioned to make another hundred million. Somehow making millions didn't give him the pleasure he was looking for.

Saul knew that he would never again fine pleasure until he gained the courage to go to the woman he loved. He owed Coco an apology for the hurt that he caused, and he owed her the truth about his feelings. He loved her and he wanted to be the only man in her life, for the rest of her life.

Chapter 54

Coco awoke the next morning, still angry and depressed. She could not believe the turn of events. How could this have happened? Why had Saul thought so little of her? Like a fool, she had given her heart away to another man who didn't really want her.

Until she could think of what to do next, her plan was just to keep busy—so busy, in fact, that she wouldn't think about Saul or how he had broken her heart. She went to her desk and started going through piles of mail, most of it invitations to events she could not afford to attend and the normal monthly bills.

Just as she was about to call it a day, she came across an invitation to a reception being held at the home of Senator Moyer to benefit cancer research. The event was taking place that evening, so she needed to hurry up and get things in motion. She thought, "*This is perfect timing. An evening with the senator is just what I need.*"

She immediately called the charity office, made a pledge and was added to the guests list. There was no time to shop for a new outfit. She would have to wear something that she already had hanging in the closet. What she needed was a quick trip to Karma for hair and make-up, so that was her next call.

Coco's mind kept wondering back to Saul, what was he doing, did he miss her, was he as lonely as she was? As much as she wanted to hear his voice she could not bring herself to dial his number. She had always been the one in past relationships who gave in and made amends. She would not do the same things that she had done before.

Her relationship with Saul was unlike anything she had experienced. There were no rules to follow, just raw feelings. The fear of failure was suddenly overwhelming. All she knew was that she was hurt and afraid, that she would never hear from him again.

Time was moving fast. After her hair, face, and nails at Karma, she needed to take care of a couple of errands and then it would be time to get dressed.

Coco was usually overjoyed to be anywhere the senator was, but tonight her heart was just not in it. Her thoughts of Saul held her captive.

She just kept telling herself, "Not again…not another minute wasted on a man who does not want to make me his number one and who does not respect me, not again."

She slipped into an understated royal-blue St. John knit pantsuit. She paired it with her sapphire-and-diamond earrings and bracelet that she had given to herself back when she was modeling. She didn't wear it much anymore because of its delicate art deco design. But tonight she didn't want to look at anything that reminded her of Mike, Saul, or anyone else. She tried to remember the last time she felt okay just being alone.

Coco arrived thirty minutes after the reception had started. Senator Moyer lived in a lovely house located across from Belle Haven Country Club in Alexandria, Virginia. It was the home he had shared with his wife and children.

The good Senator greeted her warmly saying, "Coco, I didn't see your name on the list. How kind of you to come all this way to support this cause."

Coco said, "I just learned of the event and wanted to support you."

Moyer responded, "Well, thank you so much for coming out."

She didn't know how to take the senator's remarks. Was he telling her to leave, or was he just surprised to see her there?

Oh well, she would stay and learn more about the charity and look around the house, his home was elegant and warm. She mingled with other patrons and made small talk. Suddenly it all seemed like a waste of time, and for the first time in her life, she didn't care to impress anyone. She just wanted to hear Saul's voice. She wondered what he was doing and who he was doing it with. If she had attended this event with him, they would have had a thousand things to talk about. Saul could speak on anything and to anyone. As it was, she was just a wallflower, lost and lonely in a sea of strangers.

After the standard speeches and forced smiles, Coco made her way to the ladies' room to freshen up. The event was coming to an end soon. She wanted a few minutes with Moyer to discuss the possibilities of her coming to work a couple of days a week in his office. His staff made sure that getting private ear-time with the senator was not going to happen tonight.

As she walked down the hall from the powder room, Coco slipped on the parquet floors. She wasn't hurt, but she was very humiliated when the senator's butler just looked at her, turned, and walked away. He never stopped to ask her if she was hurt or if there was anything he could do to help her. She was just lying on the hallway floor like road-kill.

She thought, "Okay, this must be a sign. It's time for me to get the hell out of here."

Guests were already leaving, and she was among the last group. She looked around but didn't see Moyer. She had wanted to say good-bye to him, but there was no one there just his staff walking people to the door.

The evening had turned out to be a waste of her time. And Coco was happy when the valet brought her car around. She was out of there and to her surprise, she never wanted to come back again.

As she was driving down South Washington Street, she noticed that her bracelet was gone. She pulled over to the side of the road, thinking it might have fallen off while she was driving. But she didn't find it on the floor of the car.

Then she remembered the last time she'd noticed the bracelet was when she was at the Senator's house. When leaving the powder room, before she'd slipped she thought, "*It must have fallen off then*." She called back to the house, but no one answered. She was only a couple of miles away, so she turned the car around and headed back.

When she arrived, no one answered the buzzer at the gate. She knew he was home, so she parked her car and walked through the side gate leading toward the house. She knocked on the door and a maid answered.

Coco said, "Good evening again. I am sorry, but it seems that I have lost my very expensive bracelet. The last time I had it was earlier this evening when I was here. Do you mind if I come in and look around?"

The maid said, "Absolutely not. I have no idea who you are, and the Senator does not like people looking around without his approval."

Coco said, "Look, lady. I was just here for the reception and I am not just somebody. I want my bracelet back."

The maid pushed Coco back and said, "Well, the party is over and if we find your belongings, we will have them sent to you. Good night. Now, please go home." And then she slammed the door in Coco's face.

Coco said, "What a bitch! I just want my bracelet."

She knocked on the door a couple more times, but no one answered, they just turned off the porch light, leaving Coco standing in the dark.

Coco thought, "*This is crazy. If the Senator had any idea how his staff treated people she was sure he would be very displeased.*" As she prepared to walk back to her car, she noticed a light, coming from a window on the side of the house. Walking around the side of the house, she looked through a window into the library. Sitting on a sofa was Senator Moyer. Just as Coco was about to knock on the window to get his attention, his trusted butler walked in.

There was something about this guy that Coco didn't like. She wanted to wait until he left the room, and then she would knock on the window. She was sure that the senator would be more than happy to help her find her bracelet.

Coco crouched down near the window and watched the two men talking. She could not make out what they were saying. She only knew they were relaxed and enjoying each other's conversation.

The senator removed his shoes and the butler went to the bar and made him a drink and then smiled as he bought the drink to Moyer. It was then that Coco felt something was just a little too comfortable between these two men.

Moyer smiled at the man and the two exchanged more pleasant conversation. Coco's knees were starting to ache. She hoped the butler would be leaving soon. So she could get into the house, get her bracelet and then be on her way home.

Just then, Moyer motioned for the butler to join him on the leather sofa. After a couple more sips of his drink, Moyer reached over and passionately kissed his butler. The man returned the kiss, then reaching down, he started massaging Moyer's private parts.

Coco could not believe what she was seeing. After a couple of seconds, passion between the two men started heating up. Both men unzipped their pants. Moyer took the man's pleasure stick into his hungry mouth and started to suck the life out of him. A couple minutes later the butler got up, walked over to the desk, and dropped his pants. And Moyer mounted him like a stallion. The two men were fucking like there was no tomorrow. Coco could not believe her eyes, she was frozen and unable to move, as she leaned against the house for support.

Coco could not take it anymore. She felt sick to her stomach. She'd spent so many nights thinking about what it would have been like to have a Congressional lover. Now she knew and it was making her stomach turn.

Witnessing the butler having a grand time taking it all in, was just too much for Coco's system. She threw up right there. Losing her footing, Coco tumbled over into the rosebushes. When she tried to get up, her hands sank into the soft mulch. There was nothing to wipe her hands on but leaves and grass. She had to get the hell out of there—and now. She looked back through the window one last time. Yes, that was really happening. Senator Moyer was having sex with his butler, all while Coco was throwing up in his garden. No longer caring about the bracelet. She got up on her shaky legs and ran to her car.

When she got to the car she was shaking all over. Suddenly she was overcome by a strong smell of shit, once again she became nauseated. She now realized what she thought was soft dirt was indeed dog shit and it was on her clothes, hands, and shoes. She opened all of the windows in the car, but the fresh air was not helping. Feeling sicker by the minute she pulled over to throw up again.

The evening had turned out to be one of the worst ones she could remember since Mike's death.

She sped down the road, wanting to put as much distance between her and this crazy night as she could. After what she had witnessed, her crush on Senator Moyer was officially over. What he wanted she could never give him, not even with a strap-on. It was clear Senator Moyer enjoyed his quiet, private life and public lies.

When Coco got home, she was still sick to her stomach. Her knees were bleeding, and her head was hurting. She took off all her clothes and threw them in the washroom. There were some things in life that you just shouldn't see, and she had just witnessed one of them.

This had to be the craziest night of her life. And the only person who would understand was Winnie. So she called her friend, but Winnie didn't answer. She could not go to bed without telling someone, so she called her sister Barbara.

When Barbara answered Coco started off the conversation with, "You will never believe what happened to me this evening."

Barbara said, "Coco, yes I will believe you, so spill the beans now. What happened?"

Coco said, "You need to sit down for this one."

After two hours of gossip, laughter and good old-fashioned sister bonding. Coco and Barbara ended the call with a promise to get together for dinner soon.

Coco took a shower and then she got herself a large bowl of sorbet and went to bed. She hoped the images she'd seen would not come back to haunt her during the night.

The next morning she called everyone she knew and repeated the story. She wanted everyone to know that Moyer was a man on the down low. Telling everybody about his sexual choices made her feel better about him not wanting her.

Chapter 55

Winnie saw that she had missed a call from Coco. She made a mental note to call her back later on. Today she just wanted to enjoy getting back to her normal routine, arriving at the station before the sun rose, doing her morning news coverage and spending the remainder of her morning working out before heading back home.

It was easy to manage her time when she didn't have a full schedule of special appearances, Winnie was thankful for some downtime.

On the drive back home, she didn't know who to call first. Winnie had to prioritize her calls according to which friend had the most urgent drama and right now that would be the Hadid family. She was very concerned about Paulina, so she placed a call to Nancy.

Nancy was grateful to hear from Winnie, "Hi Winnie, what's going on. Are you just leaving the spa?"

Winnie could hear the sadness in Nancy's voice. "Yes, I had a great work out, but I missed running into you. How are you doing? How is Salim and Paulina?"

Nancy took a deep breath while deciding where to start and said, "Well, to tell you the truth, this journey feels like we're slowly walking through hell. We are going to see the therapist you recommended. Thank you Winnie."

"Winnie said, "Is it helping? Have you made any progress?

Nancy sadly said, "Well, yes and no. But I have faith that we will soon. One thing for sure. It can't get much worse."

Winnie quickly said, "Oh Nancy it will get better. In the mean time don't lose faith."

What life had taught Winnie was that our greatest tests are our personal relationships, no matter what the definition of the relationship. Business, a family member, a lover, or a friend they all had requirements and being truthful was at the core. She really hoped Nancy could undo the damage she had done by not being truthful.

Winnie remembered the evening Nancy and Salim had fought. Nancy had drank too much and she'd told Winnie about the adoption and using a surrogate. She had asked Winnie to please never tell anyone and of course Winnie never would.

Winnie did warn Nancy that keeping such a secret would only damage her family when the truth came out and it would. You can never hide a thing like who a person's real mother is. For a smart woman, Nancy had allowed her emotions to make her act very dumb. Winnie felt bad for her friend, but all she could do was be there and listen to her. Winnie and Nancy chatted for a while, catching each other up on the latest in their lives. When they ended the call, Winnie was pulling into her drive way.

Happy to be home Winnie was feeling bad that she hadn't returned any of Coco's calls. She just could not listen to anymore complaints about Sadie. Winnie thought, "*Calling Coco back will just have to wait until after I take a long hot bath and enjoy a glass of wine before venturing into the land of Cocoism.*'"

Coco's calls were always the same, "Where have you been? Where are you going? Can you invite me?" Winnie thought, "*Bless Coco's heart. She will never change.*" That was just who and what she was. Winnie did love Coco, but sometimes she needed some space from her.

Chapter 56

As she walked into the house, the first thing Winnie saw was a large arrangement of tulips, hyacinths, dutch crocuses, loddon lilies, and irises arranged in a large straw hat. There were gardening gloves dangling from the side of the arrangement. Winnie laughed out loud; she knew right away who had sent it, dropping her shiny, red, crocodile Birkin bag on the small settee just off the kitchen. Like a honeybee she went straight to the heavenly scent of blossoms. She read the card attached:

> Dear Winnie,
> For your garden and your hands.
> Thanks for a great lunch,
> Phillip

It had been several weeks since she and Phillip had enjoyed lunch at Café Milano's. She wondered why he was sending the flowers now. Examining the arrangement again, she laughed out loud, thinking to herself, "*When you receive flowers this lovely, you are grateful,*" she walked into her bright and sunny home office.

Winnie's office had been decorated to harmonize with her beloved Theodore Earl Butler painting entitled *Manhattan*, an oil-on-canvas scene that, in the softest tones, depicted the New York City landscape with a view of the Hudson River. Winnie had fallen in love with the painting when it came up for auction at Sotheby's, and she was determined to be its new owner. She had instructed her design team to bring the painting to life. Which they accomplished with soft pastel tones throughout the room.

She loved her office, it was decorated with one large desk in the center of the room and a small desk in the corner. There were lots of silver frames pictures of Winnie with important people and keepsakes given to her from organizations that she had supported. The book shelves were lined with several Emmy's and broadcasting awards. A large bay window with a window seat lined with needlepoint pillows in pastel colors allowed a perfect view of the garden, and lots of light to shine throughout the room.

Once a week, Michelle, Winnie's personal assistant, came to the house to go over bills, handle correspondence, send out thank-you cards and gifts and go over Winnie's calendar.

Today there was a small mountain of invitations to respond to, along with important board-meeting minutes and papers that required her attention.

"Good afternoon, Ms. Winnie." Michelle had arrived on time and was ready to begin their day.

Winnie smiled and said, "Hello, Michelle. We have a lot to go over today. Look at all of this mail."

Michelle said, "Look at those beautiful flowers!"

Winnie just smiled and said, "Yes, they are lovely."

Winnie and Michelle got down to business, going over every piece of paper on Winnie's desk.

Winnie asked Michelle to send Phillip a box of chocolates in the shape of a gardener's wheelbarrow, she had seen on line. She instructed Michelle to send the gift to Phillip's office address.

Winnie smiled thinking, *"Phillip was a dashingly charming man. A class act through and through, the kind of man she would love to get to know better—if only he weren't married."*

After several hours of non-stop work. Winnie was satisfied that everything was handled, she invited Michelle to join her in the kitchen for a late lunch.

Chapter 57

While Salim was busy traveling and making speeches around the world, Nancy was spending her time working on special projects for at-risk children through her foundation. She had been getting updates from Skip Turner's office, Paulina's birth mother still had not agreed to meet her. Nancy had a sickening feeling that this woman would never agree to a meeting. She didn't know how the refusal would affect Paulina.

Nancy was sitting at her desk when her doorbell rang. She heard the voice from the vestibule and she couldn't believe the surprise it was her sister Lynn. She had flown in from England for a quick visit. What a wonderful turn of events. Family was just what Nancy needed right now. Lynn told her that when they'd last spoken, Nancy sounded so miserable that she had booked the next flight to the United States.

The two sisters chatted all day, catching up and commiserating about their problems. Nancy brought Lynn up to-date on everything that was happening with Paulina and the detective.

Lynn was careful never to say, "I told you so." She had predicted this outcome and had given Nancy plenty of warnings. But now she only wanted to help her sister find her way to the other side of this problem. They had a great time sharing memories and giving each other advice. Lynn said she was staying in the States for a couple of weeks. Nancy could not have been happier. She was lonely and loved having the company.

The next evening, Nancy took Lynn to Blue Duck Tavern on Twenty-Fourth Street for a quick pre-theater dinner and then to the Kennedy Center for a wonderful performance by the Washington Ballet. The production was set to Frank Sinatra's music, and it was absolutely brilliant. Their artistic director was a young man, full of energy, talent and with great vision. Had really infused new life into the company.

The next day Nancy and Lynn attended the Congressional Club's annual First Lady's Luncheon at the Washington Hilton Hotel. A fabulous event that was always attended by the first lady and the spouses of the entire executive cabinet. The ballroom was filled with the usual social suspects, all dressed in the latest couture.

Nancy, Sadie and Winnie were also in attendance. They all chatted with Lynn during the reception. Coco was a guest of Sarah Talcott, and she made sure to let the other ladies know just how disappointed she was that they had not included her at their table.

Coco said, "Hello, Winnie. I called you the other day, and you never called me back. I see you, Nancy, and Sadie are all here. Well, I am so thankful to have my dear friend Sarah invited me, because no one else even thought about me."

Winnie replied, "Coco, I don't have a table to invite anyone. I am a guest, just like you are. You know we all attend this event every year. You could purchase a table yourself and invite us. No one left you out. Please don't even go there."

Coco responded, very hurt, "Well, Sadie and Nancy have tables, and no one called me. I didn't even know you all were coming."

Winnie said, "Coco, I am sorry but I have been really busy lately and again, I am a guest too. Winnie was the guest of one of the most powerful lobbyist in Washington. She said, "Coco, I have to go. My hostess is looking for me. Remember the wine dinner is in a few weeks. See you then."

She walked away from Coco, wondering why had Coco gone on the attack with her famous, "Poor lonely me. My friends have forgotten me again." Winnie thought, *"Coco is far too beautiful, talented and resourceful to act like anybody's victim."*

Nancy overheard the conversation and moved herself and Lynn away as fast as possible.

Lynn asked, "Is Coco feeling sorry for herself again?"

Winnie and Nancy were trying to stay clear of the catfight between Coco and Sadie. Neither woman felt good about it. It's always hell when friends fight. Nancy hadn't invited Coco because she just didn't want to get in the middle of it. She had enough drama going on right now.

The remainder of Lynn's visit was spent close to Nancy's house. The two sisters enjoyed baking, talking with their other siblings and just catching up and sharing time together.

Two weeks went by so quickly and it was time for Lynn to head back home to her family in Oxford, England. Her husband was a Rhodes Fellow, they had two daughters Paulina's age, they lived a peaceful, quiet life. Lynn and Nancy laughed about how far they had both come from their very humble beginnings.

Lynn said, "You know what, sister dear? We should both be very grateful for our educations which got us so far in life."

Nancy said, "You know what Lynn? Saying 'I do' has done wonders for us as well. I am a firm supporter of the institution of marriage."

Lynn agreed and said, "Well, that's a good thing, because we have been married so long it's hard to remember a time when we were not Mrs."

Nancy said, "The trick is not getting married but *staying* married. That's the hard part."

Lynn pondered that statement and said, "Yep, to stay married and not kill each other."

They started laughing and couldn't stop.

The next morning Lynn sadly boarded a flight for home.

Chapter 58

When Paulina arrived home Tiffany was her usual self looking for a party. Paulina didn't want to party tonight. What she wanted was to be alone with her thoughts. The latest news from Skip kept playing in her head like a sad country western song over and over she heard Skip say, "She does not want to see you."

Tiffany said, "Hey girl, you almost missed me. Get dressed so we can go get you a drink."

Paulina told her, "Not tonight. Girl, I am too tired. How do you do it—every night out partying?"

Tiffany said she was not taking no for an answer. The party was on Capitol Hill at some millionaire's row house.

Paulina didn't have the presence of mind to fight so she just said, "Okay, just one drink and I am out of there."

Tiffany said, "I called uber our car will be here any minute, I know we will be drinking."

Paulina didn't care about the details she just said, "Okay, but let's make it an early night alright."

Paulina put on her new Dolce and Gabbana mini-dress with a large gold belt. Tiffany was wearing a pair of leather mini-shorts with a long leather and suede laser cut top, and her favorite Versace shoes. It was the craziest outfit that Paulina had seen Tiffany wear.

When they arrived the party was in full swing and Congressman Flank was front and center. There was something about the man that made Paulina uncomfortable. Lucky for her, he never saw them. He was too busy with another young woman to notice anyone. She couldn't put her finger on what it was but there was something about him that she just didn't like. She wanted to stay clear of him. Then she thought, *"I am becoming suspicious of everybody because of my own mess. Congressman Flank is most likely a cool guy."*

With no more thoughts of Congressman Flank Paulina enjoyed a couple of drinks some harmless flirting and then she and Tiff took uber home.

Chapter 59

Lonnie and Sadie were enjoying a restful weekend, so he thought it was the perfect time to lightly approach the subject of her drinking. There would never be a perfect moment to tell the woman you loved you thought she was an alcoholic. As he had expected, when he bought up the subject of her drinking, she was very offended and didn't want to talk about it.

She said, "So what are you saying, Lonnie? You think your wife is a boozer? An alcoholic? A drunk? Well? Is that what you're saying?"

Before he could answer, Sadie was on her feet, pacing back and forth. She said, "If you had as much pressure on you as I do, you would drink too. No, let me correct myself. You would soak your bony ass in a vat of vodka."

Lonnie asked her, "What pressure, baby? You have an entire staff to help you—and a budget that rivals the first lady of the United States! Sadie let me know what pressures you are speaking of so that I can make it better."

Sadie started to raise her voice, which was something that they never did. Lonnie said, "Keep your voice down. We are just talking. There is no need for you to act like this. I only want to help you. And like it or not, you are showing signs of a problem."

Sadie angrily said, "I will keep my voice down the minute my husband stops this crazy conversation. Here's the real problem, Lonnie. You have no idea what I do to keep us so—why do I even try to explain to you? You just have no idea."

She was completely disheartened that he had bought up the subject, so her only defense was to turn the matter on him. Lonnie watched her struggle to explain, he felt lost he knew that this was not going to help her.

Lonnie used his calm voice saying, "Baby, just tell me how I can help you, and I promise I will do anything to make it better."

Sadie rudely said, "You could never understand, Lonnie. You are not a woman." Then she walked out of the room.

Lonnie didn't want to fight, but he felt she'd sucker-punched him with the "you are not a woman" thing.

He followed her up the stairs. When they reached the top landing, Lonnie grabbed Sadie's thin elbow, turning her around to face him.

Lonnie said, "No, you are damn right, Sadie. I am not a woman, but please tell me, since when does having a vagina give someone permission to abuse anything? And drinking too much is a form of abuse."

She marched into their bedroom, and he followed her. Lonnie said, "Sadie, you can't run from this. We have to face it. The boys are worried about you, and so am I."

Sadie replied, "Oh my God, Lonnie. Have you been talking about me to our children? Do you have them thinking that their mother is a drunk? This is low, Lonnie—really, really low."

She walked into her dressing room and locked the door. He begged her to open the door, but she wouldn't.

Lonnie knew the conversation was over for now, but he was not going to let her off that easy.

He was sure that, whatever the problem, he could get her through it without the help of an outside person. But it was not worth the discord it had bought them, and he could not stand to see her unhappy. So for now the subject was closed.

Sadie remained locked in her dressing room until midnight. Lonnie could smell the heavy scent of alcohol on her when she came to bed. He pulled her to him and whispered in her ear that everything would be okay and that he was sorry for upsetting her.

Sadie didn't answer, she just closed her eyes and went to sleep.

The next morning after breakfast, Lonnie telephoned their sons. He explained Sadie's reaction when he'd brought up her drinking. They were more concerned than before about their mother. They promised to talk about it during their annual father-son fishing trip.

Lonnie changed the subject, asking Benny how things were progressing with his girl, and asked Tim how he was handling his breakup. Larry's relationship did not bear the thought of a conversation at this time. When it came to women, Larry had not yet matured to the point to even think about marriage. He was still in love with the fun and games of chasing women.

Lonnie thought that was what your youth was for, finding your way to the right woman. If his sons were as lucky as he had been, they would find their ladylove, and that love would change their lives. He wanted that for them. He could not imagine life without loving their mother.

Chapter 60

Lonnie could tell Sadie was not enjoying the evening. She was unusually quiet. No matter what subject he brought up, she remained distant.

Gazing out the car window, Sadie could only think about the last couple of days since she and Lonnie had talked, admitting to herself that sometimes her drinking was excessive, she needed a drink to handle the pressures of being a leader in the community. People just expected so much of her, and there was always someone asking her for something.

She was sorry for how she'd acted out the other night, but she couldn't find the strength to tell Lonnie that maybe he was right. What hurt the most was knowing that her sons were worried about her.

Lonnie was aware of how much bringing up the subject of alcohol had hurt her. But what kind of husband would he be if he didn't want to protect her?

He reached over, taking her hand in his and kissing her soft skin. Lonnie loved to touch Sadie. She had the softest skin. Every inch of his lovely wife was perfection. He often called her his Sophia Loren. Looking deep into her smoky eyes, he said, "Tonight, my bride, you look more beautiful than ever."

She was dressed in a white silk Yves Saint Laurent tuxedo-styled pantsuit, and a Cartier necklace of coral, seed pearls, and diamonds, with matching diamond-and-coral earrings, ring, and bracelet. Sadie loved coral and remembered, the Christmas when Lonnie had given her the beautiful suite. She only hoped that the mystery of coral's healing powers would work for her tonight.

When they arrived, the restaurant sparkled with the glow of candles, crystal stemware, and dramatic floral arrangements.

The executive chef, along with the culinary team responsible for the evening's epicurean feast, warmly welcomed them. Everything was to Sadie's liking. She smiled at all the right times, and no one but Lonnie could tell that she was brokenhearted.

As the waiter brought over her favorite gin martini, very cold with three large olives, Sadie took the drink and looked away from Lonnie.

Winnie and Nancy were the next to arrive. They both looked great and were enjoying a lighthearted conversation. After greeting Lonnie and Sadie, Nancy shared a joke, and they all laughed. Sadie was so happy to see them, it seemed like such a long time since they had all been together. Nancy and Winnie's arrival changed Sadie's mood.

Winnie said, "Oh Sadie, everything looks wonderful."

Sadie smiled and said, "Well, Winnie, if you give it your stamp of approval, I know I have done something right."

Nancy asked if anyone had heard from Coco today. No one had. She then asked Sadie if she and Coco were okay.

Sadie said, "I will never be okay with Coco again after what she did, I will be polite, and I will forgive her, but I will never forget her display of green-eyed jealousy."

Nancy replied, "Oh Sadie, I do hope you can forgive her, Coco does love you, and I know she is very sorry."

Wanting to keep the conversation light and friendly, Winnie quickly changed the subject. Asking them about the first lady's fashion choice at the White House State dinner, that had taken place a couple of nights before. They all agreed politics aside the first lady had chosen a great American designer, and she was showcasing American businesses well.

Guests were starting to arrive and the room was quickly filling up. Coco, a master at making a grand entrance, arrived late, and as usual, she looked like a million bucks. She was wearing a pale-gray silk pantsuit from Carolina Herrera's couture collection. Her hair was pulled back to show off her aquamarine-and-diamond pendant and earrings, and her hand sparkled brightly with the display of a twenty-carat aquamarine-and-diamond ring.

When Sadie saw Coco she tensed up, but not wanting anyone to think they were at odds, Sadie made the first move, walking over to Coco and offering her a warm greeting.

Coco said, "Good evening, Sadie. The room is full. It seems our event is a grand success."

Sadie just smiled and said, "Hello Coco, I hope you enjoy the evening."

Coco said, "Sadie, do you know which table I am seated at?"

That was it. Sadie snidely replied, "Take that up with a staff member at the reservation table." She turned her head and walked away. Nancy saw the exchange and knew better than to interfere, she decided to stay away from them both.

Winnie noticed how the other women were keeping a polite distance from Coco, and she didn't like it one bit, so she made every effort to chat with Coco. Sadie had done her deed, and used her social power to make Coco an untouchable outsider.

The executive director of the charity asked everyone to please be seated, and then she thanked Lonnie and Sadie for their outstanding gift. They had made a donation to cover all of the costs of the evening, so that every penny raised would go directly to the charity. Everyone applauded, and Sadie looked right at Coco and smiled. Coco knew what that meant. Sadie was not ready to forgive her, and she might never be.

Lonnie and Sadie seemed to be enjoying the evening. They were both enjoying the wine selections which were being served with each of the seven courses.

When the dinner finally came to an end, Lonnie told Sadie they needed to leave because he had an early flight to meet the boys in Canada. When Sadie got up, she was visibly unsteady on her feet. They said their good-byes and made their way to the valet station. Lonnie asked Sadie to wait for him at the door while he used the men's room. Sadie told him she would, but as Lonnie walked away, she realized she needed some fresh air.

She walked outside of the hotel. Taking in a deep breath, the warm evening air felt wonderful. As she stood near the curb she suddenly felt ill and lightheaded. As Sadie leaned forward to catch her breath she did not see the valet backing up their Rolls-Royce Phantom. She lost her balance and fell face -down onto the cobblestone driveway. Several guests yelled out to stop the car. When the car came to a stop Sadie's head was inches away from the back tires.

When Lonnie came out of the restroom. He didn't see Sadie, thinking she'd gone back into the restaurant, he headed in that direction. He was stopped by the hotel manager, who looked very upset. He asked Lonnie to please follow him, that Mrs. Von Kinley had fallen down.

Lonnie's heart stopped for a minute. He said, "Where, where is she? Please take me to her."

As Lonnie made his way through the crowd he saw Sadie's beautiful long legs sticking out from under the car. She had hit the stone driveway hard and was unconscious. Lonnie fell to his knees. He could see she was bleeding. He called out her name, but she could not answer him.

He looked up at the manager, who said, "Mr. Von Kinley, the ambulance is on the way. I am sure she will be okay." Lonnie just dropped his head, sat down on the ground, and held Sadie's feet.

Winnie, Nancy, and Coco heard what happened and ran outside to find their friend hurt and helpless. At that moment the ambulance arrived and hotel security cleared the area.

Nancy ran inside the hotel and told a waiter to bring her a tablecloth quickly. She did not want anyone to see Sadie covered in blood. Several men were asked to please assist in pushing the car, which was the only safe way to avoid the possibility of further injury to Sadie.

When the car was moved, Sadie lay spread out on the cobblestones and blood was streaming down the driveway. Several members of the staff held up the white tablecloth to protect her from view. When the medical team started to move her, Lonnie yelled out, "Please don't hurt her! Please." His words, like his spirit, were broken.

The police arrived and asked the crowd of onlookers, "How in the world did this lady get under this car? Can anyone tell me what happened here?"

Lonnie said he needed to be with Sadie. He turned to Winnie and asked her if she would please help him.

Winnie said, "Anything, Lonnie. What hospital is she being taken to? George Washington is the closest."

Winnie stood by Lonnie's side until Sadie was in the ambulance, and then she and Nancy got on their telephones. They called the Von Kinley's house and relayed the nights events to Felix, who assured them that he would be there immediately.

Winnie told the valet to please get her car. She and Nancy would be heading to the hospital right away. Coco was standing motionless, not knowing what to do next.

Nancy looked at her and said, "Coco, are you coming to the hospital?"

Coco said, "Yes, of course. I will meet you there."

Lonnie broke down in the ambulance. Sadie still had not regained consciousness when they arrived at the emergency room. The ER team of doctors and nurses went into immediate action. Her face was covered in blood, and she had clearly broken her nose.

When Winnie and Nancy arrived at the hospital they were taken to a private waiting area where they found Lonnie. They both gave him a hug and told him they would not leave until they knew Sadie was out of danger.

When the doctor came out, he asked to speak with Lonnie in private. He was very concerned about Sadie's blood-alcohol level. The x-ray's showed she had broken her right cheekbone, nose, wrist, and she had fractured her pelvis and hip. She would need immediate surgery. They needed to know her medical history, and they asked Lonnie to sign the consent forms for the surgery.

Lonnie signed all the necessary papers, he told them he would arrange for a plastic surgeon to repair her face. The ER doctors told him that was his call but they needed to get her wrist, pelvic and hip taken care of right away.

Lonnie only had the strength to make one call, so he called Benny.

Benny answered on the first ring, saying, "Hey Dad, are you ready for some real fun? Can't wait to see you on the fishing boat. Remember what I said, I will get the biggest catch."

Lonnie could barely speak. He said, "Son, your mother has been in an accident. It's bad. We are at George Washington Hospital. They are preparing her for surgery now."

Benny said, "Dad! Oh my God! How—what? Where? Okay, I will tell Tim and Larry, and we will be right there as soon as we can get a flight."

Lonnie said, "I am sending the plane to pick you guys up…I need you, Son, and your mother needs all of us now."

Lonnie came back into the waiting room where Nancy, Winnie, and Coco were waiting for him. Lonnie only spoke to Winnie and Nancy. He didn't understand why Coco was there. She never helped anyone. He didn't have the interest or time to hear anything she had to say. This was not going to be about Coco and some more of her drama.

Winnie asked if he needed her to handle anything else. He asked her to call Felix and have their plane sent to Canada to pick up the boys.

Winnie was on it. Within minutes, she and Felix had everything arranged. Nancy was speaking with the hospital CEO. They had reserved a private VIP suite for Sadie.

Lonnie asked Winnie to come with him. He needed to speak with her in private. He said. "There are two things that I can only trust you to handle. First, right after the surgery and when she is stable, I will be moving her out of this hospital. I think you know what I am talking about, Winnie. I don't want anyone seeing her like this."

Winnie said, "Lonnie, we understand."

He then continued, "Please asked Felix to go to the lobby, and if there is anyone waiting to see or hear how Sadie is doing, ask them to please go home."

He then took a long, deep breath. Once his lungs were filled, he said, "Also, I need you to please ask Coco and Nancy to go home now."

Winnie didn't ask him why. She just did as he asked. She went back to the waiting area and asked Nancy and Coco to follow her. Once outside in the hall, she told them that Lonnie wanted to be alone. Felix arrived, and she asked him to go into the waiting area with Lonnie. After Nancy and Coco left, Winnie prepared a statement for Felix to read from, and he carried out Lonnie's instructions.

Sadie was in surgery for several hours. She was being monitored closely.

Chapter 61

Benny, Larry and Tim arrived at four o'clock in the morning. Sadie regained consciousness shortly after her surgery. She was in extreme pain, and her sons were heartbroken to see their mother so battered and bruised. Benny was still not clear on exactly what had happened, and his father was in no condition to pressure for information.

Winnie was the only friend that Benny was comfortable with. She was very honest and didn't have a hidden agenda like most of his mother's social friends. So Benny called her to get all of the details. She said she would meet him at the hospital. She wanted to speak with him and his brothers. They had to get some help for Sadie, and now. She knew what Lonnie had said, but she wanted to reinforce the urgency of her friends situation. She went to the hospital as soon as she was off the air.

Benny, Tim, and Larry were waiting for her when she arrived, and they went to a private area to speak. She told them everything she knew. Larry's eyes filled with tears; he couldn't say a word. Tim hugged him. Winnie started to cry. They were such a loving, close-knit family, and this was taking a toll on them.

She didn't want to overstay her time or keep them from their parents, so she made the meeting quick. They thanked her for being a loyal friend to their mother. They said she was the only friend that their mother truly trusted. Winnie was touched. She hugged them and made her exit.

The next day as Tim was ending a business call with a client, a beautiful young woman carrying a covered dish asked, "Is this Mrs. Von Kinley's room?"

She said that she'd heard about the accident and knew how much Mrs. Von Kinley liked her homemade fudge, so she wanted to bring her some. She didn't want to see her but just asked if he would be so kind as to give her the fudge and the card, and to tell her that Paulina Hadid had come by for a visit.

There was something about this woman that felt familiar, as if he had met her before. She was beautiful but very sad. Her large eyes were filled with sadness. He told her she was in the right place and thanked her for taking the time to prepare something from her home that his mother loved.

He said, "I know she will enjoy this, thank you so much." When she turned to walk away, something hit him. He remembered the beautiful creature from Aspen, the sick girl. He laid the dish down and ran out the door. She was about to get into the elevator when he said, "You are the young woman from Aspen. You were sick, and you almost threw up on me." Paulina just stood there, not knowing what to say. She didn't remember him at all, but she did remember being very sick.

There were other hospital visitors standing around them, so he asked her to please step to the side.

Paulina thought this had to be the handsome man that Kimberly had spoke of. He was alluring and well groomed, and when he spoke, his voice was strong but very comforting. It revealed his tender heart. His eyes were piercing. She was finding it hard to look away from him. There was something very formal and proper about the way he carried himself. He had a royal presence and all the markings of a prep-school education.

She shared with him that his mother had always been very kind to her and that Sadie had reached out to her often during her recent family problems. Paulina apologized that she didn't remember anything about meeting him in Aspen, but she thanked him for helping her and her friend.

As they stood there, she could not help staring into his eyes. He had a calm, peaceful spirit. She told him he had the best mother in the world. She was so very kind to everyone. Tim thanked her again. He asked Paulina for a number where he could have his mother call her to say thanks. When Tim and Paulina's hands touched, electricity passed between them.

Paulina said, "Oh, I am sorry. There is a lot of static electricity in the air."

Tim said, "Yes, I guess so. I am sorry. Can you tell me how you know my mother?"

Paulina said, "Our mothers are best friends. Oh, my adopted mother, oh—well anyway, my mother is Nancy Hadid. She was at the event when your mother had the accident."

Tim looked at Paulina as if he was trying to see into her very soul. He wanted to know more about her, why she seemed so uncomfortable in her own skin, and why she seemed so sad and afraid.

Paulina said, "I am sorry. Did I offend you by coming to bring your mother a gift? If I did, please forgive me. I didn't mean to, it's just that your mother has been so kind to me. She calls me to check to see if I am okay. She even sent me chicken soup when I had the flu."

Tim said, "How are you feeling now? My mother makes the best soup. We my brothers, and I, joke with her. We call it her penicillin." When he smiled Paulina could feel her heart melting.

She felt like he could read her mind. Dropping her head, she quickly said good-bye, and before he could stop her, she was gone.

Tim thought, "*Damn, she is gone again. What is it about this girl? Why do I want to help her?*"

He walked back into Sadie's room. Larry was in the room, and Sadie had come back from having more test and was now fast asleep. Larry said she had just taken some pain meds and would likely be out for a few hours. He asked about the dish of fudge, and Tim said the Aspen girl had brought it to their mother.

Larry said, "Oh damn, the sick one? Is it safe to eat? Is she still sick?"

Tim told him, "She is not sick anymore, and it seems that our mother keeps in touch with her."

Larry said, "It's a small world, man." He then noticed that Tim seemed a little taken with the Aspen girl, so he asked him more about her.

Tim said, "I don't know much. Just that her mother is Nancy Hadid and she and Mother are best friends. She doesn't remember me from Aspen, and she is the most beautiful girl I have ever met, and for the life of me I can't—oh, never mind."

Larry said, "Well, she sounds like a lot of drama, if you ask me, Bro, but what do I know about women? I am dating a bunch of them right now."

Tim corrected him, saying, "No. You are sleeping with a bunch of them. When you find the right one, the universe will let you know."

Tim asked him if he was hungry. Larry said he was, but he didn't want to leave Sadie alone. Benny and Lonnie would be back any minute. A few minutes later, Benny and Lonnie came through the door. They checked on Sadie, who was still sleeping. Tim said he and Larry were going to get something to eat and asked Benny and Lonnie if they wanted anything. Before they could make any suggestions about lunch, Felix walked in and said that would not be necessary. Hattie and the chef had prepared lunch for the family. He set a table in the room with delicious crispy fried chicken, potato salad, shrimp salad, tender roast-beef sandwiches, pasta salad, and individual apple pies that were coated in cinnamon sugar.

They all thanked Felix, and as soon as the food was set up, they dived in. They were all hungry, worried, and tired. It had been a long thirty six hours.

When they had satisfied their hunger, Lonnie announced the plans he and Benny had been working on for Sadie. As soon as the doctors declared her stable enough to travel, she would be flown to a medical treatment center in Los Angeles, California.

They knew that the treatments would take care of her physical problems, but it was now time to have the family conversation about her drinking. And like it or not, Sadie would have to be present.

Lonnie had been in contact with the best physicians and surgeons in their respective disciplines in Beverly Hills, California. They would be expecting Sadie within a day or so. Everyone was on board with the plan, and together they would be flying with her to the West Coast, and staying as long as they had to.

Lonnie told them he would be with her, and they could return to their jobs. Tim, Larry, and Benny protested that they needed to be with their mother. Lonnie told them Sadie needed some time to come to terms with her demons and address some things alone. They could only do so much for her.

Lonnie said, "My sons, I love you all so much, but your mother needs to face this part of her life without us holding her hand. She must admit that she needs help and also face what is at the root of her drinking."

Lonnie's eyes filled with tears as he looked over at Sadie and then back at his brave sons. He felt that he had let them all down. It was his job to protect her—and *now* look at what had happened. He dropped his face in his hands and said, "I failed her. She is sick. I was too afraid to face the truth, and look at what has happened to love of my life. Look at what I let happen to her."

The boys had never seen their father this broken. He had always been a tower of strength. Larry went to his father and wrapped his arms around him. It was a sad moment for the Von Kinley family.

The telephone rang and broke the silence in the room. It was Coco calling to check up on Sadie. Tim answered the telephone, and Lonnie said, "No calls right now." He didn't want to speak with anyone right now, no matter how close they felt they were to Sadie. Lonnie had circled his wagons, and no one was getting in but his sons.

Later that evening a private-duty medical team prepared Sadie for the trip to the West Coast.

Winnie was the only person who knew where Sadie had been taken, and she had told Lonnie she would never tell. And so she didn't.

When the news got out that Sadie had been moved in the middle of the night and no one had let Nancy and Coco know, they were both upset but Nancy understood that Lonnie was in charge and she respected his decision.

Coco made a big deal about it that she was being singled out because they were still upset with her. Nancy told her to get over herself. She said, "Coco, Sadie has a large family, and a very protective husband. He has taken her away so the family can deal with her problem. We will just pray for her and be there should she need us."

They asked Winnie, and she told them she didn't know any more than they did. Winnie told Coco, "Sadie needs her family, and when she is strong enough, she will reach out to us. For now, let's all just pray for our friend."

Chapter 62

When the Von Kinley's arrived at Cedars-Sinai Medical Center in Los Angeles, Sadie was taken immediately to a private suite. The family met with her new team of surgeons, therapists, and addiction counselors, who told them that the road ahead would not be easy, but they would get Sadie back on track.

Sadie was scheduled for several procedures, and they would be following a very strict protocol for her care. Everyone was in agreement. Once she was comfortable and sedated with pain meds. Lonnie, Benny, Tim, and Larry, along with Felix made their way to the Beverly Hills Hotel, where they would be staying until Sadie was ready to return home. They were emotionally and physically worn out. Lonnie felt somewhat better knowing that the next step of Sadie's care had begun.

Benny was staying in Bungalow 10, and when he arrived there was a message waiting for him to please come to the lobby lounge. There was someone there to meet him. He wondered who knew he was there, and furthermore, who would be waiting for him at such an ungodly hour. He telephoned the lobby lounge to confirm that there was in fact someone there and the message had not been sent to him by mistake. The gentleman on the phone confirmed that there was, someone waiting for him, and she had been there for several hours.

Benny couldn't think of a soul who would be waiting for him, unless maybe it was Winnie. She was the only person he had told of their plans. Benny looked worried and tired but still handsome. His face lit up when he saw it was Amy.

He said, "My love, what are you doing here? Why didn't you tell me you were coming?" She just hugged him and said, "I can't let you go through this alone. I love you Benny. Please don't shut me out."

Benny could not express how deeply grateful he was to her. He needed her so much right now. It wasn't until that moment that he knew for sure that she was the love of his life. He hugged her so hard he lifted her off the floor. He could hardly hold back his emotions. Once he released her and Amy was back on solid ground, he looked for her luggage. She was only carrying one LV bag. He scooped her bag up, and with his arm around her small waist, he led her to his bungalow.

Once inside, he ordered them some champagne, a crab-and-shrimp frittata with extra cheese. Room service brought their mid-night dinner, and set it up in front of the fireplace. Amy prepared their plates as Benny told her everything that had happened and the plans they had for his mother. Amy was very proud of him and all the Von Kinley men for protecting Mrs. Von Kinley.

Amy gently brushed Benny's hair with her fingers and softly kissed his tired eyes. She laid his head on her chest and told him it would be okay. His mother would come through this stronger than before. Benny buried his head in her chest. He had been so strong for his father and his brothers. Now in this moment with the woman he loved, he could no longer be strong.

Benny was surprised at just how much Amy had come to mean to him. She had become his anchor, with her he felt his heart was safe. He needed her more than anyone in his life. Amy was his soul mate and he loved her more than words could convey.

They talked for a while until the late hour caught up with them. Then falling asleep in each other's arms, and for the first time since the accident, Benny had a restful sleep. When he woke up, he was delighted to see it hadn't been a dream. Amy was sleeping in his arms.

He snuggled closer to her breathing in her lavender scent. She felt him move and woke up. He whispered in her ear to please join him in the shower. She was more than happy to do so. They made sweet, beautiful love under the warm water. After they showered, Benny ordered them breakfast.

Over coffee, puffy eggs, maple sausage, and lemon pancakes, they talked about the day's activities. Amy told him she didn't want to get in the way. It was not the right time for a family meet and greet, so she would stay behind and meet the family at a later time.

Benny could not believe how selfless, kind, and honorable Amy was. She had flown across the country, waited in the lobby for hours, and given him back the strength he needed. And now she would stay behind to give him the space necessary to handle his difficult family matters.

Benny just looked at her. He had never felt such love for any woman except his mother, and right now his world was spinning around with both of them. He kissed her and said thank you. Looking at the time, he told her he had to go. He was meeting his father and brothers in the lobby in ten minutes. They planned to meet with doctors before his mother was taken into surgery that morning. He asked her if she was sure she would be okay. He also told her how much he loved her. He got dressed and rushed out to meet his family.

As promised, Amy stayed out of sight. She went back to sleep, and around lunchtime she woke up and went to the gym for a workout and then to the pool for a long swim.

Lonnie and his sons were at Sadie's bedside all day. They arrived as Sadie was being prepared for surgery. She was happy to see them, and for the first time, she gave a small smile. With her good hand, she gave them a thumbs-up sign. It was the first ray of sunshine that gave Lonnie some hope that he was doing the right thing.

Lonnie had not called any of Sadie's family. He didn't think she would want them to know. So for now it was just him and the boys by her bedside.

Over lunch Benny told his brothers about Amy, and they were blown away with her courage and dedication to him.

Tim said, "Now that's a real woman, Bro. That's the kind of woman you marry."

Benny felt the same way. Tim and Larry said they really liked Amy and wanted to have dinner with her. Benny said he didn't think Lonnie would be ready to meet her under these circumstances.

Tim said, "Try him, Benny. Just tell him what's going on and try him."

When they went back to the hotel, Tim and Larry left Benny alone with Lonnie, and he told him about the wonderful woman who had entered his life.

Lonnie said, "This is a hard time. I am not at my best, but this young woman sounds too good to believe. And Son, that is something your mother would have done for me. Please bring her to dinner. We will dine at the Polo Lounge, if that is okay with you."

As promised, Benny brought Amy to dinner. Lonnie was delighted to meet her. She was everything that Benny had said she was and more. She was compassionate, kind, gracious, and very thoughtful. Lonnie saw a graceful elegance about Amy that reminded him of Sadie. But more importantly Lonnie could see how completely in love she was with his son.

Larry and Tim seemed to really like her as well. They all got along perfectly. Lonnie thought, *"It's official, Amy is Benny's girl. She is lovely, hopefully she will be joining the Von Kinley clan soon."*

Things were the same for the rest of that week. At the end of the second week, the boys had to return home. Amy had left the week before, and Benny was not the same without her. She sent flowers, and boxes of chocolates, along with a beautiful nightgown with a matching bed jacket that her designer had made especially for Sadie. Sadie loved the gifts and was looking forward to meeting Amy. She'd heard wonderful things about her. She was thrilled that Amy was making Benny happy. One thing Sadie knew for sure was that she had good taste and a great deal of class for such a young woman.

Once the boys left, Lonnie spent even more time at Sadie's bedside. She was recovering well from the physical breaks, but he knew her hardest challenge was just around the corner. She now had to deal with her drinking. Lonnie was facing the fact that he had ignored the warning sign's because he was afraid of hurting Sadie's feelings.

He'd known that Sadie needed an intervention long before the accident, and the guilt of that was weighing on him like a ton of bricks. For him this revelation was a turning point. From this moment for the rest of their lives together. He would never protect her to the point of losing her. Lonnie vowed to never let anything like this happen again.

When Lonnie made his early morning visit. Sadie said, "Good morning darling, I have been waiting for you to arrive. Please have a seat I really want to talk to you."

Lonnie pulled a chair close and took her hand gently in his. "What is it my love, what do you need."

Sadie said, "I need help with the drinking. Lonnie, I never want to be drunk again."

Now that she had said those words, Lonnie felt that he could speak freely. He said, "Sadie, are you sure you feel strong enough to have this conversation? If you do can you tell me why? Or what is happening in our lives that makes you need to numb yourself with liquor?"

Just as she begin to speak, her therapist knocked on the door. With sadness in her eyes Sadie told Lonnie they would speak about this later once her therapy session was over.

Lonnie wanted so much to hear what was really bothering Sadie, and he was glad that she was ready to face the ugly truth. As he left the room he felt that a weight had been lifted, he was glad that Sadie was ready to talk about what was really bothering her.

To keep up with the demands of his company, Lonnie had set up a small command center in his hotel suite. He had flown his secretary in, and to make Sadie feel more comfortable, he had also flown Hattie in to be with her.

Sadie's days were long with grueling physical therapy sessions and today she would be meeting with her addiction counselor. Facing every task with courage, she was determine to get to the other side of her problems.

Benny and Amy were now living together, and enjoying every minute of their new blissful arrangement. He could not wait until his workday was over, so he could come home to her.

He now understood his parent's love for each other. When you find that special person you develop a forever kind of love, which gives you a feeling of completeness and security.

Benny knew that no matter what else happened in his life, he had Amy, and together they could make it through anything.

Having purchased her a ring during his recent travels, it was three carats of perfection with each carat holding a special meaning, one for her, one for their love and one for the family they would build together.

Now he was just waiting for the right time. He wanted the moment to be perfect. She had given him so much. He wanted to give her a memory that would last as long as their love for each other.

Chapter 63

Tim had been unable to get Paulina out of his head, so he placed a call to thank her for bringing the sweet treat to his mother's hospital room. When she answered the phone, her voice was soft, and inviting. Like creamy butter on a hot biscuit, Tim's poor heart was melting away.

He asked her if she would be interested in meeting him for a drink. She said, "No, I am sorry but I have too much homework, maybe another time."

Not wanting the conversation to come to a quick end. He asked, "What college are you attending".

Paulina proudly said, "Well, only the best, American University, of course."

Tim said, "Hey, watch out. I am proud grad of the best, Georgetown Law."

She told him she was studying to become a lawyer. He responded with great pride, "I, majored in corporate law. I highly recommend a career in the legal field."

Paulina was vastly interested in anything having to do with the judicial system. The entire legal process fascinated her.

Tim said, "So what do you think about *Fisher vs. University of Texas at Austin?*"

Paulina said, "The oral arguments presented today were interesting. I have been following the case. Well, between studying and other stuff."

Tim said, "I will be in town soon maybe we could talk about it more over drinks."

The thought of discussing cases excited her and she quickly changed her mind saying, "I would love to discuss some of the cases I am studying now."

Tim smiled and said, "It will be my pleasure."

He would do anything to find out more about this lovely young woman who had taken possession of his heart.

They met at the Ritz Carlton hotel in Georgetown on South Street, for the first time she appeared happy. Her long, shiny hair was pulled back in an elegant ponytail that showed off her magnificently beautiful face. Her large brown eyes were clear, the traces of pain were no longer there. She was wearing brown suede jeans, a long tan-colored top, pink pearl earrings, and very little make-up.

He asked her how she was doing, and she said, "Just okay…but that's better than I have been."

Tim said, "I don't understand."

Paulina said, "Well, I understand how that might sound at this moment, but believe me when I say I have a lot going on right now." Suddenly, she looked very reflective. Tim was just not going to let her do that to him, not this time. He had flown from Texas just to have a drink with her.

The fact that he could not get her out of his head had something to do with him not wanting her to shut down. He was also very afraid that she would not want to stay for dinner. He wanted and needed to stay in her presence as long as he could.

Tim said, "Paulina, please don't get silent on me. We have a lot in common. For starters, our mothers know each other and are friends. You and I have met before, although you don't remember me. And I want you to know I was a grand gentleman that night."

He then turned very serious as he said, "Paulina, my mother was face down on the cobblestone driveway, and your mother helped her. For those reasons alone, we can speak freely with each other. Oh, and by the way, I loved your fudge." He smiled, and Paulina relaxed a little.

"Okay, my lady what would you like to drink."

Paulina smiled and said, "How about a glass of Pinot Noir."

He placed their drink orders, and they started to chat about law school. Paulina relaxed, Tim was great to talk too. After they finished their glass of wine, Tim said, "So tell me something more about your life Paulina. There has to be more than just studying and making delicious fudge."

She said, "Well, Timothy, since you are an attorney and very well trained at listening to people's problems, I have this friend who's having a major problem dealing with a family lie." Then she told him the story about her so-called friend who had found out she was adopted only after she went through some papers in her father's wall safe. She had found the papers by accident, and now she wanted nothing to do with her parents. But she still loved them very much, and she missed them greatly.

Tim knew at once whom she was speaking of. He also understood that sometimes telling the truth was painful, especially when it was wrapped up in so many emotions. So for that reason alone, he would go along with her game for now. He also wanted to get behind the sadness that he had seen before in her beautiful eyes.

He asked her questions, and she kept the conversation in the third person until she had told him everything.

Paulina was enjoying the ease that she felt with him. Now she noticed what Kimberly had said, he was drop-dead handsome and very well-groomed, and his manners were that of an older, very English gentleman. She wondered if he had attended a finishing school somewhere in Europe. She then asked him a question that he was not prepared to answer, "So tell me, Tim, why did you fly across several states to have this meeting with me?"

He liked her honesty and directness. Tim laughed and then looked deep into her eyes and said, "My dear young lady, you have stolen my heart, and I would like to get it back. And now I am hoping that you do or say something that will make it leave your possession and return to my chest."

Paulina laughed out loud. Tim was delightfully charming. She was enjoying herself for the first time in almost a year.

She leaned into him, telling him to come close. She needed to whisper something in his ear. He smiled and did as she asked.

Once she had his ear, she said, "Tim, I am a mess, a complete mess. So I give you your heart back." She then placed her hand on his chest and said, "Magic heart please return to Timothy Von Kinley's chest at once." She sat back in her seat and then asked, "Well, did you get your heart back?"

He put on a brokenhearted face and said, "Sadly, you have a bigger hold on it, and the only way it will return is if you will have dinner with me. And if you say no, I feel I shall never get my heart back again."

They both laughed. She said she was very hungry and that the chef there made the best burgers in town. She could never decide which one to order.

Tim said, "Not a problem. We can order one of everything and have a little taste test."

Paulina smiled and said, "Not sure if I'm that hungry, but it sounds like a delicious problem to have. Let's go for it."

They both smiled. Tim ordered for them both.

During dinner they talked about his mother and what she meant to Paulina. He had no idea that his mother had shown so much kindness to this young woman. He sometimes wondered where his mother found the time to do so much for so many people. She was always there for anyone who had a problem.

Paulina noticed that a sadness came over him when she mentioned his mother. She told him that Sadie would be okay, that God always takes care of angels, and Sadie was the most beautiful loving angel she had ever met. That seemed to lighten the heaviness that had come over him.

Then the waiter came to the table and asked if they wanted dessert. Tim looked at the array of dishes and wine glasses on the table. Then he looked at Paulina, and the two broke into a deep belly laugh.

Tim said, "Yes, but only if this lovely lady will join me."

Paulina suddenly realized that she didn't want the evening to end. She said, "Yes, I would love anything chocolate."

The chef prepared them a sampler plate of desserts, which they enjoyed with after-dinner drinks.

Finally, the evening came to an end. As they walked to the valet, Tim asked her if there was any place he could drop her off. She wondered how he knew she had taken a cab. Her car was in the shop and had not been returned to her.

She told him she would love a lift if it was no trouble and gave him her address. He drove her home and made sure she was safely inside. He thanked her for the opportunity to learn more about her and wished her a restful night's sleep. Just as he was about to walk away, Tiffany walked out the door, dressed in her finest club attire. Paulina was so embarrassed. Tim took it lightly. He said, "You only told me about one friend tonight. There has to be plenty of stories for our next dinner, and I am looking forward to hearing about this friend."

They both laughed. She introduced him to Tiffany, who told him she was heading downtown to a party and asked him if he was interested in coming with her. He answered as only a gentleman would saying, "I am sorry but I must regret your kind invitation. But I do hope you have a wonderful time." Then he bid them both a good night. He looked at Paulina and said, "Please be safe."

As he walked away, he suddenly felt very old. Maybe he was too mature for Paulina. Could Larry have been right when he warned him about the drama that seemed to follow Paulina?

Well, whatever it was, his heart wanted nothing more than for him to go running back down the hall, take her in his arms, and never let her go.

Chapter 64

Nancy and Salim were making some progress with their counseling sessions. Little by little, they were getting to the truth, unmasking demons and disappointments that had been building up for years. It was a gut-wrenching process that left them exhausted after each session. They both admitted that they wanted their marriage to work.

Salim said, "I can only work at this if there is a chance I can get my old Nancy back."

Nancy asked him, "What does that mean, your old Nancy?"

He answered, "The woman I married. The woman who wanted to be a wife and mother, not this community socialite that's more concerned about her picture in a damn magazine than about loving me."

Nancy fired back, "Well, I would like a husband who makes the time to make love to his wife and not fall asleep before she has gotten off of him. Do you think I can get that husband back? Well, do you? Doctor Perfect? *Well, do you?*"

Their sessions were heated, confirming several things which had broken down in their relationship. However, the counselor explained that sometimes it was the only way to find what was at the root of their problem.

Salim was angry with Nancy about not telling Paulina, but the counselor told him they were both at fault. They had to equally share the blame of hurting their daughter. She told him it was the father's job to protect, and he could have at any time stepped up and told Paulina himself. Throwing that burden on Nancy was simply a cop-out. Their difference about the secret of Paulina's true parentage was not the only thing wrong in their relationship and they both needed to face that fact.

Eventually Salim opened up about Nancy being so busy with her charity work. The gloves were off when that subject came up. Again, the counselor told Nancy and Salim they again were both to blame for this. They were blaming each other for what each of them was too afraid to face.

When Paulina was small Nancy wanted to stay home but as the years went by she put community projects ahead of their marriage and her family.

Salim had become addicted to the spotlight of being a national expert in the world of medicine, and he used his schedule to punish Nancy. The counselor asked Salim to tell Nancy what he really needed and expected out of their marriage.

Salim said, "Your disinterest in me hurt me greatly, you never seem to need me anymore. You quickly replaced me with community activities. I no longer feel like I am her main concern."

Nancy said, "I feel the same way about your demanding career."

The counselor asked Nancy to look outside of herself and try to see and feel things from Salim's side. She asked Salim to do the same. Believing that this was the only way either of them would be able to see what she saw, two people who still loved each other but were very stubborn, to the point of losing it all. If they really wanted their marriage to work, she needed them to want to work on a compromise.

Finally, Salim brought up the money that Nancy had made and never told him. She told him it was something that she and her sister Lynn had invested in. She said she'd never used that money for anything other than charitable donations.

She knew how much being a provider meant to Salim, so she wanted to reassure him that it was his money that she and Paulina lived on, not her foundation money.

The counselor asked her why. Nancy said that Salim was the provider and the head of their home. She only invested in the stock market for fun. She was surprised when she and Lynn made such great returns.

Salim was quiet. When the counselor asked why, he said, "Well, I wish you would have shared that with me, Nancy. Why do you keep secrets? I am very proud of you, but I don't understand you sometimes."

The counselor asked him why was he proud.

Fighting back tears, he said, "Nancy is the smartest woman that I know, and when she puts her mind to something, she can move heaven and hell to make it work."

Then the counselor asked them if they still loved each other, and they both said, "Yes, very much."

Nancy looked at Salim and said, "I have never loved anyone the way that I love you. But Salim, do you still love me the same way?"

Salim said, "It hurts me that you even have to ask me that. Yes, Nancy, I love you the same as I did when we got married."

They knew they had more work to do, but they were getting to the heart of it and starting to feel like they could make their marriage work.

Chapter 65

Paulina and Nancy met with Skip. As promised, he delivered all the information that Paulina wanted about her birth mother, including photos. Skip had made contact with Paula, and she didn't want to meet Paulina, but she did send a letter:

> Dear Paulina,
> I know this may be hard for you to understand, but please except that I was never your mother. I was just the vehicle God used to get you here. Nancy is and has always been your mother. You must forgive her for keeping this from you. She loves you too much to ever hurt you. Did she tell you that she took me to every doctor's appointment? She was there for the sonograms and the morning sickness, and she and Salim, your dear father, were there when you were born. They cut the cord, and it was her chest that you rested on, not mine. She gave you your first bottle, and she changed every diaper. I did them the favor of carrying you, but my dear girl, they are your parents—not me. Don't waste your precious time on this earth longing for what is right in front of you. Be thankful for the love you already have. You have your mother and your father. And they love you more than life itself.
>
> It is for this reason that I will not meet with you, and if you open your heart you will realize that we have nothing to discuss. You are already with your parents. I was never

a surrogate for anyone else but Nancy and Salim. You don't have any other brothers or sisters. And for the record, you look nothing like me. You look just like your Grandmother Hadid and your father.

Paulina, forgive them, love them, and move past this, because no one on this earth will ever love you as much as they do. You were named Paulina out of respect for the gift that I had given them: the Pau is from Paula, and the Lina is from Carolina, Nancy's mother's name. It represents the two roads that brought you into the world.

Love them and find the peace you need, and please allow me to live my life with my family. Paulina, Nancy is your mother. She always has been and she always will be.

Paula Crumbly

After she read the letter, Paulina broke down crying. She could not believe Paula would not meet with her, or that she wanted nothing to do with her.

Nancy said, "Oh baby, what does the letter say? Paulina, please tell me." Paulina handed the note to Nancy. She read it, and then she said, "Oh baby, I am so sorry."

Paulina said, "I need to be alone." She walked out of Skip's office that day, knowing she would never return. Nancy followed her, begging her to come home with her. Paulina said, "No, I just want to be alone now." She could not believe how hard it was to breathe. She opened the windows of her car, but she could not get enough air. She drove to the apartment. She needed someone to talk to. Tiffany was out on another date with some boy, so she just sat in the apartment and reread the letter, over and over again.

Around nine o'clock, her cell phone rang. It was Tim. He could tell something was wrong.

He gently asked her, "Is it about your friend with the adoption problem?"

She told him yes, but it was too much to talk about right now. She asked him how his mother was.

He told her she was doing much better, but there was still a lot of work to be done.

They talked for hours. Paulina found more comfort in her conversation with Tim than she had ever found with anyone. He told her he would be coming to town at the end of the week, and he wondered if they could have dinner together. She said, "Yes". So they made plans to meet on Friday evening.

Nancy called Paulina several times that evening to check up on her. Salim also called. They were very worried about her. Around midnight, she returned their calls and told them she just wanted some time alone.

Salim said, "What does that mean, Paulina?"

Paulina said, "I don't understand what any of this means. I don't know who I am anymore. Do you understand that? I just don't understand any of this right now."

Salim said, "I am sorry baby. One day I hope you will except that I love you."

Chapter 66

The next morning, Nancy turned on the morning news show. Winnie was reporting on a young woman who had been found in Rock Creek Park, beaten and raped.

The police would not release her identity until her family had been notified. It was the second incident of a young woman being found raped, beaten and left for dead.

Nancy called Paulina at once. Nancy kept her voice even and causal, "Hello Paulina, good morning, how are you feeling today. I know yesterday was rough on you. But everything the letter says is true."

Paulina didn't want to start her day feeling bad, and this telephone call from Nancy was making her want to cry. So she said, "I, just need some time."

Nancy quickly said, "I understand but if you want to talk I am here for you. Also I wanted to let you know that you received some mail the other day, and I was wondering if you would like me to bring it to you."

Paulina said, "Does it look important."

Nancy said, "I don't think so, but I will be in your neighborhood today and I can drop it off." Paulina thought for a minute, "No that's okay just drop it in the mail if you think it's important or I can pick it up the next time I come by."

Nancy was so grateful that Paulina sounded better she would have agreed to anything. "Okay I will leave it on the bakers rack in the kitchen."

Paulina agreed, "Sounds great."

Nancy said, "Okay darling have a good day."

Paulina quickly replied, "Yea, you do the same." With that they ended the brief call.

Now that she knew Paulina was okay, Nancy went about her daily activities, which always included sending food over to Paulina's apartment. Today she would have chef prepare a wonderful chicken and strawberry salad that she knew Paulina loved and a small lemon layer cake with thick lemon frosting. Sending food to Paulina's apartment gave Nancy a feeling of being part of her life. It helped Nancy deal with the loneliness and her constant feelings of guilt and failure.

Nancy had a busy day, with meetings with her financial planner, and then a quick dinner with Winnie later that evening. She was looking forward to catching up with Winnie, it was the break that she needed right now.

Chapter 67

Coco hadn't spoken to Saul since they'd returned home from New York. Her feelings for him were intense. Her longing for him was overpowering her senses. She wanted to run into his arms and tell him everything that she was feeling. But she couldn't risk rejection.

She was surprised when he sent her ten dozen roses. Each bouquet had a card with a sincere sentiment. One card read, "I miss you." Another read, "I am sorry." Others read, "Forgive me" and "Let's start over."

Coco was just not sure what to think about it all. She was uncertain of his real motives. Thinking to herself, *"Can I risk my heart again? Should I believe him? Does he really miss me or is he just horny?"*

Whatever his real motivation, Saul's floral apology had been on display for a full three days. She had fallen deeply in love with Saul. And the only thing she was certain of was that she really missed him.

Early one morning, her doorbell rang. When she looked out the window, all she could see were flowers. Thinking it was just another delivery, Coco opened the door. To her surprise, standing behind an enormous arrangement of spring blossoms, was Saul.

Her one and only fish face lover now looked more like her heart's anchor. He asked her if she would just give him a minute. He wanted to make her understand his feelings.

Saul had accepted the fact that he truly loved Coco. He no longer wanted just a sexual relationship with her. He wanted, and he needed a real grow old together kind of relationship. He didn't want her seeing other men. He wanted to be the only man she saw for the rest of their lives.

Seeing him standing there Coco was feeling so many emotions, but she was still uncertain. Should she listen to what he had to say? Or should she protect her heart and ask him to leave? She needed to know what had brought him to her door. She softly said, "Please come in."

As Saul stepped inside he looked around. Coco's house was decorated in soft hues, it was very elegant and there were no signs of another man. Saul had stood before major titans of business and world leaders, but never had he felt so overwhelmingly unprepared to present his case. His mouth was dry, and his hands were sweaty. He steadied himself and prayed for the strength to tell Coco how much he loved her. Just to be in her presence was all he needed.

Saul was never someone to beat around the bush. He believed in the direct approach to everything. So after she invited him to have a seat, he said, "Coco, I am sorry I hurt you. It was never my intent to do such a thing. Can you please forgive me?"

Coco knew that for Saul Baumann to drive out to Potomac, Maryland, and cover her house with flowers meant that he really had feelings for her, and she had him on the ropes.

She now would play her hand. So she said, "I am not sure if I can. You really cut me deeply. For the record, I no longer have any desire to be your sex toy."

He quickly responded, "Great, because I want so much more from you—from us."

Coco thought for a minute then responded, "Us? Really us. There was never an '*us*,' until New York. I loved that Saul. But when we got back home, you became demanding and you discarded me with your gift. I never asked you for a penny, and Saul Baumann, I am not your whore. Do you understand that? Coco is not a whore. Yes, we have played sexual games, and we both have enjoyed them. But your behavior was disrespectful, hurtful and most of all unacceptable. No, Saul, I am not sure if I can forgive you."

Saul got up from the chair, walked over to her, and gently wrapped his arms around her. As she smelled the scent of Cartier Roadster, she was overwhelmed by the strain of being without him. Now she realized without a doubt that this man was her future.

Coco started to cry. She wanted a forever kind of love with Saul. She no longer wanted to be alone.

Saul tilted her chin so that she looked directly at him as he said, "Coco my love I am not playing any games. Are you ready for a real relationship and everything that it means."

Coco said, "Yes, Saul I am and I have been for some time." Holding her as tight as he could, he gently and tenderly kissed her tears away.

He asked her to pack a bag and come with him. Or better yet, just come along with him. He would purchase her everything she needed, if that was okay with her. Coco could not speak through her tears.

After a minute she said, "Come with me, I need to get my make-up."

Saul didn't want to see the bedroom she had shared with another man so he said, "I will wait here for you."

Coco rushed up the stairs and packed an overnight bag, and called Anita and told her she would be out of town for a couple of days.

She locked up the house, and they went directly to the airport. Saul took her to his house in East Hampton, New York. Coco was overwhelmed at the splendor of the five bedroom home.

Once they had unpacked and were comfortable, Saul asked Coco again if she was truly ready for a life with him, and if she understood what being with him really meant?

Coco said, "What do you mean? I am not dating or seeing anyone else."

Saul said, "To be my woman, my life partner, my soul mate—whatever word or title fits best—you will have to sell any and everything that you have from your past relationship with Mike DeSalis. You have to sell your house and your car. I can never accept you keeping another man's gifts and being in my life, Coco that is what I mean."

Coco stood up, walked over to the sliding glass doors, looking out at the beautiful oceans waves. For several minutes there was silence, then she turned to Saul and said, "I will sell my house, car and every piece of clothing I own."

Saul smiled and said, "Well, you can re-decorate this house any way you would like. I want you to feel at home here. In fact my love you can re-decorate all of our homes."

Coco could not believe what he was saying she couldn't imagine being more in love with anyone. She walked over to him and wrapped her arms around him looking into his eyes she said, "Saul I love everything about this house, but most importantly I love you."

Saul answered her saying, "Coco I love you too."

They stayed there for two weeks, making passionate love—and making up for lost time.

As Coco got to know more about Saul's empire she was surprised that he owned four homes, and he wanted Coco to visit each one of them. He wanted Coco to be the lady of his houses, his life, and his bed. Coco had waited for so long for her happiness to arrive. Now she was afraid this was all a dream, she would no longer be the one longing for what she could never have, she would now be the head and not the tail.

Coco was making coffee on their last morning in the Hampton's. When Saul surprised her with a marriage proposal and a Van Cleef and Arpel fifteen-point-nine-carat ring, flanked on either side by pear-shaped diamonds, along with a prenuptial agreement. She signed the agreement without reading a word. Saul was impressed. Coco agreed to a quick, quiet wedding, and when she did, Saul carried her to the bedroom, they made love and talked about their new life together.

The next morning Saul and Coco applied for their marriage license and by the end of the week they were married in front of the justice of the peace in New York. Saul's secretary sent out announcements for the happy couple.

When they returned to the city Saul went back to work and Coco was busy making plans for their new living arrangements. She called Anita, "Hello Anita, I am back in town and guess what.... I am married."

Anita said, "I read it in the paper. I am so happy for you Ms. Coco, Mr. Saul will make you happy."

Coco agreed saying, "Oh Anita, he has already made me so very happy. Now I have to get to work. Can you meet me at the townhouse today?"

Coco wanted to let Saul know she respected his wishes and she also wanted to move forward with her new life.

When they met Coco caught Anita up on everything that had taken place, and then she gave Anita a long list of things that needed to be taken care of. Time was moving fast and Coco still had a great deal of things on her to-do list to complete.

She called Apple Transfers to arrange to have her furniture and antiques moved to a consignment shop in Germantown, Maryland. Next she called Washington Fine Properties and arranged a meeting to list the property for sale. After that she headed to the bank to place her jewelry in a safe deposit box.

Her next call was to Neiman Marcus Mazza Galleria. She said, "Hello would you please connect me with Andre in the couture salon. Hello Andre, it Coco Runni, oh I mean Coco Baumann. I am in need of a entire new wardrobe. When are you available to meet with me?" They scheduled an appointment for the following day. She repeated the same call to Saks Jandel's making an appointment with her sales lady for some serious shopping.

Feeling great that she was getting things completed Coco headed home. Saul had presented Coco with another house that would be their primary residence. In fact now she was the mistress of four homes, there was their primary residence, the lovely penthouse apartment at the Ritz Carlton in Georgetown, their weekend home in Middleburg, Virginia, their East Hampton, New York, home and their Palm Beach, Florida home. Just down the road from Sadie and Lonnie's Jewels.

Coco so wanted to hear what the girls thought of their broke friend now, her empire rivaled theirs, she wondered if she would still be considered the poor underling?

Nancy was the first to call with congratulations. Their marriage announcement had been printed in every social column on the east coast.

Nancy said, "Nice work, Coco you did it. You moved on with your life. I am proud of you. When life gives you lemons, you make lemonade. I wish you every minute of happiness." Nancy didn't personally know Saul, but she had heard about him. He was a very highly respected gentleman. Nancy thought this union was just what Coco needed.

Coco asked if anyone had heard from Sadie. Was there any more news of her condition? Nancy told her no, but she was sure that Sadie was getting the best care known to mankind.

Sarah Talcott was the next to send Coco congratulations. She was truly happy for her and offered to host a small luncheon in her honor when she returned from her honeymoon.

Winnie was next to call. She too congratulated Coco and wished her the best. Winnie was not sure about this marriage, but if it worked for Coco, she was just happy her friend would not be lonely anymore.

Every member of Saul's family called to congratulate them, the only person that Coco wanted to hear from was her sister. But Barbara never tried to reach Coco, it was just as it had always been. No one in Coco's family had ever really been happy for her, which made her even more grateful for the love, that she and Saul would share for the rest of their lives.

Coco and Saul left on a six-month honeymoon. Around the world on a five-star Crystal Cruise ship.

Chapter 68

Tiffany invited Paulina to a fundraising party on Capitol Hill for the new young congressman from Wisconsin. Paulina didn't want to go, but as usual Tiffany talked her into it. Paulina had not shared with Tiffany any details about Tim, but they had been spending a lot of time talking on the phone every night and texting each other. He was smart, funny and a great listener.

She somehow felt disloyal to him by going out with Tiffany. It was crazy because Tim hadn't made any moves on her, but she had developed feelings for him. She treasured their time together and didn't want to do anything that would seem unworthy of their friendship. The party was taking place at a roof top restaurant, even though it had just gotten started it was already overcrowded, the music was loud and there was no place to sit down or even enough space to get to the bar. After a few minutes Paulina lost Tiffany in the sea of well dressed people. Paulina felt a sense of deja vu, once again she was standing alone in a room full with strangers.

Paulina had enough of this scene. She walked out of the crowded affair making herself a promise that this would be the last time she would be attending any more parties with Tiffany. Once outside she sent Tiffany a text, "I am leaving...too crowded for me. See you back home." As she was contemplating walking a few blocks to Union Station where she was sure to catch a cab. A limo pulled up in front of her, as the window went down Paulina recognized Congressman Flank.

He said, "Hi, do you need a ride. I can drop you off somewhere? It's not a problem."

Paulina said, "Thank you but no, I will be okay. I am just trying to catch a cab."

He would not leave. He tried making small talk about how Washington, D.C., was the only place he knew that every night there was a party for someone or some cause. After a couple minutes he said, "Look this is a busy night and I am in this big car all alone. You will be safe with me. Let me give you a lift home."

Paulina looked around and there were no available cabs, so against her better judgment, she got into his limo. As soon as she was seated and the limo started moving he closed the window that divided the front and back seats and locked the doors. He offered her a drink, when she refused that he offered her some cocaine. When she told him she didn't do coke he said, "Hell, why not! Everyone else does. I am sure all of your friends do it." He then sniffed a line of coke, and within seconds his personality changed.

She told him that he could stop the car at the next light. She could catch a cab in front of Union Station. But the car drove past the stop and turned onto a side street off of New Jersey Avenue and then made another turn onto "E" Street. The congressman told the driver to park, take a walk but not to be too long. He wanted to speak with the lady alone.

Paulina said, "Oh, really I don't think we have anything to talk about, how about I just get out here and you and your driver can go to wherever you were going."

Flank said, "Well now when a congressman tells you he wants to talk to you, guess what, you listen. You know what you are very pretty, and very hot."

Paulina said, "No, I am not, but I really need to be getting out of here, so how about I just say good night, now can you please unlock this door."

Flank sharply responded, "You leave when I tell you to leave."

Paulina said, "You are a congressman you really shouldn't be acting like this, taking drugs and holding me in your car when I have asked you I want out. Now really I have to go, unlock this damn door... now."

Paulina tried to open the car door again, but it would not open. The hairs on the back of her neck were standing up. She knew she had to get the hell out of his car. The Congressman started to lean towards her. She was not going to take any shit off of him even if it meant she would have to fight for her freedom. When he tried to kiss her, she pushed him away, but it seemed to turn him on.

He said, "Oh, you like to play games, do you?" Then he hit Paulina so hard that she saw stars and tasted blood. Paulina looked around for something to hit him with. Before she could do anything he was on her, so she started hitting him with her purse, but that was not enough, she needed a weapon.

He was on top of her, pulling at her clothes and trying to push her legs apart. She was fighting him with everything she had but the little congressional monkey was stronger than she was.

Paulina struggled and maneuvered her body so that she could reach between them. When she finally found his balls she pulled with one hand as hard as she could. When he loosened his grip on her, she kneed him right in the family jewels as hard as she could. He yelled out and rolled over in pain. She tried to make a break for it, reaching for the door handle, but he recovered quickly, and this time he was mad as hell. He grabbed her by the hair and hit her across the face.

She knew if she didn't find something to hit him with, he was going to rape her. From the corner of her eye, she saw the ice bucket. She grabbed it and hit him with all her might. He fell back. Then she pushed a button, and the doors unlocked. As she was pushing the door open, he grabbed her ankle. She kicked him in the face and ran as fast as she could. Screaming "Help me somebody please help me."

She heard a voice calling for her to come. "Hey little lady come over here." It was an older gentleman. He had just parked his cab on the side street and was taking a break playing with his camera. He had seen the limo rocking back and forth. He said, "I saw that car rocking, but I don't get involved in people's business, I knew something was wrong."

Just as Paulina was getting into the cab, the congressman opened the limo door. He yelled, "I am not finished with you, bitch!" His driver heard what was happening and ran back to the limo.

Then he told his driver, "Get me the hell out of here."

Paulina fell into the back seat of the cab and pressed the lock button several times. The cab driver could see that she had been hurt. He said, "Good lord little lady, you been fighting. Do you need to go to the hospital." He passed her a box of tissues as she took the box, her body began to tremor. Paulina didn't know where to go. She was shaking all over, and her mouth was bleeding. She didn't want to go to the apartment.

Paulina said, "No, but can you take me to 2329 "S" Street, North West." He said, "Yes, I will take you anywhere but I think the police station or the hospital would be best."

Once she reached home, she realized that she had left her handbag in the back seat of the limo, so she couldn't pay the driver. She asked him to please wait there, while she ran into the house to get some money to pay him.

He said "No, I wouldn't take a penny from you. I just want you to be safe and go to the doctor. And please stay away from the man in the limo."

She started to cry and thanked him. As he drove off, she walked around to the back of the house. She knew the codes so she was able to get in the gates, and as luck would have it, Nancy was up when she knocked on the back door.

Nancy yelled, "What happened to you, Paulina? Oh dear God, you are hurt!"

Paulina was so happy to see her mother that she just started crying and told her that she had gone to a party with Tiffany, who left her, and she had been mugged after the party. She didn't think Nancy needed to know the entire story.

Nancy helped her upstairs into her old bedroom. Paulina needed something for pain. Her face was hurting. But she could not shake the fact that she had left her purse with her ID, he would know exactly where to look for her, and the thought terrified Paulina. She asked Nancy to please cancel her debit card and her Amex card.

Paulina quickly showered, she needed to wash off the smell and the feel of that son-of-bitch Flank. Afterwards she changed into some old clothes that she had left behind when she moved out. Nancy made her a cold compress for her face and gave her an ointment made from witch hazel, fresh mint, and aloe vera. She told Paulina to put it on her face. It would help with the bruising. Nancy begged her to let her take her to the hospital.

Paulina was firm. She didn't want to go to the hospital, "No, I just want to stay here with you if that is okay."

Nancy quickly replied, "Of course darling this will always be your home, but I think you need to get checked out. Paulina where did this happen, we need to call the Police, do you know who attacked you?"

Paulina said, "It all happened so fast. I don't know why this happened to me, I was just trying to get a ride back to the condo, I can't talk about it anymore please... please."

Nancy was very concerned. She could tell that Paulina was hiding something, "Okay sweetie calm down, you are okay, you're safe now. Do you need anything else."

Paulina hugged her and whispered, "Yes, I need my mother. I need you. Can you please be my mother again?"

Nancy smiled and answered as only a mother would, "I have always been your mother."

Paulina was so shaken up that she was afraid to be alone in her own room. She asked Nancy if she would please stay with her until she fell asleep.

Nancy asked her about Tiffany, and what kind of party they had gone to. Paulina said, "I am really pissed with Tiff, and that is the last time I will go to any party with her, she just left me and went off with some guy." Nancy and Paulina talked for a while until Paulina started to fall asleep.

When morning came, Paulina was in pain. She had bruises and a swollen lip, but she still refused to go to a doctor, the emergency room, or the police station.

Nancy felt like she was only getting part of the story, but she was afraid to push her anymore. She feared Paulina would take off if she applied any more pressure. So far all Paulina had asked her for was a ride to the store to get a new cell phone.

When they were in the car heading to the Apple store in Georgetown, Paulina said, "If it's okay with you, I would like to come back home. I can't deal with Tiffany right now."

Nancy said, "Anything you need, baby. Now, are you sure about the doctor?"

Paulina firmly said, "Yes, yes I am sure." Nancy tried to ask more questions, but Paulina didn't want to talk about it. As they walked through the Apple store Nancy watched Paulina's every move. She wanted to see if Paulina recognized anyone of the young people that were crowded into the store.

After about two hours of shopping. Nancy and Paulina picked up a new cell phone and canceled the service on the old one. Tim had called and texted her several times. He was worried about her. He was due to come into town on Friday. She didn't want to break their date, so she asked Nancy if she thought make-up would be able to cover up her bruises.

The two women talked a lot on the ride home. Nancy said, "Paulina, would you please allow me to take you to the police station? We don't want something like this to happen to another young woman, and it will if you don't help the police find this crazed man."

Paulina's eyes filled with tears. "I never should have gone out with Tiffany. I just want this whole mess to be over with."

Nancy said, "Oh baby. I don't know Tiffany that well, but I have been so afraid for both of you. There is a madman out there beating and raping young women. As bad as this is, it could have been so much worse. I am grateful that you were only robbed. We can get money back, but we cannot get another *you* back."

Paulina just looked out the window the remainder of the ride. Her mind was racing. Should she go to the police and tell the world what kind of creepy, cokehead Congressman Flack really was? He was one sick motherfucker, for sure, but Paulina didn't want any attention placed on her, she also couldn't stand the thought of having to defend herself in front of the press. If she had never gone to that damn party with Tiffany none of this would have happened.

As soon as they returned home, Nancy had the butler go to the apartment on New Mexico Avenue and bring some of Paulina's things home. She needed her computer, all of her schoolwork, and some of her clothes, along with her personal items.

As Paulina settled back into her old room, Tiffany called and asked if she could please come by.

Paulina said, "No, Tiff. I am sorry, but you are the last person I want to see right now."

Tiffany was clueless. "Pauly, what happened to you? Why are you being so uptight with me?"

Paulina charged in, saying, "Tiff, you party too damn much, and because of you, I got my ass beat last night by that fucking creep. And by the way, I am never moving back in with you again."

Tiffany was about to ask Paulina what creep she was talking about when Paulina ended the call. When Tiffany called back, Paulina would not answer.

Tiffany was at a lost as to what the hell happened. All she knew was that Paulina was being a high-drama bitch. She thought that she and Paulina were close, and Paulina's rejection really hurt. But in usual Tiffany fashion she just brushed off the hurt and said, "Next…I will find someone else to be my roomy."

Paulina was beyond pissed off. She thought if Tiffany wanted to party every night, that was one thing, but this was the second time that she had almost been raped—and it would be the last.

When her phone rang again it was Tim. She calmed herself and answered sweetly.

Tim felt much better when he heard Paulina's voice, but again he could tell something was wrong. He began to think that maybe Larry had been right, Paulina had a lot going on in her life. And Tim couldn't handle a high-drama woman. He just wanted someone that needed the same things out of life that he did.

He told her that he was looking forward to seeing her on Saturday. She said she had been looking forward to it as well. Tim wanted to spend some time with his family during the weekend but he had planned some time with Paulina as well.

On Saturday evening they met for dinner, and although Paulina tried to cover up the bruises, you could still see them.

Tim immediately knew she had been hurt. He took her thin body into his arms and held her as tight as possible. Saying, "Paulina, what happened? Who did this to you?"

Paulina felt safer than she had in weeks. Trying to sound stronger than she was she said, "The other guy looks worst. I was mugged leaving an event on Tuesday evening, I am okay and I will tell you everything over dinner."

When they were seated Paulina started to talk, everything just spilled out. She told him everything about the adoption, how she felt about Tiffany being a party girl, about being mugged and fighting back, and finally she spoke about the letter from her surrogate mother."

Tim said, "My, that is more than most people experience in a lifetime."

Something about Paulina's story was not sitting well with him, he could tell that she was trying to protect someone. He then questioned her about not filing a police report.

Tim bluntly asked, "Paulina why didn't you report this to the police."

Paulina thought Tim would sense her dishonesty if she told him anything but the truth, but as she explained the events that had taken place, she only told him a partial truth.

"Tim, it all happened so fast. I started running as fast as I could and jumped into the first cab that I saw. I told the driver to get me out of there. When I was safe, I just wanted to have the whole ugly thing behind me."

She told him she had moved out of the apartment and was now living back with her parents.

Tim told her he thought that was the best plan for now. As she talked he stared at her wondering if anything would make him walk away from this beautiful mess of a woman. He was already feeling torn, part of him thought he should wish her well and walk out of her life, however there was a part of him that wanted to love her and keep her safe. He had felt that way since he first saw her.

Instinctually Tim knew that he could not find the inner-strength to walk away because he was falling in love with Paulina. So he simply told her that they would work through each problem together.

As they enjoyed their dinner the conversation changed to a subject that interested them both legal cases. Tim talked about some new Supreme Court cases that they were both interested in. When dinner was over they took a late night stroll around the White House and over to the Washington Monument. Tim gently held Paulina's hand wanting to protect her from anything or anyone that may harm her. They were both sad when the date came to an end. Paulina drove herself home, and Tim called her later to make sure she was home and safe.

They enjoyed a lovely weekend filled with all the things they enjoyed and long walks along the city. On Sunday Tim took her to dinner at Blue Duck Tavern where they enjoyed a wonderful dinner of Chesapeake Bay crab cakes. The weekend went by fast and Tim and Paulina hated to see it come to an end. As they said sweet goodbye's Tim said, "I am almost afraid to leave you, I could not take something else happening to you my love."

Those were the sweetest words Paulina had heard, as she reached up to softly kiss him goodnight. She said, "Nothing bad will happen to me I have you to protect me." They kissed more passionately then. Within minutes they were outside of the Hadid house. Paulina said she wanted to say goodbye there and wished him a safe flight back to Texas.

He called her the next morning just to say hello. She had started to look forward to his morning and late-night calls, in which he always wished her a great day or sweet dreams.

Things between Paulina and her parents were getting better. They were still seeing the family therapist and Paulina was working through her mother issues, and finding peace with the outcome.

One evening when Paulina was in her room studying, Nancy knocked on her door. She just wanted to know how she was doing and if she was interested in going out to the movies.

Paulina jokingly said, "Let me guess…the new Brad Pitt movie, right? And Winnie is going with you? You two are true Brad Pitt fans."

Nancy said, "Oh, how well you know me." Then they both laughed.

Paulina asked her if she had a minute, and of course she did. She had as long as Paulina needed.

Paulina asked her to sit down. She handed her the letter that Paula had written to her. Nancy read the letter again, then she said, "Darling, every word in this letter is true. How does it make you feel? I know we hurt you...I hurt you, and for that I will be forever sorry. But please understand that I never meant to. It was selfish of me. I just never wanted you to think of anyone but me as your mother, because I could never think of you as anything other than a part of me."

Nancy told her that not for a minute since she'd found out that Paula was carrying her did she not love her, and there was nothing in the world that could break that love. She said, "A mother's love is stronger than anything in the world."

Paulina thanked her. She told her to please put the letter away with the adoption papers. She no longer needed to read or see it again. Then she told Nancy she needed to get back to her studies, and she hoped she and Winnie would have fun at the movies. She would be there when Nancy returned.

Nancy said, "If it's not asking too much, could I please give you a hug."

Paulina, said, "I would love that."

The two women shared a mother-daughter moment.

Paulina smiled and said, "Do I smell what I think? Chef is baking, and it smells like cookies."

Nancy said, "We are all celebrating you being home."

Paulina said, "Oh no, I will not be able to study with that wonderful smell in the air. Chef makes the best cookies in the world."

Nancy quickly said, "Well, you know he uses our recipes."

They both laughed.

Nancy said, "How about we meet down in the kitchen when I come back from the movies, and you and I can have some cookies and ice cream?"

Paulina said, "It's a date."

Nancy wished her good luck with her studies and left the room. She went to her room to get ready for the movies. She called Winnie and told her it would just be the two of them. Nancy was so happy that Paulina was making peace with herself and finding a way to forgive her. Nancy dressed and was heading down the stairs when she heard Paulina on the phone. Her voice was raised; she sounded upset. Nancy poked her head in the room and saw Paulina was in tears. She asked, "What's happened."

Paulina said, "It's about my friend, Tiffany. She was raped, robbed, and beaten, sometime today. She's in Georgetown Hospital. I need to go to her. I was afraid something like this would happen. Maybe I should have never left her alone in the apartment."

Nancy told her that she would cancel the movie with Winnie and take her to the hospital.

Paulina thanked her, she was glad to have Nancy by her side.

When they arrived, Tiffany was in very bad shape. She had taken a brutal beating. Her eyes were swollen almost closed, and her front teeth were missing. Because of the brutal rape, she needed immediate surgery. Tiffany had been repeatedly sodomized, and she'd lost a lot of blood. Paulina could not believe how badly Tiffany looked; she was almost unrecognizable.

The police wanted to speak with Tiffany, but in her condition she was unable to tell them anything. The doorman had called the ambulance after a neighbor found Tiffany collapsed in the hallway. The apartment doorman had called Paulina.

The officers wanted to question Paulina, Nancy asked if she could be present. The officer said, "Yes as long as you do not interfere." The officer asked Paulina, "Do you know if Tiffany has any enemies? Who would do this to her?" Paulina said, "I don't know what you mean by enemies? But if you're asking me about Tiffany's male friends. Tiffany sees a lot of guys and she parties a lot it could be anyone. I am sorry officers, I can't think of anyone who would have done this."

Nancy was about to say something when Paulina squeezed her hand as hard as she could. Nancy knew how frightened Paulina was, so she just put her arms around her.

"Officer, my daughter has told you everything that she knows. Can you please give us some time together?" asked Nancy.

After the police left, Nancy said, "Paulina, this is crazy. Who are you protecting and why? This could have been you, Paulina. If you know something, please tell the police. Let's get this monster off the streets."

Paulina just looked down at the floor. She said, " I know it could have been me. Oh my God poor Tiffany."

Nancy said, "What do you mean it could have been you. Damn-it Paulina what are you not telling me? And Why?"

Paulina said, "I don't know who did this, really I don't know."

As Paulina started to cry, Nancy hugged her and said that they would get through this.

Tiffany's parents hadn't arrived, so Nancy and Paulina stayed with her until her mother finally showed up. Tiffany's mother appeared unconcerned and somewhat angry with Tiffany. She complained that this turn of events had interrupted her vacation.

Nancy could not believe what she had just heard. She said, "To hell with your vacation! Your daughter needs you. She has just been through a hell of an ordeal, and all you can say is something about your fucking vacation? Lady, it's women like you that give mothers a bad name."

Paulina was so proud of Nancy—she was suddenly ashamed that she ever doubted Nancy as her mother.

Nancy promised Tiffany that she would come to see her everyday but if she needed anything to please call the house. Nancy had served on the board of the hospital, so she used her influence to make additional arrangements to ensure that Tiffany received the best care possible.

When they walked out of the room, Paulina took Nancy's hand, and they walked out of hospital together. Paulina thought, *"Maybe I should tell her that I think Congressman Flank did this to Tiffany. But I know my Mother she will have every television reporter and camera telling the story. She will not stop until justice is served and she is not above using the court of public opinion to nail Flank to the cross. But I can't handle the media making me out to be some wanna- be slut. No the best plan is to keep quiet. I am sorry about Tiffany. Damn what should I do. I don't want anyone to know that I was so stupid as to get in that freaks car and what if Tim finds out, I can tell that he already does not believe my story. Now he will know that I lied to him. I can't let that happen. Oh, Tiffany I am so sorry."*

On the ride back home, Paulina didn't say much, which confirmed Nancy's suspicion that Paulina may have known the attacker. Throughout the night Nancy called to check up on Tiffany. She was stable, and things were looking better for the young woman. Nancy also checked on Paulina. Around midnight, Salim came home. He was tired, but when Nancy filled him in on what had happened.

He said, "This is a father's worst nightmare." He picked up his phone, sent a text message to his secretary, and told her to clear his calendar for the rest of the week. His family needed him.

Nancy was so proud that he was willing to meet their needs, and put them first.

Tim called Paulina and asked her if she would be interested in accompanying him to a charitable event in East Hampton, New York. He knew the timing was bad, but he also felt that when Paulina was with him he could keep her safe. He told her they would be staying at his family's home in Water Mill. She agreed, and he made all of the arrangements.

Over breakfast Paulina said, "This is the worst possible timing, but I need to go with a friend to the Hampton's just for the weekend. Not to worry I will be safe. But I need you to look in on Tiffany for me please. I will be back before you can miss me."

Salim said, "Your friend has just been attacked and you are going away for the weekend? Paulina I want to trust your judgment but the timing as you just said is bad. But you are an adult now so I can't tell you not to go."

Nancy said, "I will look after Tiffany will you be back by Sunday? I think if she is stable they will more than likely be discharging her soon."

Salim said, "Can I ask who are you going with and where will you be staying? I am just a little overprotective right now. I hope you understand."

Paulina did understand but she was not willing to telling them anything about Timothy just yet.

Salim asked her a few questions about Tiffany. Paulina became noticeably shaken. Salim asked her if she knew who had hurt her friend. Paulina said she didn't and she confessed about the night that she fought two guys.

Salim said, "Well, I am glad you were there and neither of you got hurt that day. Paulina, I am sorry that this happened and that I was not there to protect you and Tiffany."

Paulina said, "Oh Dad, you were there! I used your golf club to fight them off. I think I may have a future on the links if this legal thing doesn't work out." She smiled at him and reached out and took his hand.

Salim could not hide his tears. He said, "Your my child no matter how old you get and I can't help it I worry about you."

Paulina said, "I will be fine, but please look after Tiffany."

Tim arrived in Washington on Thursday afternoon. He picked Paulina up from her home. She made an extra effort to slip out of the house before Tim could have a meet-and-greet with Nancy. But Salim was watching from the bedroom window. He saw Tim Von Kinley and immediately he felt better, he knew that Paulina would be safe on her trip.

Tim had arranged to use his family's private plane to take them to the Hamptons. Paulina and Tim never seemed to run out of things to say to each other. They laughed at each other's jokes, and they talked the entire flight. He asked about her family, and she brought him up-to-date. She asked about Sadie, and he told her she was much better, but it would still be some time before she was ready to return home. Being with Tim allowed Paulina to forget about her troubles and when she was with him she didn't feel afraid. Pushing the thoughts of her attack and the attack on Tiffany out of her head if only for a couple of days.

Felix had a member of the staff prepare the Hampton property for young Mr. Von Kinley's visit. Felix suspected it would be a female guest, so he placed lots of flowers throughout the house and all the things that a lady guest might possibly need for a long weekend.

They had a quiet dinner the first night, and the next day they attended several events. Paulina thought, *"I have never felt like this before. I am happier than I have ever been in my entire life."* Every minute with Tim was a delightful experience. He thought of everything, which made it easy being with him. They stayed up all night, just talking about their families, what mattered most to them, the kind of partner they wanted to share their lives with, their favorite foods and music, and their favorite time of year. They took late night walks on the beach and watched the moons' reflection on the ocean.

On their second night Tim cooked dinner for Paulina, lobster BLT's and corn on the cob it was a perfect evening and when he walked her to her bedroom door, she turned and kissed him. He responded and before they knew it they were undressing each other with a feverish hunger. The feeling had been building up the entire trip. They had waited long enough. She wanted Tim more than the air she was breathing and he felt the same. They made love all night, and the next morning started the day the same way. Paulina was completely open to him, her heart, her mind, and her body. Tim was worried that maybe they had taken the next step too soon, but he had no regrets, he was happy. It was the beginning of a new life, and he felt for sure that they were in it for the long haul.

Chapter 69

Winnie received a special-delivery package from Vince Payne, the elderly cab driver that she had helped. Inside the package was a note that read:

> Ms. Winnie,
> I don't know if this will be of interest to you but please watch this tape. I saw this cat on television talking about how he was in love and planning his wedding to some rich girl, but he was not acting in love the other night. I used my new video recording camera. The pictures are not too bad. Take a look-see...
> I hope this helps you break a story,
> Vince Payne

The first few minutes of the video were just a limo rocking back and forth. She had no idea what kind of story he expected her to get from this footage. Just as she was about to give up and trash the tape, the limo door opened. She could clearly see Congressman Flank fighting with a young woman and pulling her back into the limo. The door was open just long enough for the camera to catch a glimpse of his unzipped pants, and his fully displayed penis.

Winnie looked at the video several times. There was something very familiar about the young woman. When she enlarged the frames, she recognized Paulina Hadid, she was hurt and bleeding.

Winnie said, "What the hell? Oh my God, what has happened to this poor child?" Winnie thought, *"If I use this tape, I will have to show Paulina, and that would hurt Nancy and Salim. But if I don't, the congressman will be getting off the hook for assault. That would be giving him a pass to possibly hurt another young woman."*

The first thing she needed to do was make sure there were no other copies of this tape. She placed a call to Mr. Payne, after thanking him for the tape, she asked several questions about what he witnessed that evening.

He gave her all the details, including the address where he had dropped the injured girl off, Winnie knew it was Nancy's home. She asked Mr. Payne to promise her that he would not tell this story to anyone else, and she meant no one. He said his word was his bond, and he again thanked her for everything she had done for him and his family.

Winnie took the video home and watched it again. There was no way to tell this story and protect Paulina at the same time. The story would rock Congressman Flank, and possibly get him kicked out of Congress. It was clear he had every intention of raping Paulina. Who knew how many times he may have tried this with other young woman and gotten away with it? He needed to be stopped.

Winnie called Nancy and gave her an update on Sadie, and then casually asked about Paulina. Nancy said Paulina was okay, and that she should be getting back into town soon. She was away for the weekend with a friend.

She also told Winnie that she was worried because Paulina had been mugged recently. She told her everything about that evening that she knew. Winnie asked a few more questions, her answers filled in the missing pieces to the video puzzle.

Paulina had attended a fundraiser and had gotten left behind by her roommate. Flank offered her a ride home and had the car parked on E Street, where he assaulted Paulina. She needed to speak with Paulina, but she knew how protective Nancy was of her, speaking with Paulina would not be easy.

Paulina had just returned from her weekend with Tim. Nancy asked her if she wanted to go to the hospital and visit Tiffany. Paulina said she would, so they headed out. When they arrived, Tiffany was all alone. It looked like they were the only people visiting her.

Nancy sent Paulina down to the cafeteria to get some frozen yogurt. When Paulina was gone, Nancy asked Tiffany who did this to her. Tiffany became very anxious. Nancy assured her that no one would know; it would be between the two of them.

Tiffany just started shaking, and she asked Nancy to please get her out of the hospital before the person came back and finished her off. Nancy asked her who she meant. Tiffany begged Nancy to please get her out now. She said, "They are watching me, and they will come back here and kill me. Don't you understand? I am not safe here."

Nancy said she would not allow anything to happen to her, but she needed to tell her the truth. Tiffany said she was too afraid.

Nancy calmly said, "Tiffany, to help you I need to know the truth. Who are you so afraid of? And where are your parents?

Tiffany quietly answered, "I don't know who did this, but please I beg you help me get out of here. My parents gave me a stack of cash, my mother arranged for me to get new dental implants. And then she told me to handle the rest of it. She and my Father left for a trip to China."

Nancy was in shock, she had never heard of such neglect. She looked at Tiffany and said, "What, what are you saying? I can't believe this. Yes Tiffany I will help you."

Then she said, "Tiffany the police have questioned you but you have denied knowing anything, but sweetheart I know that you have to remember something about this monster."

When Paulina walked back into the room, she could tell something had happened.

Tiffany started crying and asked Nancy and Paulina to please get her out of the hospital. She could not go back to the apartment, because he had keys—and he was powerful. She said, "I am sure he will kill me next time."

Nancy called the doctors and asked if Tiffany could be discharged in her care. The doctor agreed. So Paulina, Tiffany, and Nancy left the hospital together.

Tiffany was happy and thankful. For the first time since the attack, she felt somewhat safe. But Paulina was not feeling safe at all. Having Tiffany this close to her again was giving her a feeling of complete anxiety.

Nancy noticed the change in Paulina and thought it best to have Tiffany stay in a room on the fourth-floor guest wing of the house. That way Paulina would not have to see her every time she came or went to her room. Nancy assured Paulina that Tiffany would only be with them until she could figure something out.

Salim was attending a lecture in Chicago, and was not expected home until the end of the week. Nancy called to tell him that Tiffany was now a guest in their home. Salim was glad she was with them but as a precaution he increased security around the house.

As soon as Tiffany was in her new room, she fell fast asleep. Nancy placed a call to Winnie. She told her she sensed something majorly wrong with this situation. She repeated what Tiffany had said to her about someone coming to finish her off.

Winnie said, "We need to get into the apartment."

Nancy said, "Do you think we can, there are police there now, it's a crime scene."

Winnie thought quickly, "We can try. If I have to I will use my press credentials. Whatever we do we will have to move fast. Nancy we have to find out who did this."

Nancy agreed saying, "Winnie, I will do anything to find out who did this. But I don't understand why the police haven't found something to go on yet? The building has security and is normally a very safe place."

Winnie said, "Nancy this is no random act, this monster knows what he is doing, which makes him even more dangerous." Winnie asked Nancy if she had left a forwarding address with the hospital. She said she had. Winnie quickly told Nancy to increase her security until they found out something. Nancy said, "Salim has already taken care of that."

Winnie asked Nancy to keep quiet about where she was going. If anyone asked to just say she had to run an errand and meet her on New Mexico Avenue in twenty minutes."

Nancy did as instructed. She wanted to find answers to her questions and if Winnie could provide some insight Nancy was ready, willing and able to do whatever she had to.

Nancy used her parking pass to gain access to the garage and the two used the building elevator as not to attract attention from the doorman and front desk staff.

Winnie said, "Nancy if there are detectives in the apartment, we will have to leave."

Nancy answered, " Well, I hope luck is with us Tiffany needs some clothes and some of her personal items. I hope we can get everything in these two bags."

There were no police or detectives in sight, Nancy used her key to get in the apartment. The place was in shambles, it was clear that Tiffany had put up a major fight. Nancy said, "Oh my GOD, this place is a mess."

Winnie said, "Will you be able to handle the packing? The police could come back here any minute."

Nancy quickly started packing Tiffany's personal items along with her enormous collection of makeup. Winnie packed some of the young woman's clothes and shoes then moved into the other room to look around for any clues that may have been left behind by the perpetrator.

Nancy had packed as much as the bags could hold and she placed them close to the front door. She looked around again and then she said, "It feels so creepy to be in here, I have as much as these bags can hold. Let's get going, oh Winnie can you grab that orchid plant and then we can go."

As they were about to leave, Winnie noticed something when she picked up the plant. She used a napkin to dig it out of the soil. It was a cuff link engraved with the image of the US Capital. Winnie knew this could be a valuable clue that was missed by the police, so she carefully wrapped it and placed it in her handbag.

As they headed back down to the garage. Winnie said, "Nancy please be careful. If I am right, sending someone to kill Tiffany would not be a problem for this person."

The hair on the back of Nancy's neck stood up. She said, "Winnie, do you know who did this? Can we call the police now and tell them about your suspicions? It may be a great lead."

Winnie said, "I am not sure. I don't have enough evidence but I am working on something. Whoever did this to Tiffany was a professional, there are surveillance cameras in the garage and in front of the elevators and the police have said that at the time of Tiffany's attack the camera and security system had been broken. That lets me know that this is a pro. For now, I just want you, Tiffany and Paulina to be very careful."

Nancy asked Winnie if she should take Paulina and Tiffany and leave the city for a while. Winnie told her that may be a good idea. But that whatever she did to please be careful and keep her alarm on.

Winnie said, "Nancy please inform your staff to be careful and not let anyone outside of your household know that Tiffany is staying with you."

Nancy was shaken. When she got home, Paulina startled her, and she almost jumped out of her clothes. Paulina noticed her fright and asked what was going on. Had something else happened? Nancy told her that she needed to speak with her and Tiffany now.

When they went to Tiffany's room, they found her resting, she looked much better. She appeared much calmer and she thanked them both again for their hospitality in welcoming her into their home. Nancy told her she just wanted her to be safe, but then she asked her, "Tiffany are you sure you still have no memory of your attacker?"

Tiffany's face became as white as a ghost. She said, "I don't know. It happened so fast, all I can remember is the smell of his cologne. He was wearing Clive Christian X for Men. He smelled woody, and his breath was hot. He wanted more than sex. He wanted to hurt someone, this could have happened to any woman in his path, I was just the unlucky one."

Nancy said, "Young men don't wear Clive Christian X. This guy is over forty, that's for sure. What kind of random rapist wears five-hundred-dollar cologne? How do you know it was Clive Christian?"

Tiffany said, "My lawyer wears it. I buy it for him every Christmas."

Paulina said, "Was it your lawyer who did this to you?"

Tiffany said, "No, he is too old to move that fast."

Then Nancy looked at Tiffany and said, "Okay, young lady, let me give you some hard facts. Whoever did this to you may well come back and try to finish you off. I need to get you to a safe place, unfortunately I don't believe this house is safe enough."

Paulina said, "What do you mean? We might not be safe?"

Nancy told them everything that she knew, and when she finished, Paulina had a clear picture and heightened concern about getting involved with this.

Whenever she was with Tiffany, some shit was sure to happen. Now she had put her family at risk.

Paulina said, "Tiffany, can you call your parents and go to the Orient with them?"

Tiffany started to cry. Then she said, "Pauly, when will you believe me when I tell you that I don't have parents like yours. My parents don't want me around. Your parents love you. Even your parents' *friends* love you. Someone calls you every day to check up on you. No one calls for me."

Paulina quickly said, "Someone is always calling your cell."

Tiffany said, "Yeah, for me to come to a party, or well…you know what."

Paulina said, "I told you to stop the partying, Tiff, that someday something would happen to you. But I never thought it would be this bad. I am sorry you got hurt. I am so sorry I was not there to protect you…I am just so sorry for all of this."

Paulina went over to Tiffany to console her. She wanted Tiffany safe. Just not in her house.

Tiffany said, "Pauly, I was at the apartment when this happened. I woke up and he was just standing in the doorway. When I told him to get out, he said he was there to teach me a lesson, and what I would have to do before he got out. And then he started in on me. It all happened so fast. I tried to fight him, but he hit me so hard, and then he hit me with something it felt like my head had been split open. I could hear my clothes being ripped off of me, but I could not move any part of my body to help myself."

Nancy, Paulina, and Tiffany were all crying. Nancy went to Tiffany and hugged her. She made her a promise that she would get her to someplace safe.

Nancy asked her if there was anyone in her family she was close to, and Tiffany said she had an aunt in England that she loved, her name was Catherine Ladden, she was her mother's sister. Tiffany explained that she had not seen her for several years. Nancy asked her for the aunt's telephone number. It took several hours but Nancy found Tiffany's aunt. Nancy explained Tiffany's situation and her condition, and Catherine was shocked. She explained that she would do whatever was necessary to help her niece. Nancy didn't want the lady to be upset when she saw her niece. Together they made arrangements for Tiffany to fly to London and stay with her.

Nancy and Paulina would accompany Tiffany and stay over for a few days to spend some time with Lynn. Paulina loved her Auntie Lynn so much. She was happy they would have time to see her.

Tiffany's safety was a major concern for Paulina but she was looking forward to being out of the country for a while. Paulina thought, *"I know that the attacker is Congressman Flank and this is all my fault. I left her handbag in the limo and he'd used my keys to gain access to the apartment. When he didn't find me, he attacked Tiffany. Oh God look what I have done to my friend."*

Over dinner that evening the ladies chatted about Tiffany's aunt who seemed like a lovely lady, it was the first time that Tiffany sounded happy. After dinner they all went to their rooms to pack and to get some rest but Nancy and Paulina could not sleep. Around two in morning, Paulina thought she heard something and went to Nancy's room. She found Nancy wide-awake and reading. Paulina asked if Nancy had heard anything. She said she hadn't. They called down to Rex, the butler and asked him if he had heard anything. He said he was scanning the security cameras and there seemed to be nothing out of place.

Paulina told Nancy that she could not wait until they boarded the plane and got Tiffany safely in the arms of her dear aunt.

At the crack of dawn the ladies were dressed and heading out to the airport. Rex drove them and stayed with them as long as he could. They boarded the plane and for the first time in weeks, they all exhaled.

Tiffany's aunt Catherine met them when they landed at Heathrow Airport. She was the very image of a proper english lady, and the polar opposite of Tiffany's mother. She was warm, friendly and seemed to love people. She invited them all back to her home for tea. Her house was a charming old English manor decorated with lovely comfortable furniture covered in chintz fabric, lots of fresh cut flowers and lovely china. The manor was in Oxshott, England, an hour outside of London. The stately home was located on fifteen hundred lush, well-maintained acres, and was known as one of England's finest properties.

The home was large for her aunt to manage alone. Tiffany's uncle had passed away a few years earlier and the couple never had children of their own. Her aunt employed the proper amount of staff. But the property just didn't feel like home anymore she missed her husband and she longed for family to fill her days.

Catherine said, "Having you here will give this place back the life it has been missing since your uncle passed away. My dear girl, you are a blessing to me, and I feel so grateful that you have come here to live with me."

Tiffany was delighted to see her Aunt and she felt a sense of safety and family that she had never known before, as the two women hugged as tears began rolling down Tiffany's face.

Holding her aunt close and said, "I have missed you so much, and Aunt Catherine I need you more than you will ever know."

Catherine could feel Tiffany's small frame relax in her arms, she said, "My darling child, you never have to miss me again, you are home now. Together we will heal each other."

Nancy knew that Tiffany would be safe and cared for and maybe she would settle down. Her aunt served them the finest English tea, finger sandwiches, and small cakes.

Nancy and Paulina didn't visit too long. They wanted Tiffany and her aunt to bond with each other. They were also very tired from not sleeping all night and the long ten hour flight. When saying their good-byes, Paulina whispered in Tiffany's ear, "I am sorry for everything that happened to you, please forgive me for not being a better friend. I want you to be happy and safe Tiff. You have family that loves you too." Paulina could not bring herself to tell Tiffany what she believed to be the truth about the attack. She was dealing with the heavy feeling of guilt the only way she could.

Tiffany held on tight to Paulina. She knew this may be the last time for them to be together for some time. So much had happened to them both. Tiffany said, "Pauly, you take care too. I will miss you most of all. Thank you for letting me see the love of family and for bringing me here to my new home…I love you, girl."

The two young ladies knew their lives were forever changed.

Once they had said their goodbyes and made promises to stay in touch and visit whenever possible. They could not wait to get to the hotel. Nancy had reserved the Azure Suite at the May Fair Hotel on Stratton Street near Piccadilly. Having arranged to have a car and driver, she and Paulina could get around without any stress. They relaxed while viewing the wonderful english country side along the route to the hotel. Nancy said, "It really is beautiful here, I hope and pray that Tiffany and Catherine make out well." Paulina agreed and silently said a prayer for them both.

Paulina's cell phone was buzzing as was Nancy's. Salim said, "Hello, sweetheart. What's happening in England? Is everything working out?"

Nancy said, "I think everything will be just fine for Tiffany and her aunt."

Saul was feeling elated with that news saying, "That's wonderful. Now for our family, I have taken the next two weeks off and I am spending it with you." Nancy was delighted. She could not wait to see him.

Paulina returned Tim's call. She told him what had happened and that she was heading back to their hotel now with her mother. Tim said he was glad they were safe and sound, and most importantly, that they were together.

Tim wanted Paulina to come with him to a black-tie dinner in San Francisco the following week, but he also wanted to visit her this weekend.

She said, "Yes to both. I have truly missed you."

Tim ended the call by telling her that he loved her.

She said, "So do I…and you will see how much very soon."

Nancy had noticed a more mature Paulina in the last couple of months.

She wondered if it had anything to do with the new young man that she was sure Paulina was seeing. Nancy wanted to meet him, but Paulina had not introduced him yet. If he had anything to do with Paulina's new disposition, Nancy felt like she owed him a great deal.

Neither Tim nor Paulina had told their parents that they were dating, but Tim knew he would have to soon. He had shared with Benny and Larry how deep his feelings were for Paulina, they both thought the relationship was moving too fast. Paulina had too much drama going on in her life. They didn't want their brother getting hurt again. Their warning was too late. Paulina already had Timothy's heart in her hands and their lovemaking had rocked his world. She had his heart, his brain, and his body.

Chapter 70

Congressman Alfred Flank woke up to another boring, pressure-filled day in Washington. He hated everything about the city. It had never been his plan to get this involved in the process, until he met Belinda's father, the honorable David Tackett, governor of the fine state of Colorado, and the most corrupt double-dealing motherfucker who'd ever lived.

Flank had volunteered on a Tackett re-election campaign and his hard work, gained him attention from the Governor. It wasn't long before Tackett was inviting Flank to private affairs at the Governor's mansion. Tackett quickly sized Flank up as a hard working "yes man" and the perfect mule.

Tackett had worked on Flank's insecurities and his need to please, so it hadn't taken much to convince him that the party and the state would be better off with him serving in office. Tackett designed a plan to get Flank just where he was most useful to Tackett's master plan and that would be to get Flank elected to Congress. He gathered a team of smart young people and the plan was put into motion. In no time Flank won the state-level election and four years later, he was elected to a federal seat as congressman from Colorado.

Now Flank felt like he had sold his soul to the devil. Everyday there were calls about some special interest that Tackett wanted pushed through the House. If it was not a call it was a demand that Flank listen to whatever agenda Tackett wanted.

It was Flank's job to get the bill before the right person. For every bill Flank got passed a gift was given to the Tackett family. The problem with this pay to play set-up was Flank was beholden to Tackett. To avoid bringing any attention to Flank, Tackett arranged to have his friends make large donations to Flank's father's church. Tackett's sister was the church accountant. She would quietly launder the donations back to any interest that Tackett instructed her to handle. Since Alfred had been in Washington, the church had received a windfall of special gifts and building-fund donations.

As long as Tackett got what he wanted, he continued to fund the millions of dollars necessary to keep Flank in Washington and to keep him getting all of the cocaine and special perks he could handle. But with every passing day, Flank wondered if it was worth it. Since the day their engagement was made public Belinda had changed too. Now she only seemed interested in becoming a congressman's wife.

Belinda's calls weren't any better than her father's. At the beginning of their relationship everything was fine. She seemed to really care about him. Now all she wanted to do was get to the next high-profile event so that her picture would be in the local papers. No matter how much media coverage she received she still complained she was never happy. Nothing was ever good enough, especially him. She complained about everything he did. Nothing ever seemed to please her, Alfred didn't know what to do next to make her happy.

Belinda telephoned him early that morning saying, "Al, when are you coming back home? I promised the Chamber of Commerce President that you would speak at their luncheon, and it will look bad on me if you don't do it."

Al said, "Belinda, baby, I am busy up here. Please don't make promises for me when you know your father has me meeting with so many people."

Belinda demanded loudly, "I don't give a damn, Al. When I want you by my side, I should come first. We want people to see us as the next hot couple. So get here, dammit." Before he could say another word Belinda ended the call. Flank just looked out his office window, thinking "This woman is completely losing her damn mind." He could not believe how much Belinda had changed in such a short time.

The phone rang again, this time it was daddy dearest demanding that Al get his ass home and take Belinda to the damn luncheon. Tackett hung up on Al before he had a chance to respond.

Flank was damn tired of this shit. He did not know how much longer he could be the Tackett family bitch. When he and Belinda started their relationship, she was gentle and soft-spoken but as soon as he'd asked her to marry him, she had become a demanding witch. She had turned off any romance. Now their relationship was all about calendars, meetings, wedding plans, and her damn father.

His new way of dealing with the Tackett family pressure was to meet some pretty young thing who wanted career guidance once a week. They were always happy to follow him to his office. After he met with them a couple of times, he would find something in their past that he could use to control them. Most lied on their résumés or had used drugs, or something like that. When they admitted to the crime, he used their dirty deeds to exploit them as his sex slave until he found someone else to play with.

Chapter 71

Winnie called her contact at the police station, Sergeant Walter Shaw. She knew he was a little sweet on her. He was always there to help her out when she needed a favor, and today was one of those days. She wanted him to run the fingerprints on the cuff link, but keep quiet about the results.

Shaw picked up the cuff link and ran it for prints right away. When he got the results, he called Winnie on her cell phone saying, "Winnie, there are no clear prints on this cuff link. The cuff link is a mass-produced item that can be purchased online at the US Historical Society."

Winnie said, "Was there any blood on them?"

Shaw knew Winnie was messing in police business so he had to warn her to stay in her place. "Winnie where did you find this cuff link? Don't tell me that you went to the New Mexico Avenue condo and you're messing around in a sealed off crime scene."

Winnie knew that Shaw was on to her, she also knew that he took it as a personal affront if she didn't clue him in, so she needed to pick her words carefully.

Winnie softly said, "Now, now Officer Shaw, all I want to do is help you find this monster, so did the cuff link produce anything?"

Shaw was getting annoyed with Winnie, he knew she was lying to him. He said, "No I just told you what I found on that cuff link. But Winnie I am warning you not to mess with police business."

Winnie said, "Can you do some checking on Congressman Alfred Flank? I need to know where he was at the time of the attack on Tiffany."

Shaw said, "Yeah, I have some friends down at the Capitol Hill Police. They all think Flank is a wet behind the ears jerk, so they will tell me what I need to know." He promised to get back with her soon.

Without a statement from Tiffany or Paulina, Winnie didn't have much to go on, she only had the tape. Which she couldn't use without getting Paulina involved. Winnie knew she would have to keep this under wraps for a little while longer.

Shaw called her back to warn her about the seriousness of messing with police business and to be careful. He would give her a couple of days, but if there were any more attacks, he wanted full disclosure of the information she was withholding.

Winnie called Nancy, she wanted to meet with her, Paulina, and Salim. Nancy told her they were in London and would not be returning for a few days. Nancy told Winnie she needed to know what it was about first. She would not let anything hurt Paulina.

Winnie asked her to speak with Paulina about the night she came home and said she had been mugged.

Nancy asked her why and Winnie stressed the importance of her speaking with Paulina. She told her the answers to her questions were with her daughter. After she and Winnie ended the call, Nancy decided now was not the time. They had already been handling too much drama and she was not ready to open the door for more. So whatever Winnie needed, it would just have to wait.

Nancy and Paulina were sharing a lovely two bedroom suite with marvelous views of London. Nancy ordered dinner a simple and comforting meal of delicate split-pea soup and light buttery cheddar biscuits with a touch of honey. Along with a pot of tea, it was one of England's finest suppers.

Nancy kicked off her shoes and put her feet up. When she closed her eyes she thought about everything that had happened to them, she said a prayer that maybe her family could heal and head in the right direction. Before she knew it, she was drifting off to sleep.

All Paulina wanted to do was get some rest and get back to the states to see Tim. She longed to be back in the safety of his arms. Hearing a knock at the door, she called out to Nancy. When she didn't answer, Paulina walked into the living room area and saw her fast asleep. Paulina open the door, tipped and thanked the waiter and softly closed the door behind him.

When Nancy smelled dinner, she woke up. They both enjoyed some soup and quickly went to bed. The next day they were scheduled to meet with Lynn and her two daughters Brittney and Allison. Paulina was delighted. She hadn't seen her cousins in almost five years. They made plans to meet at The Georgian, on the fourth floor of Harrods on Brompton Road, for high tea and then some shopping.

Lynn, and her girls, along with Nancy, and Paulina enjoyed the next twenty-four hours of catching up and just having "girl time" together. As it always did when they were together time moved at rapid speed, they all hugged good-bye and promised to spend more time together over the upcoming summer months.

Around midnight, Nancy and Paulina fell asleep. They were scheduled on another long flight in the morning.

As their plane left Heathrow Airport, Paulina turned to Nancy and said, "I know Tiffany is safe, and I hope she finds peace."

Nancy said, "I do too."

Paulina took Nancy's hand and said, "I am so thankful to have my family."

Nancy said, "Paulina, you and Tiffany are safe but we need to talk, I know that you know more about who attacked her and I don't have any idea why you are protecting this person. I know there is more to the story about your mugging. Now Winnie is calling me and begging me to speak to you about it. Paulina tell me what is going on."

Paulina said, "No I don't know. I have answered all of your questions. I feel bad about what happened to Tiffany but I don't know anymore."

Nancy knew Paulina was too stubborn to give in and she was sure Paulina was not telling her the truth. But for now she would let the conversation rest.

Exhaustion took over and both women slept the remainder of the flight to Dulles Airport.

Chapter 72

Winnie was certain that Flank was involved in the recent attacks on young women in the city. But getting enough evidence to make charges stick was another matter. Without hard evidence or statements from the victims all Winnie really had was an inadmissible videotape and a souvenir cuff link with the US Capitol engraved on it. There was no physical proof to place Flank there. Nothing, just the damn cuff link.

Winnie asked Officer Shaw to research any cases similar to Tiffany's. She had a hunch that if the congressman had committed this crime, he would surely do it again. This whole case had serial offender written all over it. She only hoped his next victim was not taken away in a body bag.

Winnie knew that Paulina was not telling the truth, she was sticking to her story about being mugged.

But Winnie was not the type of woman to sit back and wait for anything. She needed to find out the truth, so she could keep another woman from being attacked. And that's just what she was going to do. She was certain that there was something she had overlooked. She spent the rest of the evening going over every detail of the case.

Phillip Lay telephoned Winnie and invited her to be his guest at a charity golf tournament at the prestige Bayonne Golf Club, in Bayonne, New Jersey. She happily accepted the invitation. Phillip meticulously planned every minute of her itinerary. He arranged all of her transportation, hotel accommodations, meals, spa appointments, tee times, and practice rounds. Phillip was a man of impeccable elegance. His attention to detail, was noticed and greatly appreciated.

Phillip's foursome won the tournament. Winnie won for the longest drive from the women's tee. They celebrated over a bottle of Dom Pérignon champagne at the end of the tournament.

Phillip delighted Winnie with jovial stories of his past building projects, and what it took to remodel a historic home, but the stories of his past golf victories and horrors where the best and they had Winnie laughing so hard she had tears in her eyes.

And while his flirtatious overtures were flattering to her feminine ego, Winnie was much cleverer than Phillip expected. She was prepared and stopped him at each pass. She never let him discuss anything too personal, and she retired to her room early and alone.

They both knew what he wanted. Now Phillip knew that Winnie was not that kind of girl. She was not interested in having an affair with him. He would have to work harder if he wanted her.

When she boarded the plane. Phillip looked remorseful, he said, "I hope I didn't give you the wrong impression when I invited you for a nightcap in my suite."

Winnie said, "And what impression do you think that might be?" She smiled and took her seat next to him. Smiling to herself, she thought, "*Well, well, now, Mr. Lay, I thought you would be better at playboy games. How disappointing. Oh well, you are still damn handsome.*"

They enjoyed the return trip with more light hearted laughter and all was well. Phillip enjoyed, Winnie's kind and generous spirit. It was obvious that they liked each other but Winnie was not available for what Phillip wanted, she wanted more than a fling and she was determined not to fall in love with a married man. Without either one of them saying anything they both knew that a line had been drawn defining their new relationship, and for now they would just be friends.

Once all of her surgeries were complete Sadie began her recovery treatments at the Betty Ford Treatment Center. She was feeling physically stronger every day.

Lonnie, Hattie and Felix came to visit her as often as the therapist would allow. While Sadie was away at rehab, the rest of her family and friends were moving along with their lives. Benny and Amy were now officially engaged. Sadie had not met Amy but she had been touched by the presents and notes Amy had sent her. Knowing that Benny was no longer alone made her feel better. It made Sadie feel like less of a burden. She liked knowing that Amy was caring for her firstborn and that he was moving on with his life.

Larry had shown her pictures and told her wonderful things about the young lady, her family and how much she loved and cared for Benny. She read in the society papers that Coco was now Mrs. Saul Baumann. Sadie was very happy for Coco and wished her only the best.

Sadie had requested home treatment, however the counselor believed that she would only continue to progress under the direction of the treatment staff as an inpatient. They had only started making progress on what was behind Sadie's drinking.

Lonnie and Sadie's failure to honestly speak about her drinking never allowed them to get to the root cause of their problem. The counselor told them that being afraid to face one's demons could only ensure your repeated failure.

They were now at a point where it was impossible to turn away. They had to face it and talk to each other to find a way through the disappointment and pain. They still loved each other but Lonnie could no longer show Sadie how much he loved her.

Sadie missed the physical love that Lonnie used to shower on her, she never wanted to make him feel like less of a man. So she had learned how to live in a sexless marriage. But with each day it was killing her little by little. And the only thing that stop the pain was alcohol.

Chapter 73

Coco was enjoying the reality of being a married woman. Just the sound of it was delightful. Their marriage had given her the gift of renewal. Everything seemed bright and she was optimistic about her future for the first time. She no longer was the one pressing her nose against the window and watching someone else enjoy life, while she longed for their crumbs.

As she was making plans for the holiday's, she felt a real sense of herself, and she was completely in love with being married. She wondered if Saul had any idea that he was making her dreams come true. Saul was the very reflection of the man that she loved and she was determined to make him happy.

When she finished her yoga class, she met him back in their suite. He was reading one of the many morning news and financial papers that he read daily. When she walked in, he put the paper down.

Saul said, "Hi, sweetheart. How was yoga today?"

Coco sweetly replied, "Fine. Oh darling, I wish you would join me. It's really good for you."

He loved Coco so much all he could do was smile and say, "As you know, I work out for two hours every day. I am in great shape. At least that's what my wife keeps telling me."

Coco smiled and said, "Oh yeah, your wife. Where is this wife right now?"

Saul proudly opened his arms saying, "She is right in front of me, the sight of her has me considering missing breakfast and continuing to live on love."

Saul wrapped Coco in his arms and then said, "Good morning again, Mrs. Baumann."

Coco smiled brightly and said, "Good morning, Mr. Baumann."

Within minutes they were making passionate love. Saul still could not get enough of Coco's body. She drove him crazy with desire. She made him the happiest man alive. As he filled her body, he looked into her eyes and softly said, "I love you, Coco, more than anything in this world."

There was no need for any more words. They had found what they were both missing, over-the-top passion and true commitment. Coco and Saul had found *love*. They didn't leave their suite for two days.

They spent the next six months at sea, traveling the world and continuing to get to know each other. Coco was becoming less needy and afraid, and Saul was becoming softer and more trusting.

Coco no longer cared about the next gala or ball or being in the city, she only cared about being with Saul. Together, they were building a life, one beautiful day at a time.

Chapter 74

Growing up a Von Kinley man had taught Tim that love was an action word and that a man had to be responsible for his woman's heart. He had watched his father, love, protect and provide for his mother and their family.

He now wanted to be a husband, like his dad and someday, a father with kids who wanted to grow up and be like him. He had also learned that sometimes life required a man to take the first step and not be afraid to speak the truth and once you said it, you had to honor your word.

Tim was not feeling great about taking Paulina away for long weekends and not letting her father know where she was and that she was being taken care of. He wanted her family to know that, with everything in his being, he would make sure she was safe and returned to them unharmed. He reasoned that if he was protective and loved her, then her father had to feel the same. Therefore in taking the right course of action he placed a call to Dr. Hadid and asked to meet him for a drink.

Salim was impressed with the young Von Kinley. He had noticed a difference in Paulina and now he knew the reason. He felt that Paulina had been badly hurt which caused feelings of abandonment. If this young man was honorable enough to meet with her father, well then maybe things were moving in the right direction for her to find the happiness she deserved.

Tim was the first to arrive at the Hay-Adams Hotel. On the ride over he had rehearsed what he would say to Dr. Hadid. They had met before but nothing could prepare a man for this kind of meeting. Tim had discussed the matter with Benny and Larry and they both felt it was the right thing to do. But this move was sending a strong message, that Tim was serious about his feelings for Paulina. His brothers warned him that meeting her father may lead him to ask the question, "So what's next?"

Tim was not prepared for the, "what's next." He was, however, deeply in love with Paulina and he wanted both her parents to know that his intentions were honorable.

Since their first encounter in Aspen, Tim had a desire to protect, provide and love Paulina.

Salim walked into the hotel and the two men exchanged a warm greeting. Tim asked Salim to join him for a drink in the historic bar called Off the Record. When they were seated and their drinks were served, JW Blue Label. Tim was suddenly uncertain of what to say, so he took a strong sip of the smooth drink and then just jumped in heart first.

"Dr. Hadid, I am dating Paulina and I want you to know that she is safe with me. I will never hurt her or make her cry. Her happiness means the world to me."

Salim said, "Paulina is a young woman. How can you say, you will never make her cry? Is that your reality or just your emotions for right now?"

The attorney in Tim took over the conversation. He presented his case before the judge of his heart, Dr. Salim Hadid.

Tim was a great litigator, so within minutes he had addressed all of Salim's concerns and even touched on subjects that Salim had not thought about. The two men shared their feelings about loving and protecting the women in their lives and all that meant to them. Salim asked about his family and his past relationships. And then he finally asked Tim about his plans for Paulina's future, "What are your plans for my daughter's future?"

Tim swallowed hard and spoke the truth, "Sir, we are taking it one day at a time, which is all any man in love can do. But at this moment, I can't imagine my life without Paulina. She makes me happy, we share so much in common. We read the same books, love the same music. We have the same values of family. Yes, Paulina is young but the reality is that she and I are only six years apart in age."

When Tim finished talking, there was a bit of a silence. He had given Salim a great deal to think about.

Salim said, "I think this meeting is a great first step. I am very concerned that with all of the pressures that you are both under, this might not be a good time to become so involved with my daughter."

With nerves of steel, Tim looked into Salim's eyes and said, "Dr. Hadid, do you remember when you first fell in love with Mrs. Hadid? Was everything in your life perfect? Did that stop you from loving her?"

Before Salim could answer, Tim said, "Like any man I am powerless to control my heart, I am in love with Paulina and I intend to continue being honorable, protective and loving."

Salim did not have an answer. All he could say was, "Yes, you are right, and I am proud that you are dating my daughter but please don't make me regret this meeting."

They shared another drink. Just as they were finishing up, Tim's cell phone buzzed. It was Paulina. They were meeting for dinner in less than half an hour. Letting her call go to voice mail, he told Salim he was sorry but he needed to get going. Then he thanked him for his time and paid the check. The two men exchanged a strong handshake and wished each other well.

Although Salim had some reservations about the timing of the relationship, he felt good about Tim and Paulina and he wished them both well. It was clear that they were good for each other. As a father, he just wanted what was best for his daughter.

On the drive home Salim thought about how to best tell Nancy about this new relationship. As he placed his key in the kitchen door lock, he was welcomed by the smells of dinner and the sounds of home. Nancy greeted him warmly with a hug and kiss. She told him dinner was ready and to get cleaned up. She also told him that Paulina and the staff were out, so it was just the two of them tonight.

They enjoyed dinner in front of the television. Nancy had prepared grilled salmon with brown-sugar-and-mustard-glazed, orzo salad with fresh grilled vegetables, and for dessert, fresh peach sorbet. Salim was always impressed by Nancy's culinary talents. She presented food like an artisan, and it tasted as good as it looked. She had even picked the Chassagne-Montrachet La Romanée, a delicious white wine for their dinner.

As she placed his dinner plate before him and then gently poured the wine, Salim felt like home was the only place he wanted to be. She asked him about his day and she listened intently to all he was doing in men's health research. Nancy made dinnertime all about Salim. She wanted him to feel special when he came home. He secretly wished this kind of evening and many more like it for Paulina and Tim.

He wasn't sure if he wanted to share the news about Tim and Paulina with Nancy right away but they had promised to never keep secrets from one another again.

Salim thought that since Paulina had not said a word about dating Tim, for now he would keep his mouth shut. He felt that Nancy had a tendency to get too involved in other people's lives, especially Paulina's. She could only see things from her point of view and if that didn't work with what she wanted for the person, she could not control her urge to try and fix it.

Nancy asked him if he had noticed anything different about Paulina.

He said, "What do you mean?" It was crazy how they could almost read each other's minds.

Nancy said, "Well, she seems happier than I have ever known her to be and I think there is a new young man in her life."

Salim replied, "Really? Now that you mention it she does seem happier and I am really pleased because she deserves to be happy."

For the rest of the evening, they kept the conversation light. Nancy asked him if he would be interested in looking at some properties on Kiawah Island in South Carolina. She really wanted them to find a new weekend retreat home and Kiawah offered everything they enjoyed.

Salim smiled, "Honey, I think Kiawah would be great. We should plan on going down this coming weekend."

Nancy smiled and said, "Kiawah, here we come."

When they were in bed, Salim said, "Nancy, I need to talk to you about something important. We promised each other to never keep secrets from one another again, right?"

Nancy sat up and gave Salim a puzzled look, "Yes...Oh God, what is it?" Her heart was racing.

Salim quickly said, "Nothing bad. Calm down."

His words were not coming out fast enough for her. She needed to know what was wrong. They had already been through so much. She was not sure if they could stand anything else.

Salim said, "Tonight, I met with Tim Von Kinley, Lonnie and Sadie's son." It had always taken Salim too damn long to tell a story.

Nancy said, "Yes, yes...okay."

"Nancy, please calm down. I am getting to it. It seems he and Paulina met in Aspen and then again at the hospital after Sadie's accident. They started out as friends and now they are dating. He seems like an honorable young man but Nancy, I don't want you to say a word to Paulina until she comes to us and tells us. She does not know that Tim and I met today."

Nancy was so happy. She said, "I know Timothy. He is a fine young man. How honorable of him to meet with you. Now Salim, why didn't you tell me when you came home?"

"Because, sweetheart, I know you and you can't help yourself but to get involved in other people's business. I am asking you not to do that this time. Leave Tim and Paulina alone until they tell us. Please Nancy, promise me that you will not get involved."

"Well, okay...I promise."

Nancy was full of questions and would not stop talking until Salim kissed her and told her to focus on her man and not Paulina's.

Nancy said, "Sounds like a plan."

They made beautiful love that night and all felt right with the world.

Chapter 75

Sadie felt as though she was making progress but the counselor sensed fear in her. There was still something that Sadie was afraid to deal with. They would never fully solve her problems until she found the courage to address the core of her trouble.

Lonnie was invited to join one of her sessions and Sadie asked Lonnie, "Why haven't you gone to see a doctor about your problem?"

Lonnie felt immediately ashamed, he didn't want to talk about it in front of the therapist. "Sadie, please do we have to talk about my problems?"

Sadie quickly responded, "Lonnie your problems are my problems and when you can't make love to me, it makes me feel like less of a woman."

Lonnie was hurt that Sadie had brought up his erectile dysfunction.

Lonnie dropped his head and for a minute the room was silent. Then he said, "Our marriage is about so much more than sex. Sadie are you telling me that your drinking is because we are not making love?"

The counselor watched intently as Lonnie struggled with Sadie's admission then asked Sadie if she felt like any of Lonnie's physical problems were her fault?

Sadie said, "At times I do but his lack of attention to the problem confuses me because I know that Lonnie loves me."

Sadie continued saying, "Lonnie, you never want to talk about it. When I try to you shut me down. Now I am afraid to talk about it with you, I never want to hurt you. So we just push the conversation away but I can't push away my feelings of loneliness in our marriage."

Lonnie asked, "Is that why you drink more than you should Sadie?"

Lonnie gently took Sadie's hand in his and said, "Sadie, I could never love or want anyone more than I want and need you, you have always been my life."

He also told her that seeing her completely drunk was the ultimate turn-off for him. But it was not an excuse for not seeing a doctor. He had been afraid to deal with his impotency but he knew that it could no longer be delayed.

Sadie said, "Lonnie, you have talked about fixing our love life but talk is all you have done. I am sick to death of hearing what you are going to do, you are being a coward Lonnie."

Lonnie was angry that Sadie had called him a coward, so with determination he said, "Sadie, you're right but I am surprised that you think of me as a coward when you have been finding your solace in a glass for years. If we are being honest, I believe that we have both been cowardly."

Their next few sessions were very intense, as they addressed all of their marital problems. The counselor addressed Sadie's empty nest feelings. Their son's had moved on with their lives and she felt unneeded.

Sadie said, "I want our sons to have wonderful lives with wives, children and everything that I have been so blessed to share with Lonnie. But I need to feel wanted and not just by the charities that we support, that's just not enough anymore." She loved bringing happiness to others. She was a woman who had built her life around Lonnie and her sons. Now that they were fulfilling their life missions, what was left for her to do?.

The counselor said, "The answer is not an easy one but you will never find it at the end of a bottle. Sadie you need to take control and find who you are now at this stage in your life and what you are capable of outside of your family. You and only you can be responsible for your happiness and your fulfillment."

Sadie and Lonnie progressed with each joint session. After one of Sadie's sessions, Lonnie called a Beverly Hills urologist for an appointment. After his examination he was prescribed treatment for his condition. Lonnie was certain that he would be ready to execute upon Sadie's release.

Sadie was discharged from the treatment center after ninety days of intensive therapy. Benny, Tim and Larry were at the hotel when she and Lonnie arrived.

The boys stayed with them for three days and after they left, Lonnie sent his business team back to Washington. He had arranged to take Sadie to their honeymoon spot on Half Moon Bay in Jamaica. He thought they needed this time to continue what they had learned through the therapy sessions. To put their life and marriage first.

They spent hours walking on the beach, talking about their lives, playing golf, tennis, and swimming. When they first arrived Lonnie had experienced performance anxiety. He wanted to please her and let her know that his love for her was just as strong as it had been before. Sadie's body was still beautiful. Her long arms and legs had benefited from daily yoga and pilates. Her skin was silky smooth, soft and dewy. Inch by wonderful inch, he was rediscovering his wife again. Lonnie was amazed at the powerful reconnection that brought them both to points of ecstasy they had forgotten existed. He bathed in the pool of her love and never wanted to let her go.

On their last night, Lonnie arranged to have the same dinner they'd enjoyed at their wedding, and a small wedding cake. They had renewed their love for each other and were now ready to return to their former lives minus the booze.

Lonnie and Sadie were welcomed home by their entire staff. She was missed by everyone and the staff was happy to see her looking so healthy and strong. There was a spring in her step, she appeared to be a much better Sadie and they secretly hoped that she could keep her sobriety.

Felix had the chef prepare a grand dinner. The entire family was in attendance. Benny and Amy announced their plans to wed in the next four months. Sadie fell in love with Amy the same way that Lonnie's mother had fallen in love with her. Amy was everything Sadie had envisioned she would be. She was well educated, from a lovely southern family. She had excellent fashion taste but more importantly was the love that beamed between Amy and Benny. Sadie was so proud.

Amy's mother called Sadie and the two became instant friends. They worked on the wedding together and everyone was looking forward to the big day.

The happy couple would be married in Manhattan, New York, at St. Ignatius Loyola Church on Park Avenue and the reception would be held at the St. Regis Hotel. In keeping with the Von Kinley family tradition, the wedding was over-the-top.

Sadie gave Amy a suite of pearls and diamonds that had been in the Von Kinley family for many years. It was the one Lonnie had given Sadie on their wedding day. It included a necklace, earrings, bracelet and a large cocktail ring. Sadie enclosed a note that read:

> My darling Amy,
> Welcome to our family. You have no idea how long we have waited for God to send us an angel and now we have you. Thank you for loving our firstborn son, Benny. We wish you years of love and happiness.
> With everything that love means,
> Mother Sadie, Father Lonnie,
> and the entire Von Kinley family

Sadie enlisted the help of event-planner, who created a floral wonderland. The church was decorated in all-white flowers imported from around the world. Every type of rose and lily was used to create a romantic haven of love and fantasy. Crystals and pearls were used to add that touch of purity and sparkle. Amy's wedding gown, was designed by Valentino, a dreamy creation of silk organza and delicate silk.

The hotel ballroom was adorned in white, crystal, pearl, and gold leaf. The entire ballroom ceiling was covered in flowers and crystals hung down like dancing stars. The wedding cake was prepared by Sylvia Weinstock. It was seven layers of delicious heaven. The flowers on the cake looked just as real as the ones used throughout the room.

Benny and Amy's wedding was covered by all the society media outlets. It was Sadie's first big affair since her alcohol treatment. She was so overcome with happiness that she didn't mind drinking apple cider. Seeing the world without booze was very different; it was almost too real but she was handling it.

Sadie invited Winnie and Nancy to the wedding. Coco was still traveling with Saul on their extended honeymoon. Sadie was delighted that Coco had gotten married. She was hopeful that it would bring out the best in what was left of Coco's heart. Tim invited Paulina, Sadie immediately knew that the relationship was serious.

Sadie was much less welcoming of this relationship than she had been of Amy and Benny's but she did everything she could to cover up her disappointment. She made a mental note to speak with Tim as soon as everything calmed down. She felt that Paulina was a nice girl but with all that Nancy had told her, she was not the girl that Sadie wanted for her son.

Benny and Amy honeymooned at the Von Kinley apartment in the South of France and then took the family's yacht, *Sadie Baby*, to cruise the Greek Isles for a two month honeymoon. When they came back home, Amy discovered she was six weeks pregnant. Benny was over the moon with joy. His life felt surreal. He was now a husband and soon he would be a father.

The big announcement was made at their first dinner in their new townhouse on East Seventieth Street. Sadie would soon have her first grandchild and she and Lonnie could not be happier. She cried tears of joy.

She still had misgivings about the relationship between Tim and Paulina. Nancy had called her to talk about it and Sadie could not hide her concerns. Nancy's feelings were hurt. She asked Sadie, "You don't think Paulina is good enough for Tim? Is that the real problem?"

Sadie could not find the right words to defuse the conversation and spare Nancy's feelings, so she turned the tables on her, saying, "Nancy, after everything you've told me and everything that Paulina has been through, do you think that a serious relationship is wise right now? I just don't want our kids getting hurt. How do you feel about it, Nancy?"

Nancy abruptly ended the conversation, saying, "Sadie, please don't play games with me. I know you well and if you feel that Paulina is not good enough, then maybe I am not good enough. Not everyone has been a saint like you, Mrs. Von Kinley."

Nancy had hit a nerve and Sadie refused to continue this conversation, so she said, "Nancy, please have a good day. Good-bye."

Chapter 76

Winnie was feeling good about the in-depth research she had just completed for an upcoming interview with the Comptroller of Maryland. It was part of a special series of interviews she'd been conducting entitled "An Up Close Look at our Town." The interviews took place every year during "Sweep Week". The television station had received great feedback from the community on Winnie's handling of local and national leaders and her hard hitting questions. She would be conducting the interview at the end of the week. Her non-stop schedule had her yearning for a break.

She'd been delighted when the San Francisco Opera invitation had arrived in the mail a few weeks before and now it was time for her to start packing for the trip. She looked forward to attending the gala weekend every year.

As soon as the interview wrapped, Winnie rushed home and finished up the last items on her to-do list. Then it was time to pack and head to bed. She had a very early flight in the morning.

Once she was seated on the plane, she took a deep breath to exhale. Resting her head on the headrest she closed her eyes and finally she could relax. The airplane stewardess said, "Excuse me, would you care for something to drink?"

Winnie quickly thought about her long week, smiled and said, "Yes, a glass of champagne please." Slowly sipping the cold bubbly beverage she looked out the window, going over everything she had done all week and made a mental check list of the errands she had completed. But there was one thing that she had yet to mark off the list. A handsome male companion, Winnie was once again traveling alone.

She had become increasingly lonely since Phillip had come into her life. For years she'd fought those feelings, determined to never fall in love again. But now all she could remember was the wonderful feelings of being in love and sharing her life with someone. Taking the last sip of her champagne, she closed her eyes and tried to not think of Phillip Lay. She had bought along something to read for the six hour flight but right now, she just wanted to rest her eyes and her mind.

To ensure that she had enough time to take in the sights and sounds of her favorite city she arrived a day early. She was staying at the Mandarin Oriental Hotel on Sansome Street, it was like a second home to her. When she arrived she was greeted by the hotel manager, a charming young man who was also a fan of the opera.

He said, "Welcome back to the Mandarin Oriental Ms. Pettridge, we are delighted that you are staying with us. I am Colin Hollander, the hotel manager."

Winnie smiled warmly and said, "It's a pleasure to meet you Mr. Hollander. You have no idea how happy I am to be here. I look forward to it all year."

"As do we, the entire city comes alive this time of year. Did you notice all our special displays for Tosca", he said.

Winnie had noticed the marvelous opera artwork and floral displays in the hotel lobby. As he handed her his business card he said, "We have set up a special reception area for our opera guests, please feel free to help yourself. And if there is anything that I can do for you during your stay with us, please don't hesitate to let me know."

Winnie looked at the inviting table of canapés and special treats but graciously declined. She already had plans, saying, "Thank you so much, it all looks delicious but I just want to get to my room."

"Yes, I can only imagine that you are tired. Let's get you upstairs right away. Ms. Pettridge your luggage has already been sent up, please allow me, I will show you to your room."

Winnie said, "Oh you are so kind, thank you so much, but I will be fine." She promised to let him know if she needed anything and then she headed off to catch the elevator.

Winnie's suite was beautiful, with views of both the Golden Gate Bridge and the Bay Bridge. Just looking out the window at the glorious bay was exciting. Someone had filled her room with flowers and chocolates. She made a mental note to send a handwritten thank-you note to the manager of the hotel.

After she unpacked she took a short power nap, then dressed and went for a light stroll. Taking a cable car to Union Square. She enjoyed walking the lively streets and taking in the sounds of busy people going about their day. She watched street performers playing jazz music and then she took in some shopping in the charming boutiques, her favorite was Gump's. Being in San Francisco was just what she had hoped for and remembered it to be.

After shopping for a while, she stopped by Cafe de la Presse, a french bistro for a quick bite and a glass of wine. While sitting at a corner table in the outdoor cafe, she noticed that the entire city was decorated with art from local artists. She chatted with other tourists and some locals that were enjoying lunch at the cafe, everyone was in agreement the city's art was extraordinarily brilliant. When she finished she took a taxi back to the hotel. While she was changing her clothes, preparing for a relaxing massage, she received a telephone call. It was Phillip Lay.

"Welcome to San Francisco, Winnie."

"Hello, Phillip. How kind of you to call me. How did you know that I would be staying here?"

"You told me that when you're in San Francisco, you only stay at the Mandarin, so I took a chance that it was still your favorite."

"Well, you were right. It is. Are you here for the opera weekend?"

"Yes, we just arrived. How do you like the flowers and sweets?"

"Oh Phillip, these are from you? They are beautiful. You really shouldn't have gone to so much trouble."

"It's just what we flower people do for each other."

Winnie laughed. She was stuck on the word *we*.

"Do you and Donna have plans to do anything special during your visit?"

"No, we will keep to the itinerary that the opera has planned for us."

"Well, Phillip, I can't thank you enough. My room looks lovely."

She told him she had to go. She was having a massage in a couple of minutes. He told her to enjoy and he looked forward to seeing her at some of the events that weekend.

When she got off the phone, she was taken by the fact that Phillip was showing so much interest in her likes and dislikes.

She resolved to keep Phillip out of her heart but damn it was hard. She was beginning to think about him far too often. He was so handsome, charming and manly. They had so much in common but common interests were not enough to break her down. She reminded herself to stay strong.

After a hot-stone massage, Winnie spent the evening in her room, relaxing and watching television—something she rarely did at home. She received calls from Sadie and Nancy about their children dating. She told them both the same thing. "Stay out of it, let the kids find their way and make their own choices for better or worst. As parents, you owe them that."

She knew it seemed selfish but she needed this weekend to refresh and renew her spirit, so after speaking with each of them, Winnie hung up the phone and said to herself, "No more calls."

She waited all year for San Francisco's opera season and she was not going to let anyone destroy a minute of this glorious weekend.

She attended all of the pre-ball events. The first was a welcome reception at the home of the opera president, a mind-blowing duplex apartment in the Lumina building with unmatched views of the city. While there she ran into one of the funniest women she knew Sunny Hamilton, a socialite who was five times divorced. The two friends chatted all evening and promised to get together more over the weekend.

The next day Winnie spent most of the day in the salon getting ready for the opening night performance of Puccini's *Tosca*. Winnie smiled at the reflection staring back at her in the full length mirror. Her hair was piled high and secured with white diamond clips. She wore a melon-colored silk Oscar de la Renta gown and her thirty-five-carat citrine-and-diamond necklace with matching earrings and ring were all by Australian jewelry designer Margot McKinney. Winnie had met the designer at a small cocktail party hosted by Neiman Marcus in Palm Beach, Florida.

She had fallen in love with McKinney's creations. They were all fabulous and one-of-a-kind pieces that she kept for very special occasions. Winnie carried a Judith Leiber harp bag. It's Austrian crystal and yellow metal completed her look for the evening. The effect gave her an even more regal appearance.

Winnie's love for the arts was one of the things that she was grateful her mother had instilled in her. Walking through the elegant hotel lobby she could feel eyes watching her, she smiled to herself thinking, *"Well fifty isn't so bad after all, I feel great. This is already a great evening."* She had reserved a car and driver for the weekend. "Good evening Ms. Pettridge are you ready to leave now", said her driver.

"Yes, thank you, next stop the Opera", said Winnie.

As she arrived at the Opera House, there were persons outside of the venue dressed in period customs greeting guests and a host of photographers taking pictures. Walking into the grand San Francisco War Memorial Opera House, Winnie had to take a deep breath. The building itself was like a grand old diva with golden walls and plush red-velvet chairs. The ornate designs in it's ceiling only added to the evening's grandeur. After greeting some of the opera staff members Winnie went directly to her seat.

As the emotional soprano sang, *"Vissi d'arte, vissi d'amore, non feci mai male ad anima viva"* ("I lived for art, I lived for love, I never harmed a living soul"), the powerful voice was like a mesmerizing tonic. Winnie felt as if each word was speaking to her.

She breathed a deep sigh when the curtain fell, it was a performance to remember. While the theater lights were coming up, she reached into her small crystal bag and took out a linen handkerchief to gently wipe away her tears.

Sunny said, "Hello Winnie, was that not breathtaking. I can't believe it but every time I see this performance I am always moved by it."

Winnie agreed, "Sunny, it was fabulous."

Sunny told Winnie to follow her, she wanted to introduce her to some more guests that she knew Winnie would enjoy talking to. As they mingled through the reception Winnie spotted Phillip and Donna but she was determined not to share a minute of her evening with them. Sunny and Winnie enjoyed meeting new people and catching up with old friends. Every conversation was delightful and filled with opera experiences from around the world. Sunny said, "They are ringing the chimes for dinner, it is always amazing how time flies when you are having fun."

Winnie agreed, "We had better find our seats."

Sunny smiled and said, "Winnie I have arranged for us to be at a great table." Winnie laughed and said, "Why am I not surprised. Sunny you are amazing. Thank you for taking care of the details".

As promised Sunny had invited a Baron and Baroness, along with a charming couple visiting from Rome, who had recently retired and now traveled the world with the opera. Rounding out the table was the San Francisco Mayor. Just as Winnie was introducing herself the room broke out in loud round of applause as members of the Opera cast began arriving at the post-performance dinner. Winnie was delighted that Sunny had even managed to have the lead tenor as their table guests. The evening was magical and the conversation was endless.

Winnie was able to avoid the Lay's for most of the evening. But as Winnie was leaving the restroom she ran into Donna.

"You look beautiful Winnie, are you here with a date. Well, I hope you find a partner soon. You know we are not getting any younger", said Donna.

Having shared an unpleasant exchange with Donna before. Winnie was prepared, so she looked her in the eye and said, "Oh Donna dear, you have no need to worry about me. I have everything that I need and most importantly, I am very happy with my life, are you with yours?"

Then Winnie walked away wondering how a man as gentle, kind, and polished as Phillip could end up with a bitch like Donna.

Winnie enjoyed the remainder of the evening, dancing and having a grand time with her West Coast friends. She refused to give another thought about Donna Lay.

Chapter 77

The next morning Winnie arrived to the opera annual brunch. It was held at a board member's home. Guests were still talking about the performance of Tosca and all of the glamour of the prior evening.

Sunny immediately spotted Winnie and came over, "Good morning Winnie, how are you holding up after last night?"

Winnie said, "Morning came much too fast for me. All this fun is wearing me out. But guess what, I love every minute of it."

Sunny said, "Girl, me too. Well remember after this one you are coming to my place for the tea."

Winnie smiled brightly saying, "Sunny, I know I say it all the time but how do you keep up with everything. You my friend are the seventh wonder of the world."

Sunny said, "You know I told each one of my husband's that right before they divorced me." She laughed out loud and Winnie just smiled and shook her head saying, "Sunny you are too much."

Looking around Sunny replied, "No I am not. But look at this brunch, our hostess has out done herself, my goodness it all my favorites."

Winnie said, "Let's start with coffee."

Sunny laughed, "I will make mine a bloody Mary."

The two friends had traveled the world together in support of the arts. And never seemed to run out of things to chat about and make each other laugh.

Sunny had organized a small tea party for the opera women's committee and invited Winnie to be her guest at her exquisite home on Francisco Street in the Russian Hill section of town.

It was the last event of the weekend. As Winnie enjoyed the banter and laughter between the ladies she pushed all thoughts of Phillip and her non-stop schedule out of her mind.

Sunny said, "Winnie do you have to head back to Washington, DC., tonight? If you can stay over you and I can spend some time just hanging out."

Winnie said, "Oh Sunny, that sounds like fun but I need to be getting back to work. I am working on a big story right now."

Sunny loved any insider information. She said, "Oh do tell, anyone I may know about."

Winnie laughed and said, "No Sunny not this time."

Winnie would be heading home in a few hours but for now she enjoyed the relaxed mood that Sunny always seemed to invoke.

Chapter 78

It was late in the afternoon when Winnie returned to her hotel, she needed to start packing for her return flight home. Just as she clicked on the television, she heard a knock on her door.

It was Phillip. "Hi Winnie, can you spare me a minute of your time?"

"Hello Phillip, how are you? Please come in." Winnie was not sure what he wanted.

Phillip suddenly seemed shy and at a loss for words. He said, "I wanted to wish you a safe flight home." Winnie thought, "*Phillip was sending mixed messages.*" She wasn't sure if he was flirting with her or if he was just being a concerned friend. She didn't know what to think.

They talked about the opera and San Francisco's architecture. He complimented her on everything she had done or had worn during the weekend, even the hot-pink silk pajamas she was wearing now.

Phillip said, "Winnie, you are the most beautiful woman that I have ever seen."

Winnie answered, "Phillip, thank you but I must ask you: why are you here? What is it that you need to tell me?"

"Winnie, it's no secret that I have developed feelings for you."

"Please Phillip. I have told you before that I do not have affairs with married men. Please don't say anything more."

"I will always honor you, Winnie but I have to tell you how much I have grown to care for you."

"Phillip, please stop it. I don't want to hear this. Don't you understand? I can't hear you say these words. My heart can't stand it."

Phillip could not stop himself. He had fallen for Winnie, or the idea of loving Winnie. Whatever it was, they were both feeling the same way.

Phillip and Winnie continued to talk for another hour. Being that close to him was stirring up so many emotions. She said, "Phillip, thank you for everything that you have done but I really need to get back to packing. I am sure we will see each other back home."

"I understand Winnie, I have overstayed my welcome. I truly enjoy every minute I am with you and I care deeply for you Winnie. I only came to your room because I noticed that you had been avoiding me all weekend."

Winnie said, "Phillip I have to and you understand why. I don't need any complications in my life and an affair is a complication. As much as I respect you and given the right opportunity I could care deeply for you. I cannot and will not allow this relationship to go any further than friends."

"Winnie, "My heart has a mind of its own and it has bought me to you." Winnie stood up and walked over to the door, she needed Phillip to leave and now. She said, "I am sorry Phillip. You and Donna have a safe flight home as well."

Phillip was a perfect gentleman as he followed Winnie to the door. Turning to face Winnie for a final goodbye, he suddenly reached out and gently pulled her to him and kissed her. Winnie could not resist the feel of his smooth lips and his tongue moving slowing over hers was overwhelming. Phillip's kiss and his embrace were like a magic love potion. In spite of herself, Winnie responded and gave into the feelings that had been building up. Phillip pressed her against the wall and she could feel the whole of him. Just then her senses came back to her and she pushed him away, saying, "Phillip, please, no. You are married and for the record your wife is not the nicest person in the world. She already hates me."

Phillip said, "Oh my lovely Winnie, my heart has wanted you for so long. If you had any idea how deeply I feel for you...please forgive me. I would never do anything to hurt you. But Winnie, I want you! You must know that, I will honor the fact that you are not as you say, that kind of woman to have affairs. I am not offering an affair. I want to love you for as long as you will let me. Please let me love you. Please."

Phillip moved in closer, kissing her on the forehead. Winnie just stood there. She could not speak or move. Phillip looked so good and he felt even better. She knew that if she spoke it would only be to ask him to stay and love her the way he said he would. So she remained silent and unmoved until he walked out of her suite and the door closed behind him.

Winnie was so moved by what had just happened that she needed a moment to get herself back on track. She was taking a red-eye flight back to Washington, DC., she had a few hours to rest and reflect on this amazing weekend and the new developments with Phillip.

Her telephone rang, it was Sunny wanting to re-cap the weekend activities, and talk about some of the ladies at her tea. Winnie welcomed the conversation it was the perfect distraction from her endless thoughts of Phillip.

After Winnie and Sunny promised to catch up again soon. Winnie showered and changed her clothes. She looked around the room to make sure she had packed everything.

The next knock on the door was the attendant coming to take her luggage down to her waiting car. As she rode to the airport her mind was still reliving the moments with Phillip.

She flew back to Washington, thinking of nothing but Phillip Lay. Winnie knew she would have to take control of her mind to keep her heart from giving into her feelings.

Chapter 79

When Winnie arrived home, she had tons of messages and calls to return. She knew the only way to release the hold that Phillip's kiss had on her was to overload her schedule with work and that's just what she did for the next few weeks.

She also avoided any place she thought she might run into him, including the Four Seasons. She could not take the chance that their paths would cross because she didn't trust herself. Phillip felt too good and she wanted him.

Winnie did anything to keep thoughts of Phillip out of her head. She arranged to have her trainer meet her at home for their daily workouts. She jogged for miles in Rock Creek Park and played tennis. She signed up for golf lessons at Belle Haven Country Club.

She was already a great golfer but lessons never hurt. After one of her golf lessons, she went shopping at a lovely boutique called Patrick's on North Saint Asaph Street in Old Town. It was the best place to go when you needed an elegant gift for any occasion. She was picking up several gifts for friends' upcoming birthdays, wedding showers and new baby arrivals. As she was leaving the store she ran into Coco and Saul. They had just returned from their cruise around the world and they were shopping for their new house.

Coco beamed saying, "Hello Winnie, how are you? It is so great to run into you today. Winnie this is my husband Saul."

Saul smiled and said, "Winnie I have heard so much about you, it is a pleasure to meet you face to face. I must say I watch you every morning."

Winnie hugged Coco and Saul and said, "Congratulations to you both, I am so happy for you."

Coco said, "We are just getting back from our honeymoon it was fabulous."

Winnie thought she had never seen Coco look so blissful, "I can tell Coco you never looked more happy." It seemed that marriage agreed with them.

Coco said, "Winnie I want to have you and the girls over to dinner when we finish decorating our new place."

Winnie happily said, "I would love to, just let me know when and where and I will be there."

Winnie was truly happy for them both, it appeared that the unlikely match brought them both the happiness they needed. Coco told Winnie she was converting to Judaism. That their wedding was legal but once she completed her conversion they would have a religious ceremony and reception and of course invite everyone.

Winnie wished them well and left them to do their shopping. When she stepped out of the store, she looked through the window and saw Saul gently kiss Coco's cheek and lovingly brushed a hair from her eye.

Winnie noticed that Saul held Coco's hand the entire time they chatted. Winnie smiled and thought of Phillip. She also thought that maybe it was time for her to get married again. Perhaps the third time would be the charm. She was getting really lonely and after Phillip's kiss, she was horny as hell.

The following weeks were uneventful, her overloaded schedule was not giving her the mental relief she thought it would. Memories of Phillip still crept through her mind as he continued to call and leave messages.

Chapter 80

Winnie was delighted when she received an invitation to attend her friend Sunny's birthday party. The party was being held at The Breakers resort in Palm Beach.

When she arrived she quickly discovered that to her displeasure, the Lay's were guests as well. Winnie thought, "*Oh well there are 200 guests attending this weekend celebration, I will just ignore Phillip and Donna.*"

During the gala birthday dinner dance in the Venetian ballroom, Phillip arranged to have a young man dance with Donna while he asked Winnie to join him on the dance floor.

Phillip's moves were from a different generation. He asked Winnie when she was seated around other guests, putting her in a spot where, if she said no, it would look odd to the people watching them and if she said yes, Donna would surely see them dancing. Phillip took Winnie by the arm and they danced to Natalie Cole's "Unforgettable."

He pulled Winnie closer to him, she could feel his every muscle—as he could feel her every curve. As he led them across the dance floor, Winnie was sure that her heart stopped because he felt and smelled like heaven. He whispered in her ear, "I asked the band leader to play this song for us, Winnie."

Winnie said, "Phillip this has to stop. Really Phillip I can't do this."

Phillip pulled her even closer and said, "Let me love you Winnie. I need you and I know how to make you happy."

When the music finally stopped, Winnie said, "Thank you for the dance but this is not making me happy."

She walked off the dance floor, leaving him standing alone. As she passed Donna, she got a look that would kill.

Winnie perfectly understood that Phillip's desire was only going to make her life hell and no matter how much she wanted him an affair was just not worth the risk.

The next morning as she was stepping out of the shower there was a knock at her door, wrapping herself in a thick terry robe. She quickly thought, *"Lord please don't let this be Phillip."* She didn't want a repeat of her San Francisco experience with him. She gingerly peeped through the door's peephole, there was a porter standing there. When she opened the door he said, "Sorry to bother you madam but this package was sent to you. I was asked to bring it right away."

Winnie said, "Oh well thank you so much, please come in." She quickly tipped the gentleman and closed the door.

She thought, *"Sunny must be sending everyone a gift for attending her birthday weekend. How sweet of her."*

Winnie sat down to read the card it said.

Dearest Winnie,
It was the dance of my life.
XO
Phillip

Inside the beautifully wrapped box, she found an eighteen-carat gold pendant of a dancing lady, encrusted with brilliant rose-cut white diamonds. The bodice of the dress was accented with circular-cut rubies and sapphires. As she read the card again, tears began running down Winnie's cheeks. Phillip was making her feel emotions that she wasn't prepared for. His touch, his hold, the lovely gifts—it was all too much. Her phone started to ring. She knew it was Phillip. She was not prepared to speak with him right now. She placed the pendant in the wall safe. She would handle Phillip and the gift later.

She dressed and headed out to meet up with Sunny. They were scheduled to play golf on the ocean course.

Over breakfast Sunny said, "What's happening with you and Phillip Lay? He clearly has eyes for you."

Winnie said, "Nothing. We have a lot in common, we both love the opera, gardening and we have many of the same friends. But there is nothing else. By the way I didn't know that you and the Lay's were such good friends. I was surprised to see them here."

Sunny smiled, "We have built up a good friendship, we all travel to the same spots around the world. I seem to run into them everywhere. But Winnie please don't change the subject. Phillip's attention to you is showing for all to see."

Winnie thought for a minute then she said, "Well Sunny you know me, I have never had an affair with a married man and I am not about to start now. There is nothing going on with me and Phillip."

Sunny said, "Well, maybe not for you, but what I saw on the dance floor last night said that Phillip Lay has it bad for you. I have been married five times and have had more affairs than I can count. I know when a man is in lusty love—and Mr. Lay is in deep for you, Winnie. Now what you do with that is up to you but that does not diminish the facts. I am your friend for life and I will never judge you."

Winnie said, "Can we change the subject? Are we playing golf today or what?"

Sunny laughed and said, "Well, that will be one ball getting in a hole." They both laughed and headed out to play a round of golf. The weather was perfect, bright sunny skies and a light warm breeze. After their eighteen holes, they headed to the Club house. Winnie saw Phillip teeing off at the first tee, she was determined not to show any emotions. Sunny said, "Hey, isn't that Phillip teeing off?"

Winnie said, "Oh yeah. Well, let's hope he makes a hole in one."

"Well, that's not the hole he is longing for", said Sunny.

Winnie rolled her eyes and said, "Sunny, that's just nasty."

"Nasty or not, it's the truth", smiled Sunny.

After the golf outing and luncheon, the weekend came to a gracious close and Winnie returned home on Sunday night.

As she took one last look at the delicate gold-and-diamond pendant, she knew that it meant so much more than just a kind gesture and she couldn't take a bite of that forbidden fruit.

She left a note for her secretary to return the gift with a note to Phillip that said, "It was a wonderful fantasy but this dance is too expensive for me to ever have in real life."

When Phillip received the gift back, he was wounded. Winnie had touched his heart in so many ways. If only she knew how much he cared about her. Maybe he should tell her how lonely he was in his marriage and how much he wanted out. Donna and Phillip had a public marriage and nothing else.

Phillip felt that Donna was a cold-hearted, materialistic woman who only stayed with him because of his last name and net worth. They hadn't slept together in over ten years. She had her bedroom and he had his. They didn't even eat dinner together. Donna said she, "Hated the way he chewed his food."

The real reason was that she didn't like to eat. Donna had long ago developed an eating disorder. She would chew any meat on her plate but not swallow it, leaving little balls of chewed food.

But the mannerism that broke Phillips heart was the coldness she displayed toward their children and grandchildren. Donna preferred the company of her socialite friends and only wanted to be seen with Phillip at special events. She tolerated Phillip to ensure her lifestyle and the occasional picture in one of the glossy magazines. Phillip needed to feel loved again. He thought, "*This cannot be all that there is. Somewhere there must be someone who will enjoy the things that I enjoy and who will desire me as much as I desire her.*"

Chapter 81

Winnie was back at work and Washington was alive with headline news. Just as she was about to go on the air, her phone rang. It was Officer Shaw.

"Good morning it's Winnie."

"Hey Winnie, I am just getting word another young woman has been beaten and raped. She was found by a jogger off Canal Road. I think we have a serial rapist loose in our city."

Winnie said, "How do you know."

Shaw said, "Winnie, what do you mean how do I know. I am a cop remember."

Winnie quickly answered, "Yea, I am sorry Shaw. Can you tell me anymore."

Shaw said, "The young woman's purse was found a few yards away from her body. Her cell phone, wallet, and house keys were missing. Her work identification confirmed that she worked for Senator Moyer."

"Oh no. My producer is calling me to get to the desk. I will call you as soon as we break. Shaw, I need this story. Please tell me what else you know," said Winnie.

Officer Shaw said, "Winnie, we have a sick monster out here. This young girl is bad off. I am going to find this bastard."

"Give me everything you have. The station is sending a news truck over to the scene now but I need to know everything about this young woman. Can you get me in to see her?", said Winnie.

Shaw said, "Damn, Winnie, slow down. I am not sure if this kid will make it. She is at Georgetown Hospital."

Rushing to get in position for the live broadcast Winnie said, "I will be there as soon as I sign off. Shaw, get me in to see her, please."

Shaw said, "Okay, Winnie, you know I will try. Later." With that Officer Shaw ended their call.

Within minutes she received a text from Shaw. It just said, "Shanne Wilks."

When Shanne arrived at the emergency room. The medical team was careful with every aspect of their examination, making sure not to corrupt important physical evidence. Shanne's attacker had removed her underwear and bra. Some latex fibers were found inside her vaginal and anal walls, indicating that her attacker had used a condom or gloves during the assault. Traces of sodium hypochlorite and polysorbate 20 were found on her body. The findings from her exam, along with results from the laboratory, didn't yield a conclusive identity of the attacker. But they did raise questions for Officer Shaw. Whoever her attacker was, he was very familiar with industrial cleaning products.

Shaw thought, *"Why would traces of chlorhexidine gluconate, an antibacterial skin cleaner found in HiBiScrub, be on areas of Shanne's body?".* These antibacterial agents were commonly used in hospitals on patients who tested positive for MRSA. Shaw immediately started running a search on recently released sex offender's that had a background in health care, who might also have a connection to Capitol Hill.

When Shanne regained consciousness, she was interviewed by the police, she was too afraid to give any names. Her injuries were bad, multiple contusions, a concussion, and a fractured jaw. The doctor warned the police to go slow because Shanne might be mentally impaired due to her concussion.

Shaw and a team of detectives were on their way to the young woman's apartment and were making contact with Senator Moyer's office and Shanne's next of kin. They were interviewing her coworkers, neighbors, and anyone who had seen her in the last forty-eight hours, looking for any lead in the case. When her landlord let them into her apartment, the evidence team combed through everything. The apartment had been cleaned out. There was no computer, cell phone, or i-Pad. Her small desk was cleaned off and her bed sheets had been removed along with all the towels in her bathroom. There was not one spot that hadn't been cleaned with strong professional cleaning products.

Shaw said, "Only a professional would clean up this good."

The chief of police, a strong willed woman who didn't take any shit was calling Shaw's cell phone. "Did you find anything?, she said."

Shaw answered, "Nothing yet but no one is that smart. I will find something. This monster moved fast. The girl hadn't been in the park that long."

The police chief said, "Stay on it. I want this bastard off our streets—and now."

Chapter 82

Winnie ran a background check on Shanne, which revealed that the young woman was born and raised in Akron, Ohio. Her parents divorced when she was only four years old and a year later her father was killed by a drunk driver. Her mother never remarried. She had been an honor student all through school and had been awarded a full four year academic scholarship to Marymount University. After graduation she took a part-time job on Capitol Hill, working as a receptionist and then as a secretary. Now she was a speech writer for Senator Moyer. Shanne had been an active member of several different young leadership groups, her facebook and twitter pages showed that she had a busy social life and many friends.

The press coverage on the attack was nonstop. Shanne's entire past was now being flashed across the television screen. The coverage was not painting a positive picture of the young woman. She was being labeled as a party girl.

Winnie interviewed Senator Moyer, who was very saddened by the news that one of his staffers was the victim of such a personal and brutal attack. He spoke highly of the young woman and asked for the public's help in finding this criminal.

When the interview was complete the senator said, "I have daughters. My God, what if it had been one of them? I can't imagine the pain that her mother is going through right now." He then said, " I want you to know Shanne is like family to me, all my staff members are an extension of my family."

He looked away. When he turned back around, he was visibly angry. He said, "I want this sexual pervert caught. He has hurt one of mine. I will not let him get away with it."

Winnie said, "The police are working hard on this case."

Senator Moyer quickly said, “That’s not enough. I want them to turn over every rock and do whatever they have to do to find this monster.”

When she finished the interview. Winnie went to the hospital. She needed to try and get into see Shanne. Officer Shaw hadn’t called her with anymore updates on the girl. She knew if she called him he’d tell her to stay out of police business, so Winnie would just go it alone.

A very despondent looking woman was standing outside of Shanne’s hospital room when Winnie arrived.

Winnie said, “Hello, you must be Shanne’s mother. I am Winnie Pettridge, I am news reporter.” Before Winnie could say another word Shanne’s mother said, “Yes I am. Can you find out who did this to my daughter? “

She grabbed Winnie’s arm and said, “Please help me.”

Winnie reached out to comfort her giving her a hug, she didn’t want to do or say anything that could further upset her. Winnie gently said, “Yes. I will do anything to help you find who did this. But first I need to speak with your daughter. Will you allow me a couple of minutes to ask her some questions?”

Shanne’s mom said, “The police have been here all day asking questions. I am not sure that she is strong enough. You know someone tried to kill my child.” Mrs. Wilks started to cry, then she said, “This is a nightmare, why would anyone want to hurt Shanne? She is the kindest, friendliest girl I know. Why has someone done this to her?”

When they entered the room Winnie introduced herself saying, “Hi Shanne, you don’t know me but I am here to help you. My name is Winnie, can we talk for a minute?”

Shanne was deathly afraid. She said, “I have seen you on TV, you help people. The police said that they will protect me and my mom but I am not sure.”

Tears started running down her bruised face she said, “If I talk to you he might kills us. I want to get out of this city, I want to be far away from here.”

Winnie said, “Shanne please tell me who did this to you? What is his name? I can help you and the police will help you but first you have to give us something to go on. We need his name.”

When Winnie pressed her to identify her attacker the young woman started to shake all over, she pressed the button for the nurse. She said she wanted Winnie to leave.

Mrs. Wilks said, "I told you not to upset her."

Winnie said, "I am sorry I didn't mean to. I only want to help but you have to help us. If Shanne knows who attacked her, she needs to tell somebody, the police, me or anyone that can help her."

Winnie left her card with her cell number on it. She told Shanne that if she had a change of heart, she could call her anytime, day or night.

Two days later as Shanne was scheduled to be discharged Mrs. Wilks was arriving early to take her daughter home. She heard a call over the hospital sound system. "Code Blue room 625, Code Blue room 625."

It was Shanne's room. Her mother ran as fast as she could up the hospital stairs until she reached Shanne's room. Nurses and doctors were busy performing a full cardiac code. She tried to push through some of the medical staff but a nurse asked Mrs. Wilks to please wait outside the room. She said, "This is my daughter, oh my GOD what happened to her."

The code team worked on Shanne for one hour but they could not bring her back. Officer Shaw arrived just as the doctor was saying, "Mrs. Wilks, I am so sorry we did everything we could. Her heart just stopped beating."

Mrs. Wilks screamed, "What do you mean, it just stopped beating. My daughter didn't have a heart problem. Someone or something killed my little girl." The doctor just kept saying how sorry he was and that they would do an autopsy to determine the cause of death.

Officer Shaw started to ask questions of the nursing staff, he wanted to know everyone that had come and gone in Shanne's room over the last few hours.

There was suddenly an eerie silence in the room as Mrs. Wilks walked over to Shanne's lifeless body. Gently she lifted Shanne in her arms and started to rock back and forth, singing to her and running her hand over Shanne's hair. She remembered when Shanne was born, the moment she looked into the face of her baby girl, the sound of her baby's first cry and every moment that had happened since then. She was very young when Shanne was born and really not ready to become a mother. After Shanne's father walked out on them, leaving her to handle everything, she quickly learned and she and Shanne had grown up together. Closing her eyes, she wept uncontrollably. How would she begin to live without her only child, her baby, her world was now dead.

There were no words that any nurse, doctor or minister can say to a grieving parent, who has just witnessed the death of their child.

Officer Shaw stood in the doorway witnessing this heartbreaking scene, he was speechless. He quickly scanned the room and noticed that there was a food tray untouched in Shanne's room. He walked out of the room, over to the nurse's station and asked the unit secretary if Shanne had been unable to eat her breakfast. The young woman said, "I am sorry officer, but that patient was not ordered any food today. There shouldn't be a tray in her room. She was NPO, that means nothing by mouth. She has a badly broken jaw and was not on solid food yet. I will ask the nurse to get the tray out of her room."

Shaw quickly said, "No, please don't touch anything in that room." He called police headquarters and gave them an update on Shanne and asked for a crime team to come over to the hospital.

An hour later as hospital transporters arrived and the nursing staff prepared to roll Shanne's body away to the morgue. Mrs. Wilks started screaming and Officer Shaw had to hold her back. Officer Shaw said, "Mrs. Wilks, I am so sorry but they have to take her, we need to have an autopsy performed to determine the cause of death."

Mrs. Wilks screamed saying, "The cause of death is clear, they killed my baby. My Shanne is dead."

Officer Shaw and Mrs. Wilks slowly walked behind the morgue gurney that was covered in black carrying Shanne.

When they got into the employee's elevator, Officer Shaw said, "Mrs. Wilks, I am sorry to have to ask you questions at a time like this but I have to know. Please tell me if you can remember anything about who Shanne was dating. Do you know who attacked your daughter?"

Mrs. Wilks said, "Officer my GOD. If I knew I would tell you but I don't know. All she ever told me was that he was some guy who worked on Capitol

Hill. Shanne had a crush on him. She talked about him all the time but she would never tell me his name. I think he was married or something. He had promised to get her a better job. That's all I know."

Shaw said, "Mrs. Wilks, I know how you must be feeling right now, I am so sorry for your loss.

Mrs. Wilks said, "No you don't, you could never understand what I am feeling right now. My child, my life, my world is dead. No Officer you don't understand. Now stop asking me these damn questions and go out and find who killed my baby."

Officer Shaw steely said, "To do that I need your help. Please think, was there ever a time when she may have mentioned his first name? Or anything about him that could help us find this creep?"

Though her sobs Mrs. Wilks answered, "Shanne would not tell me anything about the men she went out with. All she said was that he had a lot of contacts with really important people and that he was going to help her get a job, maybe in the White House."

Shaw felt bad for the woman but there was a murderer out there and he needed to find him before he killed again. He took a deep breath and then said, "From what you are telling me this could be anybody. I need a name, a picture, something, anything that will link this guy to the death of your daughter."

Mrs. Wilks said, "Officer Shaw I really can't handle any more of your questions. I need to follow them to the morgue, I just want to be with her."

Officer Shaw said, "Do you have any family that can be with you, you should not be alone right now."

Officer Shaw stayed with her until she was finished signing the final papers. Then he walked Mrs. Wilks out of the hospital, put her in a cab and told her if she remembered anything to call him day or night.

On the drive back to her hotel, she telephoned her only relatives, Aunt Jessie and Uncle Todd. They lived two hours away in a small town called Easton, Maryland they owned and operated a bait shop. As she told the elderly couple what had happened to Shanne, she herself couldn't believe that her baby was dead. Shanne had so many dreams of making a life in Washington to become a White House advisor. Shanne dreamed of having a family someday. She wanted the same things other young women wanted and now she was dead.

Aunt Jessie and Uncle Todd didn't drive anymore, they told Mrs. Wilks to come out to their house and stay with them until she knew what to do next. Mrs. Wilks was afraid and she wanted to get out of this city as fast as possible.

Aunt Jessie said, "Please come stay with us, I know we have not been much of a family to you over the years but we are here for you now."

Mrs. Wilks sobbed, "I don't know what to do right now. I will call you later."

She spent the remainder of the day making plans for Shanne's final resting place. She was receiving calls from every news outlet wanting a interview but she declined them all. She made the necessary arrangements to have Shanne's body sent home to Ohio for private burial services. Senator Moyer called her several times wanting to know what arrangements she had made and if he could say something at the services for Shanne.

Mrs. Wilks didn't want to have anything to do with anyone in Washington, so she let all the calls go to voice mail.

That night Mrs. Wilks couldn't sleep she was afraid someone would break into her hotel room and kill her like they had Shanne.

When she turned on the television, the story was receiving constant coverage and the media was portraying Shanne to be a loose party girl but that was not the person that Mrs. Wilks knew. She thought, *"Why are they doing this to my Shanne...this is not her."*

Officer Shaw called her late that evening saying, "Good evening Mrs. Wilks, I have the findings from the pathology department, I am so sorry to tell you this but a large amount of ethylene glycol was found in Shanne's blood and lungs."

Mrs. Wilks said, "What is ethylene glycol?"

Officer Shaw took a deep breath and then said, "It's antifreeze. Mrs. Wilks this is now a murder case. The entire department is working on finding your daughter's killer."

"WHY, WHY, WHY WOULD ANYONE KILL MY CHILD," Mrs. Wilks, yelled. Crying hysterically her child was dead and there was nothing that could un-break her heart or answer her questions as to Why?.

The next morning when she went outside to pick up the morning paper, there was a package at her hotel door. When she opened it there was a rat with its neck sliced open and a note that read, "Run while you can."

No one but the police, Senator Moyer and her Aunt and Uncle knew where she was staying. Someone was coming for her and she was determined not to let them find her. She quickly packed all of her clothes, wrapped the package in newspaper and wrote Officer Shaw's name on it. When she checked out of the hotel she asked the front desk clerk to please see that the Officer received the package. She left no forwarding address for herself.

She received a call from Officer Shaw saying, "What's going on? Where are you? I just called the hotel and they told me you checked out."

Mrs. Wilks said, "Oh, I just needed to find a more affordable room. When I get settled, I will call you, Officer. Please find out who killed Shanne. I left you a package at the hotel front desk."

Officer Shaw said, "What kind of package? Okay Mrs. Wilks, I am heading over to the hotel now. Tell me where you are, I will send a car for you."

She thought for a minute remembering the sight of the dead rat and then she said, "Officer please find the person that did this....that's all I ask of you."

As soon as she ended the call with Officer Shaw, her cell phone rang again. The caller was a male with a heavy voice. He said, "Shut up if you know what's good for you." She dropped the cell phone in the nearest trash can, hopped in the first cab she saw and gave them the address in Easton, Maryland.

Officer Shaw tried calling her several times but there was no answer. He rushed over to the hotel. When he reached the front desk he showed the clerk his badge and said, "Can you ring room 212 for me please?"

The front desk clerk said, "I'm sorry officer but the guest just checked out."

Officer Shaw asked, "Did she leave a forwarding address or telephone number?"

The clerk looked at the computer screen, there was no forwarding information just a note about the package. The clerk replied, "Officer Shaw, there is a package here for you." She quickly reached under the desk and grabbed the package and handed it to Shaw.

Taking the package he said, "Where is your manager?"

When the manager quickly came to the desk. Shaw said, "I need to look around room 212." The manager quickly gave Shaw the access he need and said, "Officer if there is anything else we can help you with let me know."

"Thank you", said Shaw.

As Shaw was walking to the room he opened the package and saw the dead rat he said, "Damn, what in the hell." Shaw read the note that was with the dead rodent and then reached into his pocket for an evidence bag. He would enter the entire package as evidence when he returned to the station. He scanned the room, it was clean Mrs. Wilks had been scared out of town.

Chapter 83

Winnie was haunted by the death of Shanne, which made her more determined to find the horrendous viper that was victimizing these young women. She was thankful that Tiffany and Paulina were safe but she could not shake the feeling that she was overlooking something. Her senses told her that Flank was behind these attacks.

She just needed solid evidence, something that the police could use to implicate him as their prime suspect. The tape only proved he was a freak, it was not enough to prove he was a homicidal killer. If Paulina would step-up and tell the truth about what really happened to her that night it would shed light on who Flank really was. Winnie didn't have the heart to pressure her and possibly alienate Nancy.

The situation was not looking any better at the police station, the chief of police had received several calls from higher authority concerning the case, which only meant there was something big-time going on.

Officer Shaw had compiled a list of possible suspects and Flank was at the top of the list. Flank was the only person who happen to have been at several of the events that the young women had attended and now one of the women was dead. The police chief dispatched detectives to watch Flank's every move. Officer Shaw didn't think that Flank was operating alone, the clean ups were too professional. Whomever was helping Flank had experience with industrial removal agents. Shaw thought, "*There is no way this freak is doing all of this by himself.*"

While the police and detectives were busy doing their jobs. Winnie was mounting a very intensive investigation of Flank on her own. So far she had only turned up information about his upbringing. He was raised by a Baptist minister, his mother was a Sunday school teacher who worked part-time in a drugstore. During his younger years he had dreams of playing baseball for a major team. However a skiing accident killed his dream of becoming a sports hero. He took a job in the county executive's office and a couple of years later, his name appeared on the ballot, surprising his family and friends.

As Winnie combed through research she noticed that Flank's soon-to-be father-law was in every picture with him. Governor David Allen Tackett, a hard-nosed, multimillionaire who had worked his way up the ladder to the highest office in Colorado.

Continuing her search what Winnie found even odder was that there were very few pictures of Flank with his fiancée, Belinda Tackett, a skinny, homely-looking girl.

Winnie looked up everything about Flank, his traffic record, credit report, and criminal records. When she was finished she was disappointed, Flank didn't have so much as a warning ticket. What she found surprising was how he lived, for someone on a junior congressional salary, he lived very well and employed a large staff of locals.

That confirmed part of Winnie's suspicions Flank was in good old Governor Tackett's pocket.

Chapter 84

Officer Shaw finally thought he had a break in the Canal Road rapist case when one of Shanne's co-workers called to report that they had found a picture of her on a USB drive. The picture had been taken a few days before her attack. She had attended a political fundraiser at the W hotel and then went to a private after-party, several photos showed Flank and Shanne playfully flirting with each other.

This was just the discovery Shaw needed to question the congressman about his relationship with Shanne Wilks and his whereabouts on the night she was attacked. The interview took place in the congressman's congressional office. He was accompanied by his attorney and public relations director.

"Congressman Flank, as you know, a young woman was attacked recently and we have reason to believe you knew her." Officer Shaw showed Flank a picture of Shanne taken from her employee badge and asked him if he had ever seen the young woman.

Flank quickly said, "I don't know this young woman."

Officer Shaw said, "Really", then he threw down a picture of Shanne and the congressman flirting and said, "Now do you know her."

Flank looked at his lawyer and then to his aide and said, "Well, I mean, I don't remember ever meeting her."

Flank examined the picture, and he truly could not remember the young woman. He could not even remember that evening or anything about the party. He had done a couple lines of cocaine, had two dirty martinis and was stoned out of his head.

"Hey, look here officer. I meet a lot of people and some are pretty women and they all want to take pictures with me. That does not mean anything."

His lawyer could see the puzzled look on Flank's face when he looked at the picture and he knew this was not going to end well for Flank if he did not interrupt this line of questioning, so before Flank could finish his sentence, his attorney stopped him.

"Excuse me but my client will not answer any more questions unless you have a warrant for his arrest. This interview is finished."

Shaw was tired of the bullshit with Flank. He gave Flank's attorney a hard stare and said, "That can be arranged."

Just then a young woman came through the door carrying a package. She handed it to the attorney, who carefully examined the papers and smiled.

"As I said, if you don't have a warrant, this interview is over."

Shaw said, "I need to know where your client was during the time this young woman was being raped and beaten. And I am really interested in his whereabouts during the time someone administered a lethal dose of anti-freeze into her. This young women is dead and someone killed her and I am here to find out where your client was."

Flank's attorney proudly stepped forward saying, "Well, I think you should pose those questions to someone else, because we can prove that my client had nothing to do with this or any other crime. Officer maybe you should look at our pictures. They are time-and-date stamped."

His attorney presented solid proof that Flank had been on a plane heading to Denver at the time of the attack on Shanne Wilks. There were additional photos showing Flank boarding a plane at Reagan National Airport and departing at Denver International Airport. He'd purchased a drink on the flight and the receipt was also stamped with the date and time of the purchase. There were more photos of Flank leaving a press conference at the time someone was delivering the fatal dose to Shanne.

For now there was nothing more that the police could do, Flank was cleared.

Flank said, "Officer, I think you owe me an apology for wasting my time. Like I said, I had nothing to do with this crime. Now if we are finished, I would like for you to get the hell out of my office."

Shaw was pissed off and somewhat embarrassed. Flank's attorney handed him the pictures and told him to take them with him. For sure, Shaw was back at square one.

As Shaw drove back to the station, he couldn't shake the feeling that there was a mystery surrounding Flank. He would send the photos to the lab to see if they could find any traces of photo shop or editing.

Soon after he reached his desk he got a call from the police chief.

"Shaw, in my office now." The Chief was under major pressure to solve this case.

Shaw said, "Chief, I have never in all my years seen anything like this case. We have been shut down at every turn. It's like someone knows what we are looking for."

The police chief said, "We have to look deeper. I need this case solved."

Shaw said, "I believe the same person who beat Shanne is her killer. As a matter of fact I believe the perpetrator is the same person who beat Tiffany Barnhill. We are looking for a serial rapist and we need to find him before he can hurt another woman."

The police chief said, "I agree but we are running out of time."

Shaw interviewed everybody that could have seen or heard anything the night of the attack. He searched the hospital camera footage and interviewed every hospital worker on staff the morning of Shanne's death. He interviewed the jogger who had found her body but he could not supply any additional evidence and no one else had come forward with anything.

Chapter 85

As Coco was driving down River Road, her cell phone rang. It was Nancy. She was very upset—something about a fight with Sadie over Paulina dating Timothy Von Kinley. Coco thought, "*You go, Paulina.*"The last time Coco saw Tim, she'd thought he was the perfect gentleman and very handsome.

Sadie and Lonnie had very attractive sons. They had also inherited Lonnie's elegance and Sadie's quick wit; the combination was delightful. Coco told Nancy to calm down and tell her what had happened. She reminded Nancy that she and Saul were just returning home from their honeymoon.

Nancy thought Coco would never change. She was still trying to impress. Nancy said, "Coco, I am so very happy for you and if this is a bad time, please call me back when it's better for you."

Coco said, "Well, I am rushing home. Saul and I are heading to our house in Middleburg, Virginia. Can I call you early next week? I would love for you and Salim to come and spend the weekend with us as soon as I have things together."

Nancy could not believe it. Coco was dismissing her and after everything she had done for her. Nancy said, "Good-bye Coco."

"Oh Nancy, I am sorry. Please don't say it like that. I am truly interested in what's going on. You know I have always loved you and your family", said Coco.

"It's okay, Coco. You take care of your new family. We will be okay."

Coco could tell Nancy was upset and she didn't want that so she said, "Okay, let's talk next week."

When the call ended, Coco felt like she was somehow not being supportive of her friends and they had always been there to listen to her. But right now she just wanted to be with Saul and if her friends did not understand then that would be on them.

She also thought that Nancy got too involved in other people's business. Nancy and Sadie had what she was just now getting to enjoy. Coco hoped they would understand but if they didn't she thought, *"Oh well, Saul must come first."*

When she walked in the door, Saul was waiting for her. She dropped her bags and went into his strong arms. She knew wherever they were was home. He was her life, her home, her everything.

Within an hour they were on Route 66 heading to Middleburg, Virginia, their home was located on five acres with unobstructed views of the Bull Run Mountains. The main house sat at the top of the property. The house was large but not overwhelming, with soaring ceilings and large rooms that were both formal and comfortable, it had two master-bedroom suites with super large soaking tubs and four additional guest bedrooms. There was a large country kitchen with lots of windows and French doors off the breakfast room, a tiered terrace and an outdoor kitchen that were perfect for entertaining, formal boxwood gardens and beautiful landscaped grounds, a swimming pool and a state-of-the-art barn where Saul housed four thoroughbred horses. The barn was equipped with washrooms, grooming rooms, and a tack room, all temperature-controlled and a trainer's apartment. Outside of the barn was a riding ring.

It was everything that Coco had envisioned a country estate to be and all in the heart of Virginia's hunt country. The house had been professionally decorated and the walls were filled with art by great American painters like Winslow Homer and Edward Hopper.

Saul had notified the full-time caretaker, a kind gentleman who had lived in the cottage house at the foot of the driveway that led to the main house, he and his wife had worked there for over thirty years. Saul let them know that they would be arriving late and would not be needing anything special, so they could have the evening off, but to please stock the refrigerator with food for the weekend.

It was a long drive from Washington to Middleburg and Friday evening traffic had been hell. By the time they arrived, Coco and Saul were both tired, so after a quick dinner of fresh deli meats and cheeses and a good bottle of champagne, they went to bed.

The next morning when Coco woke up, she went to the kitchen to make coffee for Saul. She could not believe how beautiful the property looked in the early morning hours. She poured herself a cup of tea and went outside to watch the morning sun and listen to the birds singing. She took in a deep breath, wanting to fill her lungs with the sweet smell of honeysuckle and lavender that bordered the property.

After about an hour, she went back into the house to get another cup of tea when she noticed a large box on the dining room table.

Coco went over to the package and read the card:

> Coco, my love
> This is for our new home. I love you more than life itself.
> XOXO Saul

Inside the beautifully wrapped box was a complete set of Dodie Thayer lovely green lettuce ware, over two hundred pieces. That had been auctioned off at Christie's. Saul had outbid everyone to get the set for Coco.

When they were in New York, Coco had seen a picture of the set in a magazine and told him about how her mother had collected only a few pieces and it was the only thing that she ever wanted from her mother. Saul remembered the conversation because it was the only time that Coco smiled when she talked about her childhood.

When Saul walked into the dining room, he found Coco in tears. She didn't give him a chance to say a word. She leaped into his arms and hugged him tightly.

Coco said, "Oh my darling, I have always wanted a set of Dodie Thayer. This is her entire collection. It is wonderful! Thank you so much. I want to display it in the breakfast room, if that is okay with you."

"Whatever makes you happy is okay with me. Coco, this is our home, your home, and you are free to do whatever you want, my love", said Saul.

Saul and Coco spent the rest of the weekend, shopping in the lovely antique shops in town, relaxing and taking walks around the property.

On Sunday evening while they were having a quiet dinner. Coco bought up her conversation with Nancy and how it had made her feel.

"Saul, I want to be there for my friends when they need me and I feel like I have let them down."

"Coco, I have been wanting to chat with you about your relationship with Sadie, Nancy and Winnie. My love it's important that we keep friendships and you all have been in each other's lives for a long time."

"What are you saying Saul? Do you agree that I have let them down."

"No, that is not what I am saying. I don't think that you meant to do it. But I feel like I have taken you away from everyone. I want to love everyone that you love Coco. That includes your family and your friends."

"Well, I have told you that I don't have much of a family. Nancy, Sadie and Winnie have been my family for years. And now I have you."

"Yes love, you have me until the day I die. But I want you to have a complete balance. Coco I want you to make things right with Sadie and spend some time caring and listening to Nancy and Winnie."

"Saul, I have tried with Sadie, she is really being unforgiving with me. I don't know what else to do."

"Try harder, if you truly want to keep her as a friend that is what you must do. Now when can I meet your sister Barbara and her family."

"Do you really want to do that."

"Yes, it's very important to me. Pick a date that will work for everyone and invite them down here for a weekend in the country. Coco, we have plenty of room."

"Okay mister togetherness. When can we spend some time with your kids and their spouses." Saul walked over to Coco wrapped her in his arms and said, "Anytime you would like, nothing would make me happier."

They spent the rest of their time just enjoying the lazy quiet that is Middleburg.

Chapter 86

Benny and Amy were delighted at the thought of becoming parents and they planned a small dinner to show off Amy's "baby bump." Now that their parents knew, they wanted the world to know, inviting only their siblings and close friends over to make the announcement.

Benny said, "Hey guys just wanted you to know we are pregnant." Everyone was excited and there was a feeling of joy and excitement that filled the room.

Tim said, "Yea, I am going to be a Uncle. Man I could not be happier for you. Benny you have it all."

Tim came to the dinner without Paulina, and he looked miserable.

Benny said, "Your time will come Tim. How is Paulina? What's happening with you two?"

Benny was happy and afraid for his brother. If it didn't work out, it would be Tim's second failed relationship. He knew how much his brother enjoyed being part of a couple. Benny said, "Tim, don't rush it, just let it happen."

Tim took a sip of his drink and said, "Is it rushing when you realized that when you are not with that person you feel like half of yourself. You want to share every good and bad thing with them first. You can't wait to hear their voice at the other end of the telephone. And when hours fly bye like seconds when you are with them. Is that rushing?"

Benny said, "That my brother is love."

Just as Tim was about to say something else Larry walked into the room.

Larry was savoring his bachelor life and it showed. His date was a Victoria's Secret model who was wearing the shortest dress Amy had ever seen.

They all enjoyed a divine dinner that Amy had prepared herself, they talked about everything that was happening in their lives. The evening ended too soon for everyone but Tim, who couldn't wait to get back to Paulina. He flew into Washington, D.C., to take Paulina for a quick dinner before heading back out of town to meet with a client.

Paulina was delighted to spend even a couple of hours with Tim, she had been studying for an upcoming final exam. Tim had been wonderful for her studies. His knowledge of law was exceptional. They grabbed a quick dinner at Ping by Charlie Chiang in Shirlington, Virginia. It was close to the airport and had the best Sushi bar in town.

Paulina had received a long email from Tiffany, it was the first time she'd heard from her since they said goodbye in England. It seemed that everything was working out well. Tiffany and her Aunt were doing fine, they had started up a goat cheese company which was keeping them both busy.

Tiffany had also met a young man who's property bordered hers. Tiffany said he was a Duke and she was enjoying getting to know him and that England was a great place to live. She invited Paulina to come for a visit.

Over dinner Paulina shared that she finally heard from Tiffany, she was excited that everything was working out for her former roommate. As Paulina told him stories of her past rebellious behavior with Tiffany.

Tim listened carefully he was thinking about what Benny had said to him he needed to feel confidante that Paulina was on the same page with him. So he asked her, "How much do you miss Tiffany. I mean do you miss her, or do you miss the partying? Do you think you have it all out of your system? Because I don't think my heart could stand finding you with another man."

Paulina hadn't meant for the conversation to turn so serious she said, "No, it's not like that Tim. Tiffany had a lot of boyfriends. I never did, I am only telling you this because, I do miss Tiffany and I received an email from her today. I guess she has been on my mind. Tim, I don't want any other boyfriend but you."

Tim became very quiet and still. He gave her a hard, piercing look and said, "My love, all of my cards are on the table. I don't play games. I have even gotten permission from your father to date you. So if you think for one minute that you need to fulfill some fantasy of partying all night, then I will have to walk away. I need a woman to be serious about her love for me. Now, my love, are you in, or out?"

"Tim, baby. I am all in. Believe me. I am in!", smiling Paulina reached across the table taking his hand and said, "Timothy I love you and only you." She had known for some time but sitting there listening to him demand to hear her intentions for their relationship. She knew for such Tim was her man for life.

However she needed to make certain that her past stayed in the past. She would not be sharing anymore stories about her partying with Tiffany. She quickly started thinking about what it would take to keep her past wild activities quiet.

She'd received several calls from Ms. Winnie. Paulina knew what she wanted and she would have no part of it. Winnie was asking questions about the night that Congressman Flank attacked her. Paulina was not sure how or what she knew but it was clear she knew something.

Paulina felt she had gotten away and for her the matter was closed. She was afraid of Flank. If he was behind the attack on Tiffany, who knew what he might do to her? Now that her life was slowly getting back on track, she didn't want anything to happen to derail her again.

Tim was now a permanent part of her life, she had seen him talking with her father at Benny's wedding and she was pleased that they seem to like each other.

Although she'd sensed a chill with Tim's mother, which was odd because they had been friends before. Mrs. Von Kinley had often called her when she was going through family trouble with Salim and Nancy. Now she could barely look at her.

Paulina decided not to read anything into it, therefore it never dawned on her that Sadie felt she was not good enough to date her son. They enjoyed the rest of their date and Paulina rode with him to the airport where they said sweet goodbyes.

Earlier the next morning as Paulina was getting her breakfast she heard Winnie's voice covering a breaking story. She turned her attention to the television just as Winnie was describing the violation of another young woman. There was no identification of the latest victim. But Winnie's coverage was chilling. Paulina listened and she thought, *"Another woman drugged, beaten and raped."* She felt panic, one of the victims worked for Moyer and she was dead. Paulina started shaking and dropped her plate of scrambled eggs all over the kitchen floor. She knew it was Flank and now she knew what Winnie wanted to talk about. As pictures of the dead woman flashed across the screen Paulina recognized her instantly she thought, *"She was a friend of Tiffany's and we had all been out to dinner together."*

Nancy walked into the kitchen and stopped in her tracks when she heard Winnie delivering the latest news. She glanced over and noticed Paulina, her face was white with fear. Nancy went to her, "Paulina are you okay?" When Paulina continued to stare at the television Nancy gently placed her arms around her. Paulina said, "Mom I need to tell you something."

Nancy said, "Okay darling, let's go to the library." She didn't want the staff to overhear anything. Paulina was completely honest about what happened to her the night she was almost raped.

Nancy was chilled to the bone. As Paulina spoke she could see that there was a connection among all of these cases. She also realized that Winnie knew the connection as well. Nancy asked Paulina if anyone had seen her with the congressman. Paulina told her no, and then Nancy told her that she thought Winnie knew and maybe she should speak with her. Paulina started crying uncontrollably and told her mother of her fear, not only for her safety, but that Tim would find out and no longer want her.

Nancy said, "If nothing happened, then why are you so afraid? And why would Tim not understand?"

Paulina said, "You know how men are."

Nancy agreed but said, "You should not keep any secrets from him. If you love him as much as you say and nothing happened, then tell him the truth. If he finds out some other way, it will be hard for him to understand."

Paulina looked into Nancy's eyes and said, "I love him more than I have loved anyone. I want to spend my life with him." Paulina suddenly felt sick to her stomach and ran to the powder room to throw up. Just then, Salim walked in and said, "Good morning sweetheart. Do you want to have breakfast with me this morning? Is Paulina okay?"

He'd heard Paulina in the restroom and wondered if she had eaten something bad. He noticed that she was sick a lot lately.

When Paulina came out of the powder room, she looked pale and tired.

"Good morning, Daddy. I am not feeling good. I am going to my room. No breakfast for me."

Salim looked very concerned. "Sweetie, do you need me to call the doctor? You have not been feeling well lately. What's wrong?"

"Oh, I just overdid it today. I will be fine, I promise." Paulina made a quick exit to the safety of her room.

Salim again asked Nancy what was going on. She was now in a very difficult position. They had promised never to keep secrets and she was telling him a lie. She wondered why life was filled with these types of choices. So she told him it was nothing and changed the subject saying, "I am ready for a big cup of coffee. How about you? Oh, tell me sweetheart do you have a lot of appointments today, I was hoping we could meet for lunch."

Salim knew damn well that something was wrong. But he would give Nancy a few hours to get her nerve up to tell the truth, so he played along.

He said, "My day was filled with meetings. How about yours?"

Nancy said, "No, I think I will give Sadie a call today. I truly miss her."

Salim said, "Nancy I am proud of you for reaching out first. You have been friends for far too long to have such a disagreement. You know that Sadie loves you." Nancy smiled and said, "So how do you want your eggs today?"

Chapter 87

Sadie was finding it increasingly difficult to keep her sobriety. She never dreamed living without a drink would be the hardest thing she had ever done. Lonnie had resumed his habit of working long hours leaving Sadie alone in the large empty house.

She wasn't ready to pick up the pace with projects outside of the house, because she was afraid someone might ask about her accident or her sobriety. So she worked on remodeling and reorganizing her gift room, their pool house and the guest bedrooms. When those mindless tasks were completed, she invited Amy's mother to join her in London, so they could do some shopping for the baby.

The two future grandmothers were building a great friendship. They shared great deal in common both enjoyed musicals and the ballet and they were both married to workaholics which meant they were often alone.

Sadie missed her friends but she thought, *"Maybe we just need sometime apart."* Everything had become so crazy and there was a lot of tension between them. Well, with everyone but Winnie. No one was ever upset or angry with Winnie, she was a master at staying out of stuff.

Sensing that she needed more activity to keep herself on track, Sadie decided to take on a major project. The redecoration and remodeling of their house in Jackson Hole, enlisting the help of a world-renowned interior designer.

The Jackson Hole estate was once owned by an American icon and former US president. It sat on one hundred sixty-seven acres located just minutes from Grand Teton National Park, with marvelous views from every window.

Lonnie had not given Sadie a budget for the project. He just told her, "Have at it, and enjoy every minute." She wanted to up-date a few rooms along with the kitchen and guesthouse.

Earlier one morning Nancy called her, Sadie was delighted to hear from her. Nancy said, "Sadie, this is crazy. You are my best friend. I never want to fight with you and I don't want to fight over our children."

Sadie said, "Oh Nancy, I don't want to fight with you either. I just want you to keep an open mind. I am so afraid that if this relationship between Tim and Paulina doesn't work out they will both be hurt."

Nancy listened and then she said, "All we can do is love them and let them live their lives. And be there if and when they need us. But Sadie I am calling because I need my friend back."

Sadie smiled brightly and said, "I'm here soul sister. Now tell me everything that is going on in our town."

Nancy and Sadie chatted for over an hour. It was just like old times and it was something they both needed. Sadie said, "Nancy I would love for you to come out to Jackson Hole for a visit. How about it?"

Nancy said, "Only on one condition we don't talk about our children".

Sadie said, "It's a promise."

Sadie's revelation was the result of a phone conversation with Tim.

Earlier that morning Tim had called and they talked about trust and letting go. Tim said, "Mother, "I am no longer a little boy. I know what is best for me. And whether you believe it, or not Paulina is what is best for me."

Sadie heard the change in his voice when he spoke about Paulina and she knew how deeply he cared for the young woman.

It then became crystal-clear that Sadie could do nothing to stop this love affair. She could only hope that it was short-lived and that no one got hurt.

Tim also told her that he had met with Dr. Hadid and asked for permission to date Paulina.

Sadie said, "You did." Just as Sadie was about to say more. Tim said, "I know what you are about to say, and I need for you to hear me. Please be my Mother, and not my protector. You have to trust me."

Sadie was hurt she said, "Letting go is hard son but I will mind my own business. I can only wish you all the love that I have shared with your father."

When she got off the telephone she wondered when this change had happened—that now her sons were telling her what to do. She had to laugh to herself and admire who they had become as grown-up's.

She placed a call to Lonnie, his secretary told her he was in an important meeting and she would have him call her later. Sadie told her that was okay and that she would speak with him later.

She wondered if Lonnie would ever retire and if he would ever have enough. She felt they already had everything that any human being could need.

Chapter 88

Nancy still hadn't discussed the congressman and Paulina with Salim. She continued to fight against her natural reaction, to hide the truth from the man she loved. She knew she should tell Salim.

She thought to herself, *"This moment was another life lesson: never start lying, and then you won't have to worry about an uncomfortable conversation with your husband about your daughter almost getting raped by a member of the US Congress."*

After dinner that evening, once they were in bed, Salim was relaxed and reading one of his favorite books. Nancy said, "Darling, I need to tell you something but I also need you to promise me you will do nothing with this information. Can you promise me that?"

Salim had been waiting for this moment. He knew that there was something going on. He put down his book and turned his attention to her. He said, "Yes, my sweet, what is this about, or what do you have to tell me? And within reason I will not do anything with this information."

Nancy kissed him and said, "Thank you, darling. Now, this may sound a bit complicated but several months ago, it seems that Paulina went to a party on Capitol Hill for some junior congressman from Wisconsin. She left the party early, but could not find a cab to take her home, and congressman Flank offered her a ride. Once she was in his car…oh Salim…he tried to rape her. She fought him off and got out of the car. She told us she had been mugged but that was not the truth. That was the night she moved back here with us. Paulina believes that the congressman might be behind the recent Canal Road attack's, and the attack on Tiffany. She is afraid that if she tells anyone, he will come after her."

Salim was not sure if he should be angry because Nancy had kept such a gigantic problem from him or because she was asking him to do nothing with the information. He said, "I can't believe you and Paulina kept this from me. Does Tim know?"

Nancy said, "I am sorry. No, Tim does not know the truth."

Salim said, "This is not the kind of matter that you two should have kept from me. Nancy, I am disappointed but I also understand what position this has put you in. But Tim *must* be told, and we should speak with Paulina and him together about this. No more secrets Nancy."

Nancy said, "There is one more thing. Winnie has called several times asking to speak with Paulina, we think she knows something."

Salim said, "Then she must speak with her. Paulina could be withholding information that could keep another young woman from being attacked. We have to convince Paulina to speak with Winnie. If Paulina does not tell Tim then she is setting a precedence for secrets, if she really loves him, she must tell Tim everything. I really can't believe the two of you. Has this past couple of years taught you anything?"

Nancy felt as though a weight had been lifted. She moved closer to Salim wrapped her arms around him, and looked directly into his eyes then she softly spoke, " Yes it has, I really am sorry. I love you so much."

Over breakfast the next morning, Salim clicked on the television to watch the early morning news, he then said, "Winnie is really doing an exceptional job reporting on the Canal attacks."

Paulina became noticeably nervous. She looked at Nancy and then back to Salim, she knew that Nancy had told him and she didn't want to talk about that night, what had happened, or who she thought was behind it all.

Salim reached across the table and took Paulina's hand. "Honey, I think you need to speak with Winnie and tell her everything that you know." Paulina couldn't handle this. Every moment since the attack was playing back in her mind like a horror movie. She was remembering, "*Being in the congressman's car, fighting for her life, seeing Tiffany so beaten in the hospital and the guilt of knowing that if the congressman was behind all of these attacks, then she was his target victim and Tiffany had been beaten because of her and that Nancy and Salim's house keys were also on her key ring that was left in the congressman's car. And now Shanne was dead.*"

Paulina looked at Nancy, Salim and then over to Winnie on the television screen. Suddenly the smell of breakfast was making her nauseated. Paulina felt like the walls were closing in around her. She stood up, intending to go back to bed, and the room started spinning. She fainted. Falling hard, hitting her head on the marble floor. Salim and Nancy rushed to her, Paulina was pale and unresponsive. Salim yelled out to the staff, "Call for an ambulance."

When help arrived, Paulina was transported to the Hospital. Salim and Nancy waited several hours before the doctor appeared, he diagnosed her with "a very mild concussion." They both felt that something was missing because the doctor failed to address what was causing Paulina's nauseous symptoms.

Salim said, "I am worried about her, she has been complaining about not feeling well a lot recently. Have all of the test come back okay."

The doctor assured him that Paulina was well. He said, "I understand your concern but Paulina just needs to take it easy for a couple of days. She will have a headache but she will be just fine. When she gets home if she starts feeling bad, she can call my office. We are keeping her overnight to be on the safe side, but all and all she is in great shape."

Nancy said, "Can we see her now?"

The doctor said, "Yes you can, please follow me." They followed him to the treatment area and were delighted to see Paulina awake and speaking with a nurse in the room. She looked better, although very weak. Nancy asked Salim to go and get her something to drink. She wanted a minute to speak to Paulina alone. When he was gone and the coast was clear, she asked Paulina, "My baby girl, how far along are you?"

Paulina was shocked. She asked her how she knew and if her father knew as well.

Nancy smiled and said, "No your father does not know. Every father wants to believe their daughters are virgins until they die. But I am a mother, and mothers always know about these things. Then she said, "Does Tim know about the baby?"

Paulina looked at Nancy and she realized that the child in her womb would have the unconditional love that she had been shown all of her life. She thought, *"Love has nothing to do with paper or certificate, it's the people that make you feel as though anything is possible."*

Paulina said, "No, he does not know and please don't tell Dad. He cannot keep a secret."

Nancy said, "Quickly while your father is gone. I will continue to try to keep you from having to speak with Winnie. But I want you to know that your father wants complete disclosure on that subject matter. Paulina I agree with him and I think you will feel so much better after you speak with Winnie. She will protect you."

Paulina said, "I can't handle that right now."

Nancy said, "Okay, I don't want you getting upset. It will be okay sweetie I promise you that."

When Salim walked back in the room the two women were having a warm embrace. The doctor stepped back in and announced that Paulina had been assigned to a room and would be taken there shortly.

Salim said, "Has anyone called Tim?"

Paulina quickly responded, "I will call him tonight when we get back home." She turned to the doctor and told him, "I would like to be discharged I want to be in the serenity of my home with my parents. You need this bed for someone who is really sick....I only have a bump on the head." They all smiled and the doctor signed her discharge papers.

Paulina called Tim as soon as they got home. She told him what had happened and he told her he was heading to DC and would be at their house around dinnertime.

When Salim and Nancy were alone, Salim asked her if Paulina was pregnant. Nancy laughed and said, "It's was a secret. Tim doesn't know yet".

Nancy's thoughts went to Sadie she thought, *"How will Sadie react to this news? Well right now was the time to enjoy their blessings of happiness, she was going to be a grandma soon."*

Salim said, "This family just never has a dull moment."

Nancy and Salim looked at each other and laughed. Later, they went to check on Paulina. "Hi there how are you feeling? Would you like anything for lunch?"

Paulina said, "Yes some fruit would be great but I think I will just take a nap."

Nancy said, "Okay that sounds like a great plan, I will have a small fruit salad sent up to you. But for now you get your rest."

Nancy and Salim pushed all other thoughts out of their minds for the moment and enjoyed a late lunch of salad and wine.

Salim said, "I want to be a better grandfather than I was a father? Do you think I will get a second chance?"

Nancy said, "This is our second chance and we can't make any mistakes this time around."

Paulina dozed on and off for hours, finding it hard to sleep with all the thoughts running around in her head. She was unsure of how to tell Tim about the baby. What if he didn't want her to keep it? What would she do then? How would she handle it? What if he thought she was using the baby to trap him? She was not looking forward to the conversation.

She was sure of one thing, no matter what Tim said or did, she would not get rid of her child. She would never have an abortion. She placed her hand on her stomach and made a promise to her unborn child. She would be a wonderful mother to her baby girl or boy and they would never be parted.

Chapter 89

Tim called Paulina as soon as he landed, and asked, "How are you feeling love? Are you hungry? Should I pick up dinner?"

Paulina replied, "I only need you."

Tim then asked, "Do you think we can have some private time together, I have something important to discuss with you."

Paulina told him everyone was home and asked him if there was something wrong. Tim replied, "Paulina I only know that you were taken to the hospital. You need to tell me everything when I get there. I am heading to you now."

Paulina said, "I am fine now. Really Tim I am good."

"Tim said, "Baby, are you sure?"

Paulina smiled, "Well, I am as good as a girl can be without her lover beside her."

Tim smiled and said, "I love you, baby and I will be with you very soon."

Tim wanted to speak with Nancy and Salim, to tell them how much he loved Paulina and that he wanted to marry her. He also wanted them to know he had accepted a position as assistant general counsel in his family's company and he would be moving back to Washington, DC, within the next few months.

If Paulina would have him, he wanted to purchase a house for them, so that when she finished school, they would have a place of their own.

Nancy set drinks and canapés in the family room. When Tim arrived, Paulina came down and they hugged. The atmosphere changed, you could feel the love between these two young people. It was like a bolt of lightning shooting across the summer sky. As they gathered in the family room the conversation was mostly about Paulina's recent visit to the emergency room.

Then Tim asked to speak with Salim alone and the two men went into the library. Salim said, "Tim is everything okay?"

Tim cleared his throat and said, "Yes Dr. Hadid, it couldn't be better. I wanted to speak with you privately because I want to marry Paulina. I would like your blessing."

Salim could not believe it. He sat down in the nearest chair. Tim said, "I love Paulina more than anything or anyone and I will take good care of her."

Salim told him he would be honored. When the two men hugged and talked for a few minutes more. Then when they came out, Salim was all smiles. Nancy knew right away what was going on.

Salim told Paulina and Tim that he and Nancy had to make an important telephone call, something to do with the sale of their Maine property and they would be right back. Nancy just looked at Salim. He took her hand and she followed him upstairs. When they got to their room, Salim said, "Tim just asked for Paulina's hand in marriage."

Tim knew what they were doing and he appreciated it. Paulina and Tim started to speak at the same time. Then they laughed.

Tim said, "You go first."

Paulina, said, "I don't know how to tell you this, so I will just say it. Tim, I love you…and I am pregnant."

Tim said, "What. What did you just say? I love you and I want to marry you. How pregnant are you, I mean how far along?"

Paulina said, "Two months. Remember our romantic weekend? Well, I'm carrying the proof of our love."

He ran and picked her up. They hugged and kissed. Then he stopped, stepped back, and said, "You didn't answer my proposal."

Paulina said, "Yes, yes, yes!" She went to the intercom and told her parents to get back downstairs. They all needed to celebrate.

Salim and Nancy ran downstairs and they all hugged. Paulina saw a large chocolate cake on the counter. She pointed to it, and Nancy said, "Yes, I will get the forks." They sat down at the breakfast table and the four of them ate cake and talked about wedding plans.

All of a sudden, Paulina's face became very sad.

Tim said, "Baby, what's wrong? Do you feel sick?"

Paulina said, "No, I am not sick, just worried about your mother."

Tim said, "I will take care of her. Not to worry."

He then told them his other great news. He had taken the position of assisted general counsel working for his Father and would be living in Washington, D.C.

Paulina said, "Oh Tim, I'm so sorry, I will be coming to this marriage without a job but I will get one by the time we are married."

Tim smiled and said, "Yes, my love, you have a job. You are the mother of my child and for the record, I am hoping for at least two more after this one is born."

Paulina said, "So noted, my dear man."

Tim smiled, "We have to start planning our future."

Paulina kissed him and said, "Sounds wonderful to me."

The happy group celebrated until Paulina started feeling sleepy. Tim noticed and said he would like to spend the remainder of the evening with Paulina if she would care to join him. Paulina kissed her parents good night and went to join her future husband at the Hay-Adams hotel. They stayed up most of the night, talking about their future.

Paulina looked out the window at the perfect moon. As tears began running down her face, she turned to Tim and said, "I will be the best mother to our child. I promise you this baby will never wonder about how much it is loved."

They went to sleep that night, thankful for what life was giving them. The next morning Tim took Paulina shopping at Charles Schwartz in Mazza Gallerie. He purchased her a sapphire-and-diamond three-stone ring each stone was three carats. Paulina loved the ring, it was perfect for her. As he slid the ring on her finger, he said, "Paulina I will love you forever."

She answered him, "You are my forever."

Chapter 90

The following week. Winnie was off the air for three days due to a nasty strain of the flu. She'd been working long hours and was completely exhausted and rundown. On day two Phillip noticed and called her cell phone. When she didn't answer, he called her house. When Maria answered, Phillip said, "Good morning. I am Phillip Lay. Would it be possible for me to speak with Winnie?"

Maria quickly said, "No, I am so sorry, but Ms. Winnie is resting now."

"Well, you see, I am a very good friend and I am concerned about her", said Phillip.

Maria remembered him from all of the flowers and gifts he'd sent to Winnie and she knew that Winnie was fond of him. So she told him that Winnie was under a doctor's care and had been ordered to stay in bed for the next couple of days. Seeing this as an opportunity to get closer to Winnie, Phillip asked if it would be okay for him to bring her dinner.

Maria said, "Mr. Lay, I am sorry, but Ms. Winnie doesn't like company when she is not feeling well. I will tell her you called."

Phillip would not be dismissed he said, "Ms. Maria, I know how much Winnie means to you. She also means a great deal to me, so please let me help you take care of her. I promise you that I will take the blame if she is upset. We can tell her that I am the crazy man that likes to bring sick ladies soup."

Maria smiled she still felt somewhat uneasy about the whole thing but she said, "Okay, but we didn't need you to bring dinner because I have already prepared a meal for Ms. Winnie."

Phillip told her to enjoy that meal herself, he would be sending over dinner.

Two hours later, a caterers truck arrived at Winnie's gate. When they buzzed the intercom, Maria told them to drive around to the service entrance in the back and she would meet them at the kitchen door.

As the food was brought in Maria noticed that it was enough for ten people and that it was some of Winnie's favorites: matzo ball soup in a rich velvety chicken broth, tender baby lamb chops with grilled vegetables and a caramel toasted-coconut cake. Phillip had also bought along beautiful flowers for the table. After everything was set up and the table was ready, Maria turned to Phillip and said, "You do understand that Ms. Winnie is sick with the flu? Lamb chops and grilled veggies are not food for a sick person. I hope Ms. Winnie doesn't get upset with me."

Phillip looked at the table and then back at Maria he said, "You're right, Maria but I just wanted this to be a special meal. Even if she just takes one spoonful of the soup or one bite of the other stuff, that will be okay with me."

Maria smiled and turned away from him. Under her breath she said, "This man is going over Fools Mountain for Ms. Winnie."

Maria went to check on Winnie. When she walked into Winnie's bedroom, she found her just getting out of bed.

"Hi there. How long have I been asleep? I feel like hell."

Maria looked very concerned. "Do you think you can stand a little food?"

"Now that you ask, I am a little hungry."

"Well, I am glad to see that you are up and looking a little better. Dinner will be ready in a minute. Why don't you come downstairs and eat, since you have been in your room for so long?"

"Let me wash my face and I will be right down. I need to check my e-mails and see what's happening. I feel like I have been away forever and it's only been a couple of days. I'll be right down."

Maria made her way back down to the kitchen, she was still uncertain about what Winnie's reaction would be to her letting this man into the house. But it was too late now.

Winnie was wearing no make-up, her silky hair was pulled back at the nape of her neck and she was in her most comfy pajamas, and her favorite, "I

Dream of Jeannie" gold bedroom slippers. To Phillip she looked delicate and beautiful.

She stopped quickly and looked around. There were two men in her kitchen and another in the dining room. Winnie didn't like surprises, she looked at Maria with a very stern expression.

Winnie asked, "What is going on? What is all of this, Maria? Who are these people? I just wanted some chicken soup. You should not have gone to such trouble. Really, Maria, this is not like you. Please tell me what is going on."

Maria could tell that Ms. Winnie was very upset with her and for life of her, she could not think of a thing to say.

"Well, Ms. Winnie, well...I just thought that maybe since you have been so sick these last couple of days...well."

Winnie knew Maria would not normally do anything like this. Walking over to the table to examine the flowers and the food, Winnie started to think quickly, and then she smiled. Knowing that only one person would be behind this kind of spread, Phillip.

She turned and looked at the waiter and said, "Thank you. That will be all. You can go now."

Everyone moved except for the gentleman standing in front of the stove.

He hadn't moved since she walked into the kitchen. Winnie looked down at his shoes and finely tailored Brioni pants, knowing that no chef wears Fratelli Rossetti hand crafted alligator shoes to work in the kitchen.

Winnie looked at Maria and shook her head and then said, "Maria please enjoy the rest of the evening and we will talk in the morning."

As Maria made her quick exit. The gentlemen in the chef's hat and coat didn't move away from the stove. Once everyone was gone, Winnie walked up behind Phillip took the chef's hat off his head. Then she said, "You can turn around, Phillip. Your cover has been blown. You know, I should really be mad at you and fire Maria for this. I am sick and I look like hell."

When Phillip turned, Winnie could see in his expression how much this meant to him. She said, "Phillip, you should not have gone to so much trouble."

He said, "I had to do something for you, Winnie. I want to take care of you and love you. Please let me."

"Oh Phillip…I can't. But for now, can you please help me eat some of this food?"

Phillip poured her a large bowl of the delicious soup. She enjoyed as much as she could. But as they ate Winnie contemplated the fact that this man had taken the time and cared enough to have all of this prepared for her. It had been a long time since anyone had treated her as if she were special. They chatted for a while. Phillip told Winnie some jokes and they both laughed. Winnie was too sick to enjoy any more of the food but she truly enjoyed the company.

As her medicine began taking its toll on her, her eyes started getting heavy. Phillip helped her back to bed and when her head hit the pillow she was fast asleep. Phillip sat in her room, just watching her sleep. Around midnight he left her and drove himself home. The next morning he called, "Good morning sunshine, how are you feeling today."

Winnie responded, "I'm much better, thank you for taking care of me."

He explained that he was scheduled to fly to Brussels the next day and would be gone for a couple of weeks. He would be in back-to-back meetings but would make time to check on her and he wanted to have dinner with her when he returned.

Winnie was touched by his concern but in the light of day, she knew that she needed to protect her heart from Phillip. She had developed feelings for this wonderful, elegant man feelings that would forever remain a secret. One thing was for sure, she was not going to become his mistress, no matter how much she cared for him.

For a brief second she closed her eyes to listen to his deep voice and imagine what it would be like to have Phillip as her man.

He said, "Winnie, are you there?"

Winnie opened her eyes and said, "Oh yes, I was just remembering when I was last in Brussels. It's a lovely country. I hope you have some time to enjoy the sites."

"I wish I could, Winnie but this trip is just all about business. I am traveling alone. I will be looking forward to returning to have dinner with you."

"Oh, Phillip you are too kind. I will see you in a couple of weeks."

"Take care, my dear Winnie. See you soon."

As she clicked off the phone, a chill ran over her body. Suddenly Winnie was finding it hard to catch her breath. The loneliness in her life was hitting her hard and suddenly she no longer wanted to be alone any more.

Chapter 91

Two weeks later. Winnie was interviewing the Police Chief she was asking the hard questions, "Chief what are you and your team of police doing to solve these horrendous attacks on our young women?" said Winnie. The Chief detailed how and where the investigation was, but Winnie would not let her off easy she went in with more hard questions. "Chief please tell our viewers what you will do to make our streets safer?" Before it was over Winnie did something that the Chief was not prepared for she opened the station telephone lines and let a few viewers ask the Police Chief questions directly. The interview lasted a full half an hour, of hard hitting facts and even harder questions.

When Winnie finished she thanked the Police Chief saying, "Chief, It was important that the community get a chance to speak with you. Thank you for answering their questions."

The Chief answered, "Well it would have been damn nice of you to let me know that you were going to open the telephone lines." The station manager stepped in, he wanted to have a word with the Police Chief. Moving Winnie away from the heated conversation.

Winnie smiled and said her goodbyes. She went to her office as she was preparing to head home she thought, "I have not heard a word from Phillip. I hope he is okay."

She had however heard from Janette a real estate agent with Waterfront Properties in Florida. Winnie had been introduced to her at Sunny's birthday party, she had told Janette that if something came on the market she might be interested in purchasing but only if it was ocean front.

Janette had telephoned Winnie early that morning before she went on air saying, "Good morning Winnie. Remember when you said that you were only interested in a unit in the Ocean Edge building. Well I have a pocket listing but you will have to move fast to get it."

Winnie smiled and said, "Are you kidding me, does it have everything that I am looking for? Are you sure? I can fly down at the end of the week."

Janette quickly said, "This unit is everything we talked about. You will love it. I am e-mailing you the pictures now." Within a couple of minutes Winnie was looking at photos of her dream condo and just as Janette had said, it was perfect. The unit had a private elevator entry, open floor plan, with four bedrooms, six bathrooms, breathtaking panoramic views of the Atlantic ocean from every room, and state of the art appliances. In total it was over five thousand square feet of living space and a extra bonus the unit came with a pool front cabana. All in the highly secured gated Ocean Edge building.

Winnie called her sister Tina to tell her about the property. Tina quickly ran the numbers, it was a good investment for Winnie. She said, "Well what are you waiting for. Make them an offer." Winnie laughed out loud and said, "I will....so what do you think, spring break on Singer Island. How does that sound to you?"

Tina said, "Wonderful, Winnie this is perfect for you. Go for it!" They laughed and chatted for a while making plans and enjoying some sister time.

When Winnie finished with her call she telephoned Janette and made an all cash offer over the phone. Janette sent her the paperwork and Winnie's offer was accepted with a ten day escrow.

Two weeks later Winnie was picking up her keys to her beach front hideaway. It had always been Winnie's dream to own her own oceanfront property, and the unit was pure heaven. She had scheduled a meeting at the property with William R. Eubanks, who would be heading up the remodeling of the unit.

Winnie said, "Hello William, thank you for meeting me here. I really want this unit to be decorated with light colors of aqua, cream and sea foam green and I want to feel like I am in the ocean."

They talked for several hours agreeing on a color scheme. Winnie completely trusted William, she knew he would make her new home a masterpiece of design and comfort. When they were finished meeting Winnie took another look around, as she stood on the balcony taking in the warm ocean air, letting the breeze blow through her silky hair, she could not help but to feel delighted, envisioning holiday's with friends and family filling up every inch of the place. She laughed to herself thinking, *"I can't wait to see what wonderful holiday meals Tina will create in this kitchen. My fabulous sister, real estate agent, gourmet chef who makes everything yummy."*

A quick look at her watch. It was getting late. She gave William a set of extra keys and they agreed to speak in a couple of days. Winnie needed to rush off she was meeting Sunny and Janette for a quick dinner at Bice on Worth Avenue. She thought, "*Bice is the Cafe Milano's of Palm Beach*." It seemed that everyone went to Bice for great food and people watching. Sunny knew the charming general manager and he took great care of her and her guests.

There were so many things Winnie needed to get done. She had only made plans to stay in Palm Beach until Sunday afternoon, then she would be flying back to Washington, D.C. Now she wished she could stay for an entire week.

As she drove over to Worth Avenue, she thought about her relationships and the one that she was missing the most was the girls. She picked up her cell phone and punched in Sadie's number.

"Hello, the Von Kinley residence how can I help you."

"Hello this is Winnie for Sadie. Is she available?"

"No I am sorry Mrs. Von Kinley is not available at this time, I will leave her a message that you telephoned."

Winnie said, "Thank you, please ask her to call my cell phone". When she ended the call she thought to herself, *"How long is this going to go on, Sadie can't hide out forever...I have had enough of this bullshit ...no one is calling me back. I have not heard a word from Phillip since he left on his trip and now I can't get Sadie on the phone.... this is crazy."*

Before the accident Sadie had been Winnie's shoulder to cry on, or get advice from.

In their friendship circle Coco had always been the single friend who she traveled and had single girl fun with. Nancy was fun and always made everyone laugh and Sadie was the friend that gave out wise counsel and Winnie was the peace keeper.

But lately things were different Sadie was trying to get herself back on track, Coco was married and unavailable to anyone and Nancy was working through her family problems.

Winnie was thankful for her blessings and she wanted to share her newest blessing with her small group of friends. She was looking forward to spending some of the winter months in Florida and wanted to make plans with Sadie.

Singer Island wasn't the only thing on Winnie's mind. She had been thinking about Phillip. She called him earlier in the week and again her call went to voice mail. She left a message, "Hello Phillip, it's Winnie, I know you are traveling and I hope your business is going well. I just wanted to thank you again for taking care of me when I was sick."

After not receiving any return calls from him since he left for his trip, she hoped everything was okay. As she was driving she placed another call to his cell phone, "Hey Phillip, it's Winnie. I hope you're okay. Guess what.. I just closed on my dream place in Florida. I will tell you all about it when we talk. Again I hope you are okay. Talk soon."

Phillip's attention had made her see that she needed someone in her life and she was ready to fall in love again. But there was that feeling of heaviness in her heart and at the same time, she knew that she needed to push away any thoughts or feelings about Phillip.

As Winnie pulled up to Bice's, she saw Sunny arriving, Winnie smiled, it was something about Sunny's light manner that just made Winnie happy to be with her. Janette arrived last. The three ladies enjoyed a delicious meal of Mediterranean seafood salad and grilled striped bass with vegetables. The conversation was non-stop through the entire meal. Jeanette and Sunny knew everyone in Palm Beach and the stories were delightful and funny.

After dinner Winnie made her way over to the Breakers Resort where she was staying. She was happy and tired at the same time. Morning came fast and Winnie needed to get to the airport.

She purchased a couple of magazines, DuJour, Costal and Royalty. To read while she waited for her flight. Flipping through the glossy papers of

Royalty magazine she saw a picture of Phillip and Donna Lay at the Royal Danish Theatre in Copenhagen, Denmark. It seems that they were guests of the royal family. Donna Lay and her royal highness of Denmark looked to be chatting in the photo. Then there was another picture of Donna and Phillip smiling, looking happy, and Donna was wearing the dancing-lady pendant that Winnie had returned to Phillip.

Winnie was overcome with jealousy. Seeing Donna Lay staring back at her from the shiny pages of the magazine, looking content, was too much for Winnie. So she took that as another sign from heaven that Phillip Lay was just as big of a rat as any other rat she'd met in her past. All she could say was, "Fuck you, Phillip Lay…fuck you." She was so disappointed in herself for allowing her emotions to make her develop real feelings for Phillip, now she felt like a complete fool she thought, *"Winnie you are better than this, what were you thinking.....he is married and he will always be married..forget you ever knew this man."*

She boarded the plane with mixed feelings, one side of her brain was happy and overjoyed about her new place in Florida, and the other side of her brain was feeling bamboozled by Phillip Lay.

The fantasy of Phillip had come to an end. Even if he returned her calls now, she would not speak with him again. She was very disappointed but determined to move forward with her plans to be happy. She remembered what her mother had always told her, *"A woman's responsibility must always be to herself to find happiness. It could never be left up to someone else."*

Being back home in Washington, DC., she was back in the swing of working long hours but there was something else that she needed to take care of. She missed her girlfriends and she knew that it would take her to make things right with them all again.

Winnie missed her friends and she knew that they missed each other but neither of them would make the first move. Sadie and Coco would both continue to be polite enemies for the rest of their lives. She loved them both too much to allow that to happen, so she arranged a BFF dinner at Charlie Palmer's Steakhouse on Capitol Hill. Nancy and Salim were away, so it would just be the three of them.

When she called Coco and Sadie, they both said they were busy and not sure if they had the time. But Winnie would not accept that, so she just said, "Meet me at Charlie Palmer's on Wednesday night for a quick dinner." Sensing she meant business, they both agreed. She told them she would be finishing up an interview around five o'clock and would meet them at six o'clock. She had reserved a table and was looking forward to it.

Sadie arrived first and as normal, Coco was twenty minutes late. The tension between the two women was electric but Winnie ignored it and moved forward with her plan. She kept them talking with lively conversation about local personalities. After everyone placed their orders, she started in, saying, "Okay, ladies, this is crazy. We have been friends too long for this to happen. I love you both and it breaks my heart to see your friendship torn apart like this."

Coco said, "It's all my fault. Sadie, I am so sorry for the way that I treated you. I was just so jealous and miserable in my own life."

Sadie said, "I know, Coco but that is not an excuse for the shitty way you behaved, and if you did it once you may do it again. I don't know if I can ever trust you again."

Winnie was silent. She wanted them to get it all out, however she noticed that Sadie had been keeping a list of offenses she felt that Coco had done to her, she appeared to enjoy reciting them one by one.

Coco's sat there looking contrite and when Sadie finished Coco's only defense was, "I am deeply sorry."

Sadie looked smugly at Coco and then replied, "Coco, please..give me something more than your, "I am sorry." Say something that will let me know that you understand what you have done. You act like a child who thinks that if you say "I am sorry," then everything should just go back to the way it was. Well unfortunately…this is going to take more than just a small gesture."

Winnie sensed it was time for her to step in, before this dinner blew up in her face.

She said, "Ladies, I think that saying 'I am sorry' is a great beginning. But Sadie, you are right. When you have been hurt, it seems like such a small thing to say. But saying 'I am sorry' must be followed by sincere actions so that the mistake never happens again. Sadie, must find a way to accept Coco, or not, but you can't go on this way."

Winnie then turned to Coco and asked her, "Coco, please tell Sadie why you want her friendship back, if you do want it."

Coco thought for a minute. She knew she needed to select her words carefully. She could tell that Sadie's feelings were raw. Finally, she said, "Sadie, in my life I never had a better friend than you and I took that for granted. My life has changed…I have changed. I have faced some hard truths and let go of false pride and the foolishness that I had before. What you see before you is the new Coco who knows how precious friendship is…and someone who will never covet what my friend has—never again. Sadie, I really have changed."

Sadie had missed Coco but she was afraid of trusting her again she quietly said, "I would like to get to know this new Coco. Can you tell me more about why you are such a new person?"

Coco said, "I am a woman who is finally complete and happy, and I want nothing from my friends but their respect and friendship. I want to share my life with my friends as an equal, not as a spoiled, selfish user. Saul has given me everything that I ever wanted in life—unconditional love—and that has made me grow. Sadie, I love you and again, I am sorry. But the rest will be up to you."

Sadie said, "Coco, I am truly happy for you and I have missed you so much. You have always been like my little sister."

Winnie saw for the second time what loving Saul had done for Coco, she truly seemed wiser, happier and I feel complete.

Sadie said, "Okay, let's take it one day or one dinner at a time. I am happy for you Coco and I would love to meet your Saul. He sounds like a good man."

Winnie said, "Okay, that's a start."

The waiters placed the food in front of them. They had ordered enough for six people. Winnie had the filet mignon with poached blue crab, Sadie the trio of Muscovy duck and Coco the citrus-basted Loch Duart salmon with roasted jumbo prawns. To share, they ordered jumbo asparagus with Dijon butter, potato gnocchi and wild mushrooms and onions. Winnie and Coco were careful not to order any wine, out of respect for Sadie.

As the tension relaxed, their conversation became very enjoyable and it reminded Winnie of why they were friends. Sadie delighted them with details of Amy and Benny, as well as Larry's wild women. She never mentioned Tim or Paulina. Coco chatted about Saul and their new life.

Sadie said, "So Winnie, tell us about your new place on Singer Island."

Winnie described her beautiful new condo in Ocean Edge and what she was going to have done to make it feel like home, with new touches here and there. She was ready to enjoy the Palm Beach lifestyle for a few months a year.

The ladies enjoyed the rest of their dinner and promised to get together soon. Coco paid the check and thanked them both for their friendship. She announced that she and Saul wanted to host a dinner for them soon. She wanted them to be the first guests that she entertained.

Winnie said, "I'm looking forward to the invitation."

Sadie just smiled.

As the ladies made their way out of the restaurant, in walked Congressman Flank. He noticed Sadie right away and thanked her for the donation to his re-election campaign. Winnie paid special attention to his every move. There was just something about him that made her uneasy. His manners were very forced. He seemed like a hungry gutter rat preparing for a grand game of bait and switch.

He greeted Sadie first saying, "Good evening, Mrs. Von Kinley. Oh, what a surprise to run into you this evening. I hope you received my thank you letter for your family's donation to my re-election."

Sadie said, "Yes, please keep up the fight for Colorado." Sadie then introduced him to Winnie and Coco.

He said, "I feel like I know this lovely woman, I wake up to your voice every morning. No introduction needed. Did I just see you interviewing the Speaker of the House?"

Winnie said, "Yes, you did."

"Well, next time you are doing a piece, please know I am available to talk about this healthcare mess", said an overly eager Flank.

Just as he started to continue, his driver stepped in between them. He said, "Sorry, Congressman, you left your phone in the car."

When he reached out to hand Flank the phone, Winnie noticed that he was wearing a French-cuff shirt and he and the congressman had on matching cuff links. A cold chill ran up Winnie's spine. She then turned her attention to every detail of the two men.

The congressman bid them good night and went into the private room at Palmer's.

As the ladies walked outside, Sadie turned and hugged them both and thanked Winnie for a delightful evening. Coco did the same.

Sadie's car and driver were waiting for her as was Coco's. It was the first time that Coco looked every inch the Washington wife. Winnie was delighted for her friend. She had finally found the peace that she always deserved and Winnie could not have been more proud of Coco.

As soon as Winnie got into her car, she telephoned Officer Shaw, asking him to run a check on Flank's driver and she explained her intuition about the cuff links.

Shaw said, "So are half the men in this city, Winnie. Give me something more than that."

She said, "Okay, goddamn it. He is always with Flank. He would know something. Can you just talk to him?"

Shaw said, "Sure, I will run a check on him and get back to you."

Winnie thanked him and made her way home. She could not sleep that night. She stayed up, researching everything she could find on Harley aka Bud Durham. Around midnight she got a call from Officer Shaw saying, "Hey, Winnie, just got something back on the driver. It's not good, there's some incriminating information, things are not looking good for him."

He told Winnie that Bud had been a former con man. He had served time in the men's correctional facility in Colorado for assault and attempted murder. After serving only a third of his sentence, he was granted an early release, he seemed to have disappeared for a couple of years, only to surface on the house staff of Governor David Tackett, Congressman Alfred Flank's future father-in-law.

Officer Shaw said, "This guy is bad news."

Winnie said, "I told you there is something there. I knew it."

Shaw said, "Okay, Winnie, leave this to the police. This guy and whoever is working with him is dangerous. Stay safe and really Winnie, leave this to the police. I will keep you updated."

Winnie said, "Okay, make sure you tell me first."

For the first time in weeks, Winnie slept restfully, knowing that soon this monster would be taken off the streets.

Chapter 92

Governor Tackett was getting calls from his spies in Washington about Congressman Flank's partying and double-dealing. Flank was making promises to everyone and not delivering on enough of them. Tackett thought, *"That is the shit that makes unnecessary enemies."* Tackett now knew he had made a mistake in pairing Harley "Bud" Durham with Flank but like most small mistakes, it could be fixed.

As Bud was driving Flank to a dinner meeting at the Mandarin Oriental Hotel in southwest section of DC., the car telephone rang. Only one person knew the number and Bud answered it on the first ring.

"Good evening, Governor. How are you doing tonight?"

Governor Tackett roughly said, "Cut the bullshit, Bud. Is Flank in the car with you?"

Bud quickly answered, "Yes sir he is."

Tackett said, "Put me on speakerphone and listen to every fucking word."

Bud did as instructed.

Flank said, "Good evening Governor, what's going on?"

Tackett said, "I will tell you what's going on. You two sons of bitches are about to destroy everything that I have been working for and I am not going to let that happen. So here is the new game plan."

Flank tried to defend himself but Tackett didn't want to hear it. The Governor quickly yelled, "I told you, when you first went to Washington not to bring attention to yourself and to keep your stupid head down and do what you were told. But you couldn't do that so listen dipshit, you no longer have any say in the matters at hand. From today forward you will follow directions or your limp body will be floating in the Potomac River."

Flank said, "Hey Governor, what in the hell has happened. I don't understand why you're so upset but let's talk about it."

Tackett said, "Shut the fuck up and listen. Drive over to 3rd Street, near Fort McNair Army Base. I have someone waiting there to meet you."

Bud turned the car around and headed in the direction of Fort McNair. He looked in the rear view mirror at Flank who just shook his head telling Bud not to say a word. They had no idea what was about to happen but they both knew it was not good. The Governor stayed on the phone with them the entire ride.

Flank said, "Governor what about my meeting tonight? I know that the pipeline deal is important to you."

Governor quickly said, "You will make the meeting dumb ass. Now shut up and listen."

When they turned on 3rd Street. There was a black sedan parked, when the headlights flashed. Bud pulled up beside the car and unlocked the doors.

A minute later a huge burley man opened the driver's door of the congressman's car and pulling Bud out.

Bud said, "Hey what the hell is going on? Get your damn hands off me." The man pushed Bud toward the parked SUV, jumped in the congressman's car and pulled off.

Before Bud could say another word an even larger man stepped out of the SUV and told Bud to get in and shut up. Bud did as he was told, he knew there was no other choice to make.

Bud said, "Hey guys I'm not sure what the hell is going on but I need to go to the congressman's house."

One of the guys gave Bud a hard stare and then said, "Look dude, the only place you are going is to the airport. He then pushed a printed airline ticket into Bud's hand. Bud needed to get back to the row house so he telephoned the Governor.

Governor Tackett answered roughly saying, "What the fuck do you want Bud."

Bud quickly thought he needed to calm the Governor down, he knew something had happened he just didn't know what. Thinking to himself,

"Damn I have been doing a good job of cleaning up behind Flank. I wondered what fuck up Flank has gotten us into now? But I must get back to the house to get my shit. Well.. let me try to reason with the old Governor and see if that works."

Bud said, "Governor please I need to get my things from the row house. Can you tell these guys to take me there. I promise I will only be a couple of minutes."

The Governor said, "Well, I will be damn. You and Flank are dumber than I thought. Here is the only plan that is working now. Flank has a new driver and Bud you are headed to the airport. Your belongings will be mailed to you. Do you understand that?"

Bud spoke up saying, "Governor I left a few items that I need to handle myself."

The governor answered, "Do you want to be brought back home in a body bag? If so, I can arrange that as well. Just let me know, Bud. One more word—just one more word." The governor ended the call and Bud knew he didn't have a prayer of getting his things. He couldn't believe this was happening or what had pushed the governor over the edge.

After Bud's stint in jail, there were not many men who made him afraid, but Governor Tackett was an exception to that rule. He scared the hell out of Bud—as did returning to prison. He'd made himself a promise that, no matter what, he would never go back to a jail cell.

While Bud was being driven to the airport Flank was getting an ear full from the Governor, "Listen you good for nothing piece of shit. You had better make this pipe line deal work out for me."

Flank quickly said, "Is this what you are all pissed off about? I have already talked to everyone concerning the pipe line deal and the off-shore oil deal. We are in a good position to get it handled and in your favor."

Governor Tackett said, "Good position my ass. The last time you told me that the bill didn't even get off the house floor. Flank, I need you to make this happen. Or I promise you, you will be sorry." Just as the governor ended the call Flank's car pulled in front of the hotel. Flank started thinking, *"How much more of this shit can I take. It's never enough no matter what I do, that son of a bitch is not happy. All this damn drama makes me nervous. Damn, I wonder what happened to*

Bud. Who in the hell is this guy driving me? He looks like Ted Bundy's, crazy father. He has not said a word to me. What the fuck is going on? Okay I need to pull myself together before that crazy ass hole Tackett has me killed."

The congressman sat in his car for a couple of minutes to gather his thoughts and then he stepped out. It was time to make the governors' special interest, Flank's only interest.

Chapter 93

At the end of another day of countless hearings and meetings with special interest groups on everything from natural gas pipelines, armed services, health care, education, to endless discussions on foreign policy, Congressman Flank returned to his rented row house. It wasn't home but right now he didn't feel as though he had much of a home, but it would just have to do for the moment.

It was better than living in a hotel but not by much. He was uncomfortable with city living. He missed the wide-open spaces that Colorado had to offer.

The row house came with a separate apartment in the lower basement area which was used by his current driver, Theo Parks. Parks was one of Tackett's henchmen and a real son of a bitch. He didn't like Flank and the feeling was mutual.

Flank had been watching his every move since Tackett's last warning.

He decided to slow down and put all of his energies into getting the job done. Belinda was still persistent in her pursuit of wanting a minute by minute account of his daily activities. Her relentless phone calls made Flank want to tell the whole Tackett family to take a flying leap and kiss his ass.

With Parks patrolling his every move, Flank had little opportunity to enjoy his guilty pleasures of coke and young hot-ass girls. Flank was thinking, *"I need something to take away some of this pressure—all I am doing is meetings and hearings, I need someone to do me. I truly hate every fucking minute in this damn city. Everyone in Washington, DC., has a agenda and these fuckers worked day and night. It was all too much for me. I need an outlet—and I need to find one fast."*

As he walked into the house, he could smell Parks. Flank said, *"That fat, lazy, nosy, motherfucker is smoking cigarettes again. I have asked him a thousand times in the last three weeks to cut that shit out."*

Flank marched downstairs to the basement apartment. Parks was on the phone, telling someone Flank's schedule. That was it, he had reached his limit with this shit.

"Who in the hell are you talking to?" asked Flank.

Parks gave a quick response. "None of your fucking business."

Flank was ready for a fight but he knew he could never win. Parks was six foot two and around two hundred eighty pounds. At Flank's best he was half that weight, so he was left to do his fighting with words.

"I don't need a fucking nanny, or a dumb-ass watchdog. What I need is for you to stop smoking in this house. And clean up! It smells like a garbage can in here. I am sick of you and your lazy shit."

Parks dropped the phone, walked over to Flank, got right up in his face, and said, "Look, you prick, if you had kept your pants up and been doing your fucking job, I wouldn't be here in the first place. Do you think I want to drive your skinny stupid ass around this concrete jungle? And if you come down here talking shit again, I am going to break your fucking face."

Flank backed up. He was now standing uncomfortably between the apartment's brick wall and Parks grease stained T-shirt and his massive body. Fearing that the next move would be him picking up his front teeth after Parks beat him to a pulp, he made a swift exit, saying on the way out, "I am going out and I don't want any damn company."

Parks yelled, "Good. You go do that. I am praying for a drive-by shooting where they use your ass as target practice, you dumb fuck. Hey, if you go get yourself in some trouble and I get a call, I am going to beat your brains out. Just so you know, there's an ass-kicking coming your way."

Flank was tired, hungry, and pretty pissed off. He wanted to get the hell out of this city....at least for a couple of hours so he grabbed a cab. He told the driver to head toward the airport. He had no idea where to go; he just wanted to be alone and away from Parks, the row house and his constant thoughts of the Tackett family.

His cell phone started buzzing. He knew immediately who it was the governor.

Flank answered, "Yeah."

Governor Tackett said, "What the fuck is wrong with you? Parks just called me. Are you on that shit again? Or are you going looking for some young ass? You unfaithful fuck. Losing your cool is the first sign of failure. Get your shit together and focus on your job. That damn pipeline bill is up for a vote in the morning. It had better go my way, you bitch."

Flank said, "I have done everything I can. I can't control every vote. This is getting out of control. Your demands are not making any sense."

Tackett said, "You will see what no sense looks like if I don't win." Click.

Flank just looked at the phone. He had met with every member on the committee and done his best to position the vote in Tacketts' favor. There was nothing left for him to do but wait and hope things worked out the way they had hoped for.

As the driver was approaching the airport exit, Flank told him to continue down GW Parkway. There was a small restaurant and bar called Indigo Landing on Marina Drive. He'd been there a couple of times before with some lobbyist. It was a very out of the way place with a great bar and it was not overpopulated with the usual Washington power players. You could get a drink and a fair dinner and talk shop without the fear of being overheard.

Flank paid the driver and walked inside. As he expected, the place was almost empty. He took a seat at the bar and ordered a very dry martini. The television was on MSNBC six o'clock news. They were showing the White House chief of staff discussing the president's position on the latest Federal Reserve action to drop interest rates and what it would mean to the American people. He downed his drink and ordered another. The bartender asked him if he wanted something to eat and handed him the menu. Flank quickly ordered a shrimp cocktail and then the Landing Burger with the works.

After three drinks he started eyeing the waitress. He needed a good quick piece of ass. Looking around, he noticed he was catching the attention of a couple of young ladies enjoying happy hour.

Flank started feeling lucky when one of the ladies nodded for him to join them. He moved fast, taking out a hundred dollar bill and telling the bartender to keep the change. The bartender thanked him and told him to be careful. Flank ignored the warning.

He swiftly introduced himself to the ladies and took a seat between them. They seemed to be having a great time. The ladies told Flank that they worked in the area and stopped off there to have a quick drink before heading home. When he asked them what they did for a living, the blonde said she was a secretary and a part-time model. The other one, a cute redhead, said she was a personal trainer and a bored housewife.

Flank ordered them another round of drinks and the threesome chatted for a couple of hours. When the pretty blonde left the table to visit the restroom, the fiery redhead told Flank she thought he was very handsome and she would like to get to know more about him. They exchanged numbers and promised to meet up later.

After a couple more drinks, the ladies told Flank they had to leave. He paid the check and they said their good-byes. Flank asked the waitress to call him a cab and he watched the pretty girls leave. He would follow up with the redhead later. He knew she would be good for a fun time.

For now, he needed to get back to the shit bath that was his life. He took a cab back to the city. When he walked into the house, he could still smell Parks cigarettes.

But he had a worse surprise. There was Belinda, sitting and waiting for him. Tackett failed to mention that his darling daughter was heading here on his last call to him.

Flank asked, "What are you doing here?"

Belinda said, "Well, that's some greeting for your fiancée. Aren't you happy to see me?"

Flank thought about his answer. A lot was riding on keeping Belinda happy. Inside he was thinking, "*Who in God's name arranged this nightmare visit from Hella the witch*?" He swallowed hard and said, "Oh no, you just surprised me."

Flank thought, *"Damn this woman is no beauty..thank GOD her father has money because it is the only thing that is helping me to get used to her flat body, no boobs, wide ass, skinny legs, thin hair, and that high voice...damn she sounds like a crying weasel."* At one time he'd thought he loved her but now he was sure it was just his fear of dying alone. Lately every time he heard her voice he envisioned jumping off the 14th street Bridge, he thought *"The pain from the fall can't be as painful as listening to her speak."*

Belinda walked over, lightly hugged him, and then she said, "Damn Al, you smell like gin and cheap perfume. Parks said you were out on a mystery run. Where have you been?"

Flank thought, "*That damn Parks.*"

He said, "Belinda, I am with people all day. Who knows what I smell like at this hour of the evening? And as for Parks, he hates me, and I feel the same way about him."

Belinda started in about everything she disliked about Flank, how he was disappointing her family, how their wedding was coming up and he hadn't spent any time with her on planning it and how she was not sure about when she wanted to start their family.

Flank was in the toilet taking a leak. When he heard her say the word *kids*, his piss dried up at once. He yelled, "*Children?*" What are you taking about *Children*? Do you even remember the last time we had sex?"

Belinda said, "Sex is overrated, maybe if you didn't smell like a piece of moldy cheese. I would not mind you being on top of me, anyway I am too busy planning our wedding. So I suggest you continue to act happy and quietly go play with yourself because there will be no sex for you until you earn it."

Flank's face flushed as he turned and slammed the bathroom door. As she was changing into her night gown Belinda said, "Al dear, if you come near me tonight, I promise you will lose those little mouse balls of yours." Flank quickly said, "Trust me Belinda, I am not in the mood."

Before Flank could close his eyes Belinda said, "You are my escort to the Friends of The Library of Congress Dinner, tomorrow night, it's black tie." She knew how much he hated black tie dinners and it was giving great pleasure to put the screws to him.

Flank said, "What Library of Congress Dinner? And why am I just hearing about it?"

Belinda said, "All you need to know is I will be ready at 6:00 p.m. Parks is driving us and you are going, and you will be gracious and interesting to everyone you talk to at the dinner. My father is a major sponsor of the event and you are representing my family."

Flank was mad as hell. He shouted, "Belinda, don't speak to me like that! I am not a dog. Show me some fucking respect, will you please?"

Belinda pulled opened the drawer to the nightstand, threw a handful of condoms in his face and said, "You have never worn these with me, so who in the fuck are you wearing them for? Now, little puppy, and I do mean *little* in every sense of the word. Turn off the lights, so I can get some rest."

She had him. He was caught in his own game. All he could do was take a blanket and pillow and go downstairs to the couch.

Belinda stayed in town for two long weeks, and their relationship didn't get any easier. They made appearances at all the local hot spots for dinner and posed for pictures at a couple of black-tie fundraisers. She talked endlessly about the wedding and the house she wanted him to buy for her. She was clearly only interested in being a congressional wife and any Congressman would do. Flank knew that Belinda didn't love him, her only interest was in a man who could make her the next Jackie Kennedy.

Flank thought, "*She just wants the title; she couldn't give a shit about me. Damn I don't think I can live with this woman. What the fuck have I gotten myself into?*"

Flank felt like a caged animal and Belinda was his angry keeper. He could not wait for Belinda to get on a plane and head back home to her family.

On her last day, Parks took Belinda to the airport while Flank was at work. In celebration of his first clear evening after Belinda's departure. Flank called the number that little redhead had given him at Indigo Landing. Her name was Penny and on her business card he noticed the words *personal assistant and companion*. He remembered her saying she was a housewife, so he asked her about her day.

He quickly dialed the telephone numbers on her card. "Hello do you remember me, Alfred or Al is what my friends call me."

Penny said, "Hi Al, I have been thinking about you. How is your day going? Are you still at work?"

"No my day is finally over. I need to get a drink what are you doing this evening? Tell me what is it that you do for a living?"

She told him, "I work part-time for very special people."

Flank asked, "That is not telling me anything. What is it that you do? And who do you do it for?"

Penny said, "I make sure my boss is never without what he needs—and that he's never lonely."

Flank asked, "Do you only work for men. You said "He", So how do you do that?"

Penny said, "I never divulge office secrets but let's just say my boss is always happy."

They talked for about half an hour. Penny again said she needed to get out and have some fun. Her husband was always away and she was lonely.

Flank said, "That's too bad. What do you do when you're lonely?"

Laughing Penny said, "Me oh well, I just get busy making other people happy. That's what makes me happy, putting a smile on someone's face. That way I am never lonely. So Al what makes you smile?" Flank quickly thought about how to best answer that question he said, "Well finding out more about you and who you are."

Penny said, "I am easy to be with, and good dinner company."

That was music to his ears. He felt comfortable with Penny, so he made arrangements to meet up at the Jefferson Hotel for a drink.

He told her he would be there around seven o'clock, and to meet him at the Quail Bar. He needed to take care of something first. She said that since it would be a late night, she would make plans to stay over in the city.

Flank could not believe his luck. This innocent, sweet, little lady had no idea what was in-store for her. If all went well as Flank planned she would not be lonely tonight. He went home and handled all of his outstanding calls and texts from Belinda and Tackett.

The Tackett's were all in New York on a shopping trip, so there was no chance of a surprise visit. Now he needed to get rid of Parks. Flank laughed to himself, *"All I need to do is send him on a food run."*

Flank called downstairs, "Hey Parks, I know how much you love crabs. How about drive out to Mike's Crab House in Annapolis and bring back some crabs? I really want some good fried soft-shells myself and some fried shrimp, too. What do you think about that?"

Parks said, "Hell, that's a long way for crabs!"

Flank said, "Hey man, do you want the best or what? Let me know, but I would really like some big, sweet crabs for dinner. I am paying."

Parks said, "I know damn well you are paying. Right on, man. I could use some good seafood. Yeah, I will drive us."

Flank told him, "No not us tonight man. I have so much reading to get done. I will stay here and catch-up on some paperwork while you are gone." He gave Parks the directions and five hundred dollars in cash.

Parks said, "Look, dipshit, don't get into any trouble while I am gone. You still have an ass-kicking coming to you."

Flank said, "Yeah, yeah…get the fuck out of here and bring me back my seafood dinner."

In the past Bud had always handled all of the details for his special dates, but now he couldn't trust Parks so he had to do it on his own. The coast was clear. The Tackett family was busy and Parks was on his way to Annapolis for the best crab dinner in town.

Flank put on black dress pants, a dress shirt and a sport coat. Penny texted him and told him she was in Room 1316 at the Jefferson Hotel. He texted back, "Wow, good thinking…I am on my way."

He took a thousand dollars in cash and a small bag of coke out of his wall safe. Hailed a cab to the hotel and went right up to the room.

Penny was dressed in a short black skirt with a red push-up bra, a black see-through blouse, and red-bottomed high-heel pumps.

Flank said, "Hello, cutie. You look good enough to eat."

Penny smiled and said, "Well, are you hungry?"

Suddenly something about Penny seemed very professional. Flank said, "How much do you charge?"

Penny said, "What are you talking about?"

Flank changed the subject. He asked her what she was drinking and if she could pour him a glass. As he watched her move he was getting more aroused. But he needed to find his groove, he needed to calm down a bit so while she was pouring his drink, he pulled out his little bag of coke and laid it on the table.

He had also brought along a blindfold and handcuffs. Making himself comfortable, he took off his jacket and shoes and sat down in the comfortable chair next to the coffee table.

He took in the atmosphere of the room. It was very expensive and not something that an innocent housewife would have thought of. He knew Penny was a professional call girl, So he thought, *"I am in good hands. She would surely show him a good time."*

Penny looked down at the bag of coke and the sex toys and smiled. She then went over to Flank, got down on her knees, and asked him, "What did you come here for?"

Flank said, "I came prepared to pay for it. I know what you are all about. I even brought along some coke, if you do drugs. Most girls like you enjoy getting high."

Penny said, "You are the smart one. But tell me, what did you come here for? What is it that you want from me?"

Flank said, "What's wrong with you, woman? Do you get turned on by words? I came here to fuck you, and I have the money to pay for every minute of it." He then took out a white envelope filled with hundred-dollar bills and threw it on the table.

Penny placed her hand on Flank's knees and said, "Congressman Alfred Flank, you are under arrest."

Flank said, "No—no, what are you talking about? You are a cop? This is a setup you bitch!"

Suddenly Flank's world started spinning out of control. Every door in the hotel room was thrown open, lights suddenly turned on everywhere. Video cameras were on him and he was being pulled up from his seat. Cops were putting handcuffs on him and reading him his rights.

Penny was nowhere to be seen.

Flank said, "No, no, this is wrong. She is a housewife! She asked me for it! This bitch set me up. This can't be happening to me!"

The arresting officer said, "She is a police officer Sir and you are under arrest."

Flank was taken down a service elevator to the ground floor and then out the side entrance where more cameras were on him. There was no way around it. He had really fucked himself up this time.

Within minutes of his arrest, video footage of him being led out of the hotel in handcuffs was broadcast on every television channel. As soon as Officer Shaw heard of the congressman's arrest he went to the judge to get a warrant to search the row house. Shaw was sure he would find something linking the congressman or one of his men to the canal road attacks.

Parks was in the car, sitting in traffic on Route 50 when he got a call from the governor.

"What in the hell is going on? Is it true?"

Parks said, "What are you talking about, boss? Why are you so upset?"

Governor Tackett said, "You shit, you fucking no-good shit. Flank has been arrested for solicitation of prostitution and possession with the intent to distribute drugs. Where are you? Why are you not with him? That's the reason I sent you to Washington to keep an eye on that dumb piece of shit."

Parks said, "I am out picking up his dinner."

Governor Tackett said, "Get your fat ass over to him now. I am sending someone there to clean this shit up."

Parks turned the car around and sped back to the city but it was already too late. When he pulled up to the house, it was surrounded by police. They had gotten a search warrant and they were tearing the house apart. He was afraid to go in, so he called the governor and told him what was happening and asked what he should do.

The governor said, "Find another job. You're fired."

Flank was being processed through the system. He asked for his lawyer a powerhouse attorney and partner at Reed Smith law firm. Who was very accustomed to high profiled cases. Flank was released after several hours of being placed in a holding cell. When he got his phone back, he called Governor Tackett.

Flank said, "Governor, this is all a big mistake. I can explain everything."

The governor said, "You are a major fuckup and now you are on your own. Don't ever call me again."

As Flank and his attorney A. Scott walked out of the police station, camera lights shined brightly from all directions, he looked around and all he saw was television trucks. For the first time he felt a sense of supreme dread, thinking to himself, "There is no one here for me, but my attorney."

A. Scott made a quick statement to the media and then the two left the police station. Flank was then taken to a hotel outside of the city at National Harbor in Maryland. He was instructed to stay out of sight until they could come up with a plan.

Flank called Parks, who could not talk without cussing. He hung up the phone. The next call was to his mother. All he could say was he was, "I am so sorry."

She told him she was on the way to Washington and they would bring him back home. She said, "I told you that city is filled with evil and now the devil has you in his trap. But I am coming to free you, Son. Momma is on the way."

Flank sat in his hotel room, looking out at the Potomac River. It all seemed like a bad dream. Everything that he had worked for was now gone. With no discussion, he had lost it all and he would more than likely be sent to jail.

Chapter 94

Officer Shaw was searching every corner of Flank's row house. There were plenty of sex toys and adult magazines and a small amount of drugs. But he hadn't found anything linked to the attacks on the Capitol Hill staffer. He went downstairs to search the apartment. Combing through every inch, he still hadn't come up with anything but old half-eaten food and some liquor.

The place was a dirty mess. As he was heading out, he noticed a crack in the wallpaper behind a console table. Shaw pushed the console away from the wall and removed some of the wallpaper and it revealed a secret closet.

Shaw could not believe it, he found the evidence he had been looking for: track phones, surgical gloves, bottles of pills, sex toys, hairbrushes and combs, notes, several sets of house keys, ladies' underwear, lipsticks in all shades of red, a dirty razor and a white envelope filled with used condoms, along with several Bibles.

Shaw bagged and logged the box as evidence and headed over to the forensic department. He asked the forensic technician to process the items as fast as possible and to compare the results against all sex offense cases between Colorado and Washington, DC.

His next call was to the Police Chief. Saying "Chief, I think we got the bastard. I need to find Bud Durham."

The Chief said, "Good I want to see this monster behind bars. Tell me what you need Shaw you have the department behind you." He explained what he believed to be the facts and what he needed. When he finished talking to the Chief his next call was to Winnie.

Winnie had suspected all along that Flank was dirty and now the world would know. She asked Shaw, "Where he believed Flank would be hiding out."

Shaw said, "I think they are taking him to National Harbor."

Winnie wanted to be the first to speak with Flank so she headed to the harbor in search of her suspect.

Winnie was relieved that evidence finally surfaced against Flank and she never had to involve Paulina.

A couple of hours later Winnie's cell phone rang. It was Officer Shaw he said, "I'm heading to Denver, in search of Bud Durham."

Winnie answered, "What happening?"

Shaw answered, "All of the DNA matches Bud Durham."

Winnie said, "Flank did not rape these girls. It was Bud? Durham was Flanks right-hand man, they are both sick!"

Shaw said, "I will keep you posted. Winnie, be careful."

"Thanks, Shaw. You do the same."

Winnie wanted to see everyone that was behind these beatings and rapes put away for life.

When Winnie arrived at National Harbor, no one would tell her anything, so she hung around the lobby, looking for signs of powerful lawyers arriving. Her plan was to follow them up to the room but after several hours, she still had nothing.

She headed home, wondering if she would be the first reporter to speak with Flank. While she was driving she telephoned Attorney A. Scott. Her call went to voice mail. She left a message that she needed to speak with him and his client.

That evening Winnie lit a small fire in her library fireplace and threw the videotape in. She felt satisfied with the knowledge that Paulina was safe and this mess could now be put behind her.

She telephoned Nancy and arranged to meet her for lunch the next day at the Four Seasons, Bourbon Steak. Over lunch she told Nancy everything she knew and she assured her that she had destroyed the only copy of the evidence between Paulina and Flank.

Winnie said, “Unless the police uncover something else, I believe that Paulina will be safe and all of this will become just a bad memory.”

Nancy reached across the table and took Winnie’s hand. She was so filled with emotion at that moment, she could only say, “Thank you for everything.”

Chapter 95

Bud had been back in Denver for only a few weeks and every day he worried about Congressman Flank. Bud thought, *"Flank was more like a kid than a grown-up. He has bad judgment and trusted too many people. There is no telling what Flank will get himself into without me there to clean up after him. I enjoy cleaning up, it's what the good Lord wants me to do. Take care of the whore's and teach them a lesson. Now I am dealing with old lady Tackett and the governor's daughters, Belinda the bitch and Wanda the goody-two-shoes college student."*

Belinda berated Bud every time she saw him. Bud thought, *"If only she was not the governor's daughter he would enjoy nothing better than teaching Belinda a lesson that she may never recover from."*

He was happy to take them all to the airport for their New York trip. That would mean a long week-end for him. He thought, *"Oh well, my private box is securely stashed away behind the console. No one will ever find it. But I would feel better if I had it with me. Maybe I should try and slip back into DC., to retrieve it. But I can't trust Parks, so I had better just pace myself and enjoy these couple of days off, I will just wait this one out."*

Bud lived in a log cabin with views of Mount Evans. The cabin was located on the edge of town near Wade lake. The property had been abandoned for years until Bud saved up enough money to pay the outstanding taxes and now he was a homeowner. He lived by himself because he had too much work to do for the Lord. Having a woman around meddling and asking questions would interfere with his Godly duties.

He'd been in the house all day, cleaning up. He thought, *"Cleanliness was next to godliness, I know for sure that I will be going to heaven after all of my work down here on earth, cleaning up and getting rid of evil women. Those lost demons needed to go bye-bye."*

Bud's lake house allowed him to commune with nature and sleep under the stars. He had a small fishing boat, when he was not on duty with the Tackett family, he would spend the entire day on the lake.

After he'd finished cleaning he packed himself a picnic-basket lunch filled with sandwiches, cold chicken and beer. He'd picked up some bait and plenty of ice and had headed out to his boat. While he was fishing he thought again about the girls that Flank liked. As he looked up at the sky, he said to himself, *"If only Flank hadn't been such a weak man, I would never have taken care of those girls. But I had to do my job."*

As the sun was beaming down on him Bud repeated a bible verse that he learned as a child. His father would say it to him every time he was bad, *"And whosever shall offend one of these little ones that believe in me, it's better that he be cast into the sea .....and if thy foot offend thee cut it off.....that's what I have always done ....I cut off the offenders. Now GOD will bless me for my good works."* He closed his eyes and drifted off to sleep.

As Bud put the last of his cleaned fish in the freezer, he realized he was getting hungry so he got dressed in his best jeans and western shirt, he added his shearling and leather vest and cowboy hat, then headed into town.

The Falling Star Tavern had a great breakfast sandwich and the best coffee in town. Bud pulled up to the bar and placed his order. The owners knew Bud and would fill him in on all of the local gossip. Today, everything seemed different. No one was making eye contact with him.

As he looked up at the television everything started moving slowly. He could not believe what they were reporting. Congressman Alfred Flank was being taken into the local police station in handcuffs. He'd been caught in a prostitution sting operation.

They were doing close-ups of Flank. The next video on the television was of police officers carrying bags of evidence out of the Capitol Hill row house and to Bud's disbelief, he saw one officer carrying his metal box. Bud almost fell out of his chair. He started sweating and breathing heavily. His world was coming to an end and he had to get out of the bar fast. He took a fifty-dollar bill out of his pocket and threw it on the counter.

He went to the restroom to vomit. His knees went weak and he had to hold onto the wall for support, the room was spinning. Somehow he mustered the strength to get back into his car. He had to get to the bank, get some money, and get out of town.

He went to the ATM, withdrew everything he could and headed back to his house to pack his bags. As he was driving down the gravel road to his house, he was thinking of a plan to get out of town. His cell phone beeped and then went dead. He opened the window and threw it out of the car. He sped up, knowing he was running out of time. When he reached his house, there were several police cars waiting for him.

Bud could not let them take him in. He would not go back to prison. He stopped the car and said a prayer saying, *"Dear Lord, I have done your work down here now forgive me and take care of my mother."*

The police had seen his car approaching the house and started towards their suspect. Bud locked the doors, opened the glove box, took out his forty-five-caliber gun, put the gun in his mouth.

Officer Shaw, saw the gun and screamed, "No, he's going to kill himself." He was too late he watched in horror as Bud's brains slid down the car window. Shaw had flown all the way into Denver to arrest this chicken shit and now this.

As news reached the Governor he quickly released a statement saying that he had no knowledge of the crimes committed by Flank and Durham and renounced his support, along with asking for Flank's immediate resignation.

Belinda canceled the wedding and left town for a long vacation.

No one ever saw or heard from Parks again.

Washington was abuzz with media coverage of the rise and fall of Congressman Alfred Flank.

The news of the arrest of Congressman Flank and the suicide of Bud Durham made Paulina feel freer than she had in sometime. She wanted Flank to get the maximum punishment, believing he deserved it after everything he'd done to her and her friend.

She now felt free to focus on her life with Tim without the fear of getting hurt. She sent an e-mail to Tiffany, telling her everything about Flank and his arrest. Tiffany responded back that she was delighted. She told Paulina that she still had nightmares about that night. She was thankful to Paulina and her family for everything they had done for her. She also told her that she had settled in well with her aunt and was becoming an expert on farming and dairy products. Running a large estate with a working farm was a full-time job, but she was surprised at how much she loved it and she loved her new life.

Paulina asked, "Okay, what's his name?"

Tiffany laughed. She then told Paulina all about her new male interest, an aristocratic gentleman who owned the neighboring estate and was good friends with the royal family. They had been spending a great deal of time together. He had shown her more love and kindness than she had ever known possible.

Paulina shared with her everything about Timothy and their love affair.

The two friends talked for some time and looked forward to seeing each other again. Life had taken them on very different paths but through their shared experiences they would always remain friends.

Chapter 96

Lonnie and Sadie's relationship had weathered the storm and life was perfect again.

Tim called his father and asked if he was free to meet with him the following morning. He had something urgent to discuss. Lonnie knew what it was. He had seen it on Tim's face at Benny's wedding.

Tim was going to marry Paulina. Lonnie was happy for his son. He knew that whatever life gave him, he was man enough to handle it.

Lonnie was proud of his sons for who they were in the present moment and for the men they were turning out to be. They knew the value of family and they wanted to build their own. He thought Paulina was smart, charming and a very pretty young woman but the most important thing to him was that she was very much in love with his son.

Lonnie had no idea how Sadie would react to the news but their family was growing and there was no choice but to accept the changes lovingly with open arms.

He called the kitchen to see if someone could prepare a small tray with Sadie's favorite tea and mini cakes. Felix said he would have it ready quickly.

Lonnie carried the delicate tray of sweets and tea to Sadie's office. When she heard him she looked up from her plans for their upcoming weekend in Florida. They would be hosting a small dinner for Lonnie's sister birthday.

Sadie said, "What is all of this? Yummy! I was just about to call for a cup of tea. Darling, you have perfect timing."

Lonnie said, "Well, my dear lady, you have been working so hard all morning, I thought it was time for a tea break and today I am your server. Let me know if I do a good job." They both laughed.

After he placed the tray on the small table next to her desk, he poured her a cup and then one for himself.

Sadie said, "Perfectly done. Now let me give you a tip." She reached up and kissed him on the cheek.

Lonnie smiled and said, "Hey, with tips like that I will do this more often."

He took a seat and then asked her about the dinner plans. They talked about it for a few minutes. He looked out onto the beautiful garden and then said, "We have lived here for over twenty years and every time I look out at your flowerbeds, I fall in love with them and you all over again."

Sadie said, "The gardener has done a fine job this year. The grounds are looking fabulous. Thank you darling for your kind words I love you, too."

Lonnie took her hand and said, "I need to speak to you about something."

Sadie said, "Lonnie, is something wrong?"

Lonnie said, "Darling, I need you to listen to me with an open heart."

Sadie sat down her teacup as Lonnie told her about Tim and Paulina and what he saw in their eyes.

Lonnie said, "Sadie, we need to give them our love and approval because Tim is a grown man. It's his life, not ours. We have to trust him and love them."

Sadie said, "Lonnie, I love Paulina but I am worried about her being so young and her having so many problems with Nancy and Salim."

Lonnie said, "Baby, have you forgotten that everything was not perfect when we fell in love but our love has gotten us through this far. I want you to let go of whatever you are feeling and trust your son."

Sadie said, "I am his mother and I just don't want him to get hurt again. Tim loves hard, Lonnie."

Lonnie took her by the hand and walked her over to the window. He pointed at the roses and said, "Each one has thorns that cut and make your hands bleed but it has never stopped you from planting them or being proud of their blossoms. You must allow our sons to live their lives roses, thorns and all. We will be there when and if they need us. But we can never stop them from living, loving, or growing. Sadie darling, they have a right to build their families, just like we did."

Sadie knew he was right and that she would never win this battle, so she walked back over to her desk, sat down and said, "This is the strongest cup of tea that I have ever had to drink."

Lonnie smiled and said, "It's tea fit for the queen of the Von Kinley men. Now drink up my darling. Your kingdom is growing."

The next morning when Tim arrived early for breakfast, Sadie was waiting for him. But before she could say a word, Lonnie walked into the room and made immediate eye contact with her.

Tim said, "Good morning, Mother and Dad."

Sadie said, "Good morning, dear. Are you hungry?"

They went into the breakfast room where Felix had a lovely breakfast set up with of all of Tim's favorites.

Lonnie said, "Well, this all looks great."

After they had filled their plates and started eating Tim said, "I need to tell you both something. It's about Paulina and me."

At that moment, Sadie would have given her entire collection of jewelry for one drink. She knew what Tim was about to say and she just did not want to hear it.

As Tim continued, he said, "Life has given me another chance at love and my dear parents, I am proud to tell you that I have asked Paulina to marry me—and she has said yes."

Sadie said, "Tim, are you sure about this?"

Lonnie gave her a stern look. Then he said, "Tim, I am happy for you and Paulina, and you have our approval and support."

Tim said, "Paulina and I are very much in love. I am also aware of the history and the heartbreak she has been through. I know the problems they have had as a family. But I believe that no family is perfect. Everyone has problems but with love, patience, prayer and respect for each other. You can get through anything together. Paulina and I will build a life together and we will raise our children together. She is my world."

Sadie said, "*Children*? Is this a shotgun wedding?"

Tim answered her quickly. "Well, we are asking everyone packing a gun to leave it at the front desk. But if you are asking me if Paulina is carrying my child, then the answer is yes. Paulina and I are pregnant and our child is due in seven months."

Lonnie jumped up and said, "Oh my God, another grandbaby is coming! I am so happy."

He hugged Tim. Sadie knew she had lost this fight, so she embraced it. She was getting a daughter in-law and another grandbaby.

She went to Tim and hugged him and told him they had her blessing. Tim told her he understood her concerns about everything but he didn't know how to live without Paulina. Sadie looked at him and she felt in her soul that he was head over heels in love. She had seen it in Paulina face at Benny's wedding. She knew there was nothing left to do but show them both respect and support.

Later that day, Sadie and Lonnie placed a call to Salim and Nancy and congratulated them and welcomed Paulina into the family.

Paulina and Nancy spent the morning planning the wedding. Paulina wanted it to be small and elegant but simple. They went to Just Paper in Georgetown for the perfect invitations. The wedding would be held at the Hay-Adams Hotel. Nancy and Paulina invited Sadie to be involved in as much of the planning as she felt she wanted to. Sadie limited it to the rehearsal dinner and out-of-town-guests' brunch.

Chapter 97

Two Months later

On the evening before the wedding they all gathered at Decanter's located in The St. Regis Hotel on 16th and K Street, for a lively rehearsal dinner. Prior to dinner Sadie sent a package to Paulina. She wanted to share a piece of her jewelry collection with the new Mrs. Von Kinley. She carefully selected a suite from the Chopard jewelry. The necklace, watch, earrings, ring and bracelet were in the shape of a heart from the Happy collection. She enclosed a note that read:

> My dearest Paulina:
> We want every moment of your life with Timothy to be happy. Timothy's father gave me this suite, and now I am honored to give it to you.
>
> It's named the Chopard Happy Suite. As you see, each piece is in the shape of a heart and in each heart there are four floating diamonds. I have four wishes for you: Love, Peace, Family, and Forever Passion.
>
> For everything that family means to all of us, we welcome you into ours. May you be forever in our family and our hearts. Your love has made our son the happiest he has ever been.
>
> With all of our love,
> The Von Kinleys'

Paulina knew this was the ultimate peace offering and she didn't want a moment to go by without acknowledging it. She telephoned Sadie right away saying, "Mrs. Von Kinley, how will I ever thank you for being such a wonderful mother? Because of your love, Timothy is a great man. I promise to be a good wife to him and a wonderful mother to our children." Paulina prayed that Sadie believed her. She wanted them to be a family.

Sadie said, "When you are comfortable, please call me Mother Sadie."

Paulina started to cry, they had come so far together and now they were on the same team: The Timothy Von Kinsley team, forever love and happiness.

The wedding ceremony was held at St. John's Church at Lafayette Square, across from the White House. The historical Church which had held so many Presidential memories had never looked more elegant and serene. The alter and pews were decorated in white lilies and roses, the services was traditional and Paulina and Tim read beautiful vows to each other.

Paulina wore a very simple lace gown designed by Dior. The design of the dress did not bring attention to her small baby bump. She looked elegant and glowed with love. Timothy wore a very tailored Tom Ford suit. His brothers were his best men, Paulina's two cousins were her bridesmaids.

After the short ceremony guest walk across the street for the reception taking place at the Hay-Adams Hotel. Nancy enlisted the help of local event planner the very handsome Andre Wells, who produced out-of-this-world elegant events. Sylvia Weinstock created a wonderful cake that not only looked marvelous but tasted like a creamy dream.

During the reception Tim asked all of the men to please bring the women they loved onto the dance floor. He then asked the band to play, "Thinking out Loud," by Ed Sheeran. The lyrics expressed everything he felt about love and life.

> When your legs don't work like they used to before,
> And I can't sweep you off of your feet,

Will your mouth still remember the taste of my love?
Will your eyes still smile from your cheeks?
And darling, I will be loving you till we're 70.
And baby, my heart could still fall as hard at 23.
And I'm thinking 'bout how people fall in love in mysterious ways,
Maybe just the touch of a hand.
Oh me, I fall in love with you every single day,
And I just wanna tell you I am.
So honey, now
Take me into your loving arms,
Kiss me under the light of a thousand stars,
Place your head on my beating heart.
I'm thinking out loud,
Maybe we found love right where we are.

Taking Paulina into his arms, he glided her smoothly across the dance floor, softly singing into her ear. She felt their baby move. As she placed her head on Tim's beating heart, tears softly ran down Paulina's cheeks. They had found a deep love that would last forever.

As Lonnie and Sadie gently moved across the dance floor, she looked around and saw her three best friends in the arms of the men they loved. Nancy and Salim had fallen back in love with each other, Saul and Coco were still in honeymoon-crazy love and Winnie was in the arms of her new love interest international billionaire and statesman Stephen Cohen. They had all gone through so much and had come full circle.

Sadie was thankful they had made it through the jaws of hell and were stronger because of it. One thing was for sure, at the end of the day, they were all better women. Their experiences had freed them from all of the stuff they once held onto so tightly, and no matter what they were friends for life.

They were four women in love with life!

Chapter 98

Thanksgiving
One Year Later

Sadie and Lonnie had finally found a happy medium with his work schedule. He was working part-time and they were spending a lot of time together with their three beautiful grandbabies. Amy and Benny had a precious baby boy, Lewis Russell Von Kinley. Tim and Paulina had been blessed with beautiful twin girls named Isabella Sadie and Shirley Rose. The twins were born on September 14, Sadie's birthday, which made Sadie the proudest grandmother ever. Tim and Paulina purchased a charming home in McLean, Virginia. Paulina and Amy had become great friends and according to Sadie they were the new, modern day Von Kinley women.

With the additions to her family, Sadie finally felt fulfilled and loved more than at any time in her life. The entire family was looking forward to Thanksgiving dinner at Jackson Hole and Lonnie had promised to help Sadie with dinner.

Coco and Saul were looking forward to celebrating the holidays in Palm Beach, at their new home on South County Road. Coco had asked Saul to invite his children for the holidays. They would be observing both the Jewish and Christian celebrations. It was the first time Coco had ever planned a big family holiday dinner and she was excited. She even invited her uptight sister, Barbara and her family to Palm Beach. Saul thought Coco was overdoing it but her energy and desire to please were a joy to watch. After the holiday's the love birds would be departing on another trip aboard the fabulous Crystal Cruise line for thirty days of wonder.

Nancy and Salim were enjoying being grandparents. Nancy began joining Salim on some of his speaking engagements, which gave them plenty of time to continue rebuilding their lives as a couple. The house in Maine was on the market and they had purchased a lovely second home with amazing ocean views on Kiawah Island in South Carolina, they were looking forward to sharing it with their growing family.

Winnie was still dating and enjoying every minute of her life. All of the ladies would be in Palm Beach at the end of January for the International Red Cross Ball. Winnie had planned a luncheon for the ladies at The Breakers Resort. Everyone was excited about this year's holiday season and looking forward to a future filled with love, happiness and friendship.

THE END

Gurdie Corell

Gurdie Corell is a native Washingtonian and former society writer Capital Ladies' Club is her first novel.

Gurdie has a great love of entertaining and travel; she resides in Washington, D.C., with her family.

From the desk of Gurdie Corell

To you my readers:

With each page you've read you have made my dreams come true ,and I will be forever grateful to you.

Please join me at www. GurdieCorell.com, and sign up for my monthly newsletter.

I look forward to meeting you when I am in your town or city. Until then please continue to, "Live your life with passion and style!"

Love and hugs,

Gurdie

Acknowledgements:

I want to thank so many people here is the short list.

I am forever grateful to my beloved Delores "Mikki" Barham, the ultimate collector of fine things.

Franco Nuschese and the entire staff at Cafe Milano in Georgetown, for over twenty years you have treated me like family and I am most grateful. I can't wait to dine at Cafe Milano, Abu Dhabi, see you March 2016.

The entire staff at the Four Seasons Hotel and Spa and the Chef and culinary team at Bourbon Steak in Washington, D.C.

To Edie Rodriguez and the army of fabulous stewards that make up Crystal Cruises, you are the finest in the world!

Thank you to Paul N. Leone and the staff of the best resort on land, The Breakers Resort and Spa, in Palm Beach, Florida.

I want to send love to my friend the fabulous Margot McKinney. Thank you for sharing your gifts as a master craftswoman, your gems shine brighter than the stars!

And a very personal thank you to all of my fabulous BFF's, you know who you are so I don't have to list your names, thank you for loving and caring for me!!

To the entire Perioperative team at Virginia Hospital Center, thank you it's been fun!

Love to all!

Gurdie

Made in the USA
Middletown, DE
03 April 2016